Little
Kerber
Creek

A Novel

Little Kerber Creek

A Novel

Pat Chamberlain Murray

SANTA FE

Sunstone books may be purchased for educational, business, or sales promotional use.
For information please write: Special Markets Department, Sunstone Press,
P.O. Box 2321, Santa Fe, New Mexico 87504-2321.

Book and Cover design › Vicki Ahl
Body typeface › Laurentine
Printed on acid-free paper
∞

Library of Congress Cataloging-in-Publication Data

Murray, Pat Chamberlain, 1939-
Little Kerber Creek : a novel / by Pat Chamberlain Murray.
    p. cm.
ISBN 978-0-86534-879-0 (softcover : alk. paper)
1. Colorado--History--1876-1950--Fiction. I. Title.
PS3613.U7736L58 2012
813'.6--dc23

                    2012011868

WWW.SUNSTONEPRESS.COM
SUNSTONE PRESS / POST OFFICE BOX 2321 / SANTA FE, NM 87504-2321 /USA
(505) 988-4418 / ORDERS ONLY (800) 243-5644 / FAX (505) 988-1025

Dedication

This book is dedicated to my husband, Mick Murray,
for encouraging me to have faith in myself and for believing
in the story and enduring the four years it took to complete.

And, in memory of my dear brother, Bob Chamberlain,
who expected me to set high goals and be the best I could be.

Acknowledgements

Research Assistance:

James Kemper Millard, Lexington History Museum
Bob Shank, Superintendent, Denver-Rio Grande Railroad
Don Shank, CEO, Denver-Rio Grande Railroad
Josephine Lobato, former Director, Fort Garland Museum
Mark Allison, former Director, Rio Grande County Museum
Elaine Woodard, Villa Grove historian, Colorado
Kenny Frye, archaeologist and historian, Del Norte, Colorado
Bob Boppe, Chief Engineer, Homestake Mining Company, Creede, Colorado
Bill Jones, Root and Norton Assayers, Silverton, Colorado
Paul Eldredge, botanist
Vince Spero, former Rio Grande National Forest archeologist
Gwen Voris, music lyrics research
Ruth McCain, widow of Buck McCain (name permission)
Mike Norris, sheriff, Saguache County, Saguache, Colorado
Lee Griffin, firearms consultant

Encouragement and Thanks:

Donna Gallegos, typist, critique
Mamie Chambers, typist, critique
Barbara Carpenter, critique
Virginia Amato, Linnea Murray, Lynn and Sandy Sewell, John and Lis
Chamberlain, Eileen Chamberlain, Art and Joyce Chamberlain, Bill and Bobbi
Briggs, Margaret Wilkinson, Julie Burke, Linda Cross, Dan and Cindy Stormer,
Paul and Becky Gilles, Judy Baker and Kay Wilson

Special Thanks:

John and Sandy Stormer, and Casey and Jane McGann

Most of all, my gratitude and appreciation to Jim Smith, Publisher at Sunstone
Press. Thank you for believing in me and my novel, and for the courtesy and
understanding you extended over the years.

1

Bonanza, Colorado
April 14, 1878

*I*t was still dark this early April morning when Rick Barnett blinked open his eyes. He lay in bed for a moment before remembering the telegram he'd received yesterday; then he flipped back his heavy quilt and swung his feet onto the small buffalo rug. He picked a match from the pile on the bedside table, struck it against the wall and lit the wick of the kerosene lamp.

Rick reached for his pants on the knob of the footboard and thrust his long legs into them up as far as his knees, then bent over and groped for his wool socks. Finding them just under the bed, he brought them to his nose, took a whiff and tossed them aside. Rising, he pulled his pants over his hips and buckled his belt.

The floorboards were cold on his bare feet as he plodded to his chest of drawers in the corner to get a clean pair of socks. Opening the top drawer, his eyes fell upon the telegram he'd placed there last night. He scratched the back of his neck and let out a troubled sigh as he stuffed the envelope into his pants' pocket.

Rick pulled a clean shirt out of the second drawer and slipped the red-checkered wool over his muscular arms and broad chest. He buttoned it up but left the tails hanging out. Clutching his socks in one hand and the lamp in the other, he sauntered barefoot down the hall.

Passing Jim's room, he cut through the parlor and into the kitchen, the light casting a warm glow over the cozy split-log room. Rick set his socks and lamp on the long oak table and slid his fingers across its smooth, shiny surface. He glanced proudly around the room at his other efforts, the carved mantle over the fieldstone fireplace, the shelves and cupboards—there was a lot of him in the whole cabin.

He touched the coffeepot with his fingers and figured it was warm enough for starters. Taking his orange earthen mug from a hook on the wall, he filled it with last night's brew and took a large gulp. Setting the mug on the sideboard, he grabbed a couple of logs from the wood box to fire up the stove. Retrieving his mug, he took another healthy slug as he headed to the table and finally sat down.

The gray in his dark brown hair sparkled from the light of the lamp, the soft glow enhancing the handsome profile of his straight nose and firm jaw line. Rick bent down to pull on his socks and reached for his boots beside the chair. He jammed his feet into the well-worn leather and reached for his pipe next to the lamp. With steady concentration, he lit it and now felt ready to tackle his problem.

Rick pulled the telegram from his pocket and spread it before him; puffing on his pipe, he slowly reread the words.

> Richard Barnett, Bonanza, Colorado
> Things impossible here. Want to move to Bonanza. Reply soon.
> Kathryn

"How do I answer this?" he muttered out loud. He tried to picture his niece Kathryn as she might be now, for he hadn't seen her since his brother John's funeral. That was almost ten years ago, and she was just a young girl then. He and Kathryn wrote to each other often, but he hadn't heard from her in over six months, until yesterday.

The door to Jim's room opened, and he heard the sound of Jim's feet shuffling toward the kitchen. "Mornin', Rick," mumbled Jim as he passed the table and headed straight for the coffeepot. Grabbing his blue enamel cup from the hook, he stood half awake in his long woolies, scratching the side of his leg as he poured coffee into his cup.

Jim was a short, stout fellow in his mid-thirties, with unruly, sandy-colored hair, devilish blue eyes and a quick grin. Rick had known Jim Miller since the Pikes Peak gold rush days and had taken an instant liking to him. Jim had not been as lucky in mining as Rick, and when Rick decided to buy land, he asked Jim to be his foreman.

The two of them and Sam, a newly-acquired hand, had built the big adobe and log ranch house, bunk house, barns and corrals. The 1,500-acre spread, the ranch now had over 500 head of longhorns and some of the finest-bred horses around.

Rick had been content with his life until, yesterday; but now he was consumed with worry over his niece.

Jim was slouched in his chair, his head bent over his cup as he looked at the paper in front of Rick. "Still don't know what to do, huh?"

"Nope." Rick emptied his mug and got up to refill it, then paced back and forth before the large window over the sink. He stared out at the horses in the corral and watched their silhouettes move about in the gray dawn as he absently wondered which one he'd give to Kathryn. Shaking that thought from his mind, he went back to the table and picked up the telegram. "What would she do stuck out here in a place like this?" he said. "She's used to city life, a big fancy house and finer things. Just don't seem fittin', this place is fine for us, Jim;" he conceded, "but I'm afraid she'd come to hate it."

Jim had been quietly studying Rick, knowing that he was wrestling with a heavy decision. Finally, he spoke up. "Do you have any idea why she wants to come out here?"

"Nope. Just says that things are impossible. The only thing I'd venture a guess on is that it's something to do with her mother, Jolene."

Rick slumped back into his chair and stared at the telegram, mulling things around in his head. "I told her once I'd always try to help her if I could.

He rose slowly and walked over to the cluttered desk. Finding a sheet of paper, he picked up his pen and ink bottle and brought them back to the lighted table.

Carefully wording his answer, Rick handed the paper to Jim. "Ride this in to Villa Grove. Have 'em wire it pronto."

Lexington, Kentucky, Three days later.

It was early afternoon and Kathryn had been out riding for quite some time. She couldn't bear being cooped up in the house with all the painful problems and emotions.

She and her mother, Jolene, had been so close, especially after her father's death. Now they were as distant as strangers, Kathryn felt it was all due to Phillip Wheeler. Oh, how she despised that man.

Needing solitude, Kathryn turned her horse down toward the brook that ran through the western side of the estate. She felt her very existence hinged upon Uncle Richard's answer to her telegram.

Reaching the stream, Kathryn commanded Jackson to halt, then quickly dismounted and tied him to a small tree. Hiking up her long pink skirt, she stepped high through the lush, green grass along the banks.

She was a spunky gal and a bit of a tomboy, which her feminine beauty defied. She had long, dark brown hair with hints of red and gold that sparkled in the sunlight. Her sensuous brown eyes had a mysterious yet almost sad gaze when she was serious and a mischievous twinkle when she was happy. She was aware that her petite, yet provocative figure turned many a. man's head, but the attention did not jade her.

Kathryn stopped near the water's edge and eased down into her usual spot beneath the great oak. The brook was moving rapidly, little whirlpools spinning as they traveled on their way. Kathryn leaned back against the tree and closed her eyes, the swooshing water, lapping against the rocks soothing her. She breathed in the heady fragrance of the blossoming white magnolias that grew in abundance and inhaled the blended scent of apple blossoms that floated through the balmy spring air.

Her thoughts drifted to a new life as her mind and body sank into a dreamy state.

The singing of a whippoorwill on a branch overhead later brought Kathryn back to reality. She got up, untied Jackson and mounted up, riding reluctantly away from her favorite spot and heading back toward the house.

Her eyes surveyed the vast expanse of the Barnett estate, and her mind wandered back ten years to the many rides she and her father had gone on together.

She was barely twelve when the heart attack killed him, two years after the Civil War; it was Uncle Richard, their only living kin, who came to the rescue. Richard left his beloved Colorado for Lexington as soon as he received word of his brother's death and stayed on for a year to reorganize the mill and help Jolene get the business affairs in order.

Kathryn had become very close to her uncle during that time, and his parting words flashed again through her thoughts. "Kathryn, if ever you need help with a problem you can't handle, just let me know. I'll always be there, if' I can"

Kathryn and Richard shared the details of their lives in frequent letters. It had only been since Phillip and her mother's romantic involvement that her letters had been few. Kathryn had felt loyal to her mother in the beginning and didn't want to dishonor her by revealing personal matters. Finally, she could take no more. Without explaining, she at last reached out to her uncle for help.

She slapped her crop across Jackson's rump, moving him into a full gallop. She was an expert rider, though sometimes unconventional. Proper ladies rode side saddle and wore a skirt and hat. Kathryn rode astride when alone and sometimes even wore trousers. Today she purposely neglected to wear a riding hat so she could feel the wind in her hair.

With her skirt billowing, exposing bare legs, she and Jackson raced through the meadows.

2

*A*ttorney Phillip Wheeler's sleek black carriage with its shiny red wheels entered the circular, evergreen-lined drive and pulled to a stop in front of the stately Barnett mansion. The entrance was adorned with marble pillars and huge pots on either side of the door that would be overflowing with flowers soon. Phillip smiled and mused. Soon, he would be the master of the Barnett mansion; Wheeler mansion, he corrected himself.

Phillip had come into Jolene Barnett's life three years ago when the family's attorney died. Knowing she was a much sought-after lady and aware of her great fortune, Philip had approached the attractive widow. By playing on Jolene's insecurities, the relationship, in time, became more than strictly business. Soon they would marry.

Phillip was strikingly handsome with gray sideburns and thick, wavy black hair. His taste in clothes was impeccable. He'd always been a ladies' man and had a fierce ambition to become one of the wealthiest men in Lexington. A man of substantial means himself, he had gained financially from shrewd investments after the war—but to own the Barnett empire would secure for him the power he craved. John Barnett had left not only a prospering lumber mill but railroad and shipping holdings, as well as a fine stock of thoroughbred horses.

Phillip wondered, as he stepped out of his carriage, why Jolene had so urgently summoned him, for the nature of business had not been disclosed.

Phillip instructed his driver to wait, then strolled up to the door, his walking stick tucked under his arm, and rapped on the gleaming brass door knocker.

Eli set down his polishing cloth and dutifully shuffled toward the front door. His white, kinky head bobbed above the black tailcoat hanging loosely over his bent frame. Eli's creased dark face remained expressionless as he opened the door. After a greeting of feigned politeness, he silently escorted Phillip to the drawing room.

"I'll inform Miss Jolene that you are here," said Eli curtly, as he took his leave, Out of sight, old Eli, slowly shook his head and longed for the days when Master Barnett was alive.

Phillip smugly surveyed the green velvet drapes, polished mahogany tables, the long brocade sofa, and maroon leather chairs on each side of the fireplace; He strutted to the liquor cabinet and poured himself a snifter of brandy, then eased himself into his favorite chair by the fire. He stretched his legs on the matching footstool and waited for Jolene. He silently rejoiced over their upcoming marriage. The only un-pleasantry was

Kathryn, who was heir to her mother's estate. Phillip had plans for Jolene; to make him a full partner in all the ventures; and eventually convince her to rewrite her will.

An evil smile crossed his lips as he pondered on ways of getting Kathryn out of the picture. He wished she would marry and move far, far away. He had always suspected she could see right through him; that made him ill at ease and on guard in her presence. His ace in the hole was Jolene, who was totally in love with him and totally dependent upon him.

Phillip sipped his brandy and wondered again about the urgency of this visit.

Jolene entered the room and he immediately stood. A petite yet commanding woman of unusual beauty, her rose-colored silk dress rustled softly as she proceeded toward him. She had a small straight nose, deep blue eyes, and long auburn hair that framed her small face. She had high cheekbones, delicate lips that teased and dimples on her cheeks when she smiled. However, she was not smiling now as she marched toward Phillip, her lips pursed tight, and her eyes bore the look of anger and frustration.

Phillip opened his arms and she went into them as he kissed her on the cheek, but her body was rigid.

"What's wrong, darling?" asked Phillip.

Jolene pulled from his embrace and waved a piece of paper in front of his face; she stomped over and sat down in the chair across from his.

"Pour me a sherry, Phillip. Then I want you to read this and tell me what you make of it."

Phillip quickly got her a glass of sherry and brought it over. She, in turn, handed him the paper. Phillip took it and sat down, noting it was a telegram.

Before he had it unfolded, Jolene said, "I know Kathryn has been very upset lately, especially about our marriage plans, but I had no idea she felt this threatened." Jolene's voice was trembling as she continued. "I don't know what she is up to, but you can see for yourself that she contacted Richard, and—" She waved a hand toward the telegram. "Just read it for yourself."

Jolene nervously sipped on her sherry and fixed her eyes on Phillip as he unfolded the telegram and read it.

Kathryn Barnett, 104 Piney Ridge Road,
Lexington, Kentucky
Fine. Let me know when to expect you on stage to Villa. Grove.
Uncle Richard

Phillip kept his eyes down and took his time in responding, for it was difficult to repress the delight he was feeling. Yet, he knew that for now he must console Jolene.

At last he looked up from the paper and forced a concerned expression. "When did this arrive, Jolene?"

"It was delivered around noon. Kathryn's been out riding, and I took the liberty of reading it—of course, thinking something might have happened to Richard. He writes to her often," she interjected. "They're very close, even though he's a long way off, and he seems to have taken the place of her father. Oh, what can she be thinking? She's planning on leaving," she proclaimed. Jolene began to cry and said through her tears, "How could she do this to me, behind my back?"

Phillip went over to comfort Jolene. With a quivering voice she declared, "I will not stand for this. If she has any intention of going out to that God-forsaken place, I will just put a stop to it."

Kathryn reined Jackson to a halt by the stable entrance. Jesse, their driver and stable master, sauntered out from the barn wearing his floppy straw hat. "Dija have a nice ride, Miss Kathryn?" he asked, as he helped her dismount.

"Yes, thank you." Kathryn straightened her skirt, then stroked Jackson's neck. "You might want to cool him down a bit. I rode him pretty fast today."

"Yes'm. Oh, Miss Kathryn? I's ta tell ya to come right up to the house, soons ya gits back. Yo mama wants to see ya right away "'

"All right. Thank you, Jesse." Now what? thought Kathryn. She hadn't been summoned for anything lately, due to the strained relations. She was curious as she started up the path that led through the gardens and up to the house. She paused to look at the flowers beginning to bud, then proceeded along the brick-lined walk and up onto the veranda, Kathryn took a deep breath of the flower-scented air, then opened the door into the large kitchen.

"Aft-noon, Miss Kathryn," greeted Franny, who was bending over a counter rolling out dough.

"Afternoon, Franny." Kathryn studied the short, rotund woman work her magic on a pie crust. Franny usually had a smile and a happy disposition. She had been their cook for as long as Kathryn could remember.

As free people after the war, Franny, her husband Jesse, and Eli still chose to remain with the Barnetts. Of course pleased with their decision, John Barnett paid them far more than the average wage and made sure that all their needs were taken care of.

Franny set her rolling pin down and Kathryn noticed a white smudge of flour across one dark cheek. Taking out her handkerchief, and with a grin on her face, she wiped it away saying, "Franny, your cheeks didn't match."

Franny chuckled, "What would I do without ya, child?" She turned back to her work and began cutting out the dough.

"Oh, lordy, I plum forgot. I's to see to it ya goes right to the drawin room soons ya gits back from yo ride. Yo mama's awaitin on ya."

"I know, Jesse told me, I wonder what can be so all-fired important?"

"I don't know. But I was walkin by the drawin room and I heard yo mama raisin her voice aplenty with Mista Wheeler."

"I should have figured he'd have something to do with this," said Kathryn disgustedly. "Franny, I just can't stand him."

"I know ah's speakin outa turn, but I tells ya, yo mama ain't been the same since that Mista Wheeler start comin' round. I smells badness with the likes a him," Franny added in a pleading tone, "Please, child, don' tell yo mama I say that. "Cause she'd done have ma hide, an me an my mista be sent apackin."

"Don't you worry, Franny. You know I feel the same. I don't even like being in the same room with him." Kathryn snarled up her face and went on. "Franny, I'm going to tell you a secret." She could keep it to herself no longer. Franny stopped her work and turned, her dark chocolate eyes wide with interest.

Kathryn bent toward her and in a low voice said, "If I receive the news I'm expecting, I'm going to be leaving soon."

Franny's mouth gaped open and her big eyes got bigger, "No," Franny pleaded. "Yo not gonna leave here. Ya can't do that."

"Yes, I can, and I hope I will. Franny, I've tried to tell mother my suspicions—but it's no use. Phillip Wheeler is as far as she can see, and I won't stay around here and watch him use her."

"My land-a-goshin, child, just where ya thinkin a goin?"

Softly she said, "A few days ago, I went to the telegraph office and sent word to Uncle Richard. If he says I can come, I'm going to move to Colorado with him."

Franny looked stunned. "Not before the weddin?" she asked.

"Maybe. If he says I can come, I'll leave right away. I'm not going to pretend I approve of their wedding when I don't." Kathryn looked into Franny's eyes and saw them fill with tears which in turn brought tears to her own.

Franny wrapped her big arms around Kathryn and held her close as she sobbed and muttered, "It's like yo banishin yo self from yo own home."

With her voice shaking, Kathryn said, "Franny, I haven't gone yet. Please, don't cry."

"Sorry, Miss Kathryn. It's just ya so special to me. Lordy, since ya been a wee, bitty thing, ya been like one of my own—if I'd been seen fit to have one." Franny pulled the end of her large white apron up and modestly wiped her tear-wetted face, then with the other corner she gently wiped Kathryn's tears away. She turned back to her baking and said with a warning, "Ya bests go see what yo mama wants. Now git." Franny waved the wooden spoon she was holding to emphasize the order.

"Yes, Ma'am," retorted Kathryn, as she mocked a deep curtsy and turned to head for the drawing room.

As Kathryn neared the drawing room, she could hear the voices of her mother and Phillip. She hesitated outside the door to hear what they were saying.

"Phillip, she should have been back by now. Be a darling and go send Eli down to the stable to see what's keeping her."

Before they could discover her eavesdropping, Kathryn breezed into the room. She stood near the door and looked directly into her mother's eyes, purposely avoiding any recognition of Philip. "Mother, you wanted to see me?" she asked coolly.

"Come and sit down, Kathryn; we have something to discuss." Jolene gestured to a chair near hers.

Kathryn hadn't seen her mother this tense or serious in a long time and she felt trapped. Slowly she walked over and eased herself into the chair, thrusting out her legs and exposing riding boots with manure stuck to the tops.

Her mother's eyes darted to the boots. Through clenched teeth she retorted, "That's disgusting. You could have at least had the decency to remove your filthy boots before coming into the house."

Kathryn shrugged her shoulders and replied, "I knew you wanted to see me, so I came right in."

"Kathryn, I'm going to get right to the point, "Jolene fixed her eyes on Kathryn and said, "I demand to know the meaning of this." Kathryn's eyes widened as her mother waved a telegram in the air.

"That's my telegram, isn't it?"

"Yes, and I can't believe what it says. Kathryn, I want to know why Richard is expecting you to come to Colorado. I want some answers, and I want them now."

Inwardly, Kathryn was beaming with joy. Richard must have said she could come. She looked away from her mother, narrowed her eyes at Phillip and fixed her gaze on the carpet by her boots. She was trying hard to subdue her anger over the invasion of her privacy and her mother's audacity to include Phillip in personal matters, even though he was the main cause of it. In almost a whisper, Kathryn said, "Mother, I do not care to discuss this in front of Phillip."

"Phillip is soon going to be your stepfather, and he has every right to be included in family matters," countered Jolene. "Now, I'm waiting for an explanation."

Kathryn jumped to her, feet and said firmly, "I'm a grown woman, and I do not have to be subjected to this questioning or be put on trial in front of your husband-to-be. As far as I'm concerned, I shall never regard him as a father, step or otherwise."

Phillip looked on in silence, feeling very nervous. He rose to get another brandy.

"Make yourself right at home, Phillip," sneered Kathryn.

Phillip stopped in his tracks repressing his contempt. "Kathryn Barnett, you apologize to Phillip this instant," commanded Jolene.

"I will apologize for nothing. And now I'd appreciate it if you'd please give me my telegram." Kathryn stood her ground. Phillip, as yet, had not dared to pour his brandy and stood clutching the snifter.

"Don't you speak to me in that manner," warned Jolene.

Kathryn realized that this bickering was getting her nowhere. More than anything she wanted to read Uncle Richard's telegram. Looking down, she said, "I'm sorry I spoke to you that way, Mother—but you've put me in an awkward position." Turning her head ever so slightly toward Phillip, she directed a weak "I apologize," although she didn't mean it.

"Apology accepted," replied Phillip, and he meant it neither. He proceeded to fill his glass and returned to his chair.

"Now, young lady," said Jolene, with forced calmness. "I want to know why you contacted Richard about going to Colorado." Before Kathryn could answer, her mother continued, "How could you even consider leaving this beautiful home and all you have here to travel to some God-forsaken place filled with ill-bred people and savage Indians in wild, dangerous country?" Jolene had tears in her eyes as she went on. "I want you to put this silly notion out of your head. This is your home, and this is where you belong." Out of the corner of her eye, Kathryn detected a wince from Phillip.

"Mother, do you really want me to explain, in front of Phillip, why I find it necessary to leave, and what I really think of you and Phillip getting married? Or would you rather I save you the embarrassment?" Kathryn studied her mother and waited for an answer.

Jolene took a sip of her sherry and stared into the glass. She knew Kathryn despised Phillip but had thought it was mainly because no one could take her father's place, and she didn't want to share her mother.

Jolene had conveniently erased from her mind how she had allowed Phillip to wrest control of the mill away from Kathryn and had put his associate in charge; she couldn't deal with that. She had taken Phillips's side because she loved him so much and didn't want to lose him. But now she could be losing her daughter. Her mind was going in circles. Why was Kathryn trying to spoil her last chance for happiness? Why was she doing this to her? She was sorry that Philip was here to witness this showdown.

Slowly Jolene raised her eyes to Kathryn and said, "No, I do not wish you to cause me embarrassment, any more than you already have. I believe this discussion has gone too far, and I will hear no more talk of you leaving. I'm sure, in time, we can settle any differences, but for now your place is here until you find a suitable husband."

Jolene leaned back in her chair and took a deep breath, satisfied that the matter was resolved.

"Mother, I still want to see my telegram," said Kathryn stubbornly.

Feeling threatened by Richard's response, Jolene panicked and flung the telegram into the fire.

Kathryn rushed to the hearth and snatched the paper from the blaze. The ends were on fire and Kathryn slapped the telegram against her skirt to squelch the flames. She spun around with a. despicable look. "How dare you try and destroy something that was sent to me, something you took the liberty of reading without my permission. This is mine. Do you see?" She waved the scorched paper and marched out of the room.

Jolene leaped up, running after her. She grabbed Kathryn's arm and spun her around. With a look of fury in her eyes, she screamed, "No matter what that says, I forbid you to go. And that is final."

Kathryn stared at her mother and jerked her arm free. "We'll just see about that." Then she quickly ran up the stairs.

Jolene stood dumbfounded, ashamed and helpless. She wished Phillip had not witnessed this scene. She felt him beside her as he slid his arm around her waist, and she fell into his arms sobbing.

"It's going to be all right," said Phillip. "Don't take this so hard. I'm sure she'll come around in time. This is probably a ploy for your attention. I'm sure she has no real intention of leaving you."

"Do you really think so?" asked Jolene in a quivering voice.

"Yes," lied Phillip, playing the concerned-stepfather role. He couldn't let Jolene know this was the break, he'd been wishing for.

"Now, let's dry those pretty blue eyes and we'll take a walk in the garden. That always seems to cheer you."

Kathryn shut and locked her bedroom door and went to sit on the window seat to read her telegram. Luckily, most of the message was still legible. Carefully, she read:

N Barnett, 104 Piney Ridgington, Kentucky
Fine. Let me know when to expect you
stage to Villa Grove.
Uncle Richard

Kathryn reread it and beamed. She tingled with anticipation of seeing her uncle again and of the journey going west. She glanced out the window and saw Phillip and her mother strolling arm in arm in the garden. Her joy turned to anger, then sadness, for her mother's betrayal and a great loneliness swept over her. This had been her home, but now she felt she didn't belong. Phillip had taken over. Kathryn knew for certain now what she had to do.

Fighting back stinging tears, she folded the telegram with her uncle's decided response and carefully tucked it into her handbag; then pulled the green, braided cord that rang in the kitchen, signaling for a servant.

Kathryn went to her large wardrobe and selected a dress suitable for town and laid it across her bed. She took off her messy boots and set them by the door and removed her riding skirt and jacket, folding them neatly. She was standing in just her camisole and bloomers when there came a knock at the door.

"Who is it?" called Kathryn.

"Sally," answered the voice on the other side.

Kathryn opened the door and ushered Sally, Franny's niece, in and quickly shut it.

Sally was a skinny girl and was wearing a red, gingham checkered dress and black stockings. Her head was decorated with tiny pigtails tied with colorful strips of cloth.

"Ya needed somethin, Miss Kathryn?" asked Sally, in a high-pitched, whiney voice.

"Yes. I want you to go down to the stables and tell. your Uncle Jesse that I want him to bring my carriage around front. Then come right back and help me with my dress."

"Yes, ma'am."

"Oh, and give him these." She picked up the soiled boots and handed them to Sally. "Tell, him I need them cleaned."

Sally wrinkled up her nose and held the boots at arm's length as she left the room.

Kathryn brushed her tangled, brown hair and pinned it to the top of her head. She sat down to put on her shoes, and just as she finished hooking the buttons, a knock sounded again on the door. She opened the door and peeked through a crack, relieved it was Sally.

"Uncle Jesse say he have yo carriage round in a few minutes." Sally went over to the bed where the blue taffeta dress lay. She picked up the mass of material by scooping her arms into the bottom all the way to the neckline, while Kathryn bent down and wiggled her body up through the dress, stretching her arms out into the long sleeves. As she straightened up, the dress cascaded down around her onto the floor. Kathryn turned around so Sally could fasten the long row of buttons that went from the waist to the back of the neck.

"That's the last button," Sally announced. "Will there be anythin more ya wants me to do?"

"No, thank you, Sally. You can go now." Sally quietly left the room.

Kathryn selected a matching bonnet, tied the satin sash under her chin, picked up her handbag and hastily made her way downstairs.

Jesse was bringing the carriage around as Kathryn stepped out the door, stopping just behind Phillip's carriage, and the two drivers nodded greetings as Jesse assisted Kathryn into her seat.

Jesse clucked his tongue and slapped gently on the reins. The sleek white horse pranced the red leather carriage with a black fringe top past Phillip's rig and around the circular drive. Jesse turned around to ask, "Which way, Miss Kathryn?"

Kathryn leaned forward and replied, "To the bank first." Jesse swung the carriage left onto the road that went past other fine estates and led into the city.

The carriage stopped in front of the bank and Jesse helped her step out. Kathryn created quite a stir when she requested the teller to withdraw $5,000 from her account. Mr. English, the bank president, offered to have the money transferred to a different bank, for safety's sake, but Kathryn was adamant she wanted the cash. Reluctantly, Mr. English instructed the teller to count up the money. He became more concerned when she informed him that she was leaving Lexington, and as soon as she was settled, would be transferring most of her account and money due her from the trust fund elsewhere. Mr. English was beside himself with anxiety and curiosity, because the Barnett account was one of his largest, but he dared not pry.

A bank guard escorted Kathryn to her, carriage. She placed the canvas bag containing her money into a compartment under the seat and said, "Now, drive me to the railroad depot, Jesse."

Jesse gave her a puzzled look as he eased the carriage out onto the busy street.

At the depot, Jesse parked in an area reserved for carriages. Kathryn walked away with determination down the brick-lined walk that led to the depot entrance. There were a lot of people milling around and she had to pass some raggedy-looking men leaning against the building. Kathryn pretended not to notice their stares which gave her an uncomfortable feeling.

As she neared the door, Kathryn noticed a tall, slim handsome gentleman wearing a black hat and sporting a trim, dark mustache, watching her approach. She felt self-conscious and lowered her eyes, but when she raised them, he was still looking at her. He swung the door open for her and smiled kindly.

"Why, thank you," stammered Kathryn. She looked into deep-brown, twinkling eyes, and little twinges danced in her stomach.

The gentleman tipped his hat, which was the kind Uncle Richard wore, and said in a slow, deep voice, "My pleasure, ma'am." Kathryn felt herself blushing and quickly walked into the depot and headed straight for the sign that read "TICKETS."

As soon as an elderly couple had completed their purchase, Kathryn eased up to the skinny bars that separated her from the ticket agent.

"Where to, ma'am?" The man was old and short with a balding head that protruded from a visor. What hair he had was white and stuck out at the sides and, resting on the bridge of his nose, were square-shaped spectacles.

"I need a ticket that gets me as close to Villa Grove, Colorado," replied Kathryn.

"Can't say as I'm familiar with Villa Grove. What's the nearest large city?"

Kathryn felt embarrassed because she really wasn't sure, "I think it's Pueblo," she ventured.

"Just a. minute," the old man said gruffly, and he shuffled over to a large map on the back wall. With his finger, he circled the air around an area on the map, then punched his finger down on a spot. Moving his finger back in the direction of Lexington, he retraced until he came to a spot left of the middle. He shuffled back to the window and said, "You take this train, the L & N, that's the Louisville, Nashville, to Louisville. Then you go on to St. Louis and catch the Wabash to Kansas City where you'll take the Santa Fe as far as La Junta. That's southeast of Pueblo and as far as she goes."

"How do I go about getting a stagecoach from there? asked Kathryn.

"That's up to you when you get there."

"When does the next train leave that I need to take?"

"Ten o'clock tonight."

Kathryn looked at the clock on the back wall. It was four o'clock already. Would that give her enough time, she wondered?

"Do you want to buy a ticket or not? Cause I got other folks to wait on."

Kathryn became aware of fidgeting feet behind her and annoying little coughs. She glanced back with an apologetic smile, only to be looking directly at the face of the handsome stranger, grinning. Quickly, she turned back to the old man and said, "All right. Please give me a ticket."

The old man looked relieved and pulled a ticket from under the counter and stamped it in two places. He pushed it toward her and said, "That'll be $62.00." Kathryn reached in her handbag and counted out the fare, handed him the money and took her ticket.

"Good day, ma'am. Next?"

Kathryn stepped aside and walked slowly out of the depot clutching her ticket. Having the ticket made leaving a reality, and now she felt afraid and unsure. Getting to Bonanza seemed difficult and complicated and, worse, she didn't have much time to get ready before she'd have to rush back here to catch her train on time. She paused and thought. She also needed more information so she could wire Uncle Richard to tell him when to meet her. She felt confused and shaken and tried to calm herself. She reasoned that somewhere along the way she would find out what day her stage would arrive in Villa Grove, then she could send her wire. Feeling somewhat more sure of herself, she headed back to her carriage, unaware that the handsome man in the western hat stood watching her.

It was nearly five o'clock when Kathryn returned home. She got the canvas bag from the compartment and descended from the carriage. Jesse drove the carriage around back, becoming upset over what he suspected Kathryn was about to do.

Clutching the heavy money bag in both arms, Kathryn entered the house. She heard her mother and Philip's voices in the drawing room, and she quickly rushed up to her room,

Kathryn tossed her bonnet on the bed and sat on the floor to divide up her money. In one pile she counted up $3,000 and in two other piles she counted up $1,000 each, then placed the stacks on her dressing table. She opened the door to the adjoining storage room and dragged out a trunk and two valises to the middle of her room.

From her wardrobe she hastily selected four of her prettiest dresses, a wool, satin-lined cape, fur muff, four bonnets, two parasols and three pair of calf-height shoes with pearl buttons and packed these in the trunk.

She took a ribbon and tied up the $3,000 and stuffed the money inside of her fur muff. Between her dresses, she placed her jewelry box, framed photographs and her baby mementos. Satisfied with its contents, Kathryn closed down the lid and latched it.

In the smaller valise, she put underclothes, nightgowns, sleeping caps, a red silk robe and stationery. Tying up one of the piles of $1,000, she tucked that into one of her sleeping caps, fastened the clasp and went to the larger valise.

She put in her riding clothes first, then chose a rose-colored, taffeta dress for her arrival. She included a change of undergarments, a petticoat, and a black knit shawl. From her vanity, she took her silver brush and mirror set and her toiletries, placing them carefully inside. Of the remaining stack of money, Kathryn divided that into two $500 piles, tying them also with ribbon. She placed one of the piles into the larger valise inside a pair of bloomers, the other in her handbag, From her bedside, she retrieved her Bible and placed it under her shawl, She didn't latch this valise because she remembered her, boots and one very important item.

Kathryn looked at the clock. It was almost seven o'clock, time for dinner. Kathryn dreaded this, but she left her room and headed for the dining room.

Jolene was sitting alone at the table when Kathryn appeared. Relieved to see that Phillip was not joining them for dinner, as he usually did, she quietly sat in her place and took a sip of tomato juice.

"I'm glad to see that I won't be dining alone," remarked her mother casually, as if nothing had occurred that afternoon. Kathryn smiled weakly.

After Eli had served their meal and the two began eating, Kathryn spoke.

"Mother, I will be leaving here tonight."

"You what?" Jolene's eyes widened as her jaw dropped.

"I'm leaving. I purchased my ticket this afternoon, and I'll be on the evening train." Kathryn picked up her coffee cup and took a deliberate sip, waiting for her mother's reaction.

Jolene's eyes narrowed and looked directly into Kathryn's. "And I forbid you to go."

"And I say I'm going."

"Why are you trying to hurt and humiliate me, Kathryn?"

"Me? Me hurt and humiliate you? What do you think your siding with Phillip has done to me? Why did you allow him to strip me of my position at the mill? Why has he suddenly taken over all decision making? And why, have you ever asked yourself, does

Phillip want to control all our finances, by carefully manipulating you, so that I have no say or power over my own affairs? Why, Mother? Why? I'll tell you why. Because your dear Phillip wants to own everything we have—everything Father worked so hard for. How can you be so blind?"

"Stop. Stop," screamed Jolene, putting her hands over her ears. "I don't want to hear another word. You don't know what you're saying. You're just jealous of the attention I give to Phillip. I've been alone too long, and I won't stand for you to spoil my chance for happiness. I won't, I won't."

Jolene jumped up and her chair toppled to the floors. She paced back and forth across from Kathryn, taking deep breaths as she opened and closed her fists. She stopped abruptly and bent over the table and hissed, "I will hear no more of you moving to Colorado; is that understood?"

"Mother," Kathryn shot back, "I am leaving. I will not stay here and watch while Phillip uses you and our money."

Jolene's eyes filled with quick, angry tears. Through clenched teeth she said, "How dare you? Phillip loves me." Jolene stood trembling and gripping the back of a chair so tightly her knuckles turned white. In an almost inaudible whisper she said, "I don't want you to go."

Kathryn stood up and slowly walked around the table and gently put her arm around her mother's shoulders. Jolene stiffened. "Mother, I love you; you know that. And I truly wish for you to be happy. But I don't think you'll find it with Phillip, and I feel sorry for you about that."

Jolene took a handkerchief from her pocket and caught the tears streaming from her eyes.

"Mother, please don't cry." Yet her own tears were coming down. "I wish we didn't have to part this way, but my mind is made up. Now, I find that I am anxious to go out west to begin a new life for myself. With or without your blessing, I will be gone tonight." Kathryn removed her arm from her mother's unyielding shoulders and left the room.

Down at the stables, Kathryn bid Jackson, her horse, a tearful goodbye. She located Jesse and said, "I am leaving here tonight, Jesse." Jesse was stunned. "I want you and Eli to come to my room and bring my things down to the carriage. I want you to have the carriage around front before 8:30 so I can catch my train."

Jesse swallowed a lump in his throat and said, "Yes, Miss Kathryn."

Kathryn spied her cleaned boots and took them with her back to her room.

Placing them in the larger valise, there was still one more thing. Kathryn left her room, walked down the long hallway, and quietly descended the staircase. At the bottom, she listened to see if anyone was about before proceeding down the hall to the side of the stairs. She opened the first door on the right, entered and closed the door.

The room was dark, and she groped for the lamp and a match. When lit, the lamp cast a glow over what had been Kathryn's father's study. The large oak desk occupied the center of the room. On one wall were shelves of books from floor to ceiling, and the other displayed mounted trophies of wild game. Kathryn looked at the stuffed animals that seemed to stare back in disapproval. She shivered as she walked past them to the back of the desk. She set the lamp down, bent over and opened the bottom right drawer. There it was, in a leather holster and cartridge belt—her father's Colt 44 revolver. Carefully, she lifted the gun and holster from the drawer.

Kathryn sat down in the chair and set the gun on her lap, recalling the first time her father let her fire it. The kick it gave almost knocked her over, but as time went by she was able to aim and shoot down targets. Her father taught her how to use all the firearms in his extensive collection, much to the chagrin of her mother. Jolene felt John was trying to turn Kathryn into the son he'd never had.

Kathryn placed the gun on the desk and went to the gun cabinet. She opened the drawer that contained ammunition and took two boxes of cartridges. Realizing she couldn't carry the gun, ammunition and open doors, too, she strapped the gun around her waist, put the cartridges in one hand, the lamp in the other, and headed for the door. She blew out the lamp and quietly opened the door, listening for sounds. She snuck down the hall and listened again. Hiking her skirt in her hand, she ran up the stairs with the gun flapping against her blue taffeta dress.

Safely back in her room, Kathryn pulled the revolver from the holster, cocked back the hammer with her thumb, spun the cylinder and eyed the empty chambers. She opened one of the boxes and took out a handful of shells. One by one she slid the shells into the six chambers. Slowly, she lowered the hammer and placed the gun back in the holster. She unbuckled the belt, wrapped it around the holster and gun, and placed them into the larger valise next to her Bible and the partially opened box of shells. The other box went into the smaller valise.

Kathryn stood and surveyed her baggage, trying to think of anything she might have missed. Her derringer. How could she have forgotten that? She opened her vanity drawer and removed the double-barreled pistol with pearl-handled grips, one of the last gifts from her father. She put the gun in her handbag along with four bullets and put the box of extras into the small valise along with the others.

She was aware of the dangers of traveling west, for she'd read many a grisly account in the newspapers. Kathryn was not going to make it easy for any thief to take her money or threaten her person.

Satisfied, she pulled the green cord two times, signaling for Franny.

While she waited for Franny, Kathryn selected her traveling outfit. A light tap sounded at the door and Kathryn opened the door to see four sad-eyed faces. One by one, they entered the room and stood huddled in death-like silence. Kathryn quietly shut the door.

Eli spoke up first. "We know why you are leaving, Miss Kathryn. We just wish you weren't going. We wanted to say goodbye together."

Kathryn looked at each of them. "I never thought I'd be saying goodbye like this. You probably know I'm going to Colorado to live with Uncle Richard," she choked, "and I'm going to miss you all so very much." Her speech was joined by gasping breaths and sniffling. Kathryn continued, "I will write as soon as I get there. And—I want all of you to promise—to look after Mother—and if anything happens you think I should know about—wire me, please."

All heads nodded.

"Now, Eli, and Jesse, please take my trunk down the back way to the carriage; and then, Jesse, you drive around front for me. And hurry, it's getting late."

The two men hoisted the trunk onto their shoulders and carried it from the room. "Sally, please help me out of this dress so I can change."

Kathryn dressed in front of Sally and Franny into a light-weight gray wool skirt and matching jacket with white lace trim on the collar and cuffs. Her bonnet was gray felt with a red plume. When she'd finished, Eli was at the door for the valises.

"Sally, you take the smaller one so Eli won't have to make two trips."

Franny had remained quiet throughout all that was going on, just sitting in a chair, slowly shaking her head.

"Well, I guess I'm ready, Franny." Kathryn looked at Franny. Her face was all puckered up, trying to hold back her tears, but it was useless, for they were streaming down her cheeks and landing on her apron top that covered her ample bosom. Kathryn went over to the bed and picked up her handbag, then reached out her hand to Franny. Together they walked to the door. Kathryn turned, taking into her mind how everything looked so she could always remember, then quietly shut the door.

Eli and Sally led the way and Kathryn and Franny held hands as they passed by Jolene's room. A light shone from under the door, and Kathryn hesitated, She wanted her mother to say goodbye, but she knew she wouldn't. Silently, the four descended the spiral staircase and out the front door.

From an upstairs window, drapes parted every so slightly as Jolene watched Kathryn hug goodbyes to the servants. She held her breath when Kathryn turned and looked directly up to her window. Kathryn gave a timid little wave and climbed into her waiting carriage.

"No," whispered Jolene "I didn't want it to be like this." Jolene watched in frozen helplessness as the carriage carrying her only child skirted the circular drive and disappeared.

As the carriage turned out of the long drive, Kathryn took one last look at the Barnett mansion, her home for all of her twenty-three years. The realization that she had chosen to leave and be on her own suddenly overwhelmed her, and she buried her face in her hands and cried.

After the tears were shed, Kathryn took her handkerchief and dried her eyes and blew her nose. She straightened herself up in her seat, determined to be brave. After all, she was going on a journey, an exciting journey to begin a new life.

The horse clip-clopped through the shadowy streets, and Jesse was feeling progressively worse the closer they got to the railroad depot.

He felt like part of a conspiracy driving Kathryn so she could leave her home. He was afraid for her safety, going off in the night by herself. A lump formed in his throat thinking about it, and he felt helpless to change it. He swallowed hard as the carriage swung onto the depot road.

Kathryn glanced at her brooch watch pinned to her jacket. It read 9:40. She was just going to make it. The carriage stopped in front of the depot, and Jesse hailed a. baggage man, and the two of them put her things onto a wheeled cart.

"Jesse, you might as well go back to the house. I can manage from here."

Jesse looked down at the ground and swallowed hard. "Ah'd rather hang round here to make sure ya gits on the train with no troubles."

Kathryn saw real concern in Jesse's eyes, and she thought maybe she would feel better, too, if someone were here to see her off, even if it could only be her driver. "Thank you, Jesse. I'd like your company."

Jesse went to park the carriage. Kathryn followed the baggage man with the cart through the depot and out the other side. She took the larger valise to have with her, and the rest of her things went to the baggage car. There were lots of people waiting for the train and almost all, including Kathryn, glanced down the long, empty set of tracks hoping to see the front of the engine rolling in from the east.

Kathryn set the valise beside her on the ground and nervously inspected her fellow passengers. There were a lot more men than women, and most of the women were with husbands or being escorted. Kathryn felt awkward standing by herself and raised her hand and patted her hair in place and made sure her bonnet was on straight. She felt the weight of the derringer in her handbag and felt a little safer.

"I see it coming," someone shouted. Kathryn took a few steps and stared down the track. Sure enough, way off in the distance, a black object positioned on the tracks was moving this way Kathryn's heart gave a flutter and she took in a deep breath.

"I see yo train's acomin, Miss Kathryn." Jesse was beside her now, and it felt comforting just having him there.

Jesse stood close to Kathryn, and they watched in silence as the oncoming train became larger. Soon they could hear the chugging of the engine, and Kathryn shivered and got goose bumps when the whistle began to blow. She felt the excitement in the air as people's voices got louder and anxiously moved about. A few cheered as the train screeched to a stop and puffs of steam poured out from between the wheels.

The conductors jumped down from the cars and placed a step in front of the doors for the departing passengers. The crowd began to swell as people stepped off the train. The passengers who were taking this train began to line up in front of different cars and waited until they heard the head conductor yell, "Now boarding for Louisville, Evansville and points west."

Kathryn looked apprehensively at Jesse, then stared at the train which was about to take her away. Jesse stood behind her clutching the valise, and they slowly inched their way to the door. Four cars down, a man waiting in line bobbed up and down searching for a face but had to board before he found the woman he was searching for.

Finally, Kathryn stepped onto the train, and Jesse followed her to her seat. He placed the valise on the floor, then awkwardly stood there, not knowing what to do or say.

Kathryn threw her arms around him and said, "I will miss you so much. Please take good care of yourself and Jackson, too."

Jesse hugged Kathryn back, and with his voice choked up, said, "Miss Kathryn, yo is gonna be missed aplenty. Don yo fret none bout ol' Jackson, neither. I'll take care o him like he was ma own." By now, most of the people in her car were watching with disapproval of this display between a black man and a white woman, but neither Jesse nor Kathryn paid them any mind.

Jesse pulled away and hurriedly said, "Bye, Miss Kathryn," and dashed from the car. Kathryn turned to seat herself and noticed the cold stares fixed upon her. She narrowed her eyes at them and they quickly turned away.

Kathryn sat down next to the window, leaving an empty seat by the aisle. She scanned the group of people waving from the platform, trying to find Jesse, and finally spotted him standing by the side of the building blowing his nose.

"All aboard." The train lunged forward and slowly crept away from the depot. Kathryn and Jesse waved until they could no longer see each other, and Kathryn slumped back in her seat with tears streaming down her face.

Through misty eyes, Kathryn watched the city of Lexington pass by in fleeting objects of sights and memories. They were now on the outskirts of the city and the whistle blew as the train picked up speed.

Meanwhile, Jolene was sitting at her opened bedroom window and heard the haunting sound of the train whistle blowing off in the distance. The sound pierced her heart, and her body shook with each gasping breath. Remorsefully, she staggered to her bed, collapsing in tears and, still fully clothed, cried herself to sleep.

Blackness covered Kathryn's window and lights were dimmed in the car. Kathryn closed her eyes in exhaustion as the train chugged on through the dark night.

3

Clint Davis scrunched down in his seat. It was too late and too dark after tickets had been taken for him to wander through the cars. He'd wait until morning to look for her. He'd heard her buy a ticket for the 10:00 pm, and her destination was confirmed after he slipped the ticket agent a dollar gold piece.

What had come over him he didn't know, but the minute he'd laid eyes on that girl, he knew she was somethin special. He wished to know her name and wondered why she was traveling alone. He worried she might be going to meet some fellow. Well, he'd soon find out.

"Breakfast will be served in the dining car at eight o'clock," announced the conductor as he strolled through Kathryn's car.

Kathryn woke with a start and blinked open her eyes. It was daylight. She could hardly believe she'd slept through the night. Moving in her seat, she discovered her body was stiff and numb.

Slowly, she stood up, and holding onto the seat backs, she worked her way down the aisle, The train jerked and swayed, making her step haltingly as she headed in the direction of the ladies comfort room.

To her dismay, the door was locked and she had to wait her turn.

Once inside the tiny room, Kathryn splashed water on her face, did some primping and smoothed out the wrinkles in her skirt. After fixing her hair, she put her bonnet back on and left to find the dining car.

Waiting in line at the door of the diner gave Kathryn a chance to look about. The car was already crowded with people seated at tables of four, compacted to accommodate as many as possible.

"Are you alone, ma'am?

"Yes."

"Follow me, please." The steward seated Kathryn at a table with two older ladies who were finishing their breakfast.

"Good morning," greeted one of the ladies.

"Good morning," answered Kathryn.

A waiter set a small menu and a glass of water in front of Kathryn and said, "I'll be back for your order." Kathryn decided on scrambled eggs, a blueberry muffin and coffee, and set the menu aside.

"My name is Agnes and this is my sister, Florence," smiled the woman with pale blue eyes, Florence, who resembled her sister, nodded a kindly hello.

After Kathryn's order was taken, Agnes inquired, "Are you traveling by yourself, dear?"

"Yes, I am."

"Well, we hope you have a safe, enjoyable journey," said Agnes. Florence nodded in agreement and the ladies rose to leave.

"We shall see each other again, I'm sure, before the journey's ended," added Florence, "Enjoy your breakfast." The sisters departed as Kathryn's food was served.

She thanked the waiter and picked up her cup of coffee, unaware of the man in the doorway.

Clint's heart began pounding when he saw the girl sitting alone. "If it's all the same to you, I'd be pleased to be seated with that young lady over there." Clint pointed.

The steward nodded his approval and Clint strolled into the diner. He cautiously lowered himself into the seat across from Kathryn, and as she glanced up, her eyes widened in surprise.

Clint removed his hat and drawled, "I don't think we've been properly introduced, I'm Clint, Clint Davis. And you are?"

Kathryn blushed as she gazed into his deep brown eyes and stammered, "Why, you're the one who opened the door for me at the depot in Lexington."

"Yup. And I still don't know your name."

"I'm Kathryn."

"Kathryn," repeated Clint. "That's a pretty name. Suits ya, too." Kathryn blushed again.

Before the waiter could set down a menu, Clint said, "I'll have a steak, rare; and eggs, runny, and coffee, black." The waiter left and Clint directed his attention back to Kathryn.

"So, yer goin to Villa Grove, are ya?"

"How did you know that?" questioned Kathryn.

"I was standing behind you in line and couldn't help but overhear. Do ya have someone there expecting ya?" he ventured.

"Yes, my uncle. He lives near Villa Grove in Bonanza, but I'm not sure just how far away that is."

"I'd say it's about twelve miles," Clint offered.

"Oh, then you're familiar with the area," said Kathryn.

"Some. Are you just going for a visit?" he pried.

"No, I'm going there to live," Kathryn answered matter-of-factly.

"Pretty rugged country out there for women," declared Clint.

"I'm sure I can manage."

Kathryn busied herself buttering her muffin. She felt self-conscious whenever their eyes met. She wondered why this man had that effect on her. No one else ever had.

Clint's breakfast was served, and he eagerly cut into his steak. "Ahh. Just the way I like it." He popped a piece into his mouth and rolled his eyes at Kathryn in delight. Kathryn grinned at him, then lowered her head to sip her coffee. Ever so slightly she raised her eyes over her cup and watched him eat and reflected that he was the handsomest man she'd ever seen.

Clint stopped his eating and looked at her thoughtfully. "So ya never been out west before?"

"No, I've never been out of Kentucky. This is my first real trip."

"Well, yer gonna be in for some mighty big surprises. You'll find life's a whole lot different than back east."

Kathryn responded brightly, "My uncle has told me all about Bonanza, so I'm pretty familiar with what it's going to be like."

Clint chuckled, "Hearin 'bout a place and livin with the hardships are two different things."

Kathryn was annoyed by his laughing and stiffened in her chair. "You make it sound like I'm going to be living in some dreadful place, and I don't like your implying that I'm incapable of making changes."

"I'm not tryin to make Bonanza sound awful, Kathryn. In fact, it's a beautiful place, all. tucked away there in the mountains. But it's gonna be a lot harder and rougher living than I reckon a well-bred lady like you is used to."

"And just how would you know what I'm used to?" said Kathryn.

"Because I saw the fancy carriage you were driven in, for one thing, and yer clothes. What ya have on is much nicer than anything I've seen on the ladies where you're goin."

Kathryn glanced down at her outfit. "What I ride in and what I wear has no bearing whatsoever on who or what I am—or, for that matter, Mr. Davis, what I'm capable of doing; And I'll thank you to keep your judgment of me to yourself." She rose abruptly and marched out of the diner.

Clint stared helplessly as he watched Kathryn disappear. He wanted to go after her and apologize, "You fool," he thought, as he poked at the food on his plate.

The train was chugging through Missouri heading for Kansas. This was Kathryn's third day riding; it was becoming tedious. From her window she'd watched cities, small towns, farms and miles and miles of nothingness pass by.

Kathryn had not seen Clint Davis since that morning in the diner. She pictured his brown eyes, mustached smile and the way he wore his hat cocked back on his head. She was sorry she'd reacted so harshly. Maybe he was just trying to be helpful. After all, he did know the country she would be living in. She tried putting him out of her mind and decided to write her mother a letter but discovered she'd forgotten to pack pen and ink. Maybe it was for the better. She'd write when she got to Bonanza.

Kathryn read her Bible for comfort and companionship, for the people in her, car were still unfriendly, due, she suspected, to her affectionate embrace with Jesse. A man sitting two rows over kept looking back at her with a sinister smile. She tried to avoid glancing in his direction whenever she felt him staring but could feel the looks from his beady eyes.

Agnes and Florence were the only ones Kathryn was acquainted with, and they had taken several meals together. Although she enjoyed their company, she longed for more excitement.

It was 2:30 in the afternoon and, fighting boredom, Kathryn decided to take a stroll through some different cars, then go to the diner for tea. This way she might run into Clint, if he was still on the train. She shoved her valise under her seat and set out for some diversion.

Kathryn found it scary as she looked down and saw the tracks whizzing by underneath her feet. The cars swayed and jerked as she attempted to get from one platform to another.

In each car people nodded and greeted her as Kathryn walked down the aisles, and soon she began to feel more cheerful. In each new car, she expected to run into Clint, but he was nowhere to be seen.

Kathryn entered the dining car and was seated at a table alone. The car was empty, save for three well-dressed older gentlemen sitting together at an adjoining table. After her tea and biscuit were served, Kathryn listened in on the men's conversation.

The eldest-looking man, portly and with thick, snow-white hair, said to his companions, "Gentlemen, I understand there is already one full table going. If we could find a couple more to play, we can start another game."

"I ran into a Frank Palmer on my way here. Said he was feeling lucky and was going to the club car in hopes of getting in on a game," replied another man, who was thinner with gray streaks in his dark hair.

"Do you know of any other interested parties?" asked the snowy-haired man.

"No," answered the third gentleman, who wore round, thick spectacles

The snowy-haired man set down his cup of tea. "From what I understand, the stakes are quite high at the table now playing. That's the game I'd like to be in on." He glanced over and noticed Kathryn, nodded and smiled. "Good afternoon, ma'am. I hope our conversation is not disturbing your solitude."

"No, not at all," Kathryn responded. "You gentlemen must be talking about poker, am I not correct?"

"Why, yes, we are," answered the snowy-haired man, "Are you familiar with the game?"

"Yes, my father taught me to play."

The snowy-haired man looked upon Kathryn with new interest. She was expensively dressed and conducted herself as one of good breeding. Could be she had money. With an endearing smile, he said, "If I may be so bold, ma'am, would you perhaps be interested in playing a few hands? Or would such a. refined young lady be offended by all male company?"

"Not at all. I'd be delighted to relieve the boredom from this long ride."

The men smiled at each other, then at Kathryn, and rose from the table. The snowy-haired man offered his arm, turned to the others, and said, "Follow us, gentlemen."

Kathryn was escorted to the end of the dining car, through another and another until they entered a smoke-filled car.

Kathryn gave a slight gasp when she recognized Clint, his back to her, playing cards at the high-stakes table. She felt strangely out of place now, as she followed the three men to a table and stopped abruptly. Seated at their table, waiting for a game, was the beady-eyed man from her car. His blond, greasy hair was parted down the middle, and his rotten-toothed grin made shivers run up her spine.

What was she thinking of, going with three strange men to play poker? This was sure to create a very unfavorable impression on Clint, but she felt it was too late to back out of this situation without causing a scene. Reluctantly, she took her place at the table next to the snowy-haired gentleman. She glanced nervously back in Clint's direction and noticed the woman playing at his table. The woman wore lots of jewelry and had on a red, low-cut dress which exposed part of her bosom. She flirted with Clint, and her high-pitched laugh carried through the car. So that was the type of woman he preferred. Now, Kathryn wasn't at all sorry for her behavior toward him.

She turned back as the snowy-haired man said, "I'm afraid, my dear, I've been remiss on introductions. My name is Charles Sawyer, and these are brothers, Norbert and Jerome Miller.

The brothers nodded.

"And I am Frank Palmer," grinned the loathsome man from her car.

Kathryn sucked in a short breath of air. "My name is Kathryn." She felt they need know no more.

"It's a pleasure, ma'am," said Frank, and a smirk crossed his boney face.

A bartender asked Kathryn if she cared for a beverage. The men had ordered whiskey and she didn't know what to answer. Finally, she stammered, "A glass of sherry, if you have it."

The chips were brought out, and Kathryn pulled some money from the handbag on her lap. She bought $250 worth and, smiling, said, "Just for starters." The men smiled back politely.

Hairs on the back of Clint's neck prickled when he heard her voice. He cocked back his hat with a thumb and turned his head slowly. He could hardly believe his eyes. What in blue blazes was that girl doing in this car? Those men would surely take what money she had. He wanted to drag her out of there, but he knew he had no right to butt in. He wished he'd gone to her before this and apologized, then he might have talked her out of such foolishness. He turned back to his game and found it hard to concentrate, which infuriated him because he'd been riding lady luck for the last five hands.

The players at Kathryn's table agreed upon five card draw. Fifty-dollar chips were placed to ante in the center of the green, felt-covered table. Jerome, on the other side of Charles, was first to deal.

Kathryn picked up her cards, slowly fanned them apart, and without moving a muscle on her face, she studied her hand. Two aces, a seven, a jack and a queen.

Charles opened the betting with another $50. Kathryn put in her chip, as did Norbert, Frank and Jerome, which brought the pot up to $500. When it came to her, Kathryn turned in her seven and the jack for two new cards. The pleasure she felt when she saw her cards was kept to herself.

Norbert, on Kathryn's left, fattened the pot with another $50. Next was Frank. He hesitated, then placed his chip in. Jerome folded.

"I'll stay and raise $50," said Charles, and he tossed in two chips

Kathryn picked up three chips. "I'll see you and raise you another $50."

Norbert slapped his cards down and said, "I'm out"

Frank pondered his hand, looked longingly at the pot, and grudgingly laid down his cards. With great interest, he looked from Charles to Kathryn, as did the others.

With a bit of ceremony, Charles laid down his cards—a pair of kings, a pair of tens and a nine. He smiled at Kathryn and waited to see her hand.

All eyes were on her as Kathryn spread out her cards, and Frank gave a low whistle when they saw her three aces and a pair of queens, a full house. A slow grin spread across Kathryn's face as she scooped up the pile of chips with both hands. Charles was not amused, but he concealed his disdain.

The game went on for two more hours, with Kathryn winning a goodly share of the pots. She could feel contempt from the men, especially Frank, who'd lost a lot of money,

The game at the other table broke up. Fortunately, Clint came out ahead, but only by a hundred. His concern for Kathryn had spoiled his game. The players stayed around to watch the tense game Kathryn was in.

She smiled sheepishly at Clint when he came to stand by her chair. He grinned down at her, amazed at her playing ability and silently cheered her on. The woman in the red dress began hanging on Clint's arm, and he shrugged her off, ignoring her overtures. She latched onto another man from their game and was visibly livid over Clint's rejection, but Kathryn was pleased.

The stakes were raised to $200. Strangely, Frank had begun winning whenever he dealt, and Kathryn was suspicious.

It was Norbert's deal and Kathryn won again. Now, it was Frank's turn. Out of the corner of her eye, Kathryn watched his hands. The cards were dealt and bets were placed. When it came back around to Kathryn, she asked for three new cards. She picked them up and fit them alongside her queen and jack of hearts. Keeping a solemn face, she inwardly rejoiced over the ten, nine and eight of hearts she'd just been dealt, giving her a straight flush.

Norbert also asked for three cards. Frank discarded two cards and gave himself two more. It was then that Kathryn was sure.

Jerome and Charles folded. Kathryn slid eight chips over to the pot, saying, "I'm in and raise $200."

"Too steep for me," said Norbert; and he, too, folded. Now the game was between Frank and Kathryn.

Frank selected eight chips, laid them in the pile, then took four more and added them saying, "I'll call. and raise you two."

Everyone waited silently to see what Kathryn would do. Holding her cards in her left hand close to her chest, she reached over and took four more chips and put them in the pot. Then, narrowing her eyes at Frank, she said, "I don't play with cheaters, so if you can beat this hand without the ace of spades, you win."

The room went deathly still. Frank glared at Kathryn and she fixed her stare on him.

"No one accuses me of cheating and gets away with it. Not even a woman."

"I saw you deal from the bottom of the deck."

"You're lying," snarled Frank.

"Oh, no, I'm not." You tipped the deck when you dealt Norbert's last card, and I saw the ace of spades."

Frank sat frozen, glaring mean and threatening at Kathryn. Ever so slowly,

Kathryn lowered her right arm to her lap and with her left hand spread her cards on the table. With her straight flush showing, she said, "Now, Frank. Beat that—without the ace of spades."

Frank didn't move, just kept on glaring.

"Lay down your cards, Frank," ordered Charles. Frank went to reach inside his coat, and Charles grabbed his arm just as Kathryn whipped her derringer over the top of the table, aiming directly at Frank's heart.

"It isn't sporting to cheat at cards, Frank," said Kathryn. "And it isn't polite to threaten a lady."

Kathryn kept the gun pointed at Frank as Charles removed the gun from Frank's coat, then reached over and took the cards out of Frank's hand. One by one, Charles laid the cards face up on the table.

All heads were bent reading the cards—a ten of spades, jack of spades, queen of spades, king of spades—and, last, the ace of spades.

Beads of sweat collected on Frank's greasy hairline, then trickled jerkily down the sides of his pocked cheeks.

Still pointing her gun, Kathryn reached with her left arm, circled the pile of chips and drew them across the table in front of her.

Frank worked his fists open and closed, then eased himself up from the chair, keeping his eyes on Kathryn and her derringer. Looking menacingly at her, he said through his teeth, "Somehow, I will get even with you for this, and you can bet on that." He stomped past the stunned crowd and left the car.

Clint squeezed his hand on Kathryn's shoulder, and she looked up at him with a look of relief. Charles broke the silence.

"I am truly sorry you were involved in this disgraceful affair," he said to Kathryn. "I had no idea the man was a scoundrel."

"I'm sure you didn't," agreed Kathryn. "I think I've had enough card playing for one day. I'd like to cash in my chips."

Kathryn had won over $2,000, and as Clint escorted her from the playing car, he proclaimed, "Whewee. I do believe I've sold ya short. Where'd ya learn to play so good?"

"From my father and Uncle Richard."

Clint paused before opening the adjoining car door and looked directly into Kathryn's eyes. "I wanna say I'm sorry as all get out fer what I said that riled ya so in the diner. I sure didn't mean anything by it. I was only thinkin about yer safety and tryin to point out that there'll be a lotta big changes fer ya to make."

"I thought you were belittling me."

"No, I wasn't. Just seein if ya knew what ya were in for, 'cause life's different, way different, from what ya. know." His dark brown eyes looked worried and sad, and Kathryn could tell he was genuinely sorry.

"I understand. I think you meant well, but I'm prepared to make any adjustments I have to."

Clint studied her expression and saw an inner strength. He admired her determination and had to suppress a. desire to put his arms around her and draw her close. Instead, he reached over and opened the door of the next car and helped her cross over.

Kathryn stopped as the door closed, and with a worried look, said, "I don't want to go back to my car. Frank is riding there. Is it possible for me to change?"

"Of course. We'll just have the conductor bring yer things to my car. That'll be all right by you, won't it? After all, we're goin to the same place."

"We are?" Kathryn was stunned.

"Yeah. I drive the stage between La Junta and Villa Grove. In fact, my dear lady, when we get off the train, I'll personally escort you."

"What do you mean?"

"I'll be drivin' yer' stage," Clint grinned.

4

Bonanza, Colorado

The oil lamp flickered dimly on the kitchen table and silhouetted the lone figure of Rick Barnett in his chair. The only sounds in the room came from the crackling logs in the fireplace that he'd lit to take out the early morning chill.

Rick was usually up before the other men. He relished the peaceful solitude that afforded him time to do his serious thinking and to plan his day.

With his large, rough hands wrapped around his orange mug, he stared intently at the hot, steaming coffee, his mind deep in thought over Kathryn. He'd been fretting over his niece since her urgent telegram had arrived. Now, he wondered if she'd gotten his reply yet, and was she going to travel all the way out here by herself? If so, when? What he really itched to know was what had forced her to make this drastic decision? Taking a slow drink of coffee as he turned toward the fire, Rick observed the dancing flames. He reassured himself that in due time he'd have his answers.

Resting his elbow on the table, Rick set his chin in the palm of his hand and continued to gaze at the fire, watching the flames change to different shapes. After watching a while, he put his mind to the day ahead.

When breakfast was over, he would ride out with Pedro to bring in strays. Pedro had spotted some yesterday at sundown as he came back from riding fence. There'd been rustlers working the area, and Rick wasn't about to make it easy for them to nab his cattle.

The sound of scratching on the door brought Rick to his feet. He opened the door for Jasper and Zeke, the black and white cow dogs. They came in wagging their tails and Rick bent down to pet them. Their arrival signaled that Sam and Pedro were up and soon would be in. Rick returned to the table, while Jasper and Zeke sprawled in front of the warm fire.

Footsteps creaked the boards on the porch and Sam burst through the door. He marched straight for the coffeepot, mumbling a "G'mornin, Rick," as he filled his cup. Taking some hearty gulps, he set down his mug to stoke the fire in the cook stove.

Sam McPeak was a burly Irishman with a mustache, a full beard, and thick, shoulder-length, red hair splashed with gray. He wore a yellow flannel shirt, and buckskin britches tucked into knee-high deerskin boots with fringe around the tops. Around his neck hung a rawhide string of elk's teeth given to him by a Shoshone chief, Sam, at fifty-two, was the oldest on the ranch but could outdo most any man. He was a seasoned mountain man and, in late fall, left the ranch for the high country to hunt and trap.

Rick met Sam six years ago at Fort Garland when each was doing separate business with the military. They joined up for the ride back toward Bonanza and, along the way, Rick offered Sam a job and a permanent place to live when he wasn't in the mountains. Liking the Idea, Sam rode back to the ranch with Rick.

Sam assumed most of the cooking chores and now took a, large knife and sliced strips from a slab of bacon. Turning to Rick, he said, "Ya know, you've been awful moody here lately. Still worryin 'bout Kathryn, ain't ya?"

"Yeah, I am. Can't help it, Sam. Just wish I knew what really was the matter."

"Ya'll find out soon's she gits here," Sam answered matter-of-factly. He laid the bacon strips into a hot skillet and immediately they began to sizzle.

"Yeah, s'pose you're right," said Rick, "but I worry 'bout her travelin to git here, too. That's a long, hard stretch of country for a young lady, 'specially if she's comin by herself."

Sam put the rest of the bacon slab back into a crock. Picking up the coffeepot, he refilled Rick's cup and said, "If she's a Barnett, she kin most likely take care of herself. Now, quit yer stewin." Sam nodded his head as if his word was final and went back to his fixins.

He got a basket of eggs from the pantry and cracked several into a bowl, Rick looked on with interest as Sam cut up onions and chile peppers and plopped them in with the eggs. He added a bit of crushed garlic, salt and pepper, then took a big fork and mixed his concoction. Setting it aside on the wood-planked counter, he picked up the bowl of dough he'd prepared last night for making biscuits.

Glancing out the window as he rolled out the dough, Sam saw Pedro coming out of the bunkhouse they shared. Pedro walked toward the house and around to the back where the outhouse stood. In a few moments he stepped onto the back porch and entered the kitchen from the door near the stone fireplace.

"Mornin, Senor Rick. Feels like it's gonna be a nice day. The air, she's smellin so good." Pedro swaggered across the wood floor, his high-heeled black boots making sharp raps with each step.

Pedro Lopez was Mexican. He was just eighteen and a hard-working', loyal hand. Short and slim, with coal-black hair and big, flashy eyes, he was dressed in Levis and a blue-and-white embroidered shirt, Perched on the back of his head was his favorite black hat. He'd killed a five-foot rattler out by the corral, tanned the hide from that ornery critter and made his prized hatband.

Taking a cup from the hook, Pedro squeezed behind Sam to reach the pot, and strolled over to the table, Proudly, he set his hat on the back of his chair and took his place to the left of Rick, his back to the fireplace, After a sip of coffee, Pedro asked, "What's the plans for today, Senor Rick?"

"Soon's we eat, you and I are goin to round up those strays. Which side of Little Kerber did you say they were on?"

"This side. So, by now, who knows? Could be across and down the other side, no?" offered Pedro.

"Chance they could be," answered Rick. Pedro nodded and went back to his coffee.

In front of the stove, Sam drank coffee with one hand and turned bacon with the other. He didn't talk much when he cooked, said he had to pay attention to what his food was doing.

Heads raised and looked toward the hall when they heard the creaking of Jim's door. Jim sauntered in, as usual for mornings, barefoot and wearing his long red woolies. Stopping to stretch and scratch, he blinked his eyes, yawned and announced, "I'd have slept longer, but the noise and smell of bacon frying made me come arunnin."

There was snickering, for if there was one thing Jim didn't do often, it was get up fast or early if he didn't have to. Jim ignored the snickers and walked over to get his cup, "Excuse me, Sam." Sam stepped aside so Jim could reach the pot. "Best eye-opener there is," remarked Jim as he trudged to the table, taking his place across from Rick, his back to the stove and Sam.

Sam checked his pan of biscuits in the oven and poured the eggs into a skillet. Opening a. cupboard, he took out four blue enameled plates and from a drawer, grabbed a handful of utensils. He plunked them down on the table and went to tend his eggs. Each man took a plate, fork and knife from the pile and waited for the grub.

Jim turned around in his chair and studied Sam. With a sly grin he drawled, "Ya know, Sam, when Kathryn gits here, we're jest gonna havta have a cookin contest to see who's the better woman at the stove. Haw-haw-haw." Jim turned back, smirking to Rick and Pedro.

Sam didn't cotton to Jim's remark. Quickly, he grabbed the basin of cold water in the sink, snuck up behind Jim and dumped it down his neck.

Jim, dripping wet, sprung from his chair, knocking it to the floor, and Rick and Pedro just sat and laughed.

"Damn. Just look whatcha did, Sam. Now I gotta change into my best underwear."

Hoots of laughter followed Jim as he strutted from the room, his woolies still dripping and sticking to his skin.

Pedro mopped up the water while Sam finished cooking. When Jim returned, he was dressed in Levis, a red flannel shirt and black boots. Pedro looked at Sam and commented, "Now we know how to git you dressed in the mornin, no?"

"But, then again," chimed in Sam, "When Kathryn comes, ya'll have to git dressed, 'cause ya'll scare the poor girl off, comin out like ya do." The men laughed good-naturedly and Jim sheepishly grinned back.

Sam brought the skillets to the table. Next came the biscuits, butter and honey, and Sam took his place across from Pedro.

While the men were eating, Rick slid his eyes around the table at the three and was grateful they got on so well. For a long time now, they'd been like a family, and Rick wondered how Kathryn would fit in, being the only lady. He sensed there would be a lot of changes after she arrived.

Rick finished his breakfast and lighted his pipe. "Sam, Jim, I want you to start cuttin out the steers goin to Fort Garland and git em penned up." Sam and Jim nodded as Rick stood up and sauntered toward the door.

Hanging to the right, on wooden pegs, were coats, hats and holstered guns. Rick reached for his battered gray Stetson and slapped it on his head and pulled his pipe from his mouth.

"Pedro, I'm goin' to get the horses ready while you finish eating." Pedro's mouth was full and he grunted a throaty uh-huh that he understood. Rick took his holster from its peg and strapped it around his slim hips, pulled out the Colt and spun the cylinder, making sure it was fully loaded, and slid it back into the holster. He put on his sheepskin coat, his pipe dangling between clenched teeth. "See ya'll later," and he went out the door.

Pausing for a moment on the roofed porch, Rick puffed slowly on the pipe and watched the sun peaking over the Sangre de Cristo Mountains. Miles of rugged, massive formations, their stern, gray, jagged peaks towered across the sky; but when the sun crested, as if by Divine command, they became majestically draped in cloaks of scarlet, wearing white helmets of snow, Never had he wearied of this awesome sight, and often in the evenings he would sit on the porch surveying the splendor when the sun cast its last light, painting the mountains in glowing hues of red and shades of blue and gray.

Rick stepped off the porch and knocked the hot ashes from his pipe against the railing, shoved it into his coat pocket and proceeded to the barn. He bridled and saddled his sorrel, Charlie, and Pedro's Midnight, a dark bay, and led them both out to the corral. The splashing sound of water caused Rick to look toward the well pump to see Pedro filling their canteens.

"Be there in a minute, Senor Rick," called Pedro. He set the filled canteens down and trotted to the bunkhouse. Going inside and quickly reappearing, he buckled his six-shooter around his hips. He scooped up the canteens and walked across the bare, packed ground to join Rick.

Pedro handed Rick his canteen as he untied Midnight's reins. Grasping the saddlehorn, he slipped his boot into the stirrup, gave a hop and swung his leg up and over, landing gently in the saddle.

Easing his tall frame astride Charlie, Rick backed him up, then turned him around. He nodded to Pedro and they trotted toward the hills.

A handsome man in his forties, Rick's tall, muscular body cut an appealing silhouette against the background of the sky, He and Pedro rode silently for a stretch off in the direction of yet-to-be-known trouble on Little Kerber Creek.

"Tell me about your niece, Senor Rick," finally asked Pedro, as they crossed the last of the hills. "What's she like, this Kathryn?"

"Well, I'll tell you. The last time I saw her she was a very pretty girl. And I suspect she's grown into a beautiful young lady." Rick closed his eyes for a moment, recalling Kathryn. Pushing his eyebrows together and biting on his lower lip, he ventured, "If she hasn't changed much, I'd say she's still a spunky gal and very strong-willed. She took after her father more so than her mother, except in looks." Rick chuckled and looked straight at Pedro. "You'll be amazed how well she can shoot for a gal. That is...if she does come."

They were riding the gulch now as it twisted around the surrounding hills. Deer, poised up the hillsides, silently observed them passing by as the wind whispered steady and gently through tall, thick pine branches. Both men kept a sharp eye, scanning the ground for signs, as they worked their way among the dry underbrush.

Reaching a. small, bright clearing, they dismounted to remove their coats and tied them to the backs of their saddles. The air had warmed considerably and they paused to drink from the canteens.

Pedro looked off into the distance. "I was near that fence." He pointed his finger to the northwest. "And back of me I hear the noise and I gits a look of them critters goin very fast 'long by the creek—like they was spooked, que no?"

"Well, if they're still around, we'll find 'em. Let's go."

They remounted and rode down a narrow, sloping path and out onto flat land, heading to where Little Kerber Creek began meandering onto Rick's ranch. Further ahead stood a small, thick grove of ponderosa pines skirting a high, rocky cliff and near the pines flowed Little Kerber Creek.

As they neared the grove, Pedro pointed and exclaimed, "Senor Rick. They are there."

"Sure enough."

Rick spotted six cows and two calves standing in the grove on the other side of the creek. They rode easy to the bank of the creek, then dismounted. The horses bent down and slurped the welcome water. Rick and Pedro knelt on the bank to also quench their thirst, scooping both hands into the noisy creek and slurping the cold, refreshing water.

Pedro wiped his mouth across his sleeve and his hands down the front of his pants, then swung back up on Midnight. Rick was still resting on his haunches when his eyes caught sight of a pile of bones just across the stream near the rocky cliff. Reaching his arm up, he nudged Pedro's leg and motioned in the direction of the bones. Pedro squinted his eyes over to the spot and looked back down at Rick with a puzzled expression.

Rick got back on Charlie. Cautiously, he and Pedro stepped the horses across the rapidly moving stream, while the cattle grouped together and watched. On the other side they tied the horses to a tree and headed over to inspect the pile.

They looked down on the fresh remains of a cow, probably Rick's. Rick studied the footprints in the soft, moist soil. The impressions were not made by boots, and among those were unshod-pony tracks.

"Pedro. Go back by the horses and keep a look out. I wanna check this out."

"Right, Senor Rick." Pedro turned back, his palm resting on the butt of his gun.

Rick slipped his gun out of the holster and followed the tracks, his boot heels sinking into the moist soil. He noticed another impression in the ground, but these were the distinct tracks made by horseshoes, and they both led into a steep, narrow canyon. Warier, he looked about and continued on into the tapering hollow.

A loud, cracking sound pierced the air and echoed through the canyon walls. Rick spun around, his gun aimed, but there was nothing there. Another shot rang out, and Rick heard the horses' high-pitched whinnies and the bawling cattle.

Running to the opening, he saw an Indian on a paint with his gun pointed toward the ground. Rick fired. The Indian jerked, then looked his way. Rick fired again as the Indian spun his pony and rode like the wind out of range.

Rick knew he'd got him, but how bad he didn't know. What the hell was going on here?

The cattle had stampeded across the creek and were headed in the direction Rick and Pedro had come. Rick looked anxiously around, but there was no sign of Pedro. Midnight was pawing the dirt and Rick ran toward the horses, his gun still drawn. He saw Pedro's boots sticking out from behind a tree and Rick's heart quickened.

Pedro lay face down, his black hat upside down in the dirt, his gun on the ground near his outstretched hand. Rick stared and bit down on his lip as he tipped his hat back with the barrel of his gun. Pedro lay so still that Rick couldn't tell if he was dead.

Rick's eyes darted about, alert for more danger. He dropped to his knees, placing his gun close on the ground. Gently, he put his left hand on Pedro's shoulder, worked his other arm under his chest and slowly turned him over.

Pedro let out an agonizing moan, and Rick breathed a heavy sigh. Pedro's face was ashen and his eyes started to blink, then popped wide open in fear. Blood trickled from the corner of his mouth and he gulped and choked out, "Se...Senor...Ri...," and lost consciousness.

Cradling Pedro's head in his lap, Rick looked down and saw blood seeping through the blue-and-white shirt, adding another color to the fabric. Rick took his knife from his belt and slit open the blood-wet shirt. The wound was on his right side and Rick prayed the bullet hadn't gone in too deep. He lay Pedro's head carefully on the ground and ran to his horse, grabbed his canteen and hastily returned.

Rick took off his yellow bandana, soaking it with water. Gently, he wiped the bloody belly, and Pedro's eyes popped open again. He looked helplessly at Rick and once more tried to speak, but all that came out was "Agh...agh."

"Don't talk, Pedro. You're gonna be all right," said Rick reassuringly, and he hoped he was right.

The laceration looked mean and deep, and this worried Rick. He squeezed the blood out of the bandana onto the dirt, rinsed it out and pressed the cloth firmly over the oozing wound.

"Agh," Pedro cried out as he winced and jerked.

"I know...it hurts like hell...sorry." Rick quickly unbuttoned his shirt and took it off. Easy now, he pushed the shirt under Pedro's back and brought the cloth around, knotting the sleeves snugly over the wound. Pedro yelped and lost consciousness again.

"I gotta get you home...but how?" said Rick, only Pedro couldn't hear him.

Rick knew if he laid him across the saddle he'd bounce on the wound and would probably bleed to death before they made it back. One way crossed his mind. He holstered his gun and went and untied the horses, led them close to the body and tied Midnight's reins to Charlie's saddlehorn. He bent to pick up Pedro when he spied the hat. He snatched it from the ground and stuffed it into a saddlebag. Rick untied his coat from the back of the saddle and put it on, then got Pedro's.

It was a struggle getting the unconscious man into his coat, but this done Rick scooped Pedro up in his arms and carried him over to Charlie. With difficulty he managed to get Pedro's leg over the saddle and keep him in an upright position while he got his boot into the stirrup and swung himself up behind.

Leaning Pedro against his chest, Rick wrapped his arms about him, while holding onto the reins. Glancing around first, he then dug his heels into Charlie's side to cross the creek, with Midnight at their side.

Charlie stepped cautiously into the stream, his hooves making a clunking sound as they landed on the stones and pebbles beneath the churning water.

It was a slow, tiring ride as Rick headed back through the gullies and over the hills. The sun was hanging in the western skies, and Rick pushed Charlie on, wanting to get back before the sky turned black. Pedro's heavy, sagging body was hard to keep upright, and every so often he would come to, moaning in pain from the jostling, then mercifully pass out again.

They passed the cattle they'd come to bring back, grazing contentedly, and Rick cursed them under his breath. Throughout the long, tedious ride, Rick tried to figure out who the Indian was. Where had he come from, and what was he doing on his land? Worst of all, why had he shot Pedro? And, where did the footprints lead?

Finally, they reached the top of the last hill. as the sun reflected off the peaks of the Sangre de Cristos. Rick's weary eyes caught the welcome sight of the ranch buildings and it perked him up. He eased the horses slowly down the hill and then onto the easy, flat ground that led them home.

When Rick was in shouting distance, he let out a holler. He saw no one and heard no answer. As he rode closer, he hollered again. All he heard was the echo of his own voice. "Damn. They're probably still out on the range."

Rick rode straight to the house and awkwardly dismounted, at the same time keeping Pedro from falling off the horse. He then slid Pedro down into his arms and carried him onto the porch. Kicking the door open with his boot, he lugged Pedro over to the sofa next to the fireplace. As he laid him down, Pedro came to, his face white and beady with sweat.

"Senor Rick," his voice rasped, "how bad..."

"Not bad, Pedro, but we gotta git you a doctor."

Rick looked at Pedro's belly and saw the blood had saturated his pants and had run down the leg. He had lost a lot of blood and Rick was worried. He glanced at himself; his clothes were also stained.

Quickly Rick built up the fires in the stove and fireplace, grabbed a kettle, filled it with water and put it on to boil. He got two clean towels and set them on the table, then stepped out on the porch to see if there was any sign of Sam or Jim.

Off to the right he saw small clouds of dust and cattle moving his way. Good, he thought, 'cause I sure need some help. Rick spun on his heel and quickly went back inside.

Rick knelt down and pulled off Pedro's boots, and with great care began to inch down the wet Levi britches, now sticky with blood. He plopped the britches on the floor and looked at Pedro lying so pitiful his black hair gray with dirt, dark smudges on his face, his nice shirt torn and bloody, and Rick's shirt, wrinkled and bulging around his middle, oozing blood.

Rick cocked his ear and heard Jasper and Zeke barking and cattle lowing. They were in. He ran outside and out to the corrals, shouting and waving his arms. Sam saw him and rode to him, with Jim close behind.

"Pedro's been shot." Both men's mouths opened in surprise, and before they could say anything, Rick ordered, "Jim, ride into town and get the doc. And hurry."

Jim spun his horse around and sped out the gate Rick opened for him, kicking up the dust as he galloped toward town.

Sam leaped off his horse, leaving him in the corral and ran after Rick up to the house.

Rick was checking the water and Sam crouched down by the sofa.

"Hey, good buddy, how ya doin?" whispered Sam in a hoarse but gentle voice. Pedro lifted his eyelids and stared at Sam, then closed them. Sam looked at Rick's bloody shirt around Pedro's middle and slowly rose and walked over to Rick by the stove.

Rick was lifting a hot towel out of the kettle with a wooden spoon, suspending it in the air while the water poured out.

"What happened out there, Rick?"

As Rick squeezed out the towel, he started relating what had gone on and what he had seen, and added, "I didn't git a good look at the Indian's face…was too far away. I don't know why, but I have this gnawing feeling in my gut that Taylor's got something to do with it."

Rick took the towel over by Pedro, and Sam got a cloth rinsed with cold water. As Sam mopped Pedro's sweaty brow and face, Rick untied the shirt. Pedro jerked in pain but remained unconscious. Rick tossed the bloodied shirt on top of the britches and gently removed the once-yellow bandana and lay the blood-dripping cloth on top of the filthy pile. With a moist, warm towel, he cleaned around the wound, then bent closer to examine it. The skin was split wide; a piece of flesh hung like a flap, and under the flap, a hole.

"Sam, get a dry towel off the table while I go get a blanket." Sam nodded as Rick went off. With tears in his eyes, Sam pressed the towel over the hole and helped Rick cover up their friend. Treading softly to the stove, he filled two cups with coffee, set them on the table and slumped down. Rick came to join him and both men sat and stared at Pedro.

In a hushed voice, Rick said, "You tell, me, Sam, what the hell is really goin on here?" Before Sam could come up with an answer, Rick went on. "Taylor's always taking cattle to sell yet he doesn't seem to be breedin em. Where's he gittin em from anyhow?"

Sam started to talk but Rick kept on. "He's rustlin from the ranches round here—we both know it." Sam nodded. "He jest ain't been caught, yet." Sam was about to jump in, but Rick continued. "And why—why all of a sudden is he so all-fired anxious in buying this spread? Remember the fat offer he made me just last month?"

Sam stuck to nodding. Rick took a gulp of coffee and shook his head, "Somethin's in the wind, and I want to know what it is. Things just aren't figurin."

Pedro let out a loud, painful groan, startling Rick and Sam. Sam rushed over with Zeke and Jasper at his heels. He placed the back of his hand on his buddy's forehead. "This boy's burnin up with the fever." Sam's husky voice couldn't disguise his fear. Grabbing another towel, he soaked it with cold water and laid it across his hot brow. "That bullet's gotta come outta there soon."

"Let's hope Jim finds the doc and gets him back here in a hurry or we'll have to take it out ourselves," answered Rick. Glancing at the clock on the mantel, he saw it was already four o'clock. His eyes shifted to the window at the dimming sky light. Knowing it would be dark soon made the situation seem worse. He filled his cup again and paced back and forth in front of the kitchen window. He cast a worried look over at Pedro as he slumped back into his chair.

"Sam? Hear that?" The sounds of clippity-clopping hooves brought Rick to his feet and heading for the door.

Rick threw open the door, expecting to see Jim and the doc, but he froze in his tracks when he saw, instead, Zeb Taylor and two of his hands perched on their horses in front of the steps. Rick's eyes narrowed and his hand automatically lighted on the butt of his gun.

"Greetings, Barnett," said Taylor through his fat lips. "Fine day to take a ride, wouldn't you say so?"

Rick shifted his weight, looking directly into Zeb's piglike eyes. "State your business here, Taylor."

"Now, that don't sound very neighborly of you, Barnett. Here we jest come to pay a sociable call, and you treat us unfriendly. Don't it seem that way to you, boys?" taunted Taylor, exposing empty spaces in his bottom teeth.

The two men nodded in agreement, saying nothing.

Zeb Taylor was a large man with a protruding gut due to the volume of liquor he consumed daily. His ruddy, puffy cheeks were divided by his flat, puggy nose, and his black, greasy hair drooped uneven under a faded, smashed sombrero. Beneath a dusty, red-and-yellow serape draped a pair of pistols that stuck out at his bulging sides.

Leaning an elbow on his saddlehorn, he said, "Before you git yer feathers all ruffled, Senor Barnett, I'd like to make you another offer on this here spread of yours."

Rick's jaw tightened, "Not at any price, Taylor. Now git off my land." Rick closed his hand around his gun butt, keeping a hawk's eye on the bunch.

Zeb's two men fidgeted in their saddles when they saw Sam, shotgun in hand, step out and take his place beside Rick. Taylor's eyes protruded. "Now, hold it. Let's not get edgy."

"Let's put it this way." Rick stepped forward, "I don't take kindly to yer Indian trespassing on my land and killing my stock. But, most of all, Taylor—shootin Pedro—today."

"Hey Barnett," drawled Taylor. "I know nothing of this. I have no Indian working for me. You, my friend, are making a mistake. My men all know to respect the fence lines. Is that not right, boys?"

The boys nodded.

"Don't insult me with your bullcrap, Taylor. The truth will come out. You'll pay for what your Indian did—one way or another. Count on it. And the next time you or your men are on my land—we'll shoot. Ya got that?" Rick whipped his gun out, pointing it between Taylor's eyes, and through his teeth said, "It'll be like this."

Taylor scowled and tiny beads of sweat formed on his forehead. Squinting his cold, gray eyes, he said, "One day, one day—my friend—you will live to regret your words." He straightened in the saddle. "You will also regret not selling to me when I give you a fair price. You can count on that." He spat a gooey, brown wad of tobacco to the ground by Rick's boots, spun his horse around, his silent hands close behind, and cantered back down the road.

Rick returned his gun to his holster and looked at Sam. Both knew this was only the beginning. They went back into the house.

It wasn't long before they heard horses coming again. Rick stepped out, and a look of relief came to his face.

Sam and Rick held Pedro down so his squirming wouldn't hamper Doc Lawton as he probed for the lodged bullet. Pedro let out guttural screams through teeth biting on a leather belt, and the shots of whiskey he'd been given seemed to have no effect in numbing him.

"Aha. There it is," announced Doc. He displayed the piece of lead between long tweezers before plopping it in the pan on the floor. He dressed and bandaged the wound and covered up the boy. Rising to his lanky six feet, he stretched and his long arms nearly touched the ceiling. He took a couple of strides to the table and shrunk himself down in Pedro's chair beside Rick. Sam brought him a steaming cup of coffee and joined them.

"I think he's going to be all right," said Doc. "From what I could tell, the bullet didn't damage anything vital, and that's lucky for him." He took a drink and continued. "He'll be down for a few days until the infection clears up. Here he reached down into his black bag and took out a bottle of pills and a package of bandages and laid them on the table. "See he takes this medicine three times a day, And make sure the bandages are changed every few hours or so, depending on the drainage. Make sure he gets plenty of rest." He glanced over to the sofa. "By the looks of him, I don't think he'll want to do much of anything anyhow."

Rick reached into his pants pocket and pulled out some bills. Peeling off a couple, he handed them to Doc. "Sure do appreciate you comin all the way out."

"My job," smiled Doc. He downed the rest of his coffee and stood up. "I best get back to town now. I've got a woman at the Canon House who's probably goin to have her baby tonight." He put on his long coat that hung sack like from his bony frame and stepped over to the sofa, checking Pedro once more. Slapping his hat atop his head and bag in hand, he headed for the door. Turning, he said, "You send for me if the lad takes a bad turn." Nodding farewell, he took his leave.

Remembering the Indian, Rick jumped up and went after Doc. "Doc," he called. "I'm sure I wounded that Indian—and if by chance you happen to treat him, I'd appreciate it if you'd let me know. It'd give me somethin to go on."

"I'll let you know, but don't count on it. They treat themselves. Got their own ways. Don't trust whites, especially when it comes to medicine."

He lifted himself into the saddle, waved and rode away. Rick watched Doc ride until he was out of sight. He turned toward the mountains in time to see the last bit of sun disappear—and there came a chill to the air.

5

Sweat beaded then trickled down the wincing face of the Indian slumped on his blanket near the fire. Weak from loss of blood and the energy he'd spent getting to his cave, the most he could do was lie motionless until the fire got hot. He tried putting his mind in a trance to lessen the sharp pain in his upper left arm, but it throbbed and burned so badly as to set him to moaning, breaking his concentration.

The Indian, named Blackhorse, had fled for cover after the surprise encounter with Barnett and his hand. He had not run from the battle just because he was hurt, but to guard against capture and possible detection of the secrets of his hideaway. At a safe distance over the crest of a hill, he'd taken refuge in a stand of ponderosa, slumped across his pony's neck, clinging to consciousness, listening for his enemy's departure. At last he'd heard the sound of horses' hooves striking the stones in the creek; still he waited to emerge until he was sure of not being seen or heard.

Cautiously, he had urged the pony up over the crest. His blurring vision tried to focus on any movement that might spell danger, while blood seeped down his wounded arm making his buckskin clammy. It dripped over his hand and between his fingers, leaving splotches of red on the white mane he clutched. Worming his way across the flatland and through the narrow canyon walls, finally he came to a stop and clumsily slid off the pony. Quivering on unsteady legs he stumbled as he led the animal to the corral. Scanning the height he must climb slumped his spirit, but up he must go where he'd be safe and could tend his wound.

Beginning the ascent, his usually sure feet now stepped uneasy, fumbling for solid rocks to place his moccasins. Using his good arm to clutch low branches, he pulled himself up and up, hesitating only when dizziness washed over him, then continued on, inch by inch. Determined, he reached the opening of the cave concealed by thick brush. Parting the bushes with his body, he crawled into his dwelling, a large cave with two tunnels at the far back. Adjusting his eyes to the darkness, he slowly made his way to the fire pit and blanket.

Blackhorse started a fire, then put himself down on the blanket. His taut, muscular body tried to relax, but the pain shook him like an aspen leaf. The glowing flames lit up the features on his fine, handsome face, which bore a look of wisdom beyond his twenty-seven years; his dark brown eyes reflected a knowing and penetrating gaze.

Feeling the heat against his body, Blackhorse rolled off his blanket, now damp from his sweat, and squatted before the fire. Maneuvering with just one arm, he struggled to remove his buckskin shirt, and the torture from this act nearly put him out. He dropped the shirt, inside out, on the dirt floor beside the blanket, then pulled his knife from the leather sheath at his side and held it over the flames. Waving it to cool a bit, he then stuck the point into the wound and began digging around the bullet.

"Eeeee-aah, eeee-aah, eeee-aah," he wailed. Sweat ran off his face. His strong jaw and neck muscles ached from his clenched and grinding teeth. Silently, he prayed to the Great Spirit for strength to stay awake and to endure. The blood spurted from his arm as he dug and probed until, at last, the bullet was torn loose from his flesh and pinged against the cave wall. Blackhorse collapsed for a moment from the tension and pain but soon regained his faculties. Wiping the bloody blade on his shirt, he reheated the knife and pressed it to the wound. "Aaaaah, eeeeeeeeee-aaah," howled Blackhorse. "Aaaaah, eeeeeeeee-aah," echoed back from the bowels of the cave, as he withered to the ground.

Regaining his strength, Blackhorse reached for his medicine pouch and gourd of water. Gently, he rinsed the blood away from the shredded hole and down his arm, making red mud of the dirt. In a small clay bowl, he sprinkled the dried tops of the yarrow plant from his pouch, and with a grinding stone he made a powder. With his fingers, he scooped up the herb and pressed the substance into his wound, which would protect him from infection and swelling. He placed a soft piece of buckskin across and secured it with a rawhide thong. Adding more leaves to the bowl, he filled it with water and placed it on a hot rock by the fire. While he waited for his medicine to brew, he thanked the Great Spirit for His help and asked that he live to fight again.

The medicine was ready. Blackhorse poured the liquid into an earthen cup and drank the contents. This would ward away fever and help him rest. He built up the fire for the night and stretched his exhausted body across the blanket and drifted off into a deep sleep.

6

Dodge City, Kansas

*T*he train slowed its speed as it neared the outskirts of Dodge City, Kansas. Clint nudged Kathryn and pointed out the open window. She saw on the prairie a sea of white billowing tops covering wagons, and men leading teams of oxen, mules and horses. Women in colorful calico dresses and poke bonnets carried armloads of supplies to sustain them along their way, while many young children played and scampered about.

Observing these courageous people prepare for their long journey west gave Kathryn a warm feeling inside and a spirit of kinship. In search of fertile new land to farm and raise their families on were most; and a few had hopes of finding riches of gold and silver; but all, like herself, had dreams of a better life and future.

The youngsters shouted and waved, and even some of the grown-ups, as the train chugged slowly by. Clint and Kathryn waved their arms out the window, wearing big smiles for these hardy, brave souls.

They'd become inseparable since the poker-game incident with Frank Palmer. Clint suspected Frank was the type who nursed a grudge until. he got even. He had no way of knowing what Frank would do to a lady, but his gut feeling told him Frank wouldn't let this slide by. He'd even the score for Kathryn catching him cheating, then besting him in front of the other players. Clint took the responsibility of guarding her, which he felt was a most pleasant task.

Clint was in love but kept these feelings to himself. He fretted, knowing she came from a fancy, well-to-do family and was used to fine things and plenty of money, while his family struggled to survive. He'd worked hard most of his life, lived simply, and had come up against many hardships. After searching for so long, he'd finally found someone-someone who'd taken his heart, someone he wanted to live with, live for, love and protect. But what kind of a woman, especially one used to a better life, would want or settle for a man who drove a stagecoach for a living? Why, he bet, she could probably have her pick of just about anyone she wanted.

These thoughts depressed him and made him feel inadequate, and he hated the turmoil they brought to his head, the anguish he felt and how deeply he cared. He knew he had to find a way to change his lot in life, turn things around, so he'd be worthy enough to win her heart as she'd won his.

The train crept slower on the rails and Clint glimpsed the depot from the window. Pulling the valise from under the seat and carrying his own leather satchel, he ushered Kathryn toward the door of the coach. There was a long hiss and screech from the brakes, a jerk, and the train was stopped. She extended her hand to the porter who helped her step down to the ground. She blinked from the brightness of the afternoon sun and opened her parasol to shade the glare. Clint stepped beside her, and she slipped her hand through his arm as they made their way through the crowded dirt streets.

Kathryn looked about in wonder at everything she saw, for this was nothing at all like Lexington. The buildings were smaller, mostly of raw, weathered boards, unpainted, and many made of adobe, sturdy and plain. Some displayed crudely-made signs and exhibited their wares in front of their stores. Mixed with these were more elaborate establishments with brick-and-,mortar fronts, some painted and trimmed in dazzling colors.

The people acted rowdy and boisterous, and the many wagons and horses going up and down the streets made the town one of noise and commotion. She noted the different clothes the people wore. Some men were dressed in buckskin that was fringed and wore their hair quite long. Even their footwear was buckskin, and Kathryn thought they looked comfortable. Others were in loose trousers with suspenders showing over simple, homemade shirts. There were lots of cowboys, on foot and on horseback, in worn denim pants, and some had on chaps. She particularly liked the unique styles and shapes of the cowboys' felt hats, each unmatched by another. The cowboys and rugged-dressed men sported guns in holsters slung low from the waist like her father's Colt 44.

The ladies, too, were in many modes of dress; many in plain, durable dresses and cotton bonnets much like she'd seen outside of town by the wagons. To her relief, there were a few dressed like herself, in the fashion of the day. But as they neared one of the saloons, Kathryn stopped, her shoes planted in the dirt. Never, never, had she seen ladies wearing so little or such revealing attire or with so much color painted on their faces as the two women standing near the door—and in broad daylight.

"What's the matter?" asked Clint.

"Why, Clint. Just look at those shameless women. Why on earth are they exposing themselves in public like that? It's simply disgraceful."

"Kathryn, I'm afraid ya'll have to git used to seein women like that from time to time."

"But what do they do, and why are they dressed like that?"

"You really don't know, do ya?" asked Clint, with a smirk.

"No, I don't, or I wouldn't have asked," said Kathryn, curtly.

"My dear," Clint cleared his throat. "Those ladies, if we can call em that, are tryin to git men to come into that there saloon ta spend their money—like gamblin, buyin drinks and the like. They dance with the fellas and give favors fer money. Now, I don't know how else to say it to ya without causing us both to blush."

Kathryn studied the women, reflected for a moment, then her face turned pink. She dropped her head down and muttered, "Oh, I know now."

Just then an airborne cowboy flew out the swinging doors of the saloon landing a few feet away. A big, burly man stood in the doorway and shouted, "And don't ya ever come back again." The man turned and disappeared back into the saloon.

Kathryn stared wide-eyed at the sprawled-.out man as they walked around him and headed for the Dodge House Hotel. They had a one night lay-over in Dodge City before going on to La Junta. The hurly-burly of the streets distracted the couple, making them unaware they were being followed.

They checked into separate but adjoining rooms on the second floor of the hotel. Clint unlocked her door. "Well, here ya are, some privacy at last. ' He smiled and pulled his watch from his pocket. "What say we meet in the lobby in two hours? Will that give you enough time to relax and clean up?"

"Yes, that's more than enough time."

He set her valise inside the door, handed her the key, and strolled to his own room, the next one down the hall.

Kathryn shut her door and looked about the tiny room. Across from the door was a window facing the street, with limp, gauze curtains, once white. Left of the window stood the bed with head and foot of thin, curved iron, adorned with a faded red quilt. On the wall across from the bed was a small bureau and a commode, with a framed mirror hanging slightly crooked above. At the foot of the bed was a large, oak rocking chair with a smoothed-leather seat and a loose pillow of patchwork cloth. It was not a fancy or particularly cheerful room and a drastic change from the rooms and furnishings she was used to, but it didn't seem to matter. She knew she had to adapt to new settings and changes, for this was what she'd chosen.

To live among lovely things yet dwell in a home where she'd been pushed to the background—aware of deceit and hearing lies—was far more intolerable than this. She smiled at the room, for with all its simpleness and wear, it seemed actually inviting and cozy, especially after the crowded and not-so-private train car.

She picked up her valise and took it over by the bureau. Opening it, she removed the rose taffeta dress and proceeded to get ready to meet with Clint. She was most anxious to wash off the grime from the long, dusty ride and feel clean again.

Clint was waiting in the lobby when Kathryn descended the stairs. He and others there could not keep from staring. Clint swelled with pride as she walked toward him, just him—smiling at just him. Holding out his arm, he escorted her out the door, knowing he was being envied.

Arm in arm they strolled about the town and found a cozy cafe where they enjoyed a long, leisurely dinner.

It was dark and late as they strolled back down the wooden sidewalk toward the Dodge House, but the town was still as lively as before. Dozens of horses were hitched to rails along the walks, waiting patiently for their owners. Buggies and wagons still traveled the streets, now at a slower pace. Music and laughter drifted out of the many saloons as people went in and out, keeping the walkway a busy place. Kathryn felt giddy from all the excitement of the goings-on in this strange, new town; and she especially enjoyed the attention she received from Clint.

It was nearly midnight as they climbed the narrow, dim-lit stairs at the hotel up to their rooms. Clint stepped into Kathryn's room and lit her oil lamp, then bid her a good night's rest. Looking tenderly into her warm, brown eyes, he held back the urge to swoop her into his arms, and even more, to press his lips upon hers, to express what words he couldn't say. Instead, he reminded her that he was just next-door should she need him, then left and shut the door.

Kathryn changed to sleep in a nightgown, for the first time since leaving home; and it felt good to be in loose-fitting clothing again. She relieved herself in the chamber pot and carefully set it back in the commode and shut its door. There was fresh water in the pitcher, and she poured it into the ceramic basin on top of the commode. After washing her face and hands, she studied herself in the mirror as she brushed her long hair with thoughtful strokes. Somehow, the image reflected, appeared older, older than the angry, sad girl who'd left her, mother and home. And the woman looking back at her had a glow that wasn't there before,

Her ear caught the sound of music drifting up and she curiously walked over and raised the window. Leaning out over the ledge, she watched the activity below. The music from the nearby saloon was loud enough to catch the melody Her bare toes began to tap as she hummed along with the piano and banjo. "Buffalo gals won't ya come out tonight?"

Above in the sky were millions of twinkling stars and a near half-moon. She wondered if Uncle Richard was an anxious for her to come as she was to get there, and she wished this journey wasn't taking so long. She thought of her mother, Jolene, and hoped by now she had come to her senses. But aside from all this, she was having a wonderful. adventure, along with Clint's company.

Just thinking of Clint made little tingles run up and down her spine, and a strange awareness of sensation in the private parts of her body. She didn't know what to make of that and felt slightly ashamed for reasons she wasn't sure of.

The window was pulled down, save for an inch to let in fresh air, and the lamp blown out. Kathryn crawled into bed and stretched her tired body out, enjoying the warmth and comfort of a real bed at last. The lights from the street lamps shown through the thin curtains and bathed the room in soft shadows. Weariness overcame the tired traveler, and with Clint in her thoughts, she drifted into a deep sleep-.so sound asleep, she didn't hear the window slide open or detect a man's leg protruding over the ledge or the rest of the body enter her room.

The dark figure stood silent and looked over at the sleeping woman. Feeling safe to proceed, he stepped slowly and cautiously across the floor toward the bureau. His hands touched the handbag, placed on top, and a satisfied smile crossed his face. Clutching the bag to his chest, he quickly turned to leave, only to trip over the valise. With a. shuffle and thud, the man sprawled onto the floor.

Kathryn woke with a start. A man was groping around on the floor. She let out an ear-piercing scream. Startled, the man froze, then made an awkward attempt to scramble to the window, just as the door was kicked open.

Clint, wearing only trousers and boots had gun in hand. Seeing the intruder, he dashed to the window and jerked the man back inside.

With a powerful left hook, he sent the man across the room, where he was stopped by the wall and slid to the floor. Clint tossed his gun onto the bed, where Kathryn sat clutching the bed clothes in fear; and, like lightning, he yanked the man to his feet. Clint planted his left fist in the man's belly, a swift right to the jaw, and the man dropped to the floor again in a stupor.

Clint groped for his gun. "Kathryn, are you all right?"

"Yes—I think so."

Clint struck a match and lit the lamp. The light shown on the man coming to; and to their surprise, they looked upon the face of Frank Palmer.

"Oh, Clint, it's that horrible Frank. Here, here—in my room. They looked from Frank to the scattered money from Kathryn's handbag.

"Thought you'd take the money anyhow, did you, Frank? That didn't belong to you then or now. Remember?"

By now, hotel guests in their nightclothes were gathered at the open doorway and in the hall, gawking in and all talking at once. Kathryn remained huddled in her bed, hiding from the unwanted attention.

"C'mon, Frank—we're goin fer a walk." Clint pulled Frank to his feet and shoved him through the crowd, keeping his gun at Frank's back, and pulled the door shut behind them.

Kathryn leaped off the bed and stared at the clutter on the floor. Realizing the window was still wide open, she went over just in time to see Clint march Frank across the street to the jail. As they reached the door, Frank turned and looked up at her window, sending a chill over Kathryn. She slammed the window down and latched it. On her hands and knees, she began picking up her money and things off the floor. She found her derringer, which had slid under the bed during the scuffle, and this time she placed it under her pillow.

A soft rap sounded on the door. "It's me, Clint."

She scurried to the door and opened it, forgetting she was only in her nightgown. Clint, still shirtless, stepped in and closed the door. He looked at Kathryn standing bare foot in white, flowing gown, her long hair falling gently around her face, ending at the tops of her bosoms, and was so taken back that he almost forgot why he'd come.

"Kathryn," he stammered. "Are you sure you're all right?" His breathing came hard, and he felt embarrassed.

"Oh, Clint. I was so scared when I saw that man on my floor. I didn't know if he was going to hurt me or what he was doing here or anything` Then to find out it was Frank, who I never thought I'd see again." All at once she started trembling and tears filled her eyes. From her throat came a mournful wail and Clint grabbed her into his arms. She wrapped her arms tightly around his waist, and her face buried in the warmth of his thick-haired chest as she sobbed, not only for tonight, but for all the unspoken fears buried within her. He stroked her hair and their bodies swayed gently, while she cried herself out.

As her sobbing ended, Kathryn suddenly was aware she was in her nightgown in front of Clint. And he did not have on a shirt. She jerked away, crossing her arms over her chest, and her tear-stained eyes looked sheepishly into his.

"You shouldn't be seeing me like this. I think you should leave now."

He smiled at her modesty and said, "I'm going, but if ya need me, jest scream—again." He winked and grinned at her as he departed from the room.

Kathryn braced the rocker against the door as the lock was broken by Clint's kick. The room went dark as she turned out the lamp and crawled back into bed; and she wondered what more was in store for her before she reached Bonanza.

7

La Junta, Colorado

*I*t was early afternoon when Clint happily reported to Kathryn that they were not very far from La Junta. She was delighted, for that meant the long train ride would be over, and soon they would be riding on the stagecoach. She was looking forward to this phase of the journey, not just because she would be riding on the stage Clint drove but because it meant she was that much closer to seeing Uncle Richard and her new home.

Although the train ride had been an adventure, of sorts, she was glad to be rid of the likes of Frank Palmer. The morning before leaving Dodge City, Clint had taken her over to the sheriff's office to explain what Frank had done in her hotel room, and then she'd signed a complaint. A strange uneasiness had come over her when she looked over into the barred cell and saw Frank lying on a cot facing the wall. Little did she know he was faking sleep, and when he overheard the sheriff inquire about her destination, a fiendish grin spread open his lips when he heard her answer—Bonanza.

Now, as the train chugged on, Kathryn leaned back in her seat and closed her eyes. Once again she tried to picture the ranch where she would be living and wondered how much it would differ from the home and lifestyle she left behind. A picture of the beautiful mansion flashed through her mind and Jackson, her beloved horse; but more vivid were the images of her mother and Franny. A lump began swelling in her throat and her eyes were gathering tears. She swallowed hard, took a deep breath, and blinked away what tears might have escaped, then drifted off to sleep.

Clint had been watching Kathryn out of the corner of his eye and could sense she was going through some private pain. Out of respect, he had kept silent; and now as she slept, his eyes drank in the features of her face. To him, she looked like a princess, and more than ever he desired this woman for his own. The idea of another man with her made his flesh hot, his jaw tighten and his stomach nervous. He thought one way or another he would have to find a way to support her in the fashion she was used to, but the how part was what upset him. He, too, closed his eyes as he tried to figure and sort out his options. Coming up with no immediate solutions, he let himself drift off to sleep, knowing he would need his strength and alertness for driving the stage. This trip was more important than the others because of the precious cargo aboard, Kathryn.

"Last stop, La Junta—ten minutes," announced the conductor going through the cars.

They woke with a start. Kathryn reached up and rearranged her tilted bonnet and grinned at Clint. Excitement filled her eyes and he grinned back, caught up in her emotions.

"Oh, Clint, I can hardly wait to be on the stage. I've never been on one before, you know." She added, with twinkling eyes, "And it will be extra special, because you will be the one driving." A boyish grin came to his face and he nervously rubbed his mustache with his thumb.

"C'mon, gal. We best get ourselves ready to git off this big buggy."

Kathryn laughed at his description, and they prepared to leave.

Adjusting her parasol to shade her from the bright sun, Kathryn waited anxiously near the train for her trunk and the other valise to be unloaded from the baggage car. Meanwhile, Clint rounded up a couple of sorry-looking lads to help tote her things to the stage depot. The boys were shabbily dressed in trousers too short and worn-out boots and were excited about earning some money.

When everyone was assembled, Clint and Kathryn led the way and the boys marched behind lugging the trunk with the valise perched on top.

This was a small town, so they didn't have far to walk. In one direction the land was quite flat, but to the west stood a small range of mountains. The cloudless sky and the brilliant sun made the air very warm. Kathryn stopped to remove her cape, with Clint's assistance, and they proceeded on. At the end of the street stood a log building with a barn at the back and a corral full of horses. Along the side stood a red stagecoach with bright yellow wheels and "Barlow-Sanderson" lettered on the door.

"Boys, ya kin just set those things down here by the bench," Clint directed. He reached into his pocket and handed each lad a two-bit piece. Their eyes lit up as they stared at the shiny coin in their dirty hands,

"Gee, mister, thanks," they said in unison. Clutching their coins, they ran off down the street.

"Hey, Clint, Thought I heard your voice" A tall, sandy-haired man in his early fifties stepped out of the building with a broad grin on his face, "I was wonderin if I'd have to get Kevin to take your place today. Sure glad ya made it back in time." The two men shook hands and Clint introduced Kathryn to Aaron Gilles.

"Glad to meet you, ma'am."

"I'm happy to meet you, too," responded Kathryn.

"So tell me, Clint. How was your sister's wedding?" asked Aaron.

"It was a real nice doin. She picked herself a mighty fine fella, too. And it sure was good to see mama again and all the rest of the folks, Yup, I had me a pretty special vacation," answered Clint, and he smiled at Kathryn and winked.

"Well, ya sure cut it close, Clint. You're due to drive outa here in about an hour," chuckled Aaron. "What are we all standin here for? Come, let's go inside. " He motioned toward the door and said to Kathryn, "My dear, you must be tired from that train ride. Agnes—that's my good wife—is fixing some tea, and I'm sure she'd be delighted for some female company and for you to join her.

Aaron led Kathryn through the main room and back to the kitchen to meet Agnes, a plain-looking but friendly woman. "If you ladies will excuse me," said Aaron, "I've got some business to discuss with Clint." He poured two cups of coffee to take out with him and left the ladies to themselves.

Clint was waiting at one of the tables, sitting with his legs stretched out, studying the room. Aaron set the coffees down and joined him. Lighting up a fat cigar, Aaron tilted back in his chair and carefully chose his words.

"Clint, it's gotten rough out here again. I'm afraid I've got some bad news for you."

"Like what?"

"Like twice in the past three weeks the stage was robbed of the payroll for the Gunnison miners." He hesitated, to let that sink in. "On the first one—Jason Long was killed."

"Jason?—Not Jason."

Aaron sadly nodded yes. Clint was visibly shaken and he hit his fist down hard on the table. He and Jason had signed on together and had become close friends. It was hard to take that his buddy was dead—gone.

"How and where did it happen?"

"Jason got it just outside of Salida—as they was headin for Gunnison." Aaron drank down some of his coffee and knocked the ashes from his cigar to the floor. "The second robbery was just south of Villa Grove. We're puttin an extra man on all the stages till they catch who's doin this. Manuel will be ridin with you," said Aaron.

"Any clues to who's behind this?"

"Guess there are three of them—from the reports—and one of 'em is an Injun."

"Thought trouble with redskins was over?"

"Guess this one's not heard about it," Aaron said.

The front door swung open, letting in a stream of light. A stout, weathered-faced Mexican and a gangly young man walked in, heading straight for Clint.

"Si. I tell you, Will—this hombre git here today," declared Manuel. They shook hands and greeted their friend and plunked themselves down at the table.

"How many passengers we got goin', Aaron?" asked Clint.

"Just a man and his wife. Maybe an older kid, if he scares up enough money for his fare. And, of course, your Kathryn."

"His Kathryn?" questioned a surprised Will.

"Hey—you find yourself a woman back east?" asked Manuel eagerly.

"Now, don't go gittin' the wrong idea, fellas; We met on the train, and it jist so happens she was going to Villa Grove. She's a very nice lady, and I want you to treat her with respect—or you'll be answerin' to me," said Clint with a pretend mad look on his face.

"Si, Bossman. We comprende. Is not so, Will?" replied Manuel. Will nodded and they both chuckled at Clint, who chose to ignore them.

Agnes and Kathryn strolled out from the kitchen carrying cups of tea and joined the men. Will and Manuel went wide in the eyes when they got a look at Kathryn and promptly stood up for their introductions, The group sat and chatted for a spell until Aaron pulled out his watch and said, "Well, fellows, let's get those horses hitched so you can be on your way—'cause it is about that time." Aaron headed out the door, and the rest followed behind. The two women remained seated to do some more visiting.

Presently, a well-dressed couple entered the depot. The man walked over toward Agnes while the elegant-looking woman remained near the door. Addressing Agnes, the man said bluntly, "We have had our things brought over from the hotel and had them placed near the other baggage outside. I trust the stage will be leaving on schedule?" The man tightened his lips waiting for his answer.

"Yes, it will," answered. Agnes sweetly. Unruffled by his pompous airs, she asked, "Perhaps you and your wife would care to be seated and join us for some tea while you wait?"

"I think not, thank you. I believe we will stroll about until departure." He tipped his brown derby, exposing a bald head, then escorted his wife back outside.

Kathryn had studied her fellow passengers and thought them stuffy and cold. She raised her eyebrows at Agnes and pursed her lips tightly, and they both broke out laughing hilariously.

Their shared laughter was interrupted by the noise and commotion outside as the horses were being hitched to the coach and the sound of many hooves and rolling wheels when the stage pulled around to the front. The ladies hurried outside. Kathryn looked at the readied coach and gazed up to see Clint sitting high in his seat holding the reins on four eager horses. He grinned down proudly at her and pulled the lever that set the brake to the wheel. Handing the reins to Will sitting next to him in the box, he jumped, landing in front of Kathryn. With an arm-sweeping motion, he removed his black hat and bowed low before her.

Extending his arm, he asked gallantly, "May I have the honor of escorting you to your seat?"

Kathryn giggled and graciously slid her arm in his. Clint snatched up her valise and with great ceremony paraded her to the door of the coach. Manuel stood gallantly at attention beside the door, and when he swung the door open for her, he, too, bowed. Holding her long skirt up in her hand, she stepped high and got into the coach and slid over to the opposite door facing the driver's seat. Clint reached in and set her valise by her feet.

"Thank you, kind sir," beamed Kathryn. Clint smiled at her and stepped aside. The stuffy-acting man and his wife had been waiting to board and looked displeased over the delay. The man helped his wife climb in and he followed, both sitting opposite Kathryn. The woman began brushing off her skirt and sleeves of her dress as if entering the coach had soiled them. They barely acknowledged Kathryn, giving just a. curt nod and quickly turning their attention out the door window. Their haughty attitude made her feel a. little apprehensive about being in their presence in a confined area and for such a long time but not enough to spoil her happiness and the excitement she was feeling.

"Everything loaded up?" hollered Aaron,

"All except the mail," answered Clint. He and Manuel went into the depot and hauled out two sacks each. They carried them to the front and placed them in the boot behind the driver's seat, then went around to the back and tied down the big leather flap. Manuel retrieved his shotgun from the bench outside and climbed up into the china seat at the rear.

Hesitating at the back of the stage, Clint tried to shake the feeling of dread that had suddenly come over him. Was it a fear of the stage being robbed and a concern for Kathryn's safety, he wondered? Or was it because, for the first time ever, he felt truly caring and responsible for a woman? He sucked in a deep breath and glanced up at Manuel who was studying him. Manuel sensed Clint's anguish and returned a consoling smile as he reached down and patted his shoulder. Clint smiled gratefully for the silent understanding. He dropped his arm to his side and tapped his six-shooter with his fingers, set back his shoulders and proceeded to the front to assume his position,. Passing Kathryn's window, he turned to give her a smile, and she peered out to see his muscular legs take him up into the driver's seat.

Will, who rode as relief driver and guard, handed the reins back to Clint.

"Wait. Wait up," came a cry down the street. The kid came running, waving and shouting.

"Hold on, Clint," yelled Aaron. "Looks like we got us one more."

"Here, I have enough money now," the kid panted, out of breath. He thrust the money at Agnes, tossed his bedroll up on top and leaped inside the stage, plopping down hard next to Kathryn. He grinned to all, pleased with himself, and settled back for the ride,

"Hee-Haah," yelled Clint, as he gently flicked the reins on the horses' backs. The coach lunged forward and they were on their way.

8

*T*he steady rhythm of clopping hooves and swaying motion of the suspended coach lulled the passengers, and they soon took to dozing, as Clint Davis guided the stagecoach west. It felt good to him to be back in the driver's seat controlling the team of powerful beasts. His eyes swept across the vast expanse of prairie and he felt vital and alive again. He bent down low to catch a glimpse of Kathryn. She was leaning against the side resting peacefully; and Clint, warmed by this sight, smiled, content with his world.

"Your girl is very pretty," said Will.

"She's not my girl. Not yet anyway." Clint turned and grinned at Will, adding, "But I do hope to change that one day.

"Where's she goin to, all by herself?"

"To live with her uncle. In Bonanza."

"That all the family she's got?" questioned Will further.

"Naw. She's got a mama back in Lexington. Guess they didn't see eye to eye on her mama's choice of a new husband. Kathryn believes he doesn't love her mother and is really after the family fortune. Kathryn said she tried to convince her mother, but she wouldn't listen. Jist took the fellow's side and shut out her own daughter. So she decided to leave and come to her uncle's. Now, don't you go repeatin any of this, to anyone—including Kathryn. What I told you is jist between me and you. Understand?"

"I understand," answered Will. He thought about all Clint said for a few minutes, and in awe, said, "Hey, we have a rich lady riding back there, don't we?" He snapped his head toward the rear to emphasize his point.

"Looks like we do." Clint remembered the sharp bend in the road that was coming up and held a tight rein on the horses. A recent downpour had left deep ruts and they hit them dead-on, bouncing the coach and jostling the passengers.

"Aah," shrieked the man's wife, as she was tossed to her knees onto the floor and landed with her face in Kathryn's lap. She tried to right herself, but the bouncing, unsteady coach kept her off balance. "Oh. Oh," she kept shouting.

Kathryn had all she could do to keep herself in her, own seat but tried to get a hold of the woman's arms to guide her up; it was no use, as another bump put the poor thing entirely on the floor.

"Harold," she yelled, thrashing about at their feet "Harold, you fool, help me."

Harold grabbed her by the waist and the kid got a hold of her arms and finally got her back into her seat. The woman was totally beside herself from fright and embarrassment. All that came from her mouth was sobbing "Ooh's." She tried to straighten out her skirt and with one look at its state began to whimper, for now it was truly soiled.

Her husband, helpless to the situation, could only say, "My dear, calm down."

"I will not calm down. Just look at my dress." She reached her hand up to discover her bonnet gone and her pinned hair had fallen down, and this upset her more. But she really wailed when the kid reached by his foot and handed her her crushed, dirty bonnet.

It took some time for her husband to calm her hysteria. Although Kathryn could sympathize with the poor woman's plight, she could not help but find this scene quite amusing. Out of the corner of her eye she detected the kid suppressing a laugh. She turned and smiled at him and noted he was not much taller than she and ventured he was not older than eighteen. He was dressed in worn but clean cowboy clothes and possessed an attitude of self-assurance. A beat-up hat of dingy brown was pulled down on the right almost covering his eye, and his light brown hair hung shaggy around a girlish-looking face. Clear blue eyes met hers as he turned his head and grinned. "My name is Billy. What's yours?"

"My name is Kathryn, Kathryn Barnett."

"Well, pleased to meet ya, Kathryn," he said, still grinning.

Kathryn looked at the couple, encouraging them with a look to join in the introductions. The man cleared his throat and said, "How do you do, Kathryn—and Billy," nodding to each. "I am Harold Bartholemew, and this is my wife, Claudette." Claudette, still fighting for composure, forced a trembling smile and bobbed her disheveled head.

"Might I," requested Harold, "inquire of your destinations?"

"I am going to Bonanza," volunteered Kathryn, "but I will be getting off in Villa Grove. My uncle is meeting the stage there."

The smile she wore suddenly vanished. Her jaw dropped and her eyes widened with the shock of remembering. Bolting from her seat, she leaned out through the window, holding her bonnet down against the wind and shouted, "Clint. Clint." until he finally turned around.

"Clint, I forgot to wire Uncle Richard," she hollered above the clamoring noise. "Now, what do I do?"

"We'll wire him at the next telegraph office, he shouted back," Don't worry. It isn't going to make much difference Other than that, how ya doin?"

"I'm fine—now," she yelled back. They exchanged knowing smiles, and she pulled herself back inside and sat down.

"Aah," she sighed with relief, "that problem is taken care of."

Harold smiled mannerly at Kathryn and resumed his questioning. "And you, Billy, are going where?"

"Silver City."

"Silver City?" he frowned, and his eyebrows nearly touched. "I can't say that I'm familiar with a town by that name. Where in Colorado is it located?"

"It's not in Colorado," he smirked.

Harold bristled over Billy's flippancy, then countered, "Well, where is it then, Billy?"

"New Mexico. Down at the southwestern end." There, he thought, now I've told the prying old geezer what he wanted. He turned his head and distracted himself with the passing scenery.

Kathryn regarded Harold and his distressed wife and inquired, "And what is your destination?" Claudette sighed and fixed to stare at the roof of the coach, as if she could not bear to hear the answer.

"We are going to Gunnison, after we stop for a few days in Villa Grove."

"Oh, then it appears we will be traveling most of the way together," said Kathryn with forced cheeriness.

"It appears so," replied Harold. He reached into a slender case and extracted a newspaper and proceeded to read.

During this time, Claudette had busied herself brushing the dirt off her dress and trying to fix her messed-up hair. She was still pouting over her ordeal and nursing a grudge toward Harold over what she felt was his lack of feeling and concern for her. Their eyes met and Kathryn gave her a sympathetic smile. Claudette's eyes revealed loneliness and despair and Kathryn felt sorry for her.

"While you are fixing your hair, why don't you let me help to get your bonnet presentable?" asked Kathryn thoughtfully. Claudette was having some difficulty managing her, hair problem, with all the bouncing and swaying. She glanced down at the sad-looking bonnet and said, "That would be very nice. I'd appreciate some help." Her eyes swiftly darted sideways in Harold's direction and back again, causing Kathryn to conceal a smirk with her hand. Both women exchanged smiles, as Claudette turned her bonnet over to Kathryn.

Billy had been craning his neck out the window pointing out the wildlife when he spotted herds of antelope and deer. They marveled as they watched a low-flying bald eagle, and they laughed at the antics of playful jackrabbits. And when the stage slowed down near a rocky pass, Billy gleefully pointed out a big coiled rattlesnake sunning itself on a ledge.

Claudette gasped and clutched her breast. "No. Not rattlesnakes, too." Pursing her lips in angry frustration, she snapped at Harold, "I told you that I did not want to come west. I do not find any part of this trip amusing. I want you to book passage on the next stage—back east."

Harold became visibly irritated. "We will discuss this later—in private." Claudette resumed her pouting.

Kathryn surmised that Claudette was not used to much discomfort and was finding it difficult to accept and adjust to this journey.

The horses slowed their pace and the coach pulled to a stop. Will got down first and opened the door for the passengers to step out. The horses were led to a trough for water. The passengers went inside the stage station where they could also get a drink.

It was a small building, put together in haste. Built of logs chinked with adobe and only hard-packed dirt for a floor, it was a welcome place of refuge nonetheless. The young couple that ran the place were most hospitable, greeting each warmly as they came through the door. They were offered bread, butter and jams and thin, funny-looking cornmeal cakes, rolled up with meat inside. Kathryn was told they were called tortillas. They were eaten by holding them firmly with both hands. She and the Bartholemews' found them quite tasty.

Clint watched Kathryn with interest as she sampled the new food but felt sorry for her when she put hot pepper sauce on her tortilla like Manuel. Her eyes watered and she began coughing. He quickly brought her some water which she downed in one big gulp. She began laughing at herself, and now that it was safe to, the rest joined in.

After all had taken advantage of the privy behind the station, they piled back into the coach and headed into the sunset toward Walsenberg. Clint drove hard, trying to put in as many miles as he could, for his eyes detected storm clouds far off in the distance.

The sky was becoming dim and after a few miles Clint stopped the stage. Will swung open the door and announced, "Clint says for ya to git out for a minute to stretch while I light the lamps fer ya."

Kathryn was happy for the news. Her back and legs were beginning to stiffen, and feeling the tension between the Bartholemews kept her from relaxing. Stepping out, she found the ground dry and sandy. Scattered here and about were strange-looking clumps of flowering plants that she had never before seen, and she crouched down to examine them.

As she was about to touch, Billy warned, "Don't touch. You'll git prickers in your fingers. They sting, and they're nasty to git out."

Seeing now all the hundreds of hair like needles among the red buds, Kathryn turned to Billy. She saw him disappearing behind a huge boulder, and around from the other side stepped Manuel. Soon Billy reappeared where Manuel had come, and Will also walked to the giant boulder. When Will came back and saw Kathryn watching the rock, he looked embarrassed, and it was then that Kathryn realized why the men had been going behind it. Her face flushed hot, and she hastily retreated inside the coach and felt ashamed of herself. Claudette and Harold climbed back in, as did Billy, and the coach was on the move again. Claudette saw Kathryn's discomfort and gave her a knowing smirk, and she smiled back sheepishly.

When Will had lit the lamps, he had also let down the thick leather curtains to protect them from the now chilling air. They blocked out the wind but blocked their view as well. The interior became snug and cozy with the glow from the large candle lights. Harold moved nearer a light and preoccupied himself concentrating on what seemed like business papers. Claudette was engrossed in a magazine she had taken from the elegant tapestry bag she carried. Billy's hat was set to cover his face, and he slept with his arm safeguarding his gun. Kathryn glanced from one to the other and fidgeted, wondering what she ought to be doing.

Kathryn eased open the leather flap just a crack and peeked out. The sky had a pink and orange cast mixed in with the fading blue as the sun prepared to set. Along with this, dark clouds were bunching together and heading their way, and above the din of the fast-moving stage, Kathryn heard them rumbling. She studied them as they grew bigger and darker and caught a flash of lightning zig-zag across the sky, followed by a sharp crack. She stuck her face through the opening and took a deep breath and could smell the oncoming rain. There was something wonderful about that smell she had always liked but could never explain exactly what the smell of rain really smelled like. She just liked it.

In a matter of minutes, large drops of rain slowly splattered unevenly onto the ground.

"Heee-Haw," sounded Clint from up front, and the stage picked up speed. As they rolled along at a faster clip, the candles swayed and flickered, giving an eerie setting to their speeding rig as it loomed on over the bumpy dirt road.

A loud bang and splitting crack opened up the skies, and the heavy rain descended upon them. The sound on the roof was like a hundred tiny drums all beating at once but not to the same song.

Billy jerked awake. "Huh...what?" He yanked his flap open and got sprayed with rain and quickly slapped it shut. Suddenly, the stage slowed. The coach heaved and swayed, then lunged downward and ceased motion.

Harold grabbed ahold of Claudette to avert a second mishap and both were thrown to the other seat. Claudette gave out a wail of dismay, and from Harold came, "Oh, my God." Kathryn clutched Billy for, support, but it was no use; she toppled to the floor taking Billy with her.

"I'm sorry, I'm sorry," apologized Billy. The door flew open, and dripping-wet Will blinked in wide-eyed wonder at the displaced passengers.

"Anybody hurt?" asked Will, shouting above the noise of the storm. No's and I-don't-think-so's came from the bewildered mess of bodies. "I hate to tell ya this but we're stuck. Ya have to git out...ta lighten the load so we can git outa this mud." Instructing in a louder tone, he said, "There's a rock shelter over there." He pointed just back and behind him. "Here, ya all can duck under this to get over there." He handed Harold a folded tarp and slammed the little door shut.

Billy pulled himself off of Kathryn and got them both back on the seat opposite from where they'd been sitting, as Harold and Claudette were taking up their space "Help me unfold this, Billy," said Harold. "Just get it started and we'll lengthen it as we get out and everybody under."

"Harold," protested Claudette, but the look from Harold stopped her cold.

Billy stepped out first with the tarp over his head, holding it tightly against the gusting wind. Carefully, the rest inched their way behind him, hanging onto the flapping material, and trudged in the squashy mud through the downpour to the cave like shelter with a long, overhanging ledge.

"Oooh, my shoes are ruined and my dress is soaked," cried Claudette.

"Stop with that, Claudette," barked Harold. Claudette froze, eyes in a full open state, as he continued. "We are all wet and miserable, too, yet you seem to be the only one complaining. Be still." Red-faced from her husband's scolding and feeling ridiculed publicly, Claudette turned her back on all and began sobbing. Kathryn put her arm around her and kept telling her that everything would soon be all right.

Billy started running back to the coach and yelled over his shoulder, "I'm goin to help."

Through the sheeting rain they watched as Manuel pulled a slicker like they all were wearing from the back boot for Billy to help keep him dry. Being so short, his dragged in the water and mud, but he didn't seem to notice. Billy and Manuel put their shoulders to the rear wheels, and Will was up ahead steadying and hanging onto the lead horses' harnesses as Clint worked the reins. At the sound of Clint's "Heave," they braced and pushed, the horses' heads bent as they snorted and pawed for steady footing. The gushing ground water washed away inches of dirt, exposing a large rock that prevented the wheel from turning and going forward. The wheels at the rear were now sunk almost to the axle and the momentum of the rain carried more soupy mud their way.

After looking on helplessly from under the protection of the tarp, Harold dashed out from cover and pulled a long, thick branch he had spied out of the mud and ran toward the stage.

Manuel saw him coming and grinned at him and stepped aside. Using the branch for a lever, Harold wedged it beneath the wheel. Manuel. got behind him and they both held tight waiting for Clint to give another command of "Heave."

"Heave." Harold and Manuel put all their muscle into it, lifting up on the wheel, as it sucked out of the mud and slowly inched across the slick rock. The coach was set free and sitting on more solid ground. A chorus of hurrahs was heard above the booming sky and cascading rain.

Clint looked over from his wet perch at Kathryn, huddled with Claudette under the rocky overhang. The women were shivering but looked relieved the coach was no longer stuck.

"Will," Clint shouted. "Git up here and hold onto the reins." Swiftly they changed places, and Clint dashed over to Kathryn, keeping pace with Harold, now soaked clean through to the skin.

"Great thing ya did there, fella," praised Clint, as he slapped Harold on his wet back. Harold grinned back happily at Clint, then down at Claudette, and she studied her husband briefly as a faint glimmer of pride slipped across her face.

Clint's arm slipped around Kathryn's shoulders. "Are you ladies all right other than wet and cold?"

"I believe that says it all, Mr. Davis," replied Claudette. The four broke out in smiles that quickly turned to laughter.

9

On into the darkened night Clint guided the soggy, muddy legged team skillfully over the three remaining miles of winding, rutted road toward the next station. The storm had quieted some and the force of rain had let up, at least for the time being. Above, the clouds thinned and parted and glimmers of moonlight peeked through, putting golden lace in the midnight sky.

Clint felt rotten about the beginnings of this ride and worse that Kathryn had to endure more hardships along with her other problems. Still, it surprised him how well she handled things, and he had yet to hear her complain.

Huddled inside the coach, damp and cold, were his four jostled and travel-worn passengers. No one said much, for they were trying to keep warm by sharing the two sorry-looking blankets Manuel had come up with. Being the wettest, Harold had wrapped his entire self into one and tucked Claudette snugly inside with him, but that didn't stop her chattering teeth. Kathryn and Billy shared the other blanket. Spread across them up to their chins, they'd tucked it behind their shoulders to keep it in place. Clutching her arms to her chest inside her gray wool cape, Kathryn thought they must look like one very fat person with two heads.

A hint of alertness and questioning eyes came over the shivering bunch when the momentum of the coach abruptly slowed, then rolled to a stop, Billy peeked out and confirmed what they hoped, that they had reached the station at last. Relieved sighs were audible as they grabbed their personal possessions and eagerly got out from their cold confinement, clutching onto their blankets. They scurried in twos through the drizzling rain, making a beeline past the held-open door to the blazing stone fireplace against the left wall.

Remaining outside, Clint, Will and Manuel unhitched the horses and led them to the barn where they'd be fed and rubbed down. In haste, the three trotted to the station to join their party of passengers. The four were milling about close to the fire, drying their clothes and enjoying the hot coffee being offered.

This place was larger than the last. The spacious central room was filled with groups of tables and chairs for taking a meal and relaxing. An archway led to a connecting room with shelves stocked with supplies, serving the surrounding area as a general store. A staircase between the main room and the kitchen curved upward to a second story with two large rooms for bedding weary travelers.

After assuring Clint that she would be just fine, he and Kathryn stepped over to where Claudette and Harold stood. Harold looked relieved by the interruption, for Claudette was giving her views regarding their journey thus far.

"Ah, Kathryn," smiled Harold. "I trust you've warmed up a bit after our drenching?"

"Yes, thank you. The chills are slowly leaving as my clothes begin to dry."

"I find the same is true," he grinned back, "If you ladies would excuse us, please, I'd like to have a word with Clint in private. Perhaps, Kathryn, you could console my poor wife."

Harold quickly ushered Clint to the other end of the room where they sat huddled at a table.

"Are you all right, Claudette?" asked Kathryn, with concern.

"No, I am not. I am cold and tired and…"

"Excusa, please, ladies." Kathryn and Claudette turned to see a smiling, short, plump Mexican woman in a bright, many-colored skirt, her long black hair tied back with an equally bright scarf.

"Yes?" said Kathryn.

"I am Senora Lopez, the lady of this house and station. If I seem not too bold. I see your beautiful dresses are soiled from bad weather. If you like—now or when you take your sleep—I will clean them off and press the wrinkles, si?"

The two looked down at the sad condition of their clothes, then at each other. Their skirts hung limp and still were damp, accented with powdery splotches of mud and crumpled around their middle. Their once-black shoes appeared tan from the caked mud.

Claudette looked at Kathryn. Grinning with a ghastly smile, she exclaimed, "Oh, just imagining what I shall see in a mirror makes my heart faint. And to think you and I are displaying ourselves in public looking as we do." She blinked back tears as she said, "I should never have let Harold convince me into making this trip."

Kathryn put her arm around the poor woman to console her and wondered just how bad she herself looked. She reached up and felt around her hair. It was bunched and tangled, with a long thick strand hanging solo down her back. Her bonnet sat crooked and the stiffness on her cheek was dried-on mud. Now she felt as badly about herself as Claudette, and to think Clint had seen her like this. She glanced over to the table where the men still sat, and he caught her eye and winked. She smiled weakly and turned back to the patiently waiting Mexican lady.

"Senora Lopez. We both need your help—now. Would you be so kind as to show us where we may wash and repair ourselves? We would be ever so grateful."

"Si," she nodded and grinned. "Bring your things I will show you. Follow me, please."

The squat, friendly lady scurried to the door situated between the main room and kitchen, Other patrons sitting at various places around the room watched as the three women made their exit, then went back to warm rum or hot stew.

Up the narrow, dimly lit stairs the three climbed, then proceeded a short ways down the hall. At the far end was an opened small window flapping against the outside of the building. As Senora Lopez reached out to grab it, a flash of lightning lit up the sky, followed by a tremulous clap of angry thunder. All three women let out startled shrieks and Claudette took a firm grip on Kathryn's arm.

Tugging against the wind, Senora Lopez managed to slam the window shut and firmly latch it. Pressing her face to the pane, she briefly stared out at the sky, remarking, "Si, it is another bad one a coming. I hope so the last one was all we have for tonight." She shook her head, adding, "But I very wrong."

Just at that moment, another flash as brilliant as before and the thundering vibrations rattled the walls. The women clung together until the rumbling temporarily ceased, but the pounding rain that followed was so noisy they had to shout in order to be heard.

Senora Lopez ushered Kathryn and Claudette into a room and promptly lit the lamp that hung from the center of the ceiling. The light revealed two large beds, a cot, an infant cradle, and a couple of commodes with pitcher and bowl atop.

"You take off dresses. I will bring you something to wear for now." Senora Lopez hastily eyed their figures, and wearing a frown, hurried from the room. Kathryn was about to tell the woman they had other clothes to put on, but the eager woman was out the door and gone.

Helping each other with buttons and the like, Kathryn and Claudette began sharing bits and pieces about themselves. Claudette revealed what misgivings she had had all along about leaving her beautiful home in Charleston, West Virginia, to travel all this way in misery and discomfort, just so Harold could make more money.

"What business is your husband in?" inquired Kathryn.

"Harold is a gold and silversmith. He had his own jewelry store and he catered to all the wealthy people in the area. Why, he even had customers from other states because of his expert work and fine detailing. I was happy just the way things were. In fact, I was in hopes that we might start our family soon." Her face saddened and she quickly looked away trying to keep her poise. She took a handkerchief from her handbag and dabbed her forehead and cheeks.

"I have suffered two miscarriages already, and I am sure this journey will do nothing to improve my health." With a forced smile, she said, "Well, at least we kept our home, so if things do not work out as Harold has planned, we at least have something to go back to."

"If I may ask, why did you choose Gunnison, Colorado, to move to?" questioned Kathryn.

"Harold is very ambitious and believes he can do even better financially owning his own source of gold. With all the discoveries of gold and silver in Colorado, he was anxious to come out here and get in on the money."

"He probably sees great opportunity in doing this. I see where it would make sense, considering his profession and all. I am sure he just wants the best for both of you," said Kathryn.

"I know...it is just that it is so difficult starting new in a strange place, especially when I do not know what to expect when we arrive there if we get there."

"I do not know either, but that is part of the adventure and excitement for me. I also left a big, beautiful home, though I left for quite different reasons. You see," Kathryn continued, her expression grown serious, "I could not convince my mother that the man she is soon to marry is truly a scoundrel. I believe he is only after her money and position. So I decided to leave and go live with my uncle, my father's brother, rather than dignify his deception and remain in a house with a man whom I despise. I do not know what is in store for me, but at least I can begin a new life away from the indifference of my once-caring mother."

Claudette shook her head sadly and said, "We both are going through much change and upheaval. Perhaps we may be of help to each other. We could even become friends..." Her voice trailed off questioningly.

"I think I would like you for a friend," smiled Kathryn.

"Thank you. I would like you for a friend, too," replied Claudette misty-eyed.

A tap on the door and in breezed Senora Lopez with her arms full of clothes. "Here," she said, as she plunked the bundle on the bed. "I am so sorry I take so long, but I try to find something nice to fit you. Here." She picked up a skirt and held it up for Claudette's inspection. "And this goes with it," she smiled as she handed her a blouse. "And this is for you," she said to Kathryn, pleased with herself for her choices.

The clothes were bright and colorful, much like what the kindly Mexican wore.

"Oh, these should be fun to wear, don't you think so, Claudette?"

Claudette looked thoughtful, then smiled broadly, showing off beautiful, fine, white teeth. "Yes, let us try them on."

The woman grinned and giggled as they donned their strange new attire and admired themselves in the small mirror.

"You both very pretty. Come now. You must come down and have some food with the others."

The women descended the narrow steps and entered the large room, heading for the table where the men, waiting on them, sat engaged in a lively discussion over ale. Billy looked up and saw them first and nudged Clint sitting to his left. Clint glanced up and grinned when he saw Kathryn in her unusual clothes. Underneath the table, Clint gently tapped Harold's leg with the toe of his boot, then pointed with his eyes in Claudette's direction. Both men exchanged sly looks as they promptly stood up to offer the ladies a chair.

"Well," said Clint to Kathryn, "got yourself some new duds, I see. Kinda becomin, I'd say. Don't you think so, Harold?"

"Why, yes. The ladies look quite charming." He winked at Claudette mischievously, causing her to blush.

A hearty bowl of wonderful-smelling stew was placed in front of them, along with warm, buttered corn bread. After they'd eaten their stew, Senora Lopez came from the kitchen carrying a whole pie. To everyone's delight, it was apple-cinnamon, still warm from the oven.

Over in the corner, an old cowboy began strummin his guitar. His buddy sitting next to him pulled a harmonica from his shirt pocket, and the strains of "Down in the Valley" floated softly through the room, while the rain hitting the windowpanes added melancholy to the tune.

Out from the kitchen strolled Senor Lopez, weaving a concertina in and out, joining in with the two. Senora Lopez tapped Clint on the shoulder and handed him a fiddle. Smiling sheepishly, he stood up and tucked the instrument under his chin. Drawing the bow easy across the strings, Clint and the three musicians filled the room with the haunting melody.

Billy and Will began singing the words, and soon everyone in the place was swaying and singing:

> Down in the valley
> Valley so low,
> Hang your head over
> Hear the wind blow.
> Hear the wind blow, dear,
> Hear the wind blow;
> Hang your head over,
> Hear the wind blow.
> Roses love sunshine
> Violets love dew
> Angels in heaven
> Know I love you.

Know I love you, dear,
Know I love you;
Angels in heaven
Know I love you.

Clint's eyes met Kathryn's on the "Know I love you" part and both smiled, then looked away. When the song was finished, they all applauded, and Will yelled, "More, more."

The cowboy began, and the unusual quartet played again. Kathryn, Claudette and Harold were unfamiliar with this song and listened as the others sang:

Carry me back
To the lone prairie,
Where the coyotes howl
And the wind blows free.
And when I die
You can bury me
'Neath the western sky
On the lone prairie.
I'm a rovin cowboy
Far away from home,
Far from the prairie
Where I used to roam.
Where the doggies wander
And the wind blows free,
Oh, my heart is yonder
On the lone prairie.

"That is enough of sad-sounding songs," proclaimed Manuel wiping away a tear. You play something lively, Clint."

"Yeah," agreed Will. "Come on."

Clint grinned at Kathryn, then scrunched one eye shut, sucked in his lower lip, and thought a moment. His eyes brightened wide as he placed his fingers to the strings. Sharply, he drew the bow across the fiddle, making a high-pitched hissing sound that led into "Turkey in the Straw."

"Si," yelled Manuel. "That is the one I like."

Hands and feet began keeping time, and the rest of the musicians played along.

Suddenly, Harold jumped up, pulling Claudette with him; and in the middle of the room they began dancing the meanest "Virginia Reel" Clint or anyone else had ever seen. Kathryn laughed merrily, clapping her hands, and the rest cheered and stomped their feet, enjoying the impromptu performance.

When the music ended, Claudette was breathless and put her hand to her chest, exclaiming, "Harold, what ever has gotten into you?" and blushed from the hooting and applause.

It was late when the group turned in for the night. Kathryn shared a bed with Claudette who'd quickly fallen asleep, but Kathryn was too full of thoughts to drift into slumber. She listened to the rain pelting the building and tingling the glass. The wind kept up its constant blowing while the thunder rumbled overhead. Now and then the room lit up from the lightning, creating an eerie effect and making Kathryn feel more uneasy.

Slowly, so as not to disturb Claudette, Kathryn eased herself from the bed. Draping a spare blanket around her, she tiptoed to the door and silently left the room. As quietly as possible, she inched her way down the steps and into the main room, heading for the comfort of the orange, glowing embers. The dark shadow of someone else already there stopped her from moving another step,

Clint felt the presence of another and cautiously turned around. Instantly, he knew the intruder upon his solitude. "Kathryn...what is the matter?" he whispered.

"Oh, Clint," she whispered back. "I am so glad it is you. I was taken aback for a moment. I was having trouble falling asleep, so I thought I would sit down by the fire for a while." She made her way across the floor and added, "With the storm and being in a strange place...well, it is making me very uneasy."

"There's still coffee in the pot on the stove. Wanna have a cup with me?"

"Yes. Something warm sounds very good. Thank you," she answered, sitting down on the bench in front of the fire.

Clint scratched a match on a stone of the fireplace and lit a lamp at the far end of the mantle, bathing the room in soft shadows. He trekked off toward the kitchen while Kathryn huddled in her blanket. She rubbed her hands up and down her arms to ward off the damp chill from the howling wind pushing through the cracks between the logs.

Hearing Clint's footsteps, she turned and extended her hand as he handed her a tin cup full of coffee. A wave of goose bumps traveled her body when he eased himself down beside her, making her shudder.

"Ya cold?" asked Clint.

"A little," she said, covering up her embarrassment. She took a sip from the cup, keeping her eyes on the low flames. When she felt warmer, she stood up, holding onto her blanket and cup, and walked to the nearby window. She stood fixed and stared out into the black night.

"Are you having regrets, Kathryn?" ventured Clint softly.

"Not really," she answered pensively. Sipping her coffee, she continued gazing into the stormy night and without turning said softly, "Sometimes I wonder what I've gotten myself into. I had no idea what this part of the country was really like. The newness and unfamiliar way of living and doing things makes me feel helpless and out of place."

She paused to watch a streak of lightning flash a sharp pattern in the distance, then continued. "It is so plain out here. I am used to greener surroundings and fancier accommodations...yet," she conceded, "people are kind and treat me friendly enough. But I am lonesome for my own kind and having all my own things around me." She sighed and added, "I suspect it is going to take me a while to adjust to all this."

The room grew strangely silent, even with the rain and rumbling clouds. Clint studied Kathryn, so small and helpless; and even wrapped in the blanket she looked beautiful to him. The light from the candle cast a golden glow on her long hair cascading down the back of the blanket, and he could no longer contain his feelings. Walking over, he nervously stood beside her. Cautiously, he put his hands on her shoulders and gently turned her to face him. Without a word he took her cup from her trembling hand and set it on the bare windowsill. From the faint light, Clint could still see deep into Kathryn's questioning eyes as he lowered his head and parted his quivering lips to meet with hers.

The warm sensation of Clint's moving, pressing mouth on hers made Kathryn's knees weak. She drew her blanketed arms about his middle, clinging to him for support. Ever so slowly he pulled his lips from hers and placed his large hand gently on the back of her head, caressing her hair with his fingers. Both of them breathed in short gasps as they felt the excitement and warmth from their bodies touching.

"Oh, Kathryn," he breathed. "So long now I have wanted to kiss you and hold you like this. I hope yer not angry with me."

"I am not angry, Clint," she whispered, not wanting to let go.

"I've wanted to tell you...fer so long, my feelings but the words would never come out." Clint stroked her hair, then her cheek with his finger curved under her chin he gently raised her face till their eyes met again. Clint said hoarsely, "I can't give ya all you've been use to. Mostly, what I have to give you is me...and all the love in my soul."

He swallowed hard. "My love can never belong to anyone else...now that I've found you."

Kathryn held him tightly and snuggled her face on his chest. Clint felt his face flush for what he had just blurted out, for he had turned his insides out and exposed his deepest feelings and he suddenly felt weak and vulnerable, and he clung to her needing help with his awkwardness.

Kathryn lifted her face. "That is the most beautiful thing anyone has ever said to me." She placed her hand on the back of his neck and drew him down, putting her velvety lips to his. The kiss she returned gave Clint the hope of her love.

They sat before the fire wrapped in each other's arms. "Clint," she said, softly. "I am afraid to fall in love with you, although I think I already have. But first I must sort out my life and feelings before I can be truly sure. Can you understand that?"

"Yeah. I know you need time. But you should know, I'll wait for as long as it takes."

"Thank you. You know that I must continue this journey to my uncle's; then, perhaps when things make more sense to me, I can deal with the feelings I have inside for you, I care very much for you Clint, more than I can tell you now."

Clint held her tight, not wanting to let go of her, but she pulled away. "I must go back upstairs before we are discovered. This would not look good for us to be found, alone, like this. In fact, it would appear shameful." She walked to the staircase without looking back and quickly disappeared.

Clint sat for a moment in a daze due to what had just transpired, unable to shake the feelings that possessed his very being. The sensational throbbing down in his loins was almost more then he could bear. He went to the door and stepped outside to suck in the cold night air.

10

Walsenburg, Colorado

*T*he gray dawn split on the horizon with the bright rays from the rising sun. Clint lent Will and Manuel a hand as they hitched the team to the coach, all the while nervously glancing toward the station door for Kathryn and the others to come out. He felt exhilarated and yet tired from only a few hours sleep. He had tossed and turned till he felt he would go mad trying to figure how things could work out as he wanted. There were so many obstacles, too many scenes still to be played out. How out of control he felt, but what had happened last night had given him hope, such hope that his heart felt as if it had left his body and taken flight like a soaring eagle.

Inside the station, Kathryn was busy wording her telegram to Uncle Richard, at last, and handed it to Senor Lopez.

"I send this off right soon. Do not worry, Senorita Barnett."

"Thank you, Senor Lopez. I am just so relieved that I am getting word to my uncle. I am sure that he must be very worried about me by now." She picked up her valise, parasol, and draw stringed handbag and walked out with Claudette to join the others.

The little group boarded the ready coach and waved goodbye to the Lopezes as the stage headed on for Walsenburg.

Meandering through the long, curved street in Walsenburg, the folks inside the stage drank in the welcome sights of the small western town.

During this lap of the journey Claudette was more at ease, which was a great relief to Harold, and at times they were seen holding hands and exchanging secret smiles. Kathryn, on the other hand, was deep in thought, pondering what had transpired between her and Clint and trying to put her new feelings in some kind of perspective. Billy was something else. Excitement of reaching his destination packed him full of energy and, halfway there, he had changed his place to back in the China seat beside Manuel, giving him breathing space and mobility for his keyed-up body.

"Hey, Billy...over here." Two fellows about Billy's age were leaning against the livery stable holding their horses' reins. Billy grabbed his bedroll from the top. "Well, goodbye everyone. Good-by, Kathryn." He strolled over at a leisurely pace and Kathryn watched him go. Above the street noise she couldn't help but hear Billy's loud, angry voice.

"You what? Jeez, how could ya do that to me? I oughta blow yer heads off. Now, what am I goin to do? Damn you." He spun on his heel, flipped his bedroll back over his shoulder and walked disgustedly away.

"Billy, come back," one of them shouted. "We can work somethin out." The other fellow started after him and grabbed hold of his arm, and Billy jerked it away and kept on walking in Kathryn's direction.

"Billy, what's wrong?" Kathryn asked.

Those dumb-heads gambled with my horse-buyin money...and lost it." He was mad in the face and had that determined look of a desperate man.

"Where are you going now?"

"Ta see if someone'll stake me in a card game. so I kin win enough to buy me a horse."

"And if you lose?"

"I won't. I can't." And off he went.

Kathryn watched the young boy. Flipping up her parasol, she marched on over and approached his friends. "I want you to catch up with Billy and keep him busy for about fifteen minutes then, tell him it's urgent to come back here. Tell him that Kathryn needs him. Now, go." The lads looked puzzled but obeyed.

Kathryn walked from the bright sun, inside to the shadowy interior of the livery stable. She hailed down the owner, who was hammering a shoe on an anvil.

"Sir, may I have a moment of your time?"

"Yes, ma'am. What kin I do fer ya?"

]"What horses have you for sale?"

"Wanna buy a horse, do ya? Well, I got a real gentle lady's horse, right over there?" He pointed with his hammer to a stall across from them to an older animal, pot-bellied and with a slight swayback. "Let ya have her for two hundred."

Kathryn looked at the horse, then at the huge-muscled man, with a round, bald head and greedy eyes. "I wouldn't give you twenty dollars for that poor, broken-down horse. Now, if you have any decent animals, at a fair price...show me. Otherwise, we are wasting each other's time." She fixed her business stare on him, and he regarded her carefully and slowly laid down his hammer.

"Follow me." He led her to the back where there were three horses in a large stall. Kathryn's keen eye and sense of horse flesh spotted a nice bay. It had good color to its coat, clear eyes and strong-looking legs and fleshed out nicely.

"I'll give you two-fifty for that bay...throw in the saddle."

"You must be out of your mind. I can't let that one go for less than three, no saddle."

"Well, I'm sure there are other horses for sale around this town besides yours. Thank you for your time." Kathryn was almost to the entrance when the man called out, "Three hundred and the saddle."

"No, thank you."

"Three hundred and the saddle is as good as it gits."

"Two seventy-five with saddle, and you got yourself a deal." Kathryn turned and waited for his answer, poised to leave.

The man scratched his bald head, looked at Kathryn and back at the horse.

"All right. Business has been off. I need the money."

Kathryn opened her handbag and pulled out the amount and handed it over. "Saddle him immediately, please, and bring him out front."

Kathryn walked to the doorway and saw Clint coming out of the stage station, and further down the walk behind him came Billy and his two friends.

Clint headed her way. "What are you doin here, Kathryn? I thought you were going with Claudette to freshen up?" They turned to the doorway as the sound of horse's hooves approached and the livery man stood holding onto the bay. "What's this all about?" asked Clint

"Just something I felt the need to do," she said slyly.

The three fellows were almost to them now, and Billy called out, "What's wrong, Kathryn? They dragged me oughta the saloon 'cause they said ya needed me?" He looked worried and concerned.

Kathryn walked over and took the reins out of the man's hands and led the horse over to Billy and handed him the reins. "Here, Billy."

Billy stood dumfounded and looked from the horse to Kathryn. "I don't understand. I thought you were in some kinda trouble or somethin."

"I am," she smiled. "I bought this horse and he needs an owner, Have a safe trip back." Kathryn put her arms around his neck and hugged him.

11

Sounds from a. fast-approaching horse brought Rick out of the barn where he'd been checking in on a foaling mare. It was Jim, yelling and waving something in his hand.

"Rick....Rick. It came." Jim reined his horse to a, sudden stop by Rick and handed over the envelope. He quickly dismounted and led his horse to the corral. to tie the reins, keeping an anxious eye on Rick as he tore open the paper. His friend seemed riveted to the ground and Jim walked over by his side.

Rick's eyes studied the paper, held in his trembling hand. A stunned voice spoke. "She should be in Villa Grove May sixteen. That's only four days from now."

Jim squinted and frowned, silently observing Rick's reaction to this long-awaited news. Through misty, brown eyes, Rick shifted his gaze to Jim, then fixed his sight toward the mountains. Choking back the lump in his throat, he turned back and said hoarsely, "She's really comin, Jim, she's really comin." A tear jerked its way down his cheek, and Rick snatched it away with the back of his hand.

Jim had never seen Rick this soulful. He'd missed his kinfolk more than he had let on, shut up those lonely feelings all these years. Jim blinked away his own tender tears as he put his rough-skinned hand upon Rick's shoulder, and the two stood silent in unspoken understanding.

"Kathryn's really comin," whispered Rick. "Kathryn's really comin," he said louder. "She's really coming," he whooped.

"Yes," Jim laughed. "Yes, she's really comin." Rick grabbed Jim's arm and they did a do-si-do. "Whaaa—hooo, " shouted Rick. "Whaaa-hooo," shouted Jim.

Hearing the commotion from inside the house, Pedro, still ailing from his gunshot wound, slowly made his way to the door. He burst out laughing, which hurt, when he saw Rick and Jim dancing, stomping their feet, kicking up the dust.

"Hey, boss," Pedro yelled, clutching his side. "What is all the dancing for?"

Arm in arm, the two danced a jig up to the house, laughing and chanting, "Kathryn is comin, Kathryn is comin, Kathryn is comin." Pedro grinned as he stepped aside, and they danced on through the doorway and plopped down in their chairs laughing at themselves.

"Pedro. Kathryn...is goin to be comin... here," said Rick between gasps for air.

"Si. I hear that," he laughed back. "Boss, that is good news, no?"

"Good news, yes. I mean, Si." And they laughed some more

"What in tarnation's goin on in here?" questioned Sam, charging through the door. "I kin hear ya clean outside." Sam, followed by Jasper and Zeke, filed into the room. They'd been out checking fence line, and the dogs, tired from the run, headed straight for the rug in front of the fireplace and plopped down, tongues dangling from the sides of their mouths.

"Sam," answered Pedro excitedly and pointing toward Rick, "Bossman got good news. His Kathryn is really goin to be comin here."

Raising his leg, Sam slapped his thigh and grinned. "Well, I'd say that calls fer a celebration. What do ya say to that?"

"I'd sure enough agree with you," said Rick. "Git a bottle, Sam. Jim, grab us some glasses...and, Pedro, you sit yerself down for ya fall down."

Sam went to the pantry and selected a bottle of fine Kentucky Bourbon from the cache behind the wall and brought it to the table.

"Do the honors, Sam," said Rick. The cork was removed and Sam filled the glasses and they raised them for a toast.

"To Kathryn," said Jim. "To Kathryn," repeated the rest. They slugged down the whiskey, and Pedro coughed and sputtered, "That is some powerful stuff, Senor Rick." Laughter filled the room as Sam went around the table and refilled the glasses, then sat down with the others.

Rick tapped his pipe on the side of his glass for attention and rose from his place, and the room became silent. "Boys," he began, clearing his throat. "I'm kinda choked up here. Knowin Kathryn will be comin to live with us. I'm so happy I could bust," he said a little sheepishly. The fellows grinned at him, and he continued. "I know having someone else move in...well, there's bound to be some changes, especially since it's a woman." The fellows nodded and grinned some more. "I jest hope it won't matter much or cause any hardships, and that we can continue to live like the family we've become. We are jest gonna add another member. I jest hope ya learn to love Kathryn as much as I do." He looked into the faces of Sam, Jim and Pedro, hoping what he said met with their approval. Each smiled and nodded at him.

"Jeez," he grinned, "yer the best buncha guys I've ever known, I'd like to toast you—all of you." Rick extended his glass, looked into the eyes of each, brought the glass to his lips and poured the whiskey down. The men cheered at Rick, their stalwart friend and boss.

Holding back a smirk, Pedro innocently widened his eyes and asked in a feminine voice, "Senor Rick? Do you mean, by changes, that Jim will no more prance into the kitchen in his woolies?" then fluttered his eyes at Jim. Everyone, but Jim, burst out laughing.

"Ya," laughed Rick, "something like that." He slammed down his empty glass. "Another round, Sam."

Sam filled his own glass and slid the bottle to Rick. It was empty when Pedro slid the bottle to Jim. "Well, that's a fine howdy-ya-do."

"Git another bottle, Jim," said Rick. "We can't let ya git short-changed, now, kin we?"

"Naw," agreed Pedro and Sam.

Jim good-naturedly went and fetched another bottle, but he stopped at the cupboard and got himself a pint canning jar and filled it nearly half full before setting the bottle back on the table.

"This way," he said, "I won't have to fret when ya guys empty the bottle on me again." This statement got a laugh, and the bunch continued to work on the second bottle, joking and having a good time, until they noticed that Sam had suddenly become quiet.

"Somethin the matter, Sam?" asked Rick.

"Well, no offense now, but I've been lookin round this here place, and it ain't exactly a palace. And, Rick, where do ya plan on havin the poor girl sleep or have space to call her own? Huh?"

Rick's face fell. "Oh, my God. Here I've been only worryin about Kathryn gittin here, and I gave no more thought about fixin things up different so's to make this bachelor's nest look more inviting to her. Jeez, and we don't have time to do much either."

"Pedro," ordered Sam. "I'll git the fire goin, and you kin git the pot of stew heated up. Jist keep yer eye on it, ya know, stir it once in a while. The rest of us better git to hustlin."

"Good idea, Sam," agreed Rick. Let's git at the spare room and see if we can't make it presentable for a lady."

"That's gonna take some doin," said Jim. "Best we git started."

The three trudged down the hall, and Rick cautiously opened the door.

"Lord love a duck," exclaimed Sam. "How the devil did we git so much crap in one place?"

"I dunno," said Jim, shaking his head. "But, by the looks of this, we didn't git here any too soon."

Rick, speechless, just stood gaping into the heaping mess of clutter.

"Well, let's do it," ordered Sam, "Here, Jim, haul this saddle outa here. Hey, whose is this anyway?"

"Mine," admitted Rick. "I was gonna repair it one of these days, Haul it back to the tack room, would ya, please, Jim? And wait, take these old boots, too." Rick stepped further into the room. "Why were we savin these old clothes? And this beat-up divan? And these busted chairs? And this falling-apart butter churn? Looks like we're gonna have us one big bonfire."

Little by little they gutted out the room, hauling most of the stuff out and piled it between the house and corral in the large, bare turn-around.

When the room was near empty, Jim got the broom and dustpan and swept up the dust and the accumulation of mouse droppings. He thought to himself, "If Rick's Kathryn saw the filth here she'd turn around and go back home." He looked about the empty, bare-floored room, save for a small chest of drawers and a single bed fashioned of twisted iron with chipped white paint missing its mattress and exposing the frame of coiled springs. Jim turned to see Rick sadly leaning against the open door.

"Looks like we still got our work cut out for us, Jim."

Sam was outside lighting the fire on the pile of junk. When it was going good, he went back into the house and told Pedro to keep an eye on the blaze, then went to the room that soon would be referred to as Kathryn's.

"Looks like we need some woman stuff in here," observed Sam.

"Yer right, Sam," agreed Rick. "This'll never do. But where are we gonna git fancy furnishings in such a short time?"

"C'mon, it's not too late to ride to town, and I think I know jest the places to go," urged Sam with enthusiasm.

"I'll go hitch up the buckboard," volunteered Jim. "And while yer gone, I'll scrub this room up nice and clean."

"Thanks, ol' buddy," said Rick. "Pedro, you and Jim eat when yer hungry; me and Sam'll git somethin in town or eat when we git back. We're goin to buy some things—girl things—for Kathryn."

"I hear that. You better be lookin for some curtains, too. Pretty ones. And another thing, Boss. My mother, she always has nice tablecloth for eating."

"Thanks for the suggestions. We'll do our best. C'mon, Sam. We best git going" Rick slapped on his Stetson and took his gun and holster off the peg, strapping it on as he went out the door followed by Sam. The buckboard was in front of the porch, with Jim holding the reins till they got there.

The buckboard sped along the curved, scenic road, its passengers bent on one mission. Rick kept the two horses at a steady clip and hoped they would find what they needed for Kathryn's room without too much confusion. Nearing town, Rick asked, "Where to, Sam? You said ya had an idea where to git the stuff."

"Yeah, I said that. Take the first right turn off the main drag and go down to the end of the road. That's where the Widow Truitt lives," added Sam. "She's livin in that big, ramblin house that's full of stuff. Figure we could take some of it off her hands and give her a little money to boot. She ain't had it so good since her old man died here a ways back. That's been about four years now, I reckon," he said casually.

"I didn't know you were so well-acquainted with the widow," replied Rick in a teasing tone.

"Well, I'm not," Sam answered defensively. "Jes that, Tommy, down at the store, has asked me different times to deliver the poor woman's groceries and well, she, naturally, being a good woman an all, has asked me to have lemonade with her, to show her appreciation fer the favor. Aw, shucks...why am I explaining all this to you anyhow? There, the white house," Sam pointed out, "the one with the little front porch and the roses climbin up the side."

Rick, chuckling inside for discovering a piece of information Sam had kept hidden, slowed the team and pulled to a stop in the road at the white house with the little porch.

"C'mon, Rick, let's see what she's got," said Sam in a positive tone. The two stopped at the door and Sam gently knocked. The lace curtain over the window parted and the Widow Truitt peeked out. She smiled when she recognized her caller and quickly unlocked and opened the door.

"Why, Mr. McPeak, I wasn't expecting to see you today. What a nice surprise. And who is this nice-looking gentleman you have brought with you?"

Sam made the introductions, and Alice Truitt invited them to step into the parlor. Rick took note of Sam's widow friend as they followed. She was on the short side and dressed in a soft-blue cotton print, which showed off her flawless complexion. Rick guessed her age to be somewhere around forty or so. He could see how Sam might be a little smitten, if indeed he was.

"Now, gentlemen, might I get you a. refreshment after your long journey to town? Coffee or tea? And I just might have some of that lemonade you like so well, Mr. McPeak," said Widow Truitt in a lilting voice.

"I think a glass of water would be just fine, ma'am," replied Sam. "We don't want to trouble you. The fact is we came to ask you a very special favor and hope you would be able to help us out."

Between Rick and Sam they told of their predicament, capturing the widow's full attention. When they finished their story, Alice rose excitedly from her chair and commanded them to follow her. The widow led them down a hall and to the staircase, which she ascended with Rick and Sam close behind. At the top she passed two doors and stopped at the third. She flung open the door and ushered them inside.

The room was beautifully furnished and very feminine, Rick was more than impressed. Pale-pink organdy curtains graced the windows, a white crocheted spread was fitted on the bed, a handsome walnut bed with a delicately carved headboard and tall posts at the foot. There was an armoire, large, sturdy and also made of walnut. A small dressing table, painted cream-colored, with a. red-velvet chair stood in the corner.

"Is there a possibility that you would be willing to sell me most of the fine furnishings in this room?" Rick asked hesitantly.

"Yes. It is time that I let these things go," Widow Truitt sadly answered. "You see, this room once belonged to my daughter. And I have, all these years, kept it just as she left it." The widow looked about in memory, then looked at Rick with pained expression. My daughter, Mr. Barnett, was only eighteen when she was killed. Natalie was her name. She was out riding, and her horse was startled by a rattlesnake. Natalie was thrown off and bitten in the neck by the snake." Tears now in her eyes clouded her vision and she blinked hard and they trickled down her creamy-white cheeks. She hastily took a handkerchief from inside her sleeve cuff and dabbed her eyes. "She was dead when my husband, Harlan, got to her...the snake coiled nearby. That was eight years ago. I think it is about time I stop cleaning and washing the things in this room. I believe that it would be a wonderful thing, Mr. Barnett, for your niece to enjoy some of Natalie's things. They are certainly doing no one much good here. And," she added somewhat brighter, "I could refurnish it differently and rent out the room."

"How much would you like for the things, Mrs. Truitt?" asked Rick. "Before you answer, I'll tell you what I'd like. The bed and the covering, the armoire, dressing table and chair, and I think the curtains would fit the window pretty good. Don't you think so, Sam?"

"Sure do. I think," Sam went on, "that these things would really please your niece and give her something real nice to wake up to."

"I don't know what price to put on these things, Mr. Barnett. Would two hundred dollars seem like too much?"

"I think two hundred sounds just fine," smiled Rick. "Would it upset you if we took them all with us now? We only have a couple of days to get ready, and we have just begun."

"No, not at all. Mr. McPeak, if you would be so kind as to remove the curtain rod, I will fold up the curtains and put them in a box with the spread so they will not get soiled on the way home."

It was a matter of over an hour before Rick and Sam had the bed, armoire and other things loaded up in the buckboard, including the time they spent having a cup of tea. They waved goodbye to the widow, Alice Truitt, as Rick turned the buckboard around and drove down the street.

"Well, that was a nice surprise, Sam. I'm real pleased with the stuff, too. There is one thing, though, that we need, and that is a rug of some sort for the floor, and a nice lamp, too. Know of any more widows we can visit?" chuckled Rick.

"Not exactly. Head for the other end of town." Sam settled back and rode with a half-smirk on his face. Rick did as instructed, carefully, so's not to scratch or damage the lovely things in the buckboard. Folks walking about on the wooden sidewalk gawked curiously as they passed, wondering what they had in the back, why, and who for. Appropriate nods and waves were exchanged as they continued on through town.

"Jest where we goin this time, Sam?"

"Y'all see, but ya probably won't like it."

"What's that?"

"Y'all see."

"Well, damn. Tell me when we git there, will ya?" said Rick grumpily.

"Yeah."

They were nearly out of town when Sam nudged Rick, "Pull round to the back of that big two-story over there," he pointed.

"What are you up to?" questioned Rick suspiciously.

"Y'all see," answered Sam firmly.

"What do ya expect to find in a whorehouse except the obvious?" asked Rick, as he eased the team around to the back.

"Y'all see. Now, ya gonna come with me or wait here?"

"I'm s'pose to see...so I guess I'll go with ya...and see."

Rick hitched the team and they went to the rear entrance. Sam cranked the bell, and shortly the door was opened by the madam. "Wha, helloo there, Sam," drawled the scantily clad woman. "And, ah see y'all brought a friend. Do come in." She had her hair heaped in clusters of curls on the top of her head with jewelry pinned in for decoration, Her overly made-up face was framed with enormous earbobs of gold beset with rubies. She had green coloring on the lids of her eyes and the thickest, longest lashes Rick had ever seen, and he wondered if they were real.

"What is your pleasure, gentlemen?" she asked through wine-colored lips.

Sam blushed and Rick grinned. "Flora," said Sam, trying to keep his composure. "What we need, my friend Rick here and me, is to see yer fancy furnishins ya have to sell. Ya see, Rick-here's niece is comin in from the east in jest a couple of days and is goin to be living with us. An, well, ya see, she's use to havin real pretty things and all around her... and we're tryin to fix her up a room...all pretty-like, an...well, ya know what I mean," stammered Sam, a little out of breath in trying to explain.

Flora smiled. "Honey," she replied in a low, seductive voice, "Ah know exactly what you mean." Turning her attention to Rick, she said, "Sweetie, what do y'all need?"

"We still need a nice rug, a lamp, and—I dunno—some fancy decorations of some kind," answered Rick matter-of-factly.

"Well, Sweetie, y'all came to the right place. Down at the end of this hall...well, you see what all I've got. Pick out what you need, then we'll talk price. If y'all excuse me, I will be right back, quick's a wink." As she departed, she turned and said, "There's a lamp to light inside the door." And she scurried off. Rick looked after her and shook his head in disbelief.

"C'mon, Rick," urged Sam. They opened the plain wooden door, found the lamp, and when it was lit, Rick stared in awe. The large room looked like a regular store—not exactly regular for it contained very fancy and expensive items. Against one wall, stacked neatly, were rolls of rugs, woven or braided. There were chairs of beautifully carved wood, upholstered in brocades, velvets and the like. Polished tables of mahogany, walnut and maple shone warmly from the lamp's glow. Shelves along one side displayed hanging lamps with designs painted on them and many of stained glass, as well as table lamps with rounded bases and globes all equally beautiful. From the ceiling were displayed chandeliers with crystals dangling gracefully down. Hanging on the walls were different sizes and shapes of mirrors with gilded frames. Taking up the center of the room were some statues of cherubs or women with naked breasts. A couple of velvet sofas completed the room.

"My God, where did this stuff come from?" was all Rick could muster to say.

"It's her second business," answered Sam. "She gits this stuff shipped in from the East Coast and sells it to folks with money."

"How come I never knew anything about this?" asked Rick curiously.

"Two reasons. The first one's obvious. Second, them uppity ladies don't want other folks and the ones they associate with to know who they gits their fancy stuff from. Think it'll put 'em in a bad light. Anyhow, ya better start lookin and pick out what ya like, so's we can git on home with the stuff."

Rick headed over to the rugs and Sam followed with the light. Immediately, Rick's eye saw what he wanted, a dark green, with pink and fuchsia rosebuds scattered throughout.

"This one, Sam. This is what I want to be on Kathryn's floor. Help me git it out to the hall." Sam set down the lamp and the two carried the long, heavy rug and set it against the wall in the hallway. Back in the room, Rick asked Sam's opinion on a mirror for above the already-purchased dressing table. Agreeing on a fairly large one with gilded scrollwork and side mirrors that could be moved, Sam removed it from the wall. They picked out a double-globed lamp with burgundy glass set on a brass base and decorated with roses with green stern and leaves.

"I see you gentlemen know just what you want," said Flora entering the room. "You have made your decisions much faster that I imagined. I am truly impressed," she smiled with false adoration.

"What am I gonna owe you here, Flora?" asked Rick, concerned that he had not brought enough cash along

"Let me see," she said, pursing her red lips together in thought. "You have selected that very beautiful rug in the hallway and..." She looked at the mirror Sam was holding and the lamp in Rick's hands, "How does a hundred fifty sound to you?"

"I'd say that sounds just fine, just fine," smiled Rick. He set the lamp down to get his money pouch, when he spied a dark green velvet chair. "How much is that chair?" he pointed.

"My," Flora cooed, "you certainly have excellent taste. That honey is a hundred, but since you are buying other things, I will sell it to you for seventy-five."

Rick thought for a moment. "We'll take it. I owe you two twenty-five, right?"

"That's right, Honey." And her hand patted his behind affectionately. As Rick handed Flora the money, she twinkled her eyes and added, "Since you have bought so much from me, I'd like to invite both of you to enjoy a night on the house, free of charge, of course. How about tonight, Honey?"

"Thank you, but we gotta git this stuff back and set up." Then, shrewdly, Rick offered, "Flora, since Sam steered me onto your wonderful place, why don't I let him have my night? That way he'll have one and one to look forward to."

Taken aback by Rick's statement, Flora quickly recovered and forced a smile and replied, "Yes, I guess that would be just fine." Taking her stunned eyes off Rick and looking at Sam, she added, "You'd like that, wouldn't you, Sam? Besides, you visit us all too seldom, and the girls really enjoy your company."

Sam tried to hold in the awkwardness he felt and mustered up a smile. "That's right nice of you to say, Flora." Looking directly into Rick's eyes, he said, "And that's right friendly of you to give me your free night, Rick."

A smirk was threatening to expose itself, and Rick quickly said, "C'mon, Sam, we best git loaded up and on our way."

The carefully-loaded buckboard eased up the slight incline at the back of the whorehouse, and they waved goodbye to Flora and headed back to town. The sun was beginning its descent signaling the close of another day. Colors of blue-gray and pink tinged with splashes of pale yellow appeared across the horizon, and the air barely stirred, giving hint to a nice evening weatherwise.

Sam finally spoke. "That was pretty sly back there, how ya turned down the invite. What ya got against a little frolickin with a pretty young gal anyhow?"

"I didn't say I was against it. It's jest that I don't care for the type of woman that frolics, as you put it, with anyone with cash in his hand. I, myself, prefer a gal who cares at least a little for me, And I gotta care for her, too. Don't git me wrong. I'm not makin judgment on you or, anybody else, 'cause I tried that, back in my gold-rushin days, but somethin jest seemed to be missin. Know what I mean?"

Sam was very thoughtful and took his time to answer. Finally, he said, "Yeah, I know. It's like it's fun when yer doin it, but ya come away with nothin here," he said, tapping his heart with his fist. "Yer feelin empty inside and alone again."

"Yeah, somethin like that," agreed Rick. They were in the middle of town and, being the dinner hour, there were few people on the street except for an occasional rider on horseback. "What say we have us a big of steak 'for we head home?" offered Rick.

"Sounds like a winner," answered Sam, slapping his hungry stomach. Rick pulled the wagon to a halt in front of the hotel, and they sauntered in to satisfy their hunger.

Night was heavy upon the two as they traveled the long road home. Nearing the end of the drive, Sam and Rick were glad to see the welcoming glow through the windows of the house. Their arrival was heard, and Jim and Pedro were out on the porch to greet them, each holding a lantern, both anxious to see what they had brought back for Kathryn's room.

It was almost midnight before they were done hauling in the things and had them set up in the room to everyone's liking. When at last they had agreed on an arrangement, they stood in a cluster in the doorway admiring their work.

"I gotta say," spoke Jim, "this here's the classiest room in the whole area."

"Think she'll be pleased?" asked Rick thoughtfully. Yet, as he viewed the now-elegant room, he suspected it was just like she would want and close to what she had been used to.

"Boss, said Pedro, "she's gonna like this room very mucho, I jest know."

"I think so, too," smiled Rick, "Well, boys, it's been quite a day. What say we turn in, Tomorrow is going to be hectic, 'cause Sam, you and Jim gotta move them cattle to Fort Garland. The fellas I hired on from town will be here bright and early."

"Hey, but Rick. We'll be gone when Kathryn gits here. That ain't fair," complained Jim.

"That's right," agreed Sam. "Can't we change the day till after she's here?"

"Wish I could, boys, but I promised the Commander he'd git his supply...before I knew about Kathryn. Ya know I gotta keep my word, or else he'll be findin someone else fer their meat. Don't know what else I kin do but go ahead as planned."

Sam and Jim grumbled as they went off to bed. Pedro said nothing, as he was staying home, and he tucked himself back on the sofa.

Rick, feeling bad about the timing of events, blew out the lamp beside his bed and drifted off to sleep, exhausted and over-anxious.

12

*T*he longhorns began to spread out. Two of the hired-ons rode their horses fast and far out to the right; Jim and Sam rode to the left and made a sweep toward the middle, and they drove the steers back into formation. Sam, riding his large white mule, Snowflake, caught up to Jim on his dapple-gray Morgan, Slicker.

"Can't say as I'll be sorry when we finally git these doggies to the fort," remarked Sam as he adjusted his seat in the saddle.

"Yeah, I know whatcha mean. Sure woulda been nice if we could be there with Rick when Kathryn gits off the stage. We're gonna miss the big day," complained Jim. He took off his beat-up brown hat and mopped his sweating brow with his arm, turned and checked the position of the sun, which was fast disappearing in the west.

"Might as well camp down around here for the night, Sam, 'less ya wanna put in some night ridin? Moon'll be nearly full tonight."

"Sure'd shorten this trip," answered Sam. "We could rest fer a while, have us some vittles..."

"Ride around an see how the other fellas are doin...then we'll decide. I'll go tell Ernie to stop and git his fire goin," said Jim.

"Sounds good to me," answered Sam. He nudged Snowflake in the sides and trotted away.

Ernie banked up his fire, and preparations began for the grub at the side of his opened chuck wagon, while most of the men rested on the ground nearby. Three of the cowhands were left guarding the grazing steers and would get their supper after their reliefs had eaten.

Jim used his saddle on the ground for a headrest, as did some of the others, and hid his face from the sun with his hat to catch a nap before supper. Sam was leaning against the wagon engaged in swapping cooking secrets with Ernie.

"I'm tellin ya, Ernie," spouted Sam, gesturing with one hand, a cup of coffee in the other, "it's the currant jelly that make the difference."

"Yer sayin...put it in the gravy makins?" questioned Ernie.

"Yeah. Jest take out a gob from a jar an dissolve it in a cup a boilin water...then ya stir it in yer drippins ya thickened with flour," instructed Sam. "I tell ya, it'll be the best venison-steak gravy ya ever tasted." He itched the back of his leg with the toe of his deerskin boot and slugged down the rest of his coffee.

"I'm gonna try it, I will," promised Ernie, checking his sourdough biscuits in his makeshift oven. "Ah, they'll be done soon."

Sam slid himself to the ground, coming to rest against the front wheel of the wagon, and observed Ernie as he was giving the big pot of stew a final stir.

Ernie Smith, in his fifties, was about as round as he was tall. A long, shaggy, salt-and-pepper beard made up for his bald-on-the-top head. What hair he did have was gray, sprouted from the back, ear to ear, and hung straight to his collar. His old boots curled up at the toes and his tan shirttails snuck out from his gun belt, due to his large, rounded belly, and the long sleeves were rolled up past his elbows.

Ernie lived with his widower brother, Herbert, on about a dozen or so acres between Rick's and Villa Grove and hired out as a trail cook and helped Herbert run their farm. They grew potatoes, melons and a variety of vegetables, raised chickens and a few pigs. Pigs, he claimed, kept the rattlesnakes away. Although he was very likable, he was mostly a solitary man. At an early age he'd learned to shift for himself when Indians attacked his parents' homestead in Kansas, leaving him, a child of twelve, and Herbert, fourteen, orphaned.

Now, as always, whether everyone was close by or not, he grabbed his angle-iron and banged the striker around and around. "Come an git it," he hollered, "afore I feeds yer's to the coyotes."

The ringing clatter gathered the men quickly behind the hanging pot, knowing Ernie got real snake-headed if his cooking efforts were ignored; he was known to do as he warned. Tin plates and forks were piled on a small table near the pot, and each man took his own and waited as Ernie dished up the stew and placed biscuits on eagerly-thrust plates.

After talking it over with Sam and the others, Jim, being trail boss, decided to drive the cattle at least a few more hours after it was light enough to see. From the time the sun sunk behind the mountains and the appearance of the moon, the night became tar black. Then one, two, and soon many dozens of stars dotted and decorated the sky overhead like diamonds on black velvet. The men gathered around the light and warmth of the friendly, blazing fire, spinning yarns and chugging down strong, hot coffee from Ernie's steady brewing pot.

Dan, one of the hands that had hired on, borrowed Ernie's guitar from the back of the wagon. He stroked a few mellow chords, then softly began singing:

"I'm a rovin cowboy
Far away-ay from home,
Far from the prairie-ee
Where I used to roam."

The familiar song brought back different memories to each man, and their minds drifted as they listened to Dan's beautiful tenor voice as he sung all the verses to "Carry Me Back to the Lone Prairie." When he started to play it over again, one by one they joined in singing until the balmy night air was filled with the hearty, blending voices of the trail riders.

When they were through, the men grew silent and thoughtful as they waited for the moonlight. The damp wood on the fire crackled and spit, sending out small threads of sparks that quickly fizzled out when they hit the dry ground. Off to the left, in the direction of the Sangres, the sound of a yipping coyote could be heard, and it soon was answered by another to their rear.

Another hour passed before the long ridge of the mountain chain illuminated, and shortly an arched slice of the moon was visible, as if capping the tip of the peak. It inched upward until the entire moon burst forth, bringing objects to sight where they hadn't seemed to be. The cattle became moving gray silhouettes as they ambled about in search of edible growth.

The men, now well-rested, saddled up and took their positions, grouping up the longhorns. The stomping hooves, lowing and bellowing, and an occasional whinny from a horse stirred up the sounds in the bright moonlit night.

Ernie squelched the fire with water and shoveled dirt on top, then threw his shovel in the back of his neatly packed wagon and climbed aboard.

"Ho-ooooo...oooooooh," hollered Jim. "Move 'em out." The movement of the cattle shifted and swept along like a dark blanket of waves, heading south, with the rattling wagon and Ernie bringing up the rear.

13

*T*he mighty Sangre de Cristo range loomed ahead; its vast expanse traveled north as far as the eye could see. The awesome, towering mountains, draped with frosty snow over their sculptured formations, ridges and valleys were beyond anything Kathryn had imagined. She was the first one inside the coach to notice them and, spellbound, she leaned her face out of the coach window for a better view. Noticing her action, Claudette and Harold leaned out, too, for a look.

"Oh, my," exclaimed Claudette.

"Why, they are simply spectacular," observed Harold.

They were traveling on a military road that snaked up and over the mountains, known as the Mosca Pass. It was used by Indians, trappers, the Army and settlers, and was crossed on foot, horseback, wagon and stagecoach, where it came out over the other side onto the enormous San Luis Park. Clint had hitched on another team at their last stop for the strenuous climb over the pass, giving him six strong horses for this phase of the journey.

Clint controlled the horses with expertise and cautiously guided them as they proceeded slowly up the ever-climbing, rough, twisted road. The ravines were hundreds of feet deep and gave one the willies just to imagine tumbling down the treacherous, rocky sides to the bottom.

As the stage inched its way toward the top, Kathryn and Claudette held on tightly to the window frames for support, and Harold's face held a grim expression when they rounded sharp curves. Kathryn knew that Billy would have some wisecrack about all of this, and she rather missed his company. Where and how was he, she wondered?

Kathryn quickly dismissed these thoughts when the coach began tilting backwards, causing Claudette and Harold to tumble over to Kathryn's side. They remained there holding on tight, not daring to move or jounce, in fear of tipping over.

They were nearing the summit and presently came to a halt. Will's face peered in through the window. "Clint says ya can git out and stretch 'fore we go down."

The ladies strolled off by themselves far enough to be hidden from view, and each held the back skirt hems off the ground for the other, making it tidier and easier to relieve themselves. In womanly modesty, they wandered back, pretending they had talked of something in private, rather than having to do something in private.

Manuel and Harold were engaged in conversation, while Will was holding the teams steady for Clint, as he picked up each horse's hooves, checking for embedded stones and loose shoes. Satisfied all was fine, Clint came to Kathryn's side and quietly slipped her hand into his. She peered up from beneath her bonnet and shyly smiled into his eyes.

Standing close, bodies touching, they drank in the magnificent view. It was breathtaking. Cascading down the sides of the mountains were thick growths of ponderosa pines, pinons and leafy aspens, and the sun darted in and out from behind fluffy white clouds casting various hues, from shadowy black to amber green, upon the panorama below. Stretching out mile after mile, the wide-open land of the San Luis Park unfolded before them.

Clint pointed to the far north end of it, and somewhere out there was Kathryn's new home. The huge, sweeping valley was surrounded by range upon range, continuous, tall, lofty mountains, lower-ranged mountains, rising and dipping, and nestled at their bottoms were clusters of rolling foothills.

"I don't think I have ever seen a sight as magnificent as this," breathed Kathryn, squeezing Clint's hand.

"This is one of my favorite spots," confided Clint. "Makes me feel good knowin you think it's beautiful, too." They stood in silence looking all about at the splendor when Clint bent down and pressed his lips to her cheek and whispered, "I love you, Kathryn...I truly do."

Kathryn turned slowly to Clint and looked into his warm, pleading eyes. "Clint?" she whispered, "I...love you." Clint pulled her to him, wrapping his arms firmly around her, his lips searching out hers, and they kissed with passion and promises.

Their audience, whom they had forgotten, were clustered together and grinned and applauded when the long kiss was finished.

Foolish grins spread across their faces, and Kathryn covered hers with her hands to hide her embarrassment.

"Now, that is what I call a very good match," commented Manuel, breaking the ice. "Don't you people agree?" A chorus of yeses answered.

"With a view like this," chided Clint, sweeping his arm toward the valley, "don't you have better things to look at?"

"We liked what we saw much better," laughed Will, and the others laughed good-naturedly at the couple.

Clint patted Kathryn's shoulder and walked over to the horses, and Claudette stepped over by Kathryn and slipped her arm about her waist. "I hope you are not angry with us, Kathryn, but there wasn't any place else for us to go; and, of course, we had no idea what was going to happen."

"That is all night, Claudette. I am not at all angry; just feeling a little foolish, I guess."

"I must tell you, Kathryn, I think you have found a wonderful, dependable man, not to mention very handsome. I am so very happy for you both."

"Thank you, Claudette."

"Are you going to marry him, Kathryn, if you do not mind my boldness for asking?"

"He hasn't asked me yet. And if he did, I am afraid it will be quite some time before I could accept. I still have a lot of personal things that have to be worked out by myself."

"I understand." They strolled back to their coach, and they were helped inside by Clint and Harold.

Securing the door, Clint said, "I'm gonna be takin it slow goin down...as slow as I kin, anyhow. I don't wanner alarm ya folks, but it's a bit scarier goin down...in places... so jest hang on tight." He winked at Kathryn, adding, "We'll be down in no time. Don't ya fret."

Kathryn watched as Clint swung his muscular body back into the driver's seat and smiled back at Claudette and Harold who were watching her. They felt the coach shifting as Clint slowly let pressure off the brakes on the wheels and gently flicked the reins as they began their descent.

Alone on the seat at the back, Kathryn was finding it difficult not to fall forward, so she placed her feet across onto the other seat and stiffened her legs to help hold her position. A glance out the window bulged her eyes and took her breath when she saw how close they were to the edge...too close...and it was such a long way down to the bottom. What if, she asked herself, the horses lost their footing and they all twisted and flopped down the side? What if? The thought brought terror to her mind and made her shudder, and a tight knot formed in her stomach. She felt as if she were going to be sick, and she swallowed down hard the saliva that formed in her mouth so as not to throw up. She shut her eyes tightly and gripped the frame on the window for dear life and prayed they'd soon reach the bottom of the pass safely.

Claudette buried her face into Harold's chest and clung to him with a death grip, afraid if she looked up that she would faint from fright. Harold tried to appear brave, but he, too, had apprehensions about their safely making it down.

The coach creaked and swayed as though it would plunge to the bottom at any given moment, when they'd feel the motion of rounding another sharp curve. Kathryn was feeling lightheaded every time she sucked in her breath and held it when she felt a tense situation. Soon she had the sensation of tipping backwards. Her eyes popped open to look. They were not hanging over the edge. The road had leveled off. She pulled her feet back onto the floor, and she bent out the window for an overall view. Flatter land spread before them, and Kathryn breathed a deep, grateful sigh of relief.

"You can look now, Claudette," Kathryn announced consolingly.

Claudette removed herself from Harold's grasp and collapsed wearily back in her seat. She smiled weakly at Kathryn as she made a half-hearted effort to smooth out her dress and straighten her bonnet.

The stagecoach was nearly out of the mountains and down to the valley. Deer scampered out of their way back near the pines, staring at the invaders of their territory with brown, soulful eyes, their large ears perked up, alert for danger. Rabbits skitted among the brush, and noisy magpies scolded from tree branches.

"Oh, look," pointed Kathryn. "Way off there...to the left. If you look close, you can see a bunch of cattle...at least they look like cattle...and some men on horseback, and a wagon at the back. See, see? Can you see them?"

"Why yes," said Harold, "I see them. They are heading the other way, it seems. Probably taking them somewhere to sell for the meat. Claudette, that's what they call a cattle drive out here."

"Oh," she answered thoughtfully. "There certainly looks like there are a lot of them." Claudette caught sight of something else on the other side of the stage, "There is a big herd of those antelope like we've seen before."

"Ooooh, look," cooed Kathryn, "there's a little baby one."

Claudette hung out the window to have a better look. "Oh, there are some more Harold, look. Aren't they just darling?"

After they'd traveled a bit on smoother terrain, the stage stopped. Again, Will, with his boyish grin, peered through the window, then opened the door, "Clint says if ya wanna, ya kin git out and walk longside the coach fer a spell and git yer kinks outa yer bones."

"Oh, Will, that sounds wonderful," replied Kathryn. Will extended his long arm to assist her out of the coach.

"It certainly does," agreed Harold. "How about you, Claudette? Care to take a stroll?"

"Yes, I would like that. I think it would do us all good."

Clint and Will. also walked, each holding the harness on the lead team, guiding the coach along the dusty stage route. Claudette held her ruffled, lavender parasol in her hand, shading herself from the glaring noon sun, holding Harold's hand with her other. She took cautious steps, not wanting to turn her ankle in her heeled shoes on the rutted road. Kathryn, also toting her parasol, walked with Manuel behind the coach, She listened politely as he talked and wondered how she could gracefully excuse herself so she could walk up front next to Clint, but Manuel, riding alone in the China seat, was starved for conversation. Thinking he had an interested person to listen to him, he went on with another story. Kathryn turned to him to comment on something he had said, when his hand grasped her arm so hard it hurt, and she froze in her tracks.

"Don't move, Senorita," ordered Manuel through his teeth. She looked, scared, into his deep-lined, pudgy face, but his eyes were fixed on the ground just past her feet. "Stay looking at me," he commanded in a whisper. Kathryn's entire body stiffened when she heard a sharp buzzing rattle near her left foot. The coach was a ways ahead of them and, very frightened now, Kathryn did as she was told.

Ever so slowly Manuel raised his right arm, then lowered his hand to the gun at his side. Sliding it easy out of the holster, he pulled the trigger as he aimed. The sudden crack made Kathryn flinch and the group ahead stop. Clint and Harold ran back toward them while Will steadied and calmed the horses.

On the ground, its head barely attached by skin but the jaws still snapping, writhed and twisted a very large rattlesnake.

"Oh. Oh," shouted Kathryn, dancing her feet backwards away from the hideous thing. Clint rushed to her and grabbed her by the arms.

"Are ya all right? Did ya git bit?" Clint demanded.

"Y-Ya Yes...and no...I don't think he bit me." Kathryn picked up her skirt hem and stared down at her high-topped leather shoes searching for signs. "The whole thing just scared me so. Oh, how I hate snakes," she declared, still shaking from the ordeal. Clint put his arms around her, and she trembled in them until the creeping feeling she had disappeared.

"Nice shooting there, Manuel," commented Harold admiringly.

"I nail him good, no?" grinned Manuel, pleased with himself.

Claudette came within ten feet and not a step further when she observed the poisonous reptile and quickly looked about on the ground where she stood in fear of there being any near her.

"Harold," cried Claudette helplessly. "Please come over by me. I'm afraid." Seeing her fear, Harold quickly went to her side. Manuel whacked off the snake's head with his knife and kicked it away from the still wiggling body. Claudette felt her knees weaken, hung onto Harold for support and turned her head away as Manuel cut off the other end where the rattles were. He proudly shook them in his raised hand, displaying his trophy. It had been a big, fat snake about four and a half feet long and a set of ten buttons of rattles.

Before anyone realized what was happening, Manuel whipped out his gun again and fired a shot between where the snake corpse lay and where Claudette and Harold stood. From near a small growth of sagebrush, another rattler flipped up, twisting in midair, then flopping to the ground. Another shot from his gun pierced the air as Manuel approached the critter.

Claudette squealed and screamed, as did Kathryn. Clutching their long dresses, they both ran like the wind, parasols bouncing above their heads as they dashed for the safety of the the coach.

Although they understood their fears, Clint and Harold laughed at the sight as the two women tried to get into the stage through the same door at the same time.

Manuel brought over the second set of rattles to show the men, and they were nearly the same size as the first, having nine buttons.

"Probably was mates," observed Manuel. "Travels in pairs, ya know," he informed Harold.

"May I have a look at one?" asked Harold. Manuel handed him the second one and Harold stared at it in his open palm. Prudently, he picked it up between his thumb and index finger and gently gave it a shake. Grinning like a young boy, he shook it some more, fascinated that it rattled for him. Clint and Manuel watched on in amusement.

"Ya kin go on an keep it if ya like," offered Manuel

"Yes, I'd like," grinned Harold. "Thanks, Manuel." The heavy Mexican smiled and patted his shoulder. Harold took his handkerchief from his breast pocket and carefully wrapped his rattles and returned the handkerchief to his pocket, patting it to be sure it was safe.

"I don't think ya oughta be showin that off to Claudette fer a while, if I was you," suggested Clint smiling. The three men burst out laughing at the thought.

"Clint, if it is all the same to you, I think I skin those varmints...make maybe a belt or headband, no?" inquired Manuel.

"Fine with me. We'll take it slow. Ya kin catch up, if that's to yer liken."

"Si, I git right to it." The stocky man strolled over to his first snake, his long Bowie blade glinting in the sunlight. Inquisitive, Harold stayed behind to watch as Manuel picked up the snake in his left hand and secured the other end under his dusty, worn boot. Holding it taut, he took the tip of the knife blade and ripped it down the length of the snake in one swift motion, spreading the skin apart, exposing its bloody innards. Manuel glanced over at Harold to see his reaction, knowing this man was as citified as ever he met one and was surprised to see a look of interest in his eyes.

"C'mon an help...if ya have a stomach for it," invited Manuel. Harold stepped forward without hesitation, setting his brown derby to the back of his head like he was about to enjoy himself.

Together they worked rapidly, gutting and peeling the skin from the meat until both snakes were stripped, "Ever eat rattlesnake meat, Senor Harold?" asked Manuel.

"No, I haven't," answered Harold, wiping his dirty hands on some leaves.

"Very tasty. It is a shame we have no way to keep this meat from getting rotten, 'cause I would cook it for you and let you know what it tastes like. Some say it tastes like a chicken," said Manuel, wiping his hands down his front pants legs.

They walked briskly to catch up to the ambling stage ahead, and what an image they portrayed, Harold dressed in a fine linen suit of dark brown topped off with his short brimmed, round derby; and Manuel, in loose-fitting blue canvas pants over his portly behind, holster, gun and knife about the waist, a badly faded red flannel shirt, and a large brimmed, high-crowned, tattered felt hat. They laughed and talked as if they were old friends.

As they caught up to the stage, Manuel stashed the fresh skins in a pouch hanging from his belt, and he ran a few fast paces, then scrambled back up to his high seat at the rear of the coach. Harold trotted up alongside the door, opened it and hopped on the step, then plunked himself down inside next to Claudette as neat as you please. Shutting the door tight, he turned and flashed her a sassy grin.

"I hope you are proud of yourself," she snapped sarcastically, "fooling around with those awful slimy creatures...ooooh."

"I am," he smiled and, unnoticed by Claudette, gently touched his breast pocket.

14

*T*he happy chirping of birds brought a smile to Blackhorse's face. Kneeling on the ledge that jutted from the left of his cave entrance, his dark brown eyes surveyed the clear blue sky, and he sucked in deeply the fresh morning air. Turning his head to his bare arm, he studied his healing wound, then flexed and tightened his arm to test his muscle tone and strength. It felt good. Easing himself to a sitting position, he leaned his back against a rock, and from his hide pouch he pulled out a carved wooden comb. He carefully untied the doeskin braid ties decorated with fancy beadwork and with long, deliberate strokes began combing out the tangles in his long, thick black hair.

Blackhorse focused his eyes on a mountain bluebird perched on the tip of a ponderosa branch just across the small canyon. Although he saw the beauty in the little colorful bird and delighted in his song, his mind was working on revenge; revenge for his painful wound, revenge against Zeb Taylor for putting him in a position to be shot at.

"Guard the cave and the land around," Zeb had said. "And I will see to it you are a wealthy man a, wealthy man by white man's standards. You, my friend, will gain respect, respect that you have never had. Recall how I saved your sorry hide from the noose. I, only I, Zeb Taylor, cared a damn for your cursed red skin. Do me this favor back, and we will be even. Then, my friend, you can do as you please, call your own shots, go your own way."

What choice had he had, he asked himself. Zeb was right, he owed him.

His mind drifted back to that cold autumn night in Gunnison and the fright he had felt. He could picture it now as if it were happening all over.

He was standing in the doorway of the livery stable showing the blacksmith some hides he hoped to sell. Coming from down the street a group of excited people headed toward them. A voice called out, "There he is...that's the dirty dog that stabbed ol' Virgil." The voice was Grover Little, a, man with a bad reputation but who now seemed to be the crowd's spokesman. Before he knew what happened, Blackhorse was mobbed and wrestled to the ground and held down while his hands were tied behind his back and a noose draped around his neck. The crowd swelled as Blackhorse was led down the street to a big old tree. Someone brought a horse, and Blackhorse was thrust upon it and the rope flipped over the hanging branch above him.

Unknown by Blackhorse, Zeb Taylor watched from across the dirt street, contemplating his move. The man stabbed was one of Zeb's men. Zeb knew from a reliable witness that Grover himself had done the killing. Since Indians were usually held in suspicion, the big buck, new in town, was a perfect scapegoat. Zeb and Grover were hated enemies and now Zeb was about to put an end to the longstanding feud.

As a fellow in the tree finished knotting the rope to the branch, Zeb gave the nod to Marty, his best shot. A sharp crack was heard above the crowd as the taut rope was parted. Out of the darkness rode Cal, another of his men, in full gallop through the crowd. Cal grabbed the reins on Blackhorse's horse, and the two sped away before a bewildered bunch of would-be hangers knew what happened. Grover Little tried to disappear down the darkened alley next to the saloon, but Zeb was already there waiting.

"No more of you and your crap, Grover." Two shots met their mark and Grover met the ground. Slipping away on his waiting horse, Zeb joined the rest of his men and Blackhorse in a canyon far from town.

The killing of Grover was never revealed to Blackhorse or that Grover had stabbed Virgil, which gave Zeb power over Blackhorse.

Since that time, Blackhorse had ridden with Zeb, robbing stages and frightening landowners around Bonanza into abandoning their property. All this made Zeb a wealthy man. But greed possessed him with a disclosure from Blackhorse.

Not liking the crowded confines of Zeb's house, Blackhorse had taken off in search of his own place not far away and more to his nature and pleasure. He found himself a wonderful cave high up enough for a. lookout and moved himself in, not knowing he had crossed over onto the Barnett land. One day when Zeb came to inspect his new home, he made a startling discovery. The cave contained, toward the rear, evidence of gold ore; and now things took a different turn. He ordered Blackhorse to guard and protect not just the cave but the land around it until Zeb could buy or force Rick Barnett off the land.

Looking again at his injured arm, Blackhorse wasn't at all sure that guarding something that wasn't his was worth the trouble. He sensed that eventually Barnett and his men would come snooping around again, and he would be caught in the middle. Blackhorse mulled over the situation. If he turned against Zeb or his men, he was still in jeopardy of being hung over the stabbing of Virgil. Who did he have or know who would believe he didn't do it?

Whenever he felt disturbed, as he was now, his thoughts went back to his people, the Shoshone. He missed them and what family he might have left. He missed living the Indian ways. But could he face them since he ran away...a coward? Would they accept him back? An acute ache came to his gut, and he felt almost as alone as he had that terrible day so long ago.

He finished knotting his braid ties around the end of his hair and closed his eyes. The warm morning sun felt good on his bare chest and he keyed his mind into enjoying the sounds of nature that filled the air. The faint rustling of the cottonwood trees and the chirping of various birds gave him a peacefulness that feeling part of could give him.

A branch snapped not far below, and his pony gave a whinny. Blackhorse sat still, eyes still closed, and listened. He heard a few more ground branches snap from the hooves of an approaching horse and detected by the movement that it had to be Zeb.

He wondered what he was being summoned for this time. Zeb had a hard time hauling his blubber body up the steep incline, and Blackhorse knew he must go down to meet with him. Slowly he made his way down the trail of the canyon wall.

"How is the arm healing, my friend?" asked Zeb when Blackhorse reached him.

"Better. Still aches at night. The chilly air."

"You up to doin a job?" questioned Zeb, his fat body still mounted on his horse.

Blackhorse, his feet spread, legs taut and his arms folded across his chest, studied his distasteful benefactor. His pudgy face and pig like eyes had always turned his stomach; and his spitting of tobacco juice, as he did just now, gave him mean thoughts of what he would really like to do to this man. Instead, like an obedient servant, he gave the man an answer to his question.

"What kind of job?"

"One to yer liking, my friend." Zeb bent slightly over and stared Blackhorse in the eye. "This will be your chance to get even for your wound." He knew he had Blackhorse's full attention now. "Yesterday, while I was in town, I overheard some very interesting news." He spat again. "Over at the general store, I gets wind that Barnett's niece is soon to arrive by stage...two days from now. Didn't know that bastard had any kin...well, never mind that. Anyway, I've been doin some thinkin on this windfall. Here's the plan.

I know from a solid source that her stage be carryin a payroll fer Gunnison miners. We want that. Got it?"

Blackhorse nodded. "Now, fer the part you may like. You, my friend, are going to git the girl and bring her to my place. When Barnett gets worried enough, we will exchange the girl...for his ranch...and that great store of gold that damn fool knows nothing about. Now, I want you, Marty and Cal to leave here today so's ya can git to Cotton Creek area jest past Bismark long before they pass there. Do what ya gotta do to git that money...but most important...most important..." he spit a stream of juice, "bring that niece of Barnett's back to me. Savvy?"

"Savvy."

"I'll be expecting you at the ranch before noon so's ya'll kin leave together. And I'll be wantin ya to take the fields and back roads to git there, so's nobody sees ya and gits suspicious." Zeb spat out a wad, spun his horse around and rode away.

Blackhorse watched until horse and rider were out of sight. Glancing back over his shoulder and up to his cave, his mind began piecing together what had just been said. If things worked out like Zeb wanted, then he, Blackhorse, would at last be free... free of his obligation. If this happened, he wondered, would he at last go meet up with his people? No answer came to him. He walked back toward the cliff and climbed up to the cave to prepare for his departure.

The small cooking fire was put out and utensils set aside. He picked up his fringed buckskin shirt and rolled it to take with him. He strapped on his shooting iron and tucked his long knife inside the belt of his holster and left the cave.

As he rode toward Zeb's place, bareback on his paint, he took a last look back and a strange feeling came over him...like an omen...as if his life were going to change somehow.

15

Clint eased the coach to a stop at the Mosca Station, not a great distance from the foot of the mighty mountains. His passengers happily stepped out to make use of more civilized facilities and accommodations and to escape from the continual motion of the stagecoach. As had been usual, there was food for the hungry, weary passengers, and it wasn't long before they were congregated around a split-log table.

It was crowded in the not-so-large room with five others besides the couple who operated the small station. There was a young couple with a small child waiting for a hack to Zapata where they would catch the stage to Alamosa to the southwest. The other two, a sorry-looking older couple, had arrived earlier and were taking Clint's stage to San Isabel, the first town beyond Crestone, next on his route.

Plates were set before them; a hearty supper of tangy venison, boiled potatoes, cobs of roasted corn, fresh bread and a cold pitcher of milk was placed in the middle of the table.

"Well," said Clint, as he buttered a fat slice of warm bread, "you three'll be glad to know we have only about thirty-three miles to go 'fore we git to Villa Grove." The three beamed as he continued, "Should be pullin in round eight o'clock. And, since we don't leave here till after lunch tomorrow, that'll give ya the morning to yerselves."

Kathryn and Claudette exchanged gleeful smiles. This was wonderful news. It would give them time to relax from the weariness of the journey and a chance to bathe and get prettied up. With heads together, they giggled as they made plans to help fix each other s hair, and Claudette confided that she had brought with her the latest *Harper's Bazaar*; and wasn't it going to be fun to look at it together?

At some point, between making fun plans with Claudette and the finishing of her supper, an unexplainable trepidation came over Kathryn. Wiping her mouth with the coarse napkin provided, she graciously excused herself from the table. Clint stood and helped her from her chair and watched, puzzled and concerned, as she took her shawl from the coat rack, wrapped it around her shoulders, and quietly went outside.

Clint spread his fingers through his dark hair as he eased himself back into his chair and leaned over toward Claudette. "Is somethin troubling her?" he asked, thinking another woman might know and sense these things.

"I don't know," answered Claudette curiously. "She seemed in happy spirits when we talked of tomorrow morning, but then she became withdrawn."

"Maybe I should go after her," said Clint.

"That's a good idea, but why don't you wait a few minutes and give her some time by herself."

"I suppose yer right," Clint responded reluctantly. He went back to the food left on his plate and tried to eat while keeping his eye on the door.

A cooling breeze stroked her face as Kathryn put distance between her and the people inside the log station. When she had walked a ways, she paused. In the foothills, the strains of yipping coyotes caught her ear. She listened with interest when, off in another direction, more coyotes answered the call. Kathryn focused her vision on the huge silhouetted chain of mountains alive with moonlight, then craned her neck as she gazed up at the winking lights above that created a dazzling, jeweled sky. Although the air was not yet chilly, she shivered and clung tightly to her shawl and stood as if in a daze, not knowing where to go.

A low whinny and the shuffling of hooves attracted her attention and she absently headed in that direction, dragging her steps on the hard-packed dirt. As she reached the corral, the horse that had whinnied came over to greet her at the fence. Stroking his muzzle, she thought of Jackson, which triggered memories she had tried to keep at the back of her mind Her thoughts flashed back to the last time she had raced her beloved horse through the meadows and how wonderful it had been. Then, the memory of her departure hit her with such force as if a big rock had been thrust to her stomach, and the terrible loneliness she had felt washed over her anew, Her mouth gaped open as she sucked in air and she pressed the palm of her hand tight against her forehead to stop the anguish and turmoil but it wouldn't stop. Although she felt she had done the only thing she could by leaving, the ache to be near her mother, Jolene, weighed too heavy on her heart. She squeezed her eyes shut to keep the tears in, but it was no use; they trickled out, one by one. She pressed her lips firmly together, blinking tears away as she stared into the big eyes of the horse. And now, now that she was nearly to her destination, a new fear attacked her. Did Uncle Richard really want her there? Or was he only being kind? What had his reason been for saying she could come and live there with him? And what if she didn't fit in? And what if she didn't like living on a ranch? But, most of all, what about Clint, now that he was in her life? What was she going to do about her feelings for him? And would she even see him again after he left her in Villa Grove? She knew, without question, that she would miss him terribly.

The onslaught of all these thoughts and emotions left her weak and confused, and she lay her head on her folded arms across the fence, lost and hopeless, not sure of anything or anyone. She began to sob quietly, and the horse nuzzled her hand with his velvety nose, as if he understood. This act seemed so familiar and so special, she ceased crying and looked up through dewy eyes at the great gentle beast and managed a sad smile.

The horse's ears perked, and Kathryn's body stiffened as she listened too. The steady sound of footsteps was coming from behind her. She spun around and saw Clint walking toward her, his black hat set to the back of his head. The closer he got, the faster her heart seemed to beat.

"Kathryn? Are ya all right?" Clint asked in a soothing, caring tone.

Her jaw quivered to speak, and she was sniveling, badly in need of a handkerchief. Before she could ask, Clint pressed a hanky into her hand. She looked gratefully up at him as she wiped her face and blew her nose, louder than she intended.

"I'll be all right now," said Kathryn sheepishly.

"I was worried about you when ya jest up and left without sayin' anything."

"I guess I was just feeling confused and a little sorry for myself," she explained. "And a bit afraid of what is at the other end," motioning with her head and eyes to the north.

"I can understand that," Clint answered. "Ya've been through a lot that yer jest not use to...been a heap a changes, and knowin there's more in store would put anybody down a little low." He put his arm around her and held her close, and she bathed in the warm comfort of his strong yet gentle clutches,

"Clint?"

"Mmm?"

"What if I don't like it out here? What if I've made a bad decision?"

"Know what I think? I'll tell ya, I think yer going to grow to love this place...the west...the openness...and the challenges. Ya jest wait an see if I'm not right."

"You really think so?" she smiled.

"I really do. C'mon, let's take us a little walk." He took her hand firmly in his and they strolled around the outside of the station, not talking; just feeling close was comforting and all the communication they needed.

The main room in the station hummed with activity in preparation for departure. The men were busy reloading the trunks and valises Kathryn and Claudette had insisted they needed after breakfast.

Earlier that morning, the proprietors had furnished a large metal bathing tub, and the back end of the kitchen was blanketed off to afford ample privacy for the two women to bathe. Enjoying the luxury, they helped each other with hair washing and rinsing it with a large pitcher into a pan. Heads were wrapped in towels to dry until, time for them to be properly fixed.

Kathryn was in much brighter spirits this morning, and the warm water was such a treat when she submerged that she had not wanted to get out. But now the anticipation of seeing Uncle Richard won out, and she gingerly patted dry her shapely, dripping body. Slipping into her red robe, she hastily joined Claudette upstairs. She had already taken her bath and was anxiously waiting for Kathryn's help with her hair and clothes.

When they made their entrance into the room for lunch, their primping had been well worth the effort. All the men's heads turned and admired with their eyes. Kathryn appeared in her rose taffeta and her dark hair was gently swept up into soft curls secured with a wide, black-velvet ribbon. As she took a seat beside Clint, the aroma of wild flowers aroused his sense of smell, and he wished to himself that he could bury his nose in her neck and inhale the delicious scent even more. It had been important to Kathryn when she packed this dress that Uncle Richard see her at her best when she alighted from the coach. Now it was also important for Clint to see and admire her; although she had worn it in Dodge City, the result was still the same. Clint's eyes lit up exactly as they had before.

Claudette was decked out in a dark green silk accented with light blue panels and inserts, and at the neck, extending to a point at the bodice, was see-through ivory lace. Her wheat-colored hair was swept back at the sides with clusters of curls bunched at the back secured with a gold-and-pearl hair comb. Harold's eyes glistened and he smiled as he pulled out her chair for her and self-consciously touched his bald head where there used to be black wavy hair.

Sitting unnoticed over in the corner, the peculiar couple named George and Hanna Smith stopped their eating long enough to see what all the fuss was about. Hanna was heavyset with round, drooping bosoms that stretched the fabric of her faded, limp cotton dress. Her dull brownish-gray hair was pulled severely tight to her round head, tied with a dirty blue ribbon and hanging uneven down to the middle of her back. Her pudgy face sprouted too large a mouth and wide-apart, vague, staring eyes.

George, her husband, was a wiry grizzled man, with upper front teeth missing, narrow gray eyes, a scraggly gray beard and shaggy hair to his collar.

Hanna poked him in the leg with her boot. "Them two won't look so high-'n-mighty after they been out here fer a couple years," she snarled, exposing her badly decaying teeth.

"They's jist the uppity kind," proclaimed George. "Don't know nothin bout real life." But George was finding it hard to keep his sights off the two beautiful women. His eyes drank in their shapely bodies, shiny, done-up hair, and their gentle mannerisms and light laughter.

It was one o'clock and time to leave. Kathryn and Claudette were helped gallantly into the coach by Clint and Harold. George clomped in ahead of Hanna, letting her fend for herself. They planted themselves on Kathryn's side, taking up more than their fair share of space, pressing her against the side uncomfortably. Claudette noticed the situation and said casually, "Kathryn, come sit next to me. We can look at *Harper's* some more and see what we might have missed."

Kathryn, needing no further coaxing, got up and sat next to Claudette gladly.

"Guess we ain't good 'nuff to sit with," whispered Hanna in George's ear too loudly.

"Reckon not," he agreed. The three pretended they had not heard.

The stage stopped abruptly and Will put his head through the window. "Clint wanted to be sure you didn't miss seein the Sand Dunes on the right that's comin up." He hopped back up front, and the stage began moving again.

Soon, appearing at the foot of the Sangre de Cristos, spread out miles of mountainous white sand. "Just look at that," oohed Kathryn to the others.

"Why, Harold, isn't that amazing," said Claudette.

"It certainly is. What a fluke of nature," Harold commented.

"Why, it is like a seashore but with no ocean," exclaimed Kathryn, They looked over at Hanna and George who were not looking at all. George returned their look and said dully, "We've seen that pile a sand a hundred times. Don't see what all the fuss is fer." Hanna nodded in agreement, but when they had traveled nearly to the end of the amazing phenomena, she snuck a studied look.

There were no passengers to let off or pick up in Crestone. The passengers stretched their legs for a few minutes while the horses got water and mailbags were exchanged, and they were back on the road heading for San Isabel.

After reading a paper, Harold snoozed. The *Harper's Bazaar* had been thoroughly paged and Kathryn and Claudette talked out, so they too closed their eyes to nap. With the extra space acquired, George pulled his legs up onto the seat and reclined his shaggy head in Hanna's wide-spread lap and fell asleep. Hanna looked despondently at the bunch, first one then the other with cold, studying eyes. She was unhappy with her lot in life but had long since resigned herself, at least for now, for there was still hope. One day, she thought, the mine's bound to pay off, then I kin dress me up fancylike, even better than the likes o' them. She leaned her weary head against the side and drifted off, dreaming of riches from the elusive gold in their mine.

The sudden lack of motion woke the drowsing folks with a start. George put himself upright and poked Hanna with his elbow. "C'mon. We're home." Hanna nodded and picked her tattered carpetbag off the floor beside her and was about to open the door when Will did it for her. He extended his hand to help her step out, and she was about to refuse, then thought better of it. Hanna's tired, plain face conjured up a dignified smile as she put her, chapped, calloused hand in Will's, squared her shoulders and stepped from the coach.

This display did not go unnoticed by the others or George, and as he followed her out, he mumbled to himself about "puttin' on airs "

"We'll be here only a few minutes, but if ya'd like to git out and stretch, Clint says yer welcome to do it," Will informed the others. They gladly left the coach to move around a little and take a look at the small, mining town of San Isabel. The stage station served as a meeting place and supply depot for the inhabitants who were trying their luck with Mother Nature. There was an air of determined and serious business going on, with mules and horses pulling wagons of supplies or, ore, traveling up and down the hand-rutted roads.

Kathryn was watching this scene with great interest; and the sweaty, dirt-covered miners were watching her, also, with great interest. Clint sauntered up beside her in a manner that clearly said to the leering men, she was spoken for.

"Kathryn?"

"What?" she answered, smiling as he gently took her hand.

"Will's gonna ride in back with Manuel for a while...and I was wonderin if you'd care to ride up front with me?

Kathryn's eyes widened. "You mean it would be all right for me to ride up there?"

"Yeah. And, you know, we don't have all that far to go before you meet up with yer uncle...and I thought it'd give us time to talk. What d'ya say?"

"I'd say yes. I'd like to sit way up high and see everything straight on, instead of as it passes the window. Besides, I would love the chance to be next to you, especially for the last few miles," she answered with the unmistakable look of love.

"Good."

"Clint, is there room up there for my valise? In case there are any more passengers, I'd feel better having it with me."

"No sooner said than done," said Clint. He opened the door and removed her valise and climbed up in the seat and stashed it behind, then got down to help Kathryn.

It took a bit of doing for Clint to get her up in the high seat, what with her long, full dress and petticoats, but the task was finally accomplished, amongst cheers from the gawking bunch of onlookers.

Claudette, holding onto Harold's hand, watched her new friend, with joy in her heart for her. She hoped that, as they planned, they would be visiting one another as well as keeping in touch through letters.

Kathryn giggled as she looked down from her high perch and gave a little wave to Claudette. Claudette beamed at her and flashed a happy, knowing smile, then stepped inside the coach for they were ready to go.

The coach lunged forward, leaving San Isabel and heading for Rito Alto, just five miles away.

Clint reached down from the seat. "Here. Wear this over yer dress so it won't get dirty." He handed her a large duster, and she obligingly put it on.

They picked up speed, and Kathryn braced her feet and hung onto the metal rail at the side of the seat, grinning and laughing with delight. "This is fun," she declared.

"I thought you'd enjoy it up here," Clint answered matter-of-factly. "Sure is nice... and different to have such a pretty thing to look at...'stead of Will." Kathryn blushed a little and smiled at this man she had fallen in love with. She watched in fascination how he maneuvered the many reins of the horses. It appeared as if he were barely holding them, yet laced through his fingers they were worked independently and you could hardly see them move.

The span of scenery was beautiful as they traveled the foot of the Sangre de Cristos on their right and miles and miles of valley stretched out before them. There was a. mild breeze barely stirring the leaves on the trees and the tall grasses beside the road. The air was balmy and the sun was warming on her face. Kathryn felt happier and more content than any day since leaving Lexington. Now, she felt purpose coming back into her life, Hope and excitement filled her heart, and she moved closer to Clint and affectionately leaned her head on his firm, rounded shoulder.

For the first time in Clint's life, he knew what it felt like for your heart to swell, for his pressed against his chest and felt like it would burst through. He had met a lot of young, attractive women...in the cities back east, in the towns out west, and as passengers on his stage. Many had found him good-looking and had flirted with him, and some he had flirted back with, like a game. But that's all it had been...a game. Strangely, he never took a fancy to a one of them, until that afternoon back in Lexington. There was immediately something very special about Kathryn the moment he had laid eyes on her as she stepped out of her carriage. When he had opened the door for her at the depot and looked into her eyes and saw her face close up, there was no turning back. He knew this was the only woman for him; he had just hoped and prayed that he was the man...the right man for her. Clint shook his head now to make sure he wasn't dreaming and glanced down as Kathryn looked up and their eyes met in contentment.

"Clint?"

"What, Kathryn?"

"After you leave me off in Villa Grove, when will I get to see you again?"

"I've been meanin to talk with you about that. You see, I've been givin us a lot of thought. Maybe I was jumpin the gun, back in La Junta, but I told Aaron to find another substitute driver. I was only fillin in anyhow, and it gave me more money. In a couple of weeks, my regular route will be between Mosca Station and Villa. Grove."

"Oh, that will be very nice," Kathryn smiled. "Clint, I've been meaning to ask you something else too."

"What's that?"

"Just where do you live?" she asked in a puzzled tone.

'For the four years I've been drivin this rig, I haven't stayed put long enough to call any place home. But I'm aimin to change that."

"How?"

"Well," he grinned, "what would you say if I rented me a place in Villa Grove?"

"I would say I would like that very much," she answered, squeezing his arm.

"I figured," Clint continued, "by me living close to you, it would give us the chance to be together...and more often...'cause I know I can't go very long without seeing you."

"Oh, Clint," she said, smiling. "I'm glad you will be near. It will be not only exciting, waiting to see and be with you, but also a comfort. I realize that I have come to depend on you...I guess because you have been with me throughout this whole journey and have been there for me when I needed you,"

"I want to be there for you...in all the things that matter, Kathryn."

She beamed at him with her big brown eyes, and Clint felt the warmth cover his body.

16

*A*nxiety was mounting for Kathryn. They had stopped and gone through Rito Alto and were now leaving the station at Cotton Creek, which meant there was only thirteen miles left between her and Uncle Richard. The long, long journey was nearing its end. She could hardly wait to finally see him again and to throw her arms about his neck, just as she always had done since she was a little girl.

It was late afternoon as they neared a long grove of cottonwood trees that grew abundantly along the meandering stream called Cotton Creek. Aware of the long, curving bends flanked on one side by rocky cliffs, Clint slowed the team to maneuver the turns coming up and became acutely perceptive to the unusual stillness in the air. He glanced up and around, noting there was not a bird flying in the sky, nor had he seen any deer or antelope scampering away from the noise. Again, a sense of dread came over him, much like he had felt back in La Junta when they first started out. He tried to shake the feeling, thinking he was just reacting to his newfound sense of responsibility... until his eye detected something up ahead. A dark shape or shadow moved behind the rocks...or had he just imagined the sight of a horse's snout barely poking out? He glimpsed another out-of-place movement, and Clint straightened up, whip in hand, and cracked it above the horses' heads, and immediately they broke into a gallop.

Kathryn, as well as the others, was taken by surprise. Clint did not have to explain this abrupt action to Will or Manuel, for they instinctively knew there must be danger ahead; and with guns in hand, they readied themselves. Judging that something was amiss, Harold pushed a terrified Claudette to the floor and ordered her not to scream or get up until she was told. Sliding himself low by the open-windowed door, he pulled his Navy Pocket 36 from his hidden shoulder holster and positioned himself for trouble.

Blackhorse heard the stage from his prone position across a sun-baked boulder long before it loomed into view, and he scrambled down to his pony. He rode just a few yards up from where Cal and Marty were hidden on either side of the road. The extra horse brought along for Barnett's niece was tied a short distance back to a low-hanging branch on a pinyon tree. Although he had not counted on the rapid speed of the stage, this bothered him not, and Blackhorse gave the signal.

Cal and Marty rode out onto the rutted road with their six-shooters aimed at the oncoming stage. Kathryn, wild-eyed, hung onto the sides of the seat as the coach bounced and heaved.

"Clint. What's happening?" she yelled.

"Probably robbers. Take my gun out," Clint ordered, "use it if yaa have to."

With one hand gripping the back of the seat, Kathryn managed to reach over for his gun and free it from the holster and threw off the cumbersome duster that was draped around her.

Straddling bareback, Blackhorse's thick, muscular thighs gripped the sides of the paint, his head bent low and his gun clutched against the animal's strong neck. He was ready to do Zeb Taylor's bidding. The stage was nearly upon them, and from between the branches where he hid, Blackhorse saw what he had not expected, a woman riding up front with the driver. Could this be Barnett's niece, he thought? No matter, he would find out soon enough.

Clint saw the two horsemen. "Heeee-aaaah," he bellowed, and the whip cracked loudly as he proceeded to run the gunners off the road. Not expecting the speed-up, Cal and Marty spun their horses out of the way as the pounding team and stage clamored past them.

Blackhorse intended to grab a hold of the reins when the coach slowed down, but now found he and his cohorts, looking at two shotguns attached to the arms of able-looking guards, speeding ahead of them. Blackhorse took quick aim and the sharp crack from his gun sounded and his bullet hit its mark.

Will's shotgun flew out of his hands and landed somewhere on the ground as his body bent forward and hung over the back of the boot. His arms dangled like pendulums, while his face smacked and bounced against the wooden side spilling blood from his gaping mouth. Startled and shaken from seeing his friend shot and hanging lifeless, Manuel suddenly turned into an angry, raging man and opened fire with both barrels of his shotgun. He gritted his face in an evil smile as Cal flew backwards off his horse and thudded to the ground. Manuel whipped out his pistol as Marty closed in, but Blackhorse fired again, getting Manuel's leg. Clutching the side for support, Manuel fired back and fired again and again, finally sending a slug into Marty's shoulder, as he rode past toward the front.

With gunfire cracking around her, Kathryn scrunched down to the floor and turned around. Her eyes widened in horror when she saw the Indian galloping toward her, his expression frightening and his bare-chested appearance paralyzing her.

"Shoot," ordered Clint, driving the team at breakneck speed. Kathryn braced her shoulder against the seat, holding the revolver with both hands, but the bouncing coach made sighting her target difficult. She managed to squeeze the trigger and the explosive blast rang in her ears. The Indian was gaining...she had missed. Suddenly, she noticed the rider coming up on the other side, getting closer and closer to Clint, and she turned the gun on him. A shot rang out, but it wasn't hers.

"Aaaaagh." Kathryn's eyes darted to Clint. His face was frozen in a contorted grimace as he slowly slumped forward. Kathryn let out a shriek when she saw the back of his shirt oozing blood. The man that shot Clint was now abreast of them and she saw that blood covered his gun hand. Another shot rang out, coming from the inside of the coach, and Marty slid sideways off his saddle, then tipped toward the ground; but his boot stuck in the stirrup, and the horse galloped down the road with Marty's head thumping and twisting on the ground, splattering blood as it went.

Kathryn spun around to see the Indian with his torso turned for a backwards shot at Manuel. She aimed and fired just as the Indian did. Manuel slumped down and the Indian jerked; she had wounded him in his side. She turned quickly back to Clint and saw the reins slipping from his hands as he fell sideways onto the seat, then crumpled beside her on the floor. Dropping the gun, Kathryn grabbed the reins of the speeding horses and jerked too hard for the horses slowed their pace. Not badly hurt, as Kathryn's bullet had only split the skin at his waist, Blackhorse took advantage of her error and sped up his pony. He bent down and took hold of the lead horse's reins and brought the team gradually to a stop.

"Don't move a muscle, Claudette," whispered Harold. He slunk down in his seat, his gun aimed at the door. Kathryn, in a panic over Clint, gently turned his head and let out a grateful sigh that he was still breathing. She tried to feel for his gun, somewhere beneath all the material of her skirt. Blackhorse rode the short distance to the stage door, pointed his gun in and fired. He then turned his attention to Kathryn.

Harold had been facing the wrong way. Taken by surprise, he was shot in the back. Claudette had been biting on her arm to muffle her terrified screams and heard the close shot, then felt the weight of Harold's body drop on top of her.

Blackhorse dismounted and stood transfixed looking at Kathryn. Nervously, she stared back, sick in her stomach with fear. She had lost her bonnet and her hair hung loosely around her face and down her back. She looked beautiful to Blackhorse, even in fear. "You a Barnett?" asked Blackhorse, his dark eyes penetrating hers.

Kathryn gulped hard to speak. "Why are you asking?" she demanded, trembling.

"You are. You are niece...niece of Rick Barnett."

"What if I am?" Kathryn answered defiantly. Blackhorse kept his penetrating stare as he took a step forward. Kathryn's eyes darted over the top of the stage, and saw no one. Clint lay beside her, bleeding badly, maybe even dying, and the Indian had fired inside the coach, there was no one to help her, and she couldn't locate Clint's gun.

"Why have you done this?" she screamed, finding her voice. "What do you want?" she demanded, inching her finger under her skirt in search of the weapon.

"You." Blackhorse leaped up beside her, on the wheel, and grabbed her, bringing her off the floor, then scooped his arm around her waist and hoisted her halfway down and dropped her on the road. Kathryn tried to scramble up but his moccasined foot kicked her shoulder and she sprawled face down in the dirt. She moved her eye to see his gun pointed at her and her body froze.

"Do not move," commanded Blackhorse, taking a step back. "Do not move." Keeping his eye on her, he stepped back until he was next to the driver's seat and sprung up. Under the boot, he found the small metal box he knew to contain money and jerked it out. Clint tried to move his foot to kick the Indian off, but he had no strength. Sweat formed in droplets on his colorless face and he passed out.

The gritty sand and tiny pebbles pressed into Kathryn's cheek and bits of sand stuck in her mouth and to her tongue, but she dared not move. The particles crunched and crackled as her teeth came together sending off an irritating sensation. She gathered up saliva and spit. The white foamy glob quivered near her lips before soaking into the ground.

Blackhorse set the heavy box on the ground and slid his eyes to Kathryn. The sun gave the dark strands of her hair golden-red hues, and he longed to stroke it and see how it felt through his fingers. He admired the fancy rose dress and puzzled over the layers of petticoats and ruffles that fanned out from beneath, draping over her spreading legs. A throbbing heat spread in his groin and his hand pressed against his crotch. Still holding his gun, he turned his head to the rear of the coach, the middle and finally the front. Nothing stirred. He looked down at the woman. He wanted her. He had to have her. And he knew he must take her before he turned her over to Zeb. With his foot he rolled her over and their eyes met. Hers were dark like his own, but were wild with fear. Her mouth gaped open as she gulped for air, causing her chest to heave, and the sight of her rounded breasts as they rose and fell excited him beyond control. Swooping down, he grabbed her arm and jerked her to her feet. With a firm grasp on her wrist, he pulled her along, away from the road and coach.

Kathryn screamed as she struggled to free herself from his tight grasp. She jerked, pulled and kicked, then stumbled to her knees. Blackhorse scooped her up and flung her across his shoulder, and Kathryn shrieked and beat his back with her fists.

Clint lay in his own sticky blood, and the pain in his back and chest raged hot and sharp, causing him to fade in and out of consciousness. Off in the distance he thought he could hear Kathryn; it sounded as if she were screaming. He tried to focus his mind on the sound and then blacked out again.

Peaked with excitement, Blackhorse toted his prize around a large boulder and plopped Kathryn to the ground. She scrambled to get up, but he pounced upon her, pinning her to the ground. His hungry mouth pressed her lips hard and his teeth tore and stung her lips, bringing wincing tears to her eyes. With one hand, he held both her hands together; and with his other, he ripped open the top of her dress, exposing her breasts. Kathryn was mortified. No man had ever seen her breasts bared. Her face flushed with embarrassment, then angry indignation. She reared up and sunk her teeth into Blackhorse's arm. He yelped in pain and slapped her head hard. Dazed from the blow, her teeth released their grip.

He hadn't meant to hit her so hard, but he knew a woman like this would never willingly want the likes of him. He fixed his eyes on her luscious breasts with their quivering, protruding nipples and bent his head down, taking her right breast into his mouth. He sucked on the tit like a lost child as his hand loosened his buckskin britches, exposing his swollen, throbbing manhood.

Kathryn's body twisted and bucked beneath him, raising her legs to kick his back, and this only heightened his passion. He groped under her long dress, pulling and tearing away at her pantalets, tugging them down toward her ankles. Bracing himself up on one knee, he pushed her thighs apart with his other and began ramming his heated organ into hers. Kathryn let out a piercing scream, then mercifully passed out. Blackhorse relieved himself in a fever-pitched explosion and slowly took his mouth from the raw, tender nipple. He looked down at this woman he had just taken. Her eyes were closed and she appeared pitiful and helpless, and he almost felt ashamed. He had not wanted to hurt her, but he knew no other way. He pulled his organ out of her and viewed what he had expected...that she had had no other man before him. A shudder of pride came over him; it was now as if she was his woman.

Quickly, he pulled up his buckskin and grabbed his gun from the dirt, then trotted around the boulder for his horse and payroll box. He would put the woman on the horse with him and ride back for the extra horse, then zigzag back to Zeb's.

Far-off sounds caught his ear and he paused to listen. The team hitched to the coach swooshed their tails after flies and picked and set their hooves down anxiously, while his pony stood by the side of the road, head bent low, as it grazed on tall grass. Blackhorse cocked his head and listened intently. There was no mistaking it...the sound of horses was coming from the south. He whirled around and slapped the lead horse's rump, sending the driverless coach down the road. He dragged the strongbox and hid it behind a nearby bush and took ahold of his pony's reins. Glancing up, he saw the silhouettes of two riders loom upon the crest of the next hill. There was no time to get the woman now. He would ride away and circle back. Leaping on his pony, he sped down the road, then cut into the grove of trees.

Sam and Jim were making good time after delivering the steers to Fort Garland, They joked how they couldn't be too far behind Rick's niece's stage, not realizing how correct they were. Stopping at the Cotton Creek station, they were informed that a stage had passed through not too long ago. They were not out of Cotton Creek but a few miles when the sound of gunfire off in the distance attracted their attention. They figured it could be hunters, or it could be trouble. They opted for trouble and spurred Snowflake and Slicker to a faster pace.

"Did ya see a rider up there, Sam," asked Jim, "or are my eyes playin tricks?"

"I did...but I don't see 'em now."

"Hold up," yelled Jim. He stopped his horse and sprang to the ground, retrieving a shotgun, and quickly remounted. "Somebody's short 12-gauge," he remarked.

Sam was staring up ahead toward the side of the road. "Jim, I think I see someone layin on the ground up there." Jim squinted his eyes. "Sure looks like it, don't it? Let's go."

They rode till they were looking down at the gunshot-riddled body of Cal, lying on his back with flies swarming and landing all over his bloodied, blown-away face. "Lord lova duck," exclaimed Sam. "What in tarnation da ya s'pose went on?"

"I dunno—but I got this terrible feelin in my gut that it's got somethin to do with Kathryn's stage."

"What are we waitin for...let's ride."

With Jim going at a full gallop and Sam not far behind, they caught sight of the stage weaving around a bend further up the road. In hot pursuit, they traveled until they were only a short distance behind. They were half sickened by the sight of a man flopping deathlike over the back of the coach and looked at each other in pitied disgust. Barely able to hang on, Manuel tried to keep flat as the stage slammed his body against the floorboard, but managed to locate his gun, and it took what energy was left just to keep a grip on it. Breathing came hard and he fought to stay alert, fearing for his life. The clopping of hooves passed by followed by another, and in a short time the stage pulled to a stop. With every ounce of strength he could muster, he painfully pulled back the hammer of his 44 and laid waiting,

"Jeez, Sam," announced Jim alarmed. "It looks like a blood bath up here." Jim was standing on the wheel looking down at the driver of the stage. "I'll see if he's still alive."

"An I'll check inside." Sam opened the door and saw two bodies, one on top of the other, and the odor of urine and sweat assaulted his nostrils. "Wheew"' he muttered.

He stepped up and gently turned over the man sprawled across a woman and in doing so uncovered the face of terror. The shrieking scream that came out of the woman's mouth startled Sam and he jumped backwards out of the coach, and she did not let up. "My God," exclaimed Sam. "Help me down here, Jim. This here woman's hysterical, it could be Kathryn."

Jim had turned Clint on his side and pillowed his head with the duster he found and jumped down to assist. They carried the man out of the coach and laid him on the ground. The man was still alive with a bad shoulder wound, but he too had lost a lot of blood. They turned back to give attention to the woman who had pulled herself into a sitting position, cowering at the far side of the floor, still screaming in short gasps.

"Ma'am, we're not here to harm ya," spoke Sam in soft tones. "We're here to help ya. Please, won't ya calm down?" The woman shook and sucked for air and stared with vacant eyes. Sam reached out his hand and she shrank down, clutching her arms tight to her chest.

Sam looked at her in sympathy and said, "Are you Kathryn? Kathryn Barnett?" The woman's eyes gave a hint of recollection. She took a deep breath and tried to get control of herself.

Manuel tilted his head to listen and the sound of the voices let him know he need not fear these men. He clunked his gun on the wooden side to draw their attention for help. Jim rushed to the back, knowing that the sounds were not coming from the poor fellow draped over the back and climbed up to peer to the bottom of the China seat.

"There's another one alive," shouted Jim "and he's hurt pretty bad, too."

Sam stayed with the woman, trying to find out her identity. "Are you hurt, ma'am?" he asked.

Numbly, she answered, "Kathryn..."

"Are you Kathryn?" The woman shook her head.

"What happened to her, ma'am?" asked Sam, now frantic over Kathryn's safety. "Do you know where she is?"

"She was riding up with our driver. My husband, what have you done with my husband?"

"He's out there," pointed Sam.

Reality hit Claudette and her face went scarlet as she became aware of her soggy undergarments. Her face puckered up like a little girl's, and her lip thrust forward. "Ooooooh, oooooooh," she sobbed. "I...I don't want to get out of here...I can't."

"Ma'am...now don't take offense, but I think I know why. It don't matter. It's all right. Those things happen."

Claudette peered around Sam and her eyes lit upon Harold's stretched-out body. She scrambled to get up, and Sam lent her a hand. She bolted out of the coach and ran to her husband's side.

Jim jumped down from the back and called Sam aside. "They're all in bad shape and we gotta git 'em to a doctor, but first we gotta find out what happened to Kathryn."

"Right," agreed Sam. "Let's see if the woman is ready to tell us more."

They went over, to Claudette and Jim knelt down beside her. She was sobbing softly and stroking her husband's face, and Jim addressed her gently. "Ma'am, my name's Jim Miller. My friend Sam there and me...we work for Rick Barnett...that's Kathryn's uncle. He's expecting to meet her today at Villa Grove. Do ya know what happened to her?"

Claudette shivered and screwed up her face in thought, then looked up at Jim with pleading eyes. "Guns...shooting, all around...My Harold..." Tearing eyes stole a look down at Harold as he uttered, moaning in pain, "Please...help me...mister..."

"Please don't die, Harold...please," Claudette beseeched Jim with her eyes, "Please don't let him die, Mr. Miller."

Jim patted her shoulder gently. "Ma'am, we're gonna do all we kin...I promise. Now, can ya tell me anything that might help us find Kathryn?"

"Back there," Claudette motioned with her eyes in the direction they had come from. "She was riding up with Clint. Then lots of gunshots...then the stage stopped. I heard her scream...that was before...before Harold was shot. I was so afraid...I guess I must have fainted. The next thing I knew, the coach was moving and weaving, then you came. Kathryn must be back there...somewhere. Oh, please find her. I shudder to think that she might even be...dead." Tears streamed down her cheeks and she looked back at her husband.

"Sam, let's git these folks inside the stage, and I'll drive 'em in to Villa Grove fer help. You ride back and see if ya kin find any traces of Kathryn. When I get these wounded taken care of, I'll bring Rick back here with me. I know he'll be in town waitin fer the stage."

"Good idea."

They got Manuel and Harold loaded inside the coach and seated Claudette next to her husband. Feeling it was too difficult to get Clint down without injuring him more. Jim climbed up beside him and pulled the brake on the wheels. Sam tied Jim's horse to the back of the stage and gave him a wave as Jim clicked the team on toward Villa Grove.

Swinging his hefty frame onto his white mule, Sam turned and headed back south.

17

Kathryn was left lying alone, disgraced. Her eyelids fluttered open against the bright, slanted rays of the lateday sun. Confused, she wondered why she was lying on the ground staring up at a low, overhanging branch. She touched her damp chin and wet mouth and her fingers shone blood dripping, from her split lip. A chill crossed over her chest, and her private parts hurt. Her hand slapped across her bosoms; they were bare. Kathryn sat up quickly, and her eyes grew large when she saw her twisted, dirty pantalets hanging over her shoes, and her mind remembered. She trembled in horror and her fingers fumbled to tuck her bosoms inside her torn chemise and dress, as tears of shame inched down her cheeks. She drew her knees up and clutched them, rocking to and fro. Her head bent down and she cried low, mournful wails. In a few minutes she stopped crying abruptly. She listened, then looked, twisting her head to see all around. She was alone. Where was the heathen Indian? Clint. What happened to Clint? The stage? Were they still on the road?

Kathryn picked up her skirt to wipe off her face and saw blood smeared on the insides of her petticoats, and the tears began again, angry tears. Anger against the Indian who violated her. Anger because she no longer could go to Clint, or any man for that matter, as a pure, untouched woman. She shivered in shame and humiliation. She had not given up her virginity. It had been taken, forced, without her having a say. She felt dirty and unclean.

Her crying ceased. Instinct warned her she must not stay here. Urgently, she pulled up her soiled pantalets and on shaky, sore legs made her way around the huge boulder. Clutching her dress to her bosom, she cautiously stepped out. Nothing. No one. She gasped, blinked her eyes and looked harder. Nothing was there. She had been abandoned. All that remained visible were hooves and wheel, marks carved into the road and red splotches in the dirt of drying blood. She shuddered. Stretching her sight down the long, empty road, she hoped she would see the stage somewhere, but she saw nothing. Where had it gone? Where had they gone?

A spine-chilling thought flashed in her mind. What if that Indian came back for her, or was still somewhere close? She must hide. Where? Back into the grove she fearfully scampered, then stopped a moment to think. I need to find someone to help me help me get to Uncle Richard's. If I walk toward Villa Grove through the woods, I shouldn't get lost, she reasoned, if I keep the road in sight. Gathering her skirts close about her so as not to get tangled in the bushes, Kathryn trudged on, following the road from a safe distance, stopping to listen and looking around, then continuing on.

Concealed by a deep ravine, Blackhorse's eyes gleamed when he saw the woman come toward him. On padded feet he climbed out and slinked over to his pony tied several feet back. As he was about to mount, the sounds of pounding hooves came to his ears from down the road. Kathryn heard them, too, and froze in place, then fear overtook her. Spinning around she ran deep into the grove.

Sam's eyes darted left and right looking for signs or any traces of Kathryn. He rode past the hiding Blackhorse and came to the place in the road covered with tracks. He pulled his mule, Snowflake, to a stop and studied the ground and knew from the signs that this was where most of the trouble occurred. Sam drew his gun and dismounted, keeping ahold of the reins. Tracks and marks left the road and he followed them around the huge rock. Patterns in the dirt and flattened grass told more than he wanted to know. He stood pressing his lips tight and shaking his head, hoping what he perceived was not true.

There were more tracks, and he followed them back to the road, then back again into the grove. Branches rustled ahead and Sam positioned himself out of sight. Shadows danced through the bushes and trees and he could make out a pony and rider. Sam fingered his gun and waited. The pony moved closer. Sam squinted. It looked like an Indian, a bare-chested Indian. Was there a connection to the one that shot Pedro?

"Halt," commanded Sam, in his booming voice. He stepped out pointing his gun. The Indian stopped, looked, and fired his gun at Sam. The shot missed and split the branch above his head. Sam ducked and returned fire, and his shot did not miss. Blackhorse took the bullet in the calf of his leg.

The pain was intense. Another shot followed, whizzing past Blackhorse's ear.

Blackhorse spun his pony and rode wildly through the trees. Orders or no orders, he thought, I will not die for Taylor.

Kathryn's running feet carried her away from the horrifying noise of the guns until she had to stop and gasp for air. The shooting had stopped, but now her ears caught a different sound. She tilted her head curiously and heard the swooshing and splashing of rushing water. Mesmerized she followed the sound, going slowly until she came to a babbling creek. She stared at the water. Her memory quickly went back to her resting place next to the quiet brook back home in Lexington. Now it seemed so far away, so long ago.

Taking cautious steps toward the water, she jerked her head to check around, afraid she might still be followed. Dropping to her knees, she bent over and caught the water with her cupped hands and slurped the refreshing coldness to soothe her dry, parched throat, then splashed the water on her face. Wearily she got up and found a fresh-cut stump near the water's edge and sat down. Her temples throbbed and she was feeling light-headed. Her disheveled hair stuck in dirty, damp clumps to the back of her neck, and she slid her hand under and lifted the hair away, allowing the cool breeze to float over her skin and dry it. As she did so, she fixed her eyes on the whispering water and followed its movements downstream, Her face winced from her body's pain and the pain in her heart, and she clutched her arms about herself in private misery to comfort and protect her wounded self.

Sam let the Indian go for now. He and Rick would have to deal with him later. He had to resume his search. Aboard the mule he backtracked to where the coach had been stopped and headed further south. A horse's whinny broke the silence. He swung his stocky leg across Snowflake's rump and stepped down and tied the mule to a skinny tree. With pistol drawn he headed in the direction of the whinny. Not far off the road he spied a tan-colored horse with black mane and tail saddled up, tied to a pinyon branch. Sam paused and scratched his neck as he pondered the situation. Finding a secluded spot, he decided to wait and see who came for the animal. Removing his floppy leather hat, he drew his arm across his wet forehead and squatted on a rotten stump with his gun resting on his leg and his chin in his hand. What could have happened to Rick's niece kept churning in his mind. God, he hoped she was not hurt; but where could she be? If something happened to her, it'd kill Rick. He'd blame himself for letting her come out here. Who'd wanna harm her? Where is she, where is she? Is she all right?

The day was getting late, and Sam became edgy, and the horse was still there. He was afraid he wouldn't find Kathryn before sundown, so he left his spot, and leading his mule, headed toward the creek and followed it north.

Alerted and alarmed by the sound of snapping branches, Kathryn leaped off the stump and searched with her eyes for a safe place to hide. Grabbing her skirts up, she ran over to the large rutted base of a tree that had toppled across the stream and flattened herself on the soggy ground. She cringed as the sounds got closer, then they stopped. Who or what was near, near where she had just been sitting. Her fear became so strong that she could hear her heart beating and the air going in and out of her mouth. With shaking arms, she inched her fingers up the slimy log and pulled herself up enough to peek. Her breathing stopped and her eyes bulged at the sight of a man dressed from the waist down like the Indian. Her breath quivered and her heart pounded harder and she froze in place, staring. He was a big, stocky man with a full beard and funny looking hat. He looked around and studied the ground. Nervous perspiration covered Kathryn's body, and she felt so helpless and afraid. The big man was checking the ground again. Suddenly his head jerked up and he looked over in her direction. Their eyes met. Kathryn fainted.

Sam charged over and scooped the unconscious woman up off the damp ground and carried her over to a dry, sunny patch of grass. Carefully he lowered her down, then scooted back to the creek. With nervous fingers he untied his bandana and swished it around to remove the dirt and rinse out the sweat, then squeezed some of the water out. He listened and looked to be sure they were alone, then rushed back to the woman and knelt down beside her.

This had to be Kathryn, he reckoned. No doubt. She even had features that resembled Rick's. Besides, who else would be out here in the middle of nowhere? Sam stroked the bandana across her forehead and patted her cheeks with the cold cloth, removing some of the dirt and spattered blood. Kathryn's eyes popped open in a confused daze and when they focused on Sam's face her body stiffened with renewed fear.

Before she could let out a scream, Sam asked, "You're Kathryn, aren't ya?" in his deep, soothing voice. Kathryn had been asked her identity by the Indian, and she became afraid again. Her eyebrows knit together as she studied the face of this strange man. He had a kind expression beneath his beard and his eyes did not look menacing, yet she was still afraid.

In almost a whisper, she demanded, "Who are you?"

"Ma'am, my name's Sam, Sam McPeak, and I work fer yer Uncle Rick. Me and Jim, he's another fella that works fer yer uncle, we was comin back from delivering steers and hurryin so's we could be on hand to meet ya in Villa Grove," he explained.

"You are right," she answered hoarsely, "I am Kathryn." Tears of relief and joy came to Sam's eyes and he grinned, "Oh, Kathryn, I'm so darn glad I found ya...me and Jim's been worried sick wonderin where ya were. Are ya hurt?" That question was answered with a mixed look of fear and sadness, "What in tarnation happened anyhow?"

All the events that occurred since the stage was attacked engulfed her and she felt the horrible sensation of drowning. A cold sweat crawled over her body, and she began to shake uncontrollably. Sam slid his arm beneath her shoulders and cradled her against his broad chest tenderly.

"Atta girl," said Sam. "You g'on and cry it out...jist cry it out."

Kathryn wailed and sobbed for the fright and shame she had endured, and her panic at being left behind...abandoned. When she could cry no more, she drew back and covered her face with both hands and wiped away the wetness. Blinking her damp eyelashes, her expression became deadly serious.

"Where is the stage? What's happened to Clint? Where are the others?"

"Clint?"

"He was the driver." Sam rose up on his haunches to answer.

"Kathryn, we...me and Jim, caught up to the stage...no one was driving it...an we got it stopped. The driver, Clint, well, he's hurt pretty bad. So's the fellow inside, an one of the guards in the back is not in too gooda shape either."

"You said one of the guards...there are two."

"The other one's dead, Kathryn." Kathryn was stunned.

"Which one?" she asked.

"The young, thin one," answered Sam somberly. Kathryn's hand went to her mouth to muffle her scream.

"No, not Will?" she wailed. "He was such a nice person. Ooooh."

"I'm afraid it's so," confirmed Sam, not giving her the details of how he was when they found him. Kathryn bit her lip and blinked away rapidly collecting tears.

"Kathryn, Jim drove the stage on into Villa Grove to git em to the Doc. Then he's gonna bring Rick back so's they could help me look fer you. They sure'll be glad I found ya already," he smiled.

The idea of finally seeing her uncle hit Kathryn like a slap. She threw up her hands and her mouth dropped open. "Look at me. I had planned on stepping off the stage all prettied up. I even put on this dress." Modestly her hand went over the ripped bodice. "Especially for that occasion, Oh, what am I going to do now? I can't have Uncle Richard see me like this." She started to jump up, but she was too weak and fell against Sam.

"Missy, you've been through a lot more…ya gotta take it easy. I got a warm coat ya kin wear and it'll cover-up that torn dress. Stay still an I'll go git it." Sam went over to Snowflake and untied his coat from the back of the saddle and helped Kathryn put it on, wrapping the large front around her and rolling up the too-long sleeves. He stepped back and looked at her and grinned. "Ya look kinda cute in that," he observed and got a shy smile out of her.

Kathryn leaned wearily against the tree and Sam sat on a log nearby as she chewed on a hard biscuit that he retrieved from his saddlebag and washed it down with water from his canteen. Sam studied her and could tell she had been through a great deal to make this long journey to be with her uncle and a great deal more she was not sharing. But Sam had his hunches, and he had to know for many reasons. He cleared his throat and spoke gently. "Kathryn," he began, "I know this might be embarrassing fer ya to tell, but I gotta ask. How did yer dress git all tore like that, and who did it?"

Her eyes stared at him for the abrupt question, and she quickly lowered her head.

"Kathryn, please answer. It's important."

Still she did not answer, her face showing a definite pink blush.

"There's a Indian I encountered up the road who took a shot at me. Is he involved in the stage shooting?" Kathryn nodded he was, not looking up. "Did he hurt you, Kathryn?"

A moment passed, her head kept down, but Sam saw tears dropping on the front of his coat…the answer was given.

"Aw, no… oh, Kathryn…"

Her head stayed bent in shame as the tears splotched at a faster rate upon the coat. Sam was torn between total helplessness and inner angry rage toward the Indian, a red, hateful anger, finally he was composed enough to ask, "Did he hurt ya bad?" Her head bobbed yes.

Sam got up. He bent down and took her in his big arms, and there came tears for Rick's niece. Kathryn cried and blubbered about how he had just dragged her off and how she had screamed, but no one was able to come help her, and how ashamed she felt, how angry, too, for being forced into something so ugly. And she told how afraid she was when she discovered she was all alone, and the fear she felt when she heard gunshots again. And how she thought Sam was in with the Indian, especially wearing trousers like his. She let all these things and feelings out as she cried all over Sam's chest. Soon she could cry no more and just heaved for air, feeling weak and, oh, so tired. "Sam?" she murmured, "please don't tell anyone what the Indian did to me."

"I won't. That's up to you. After a short time Sam said, "Kathryn, do ya think ya kin ride a horse so 's we kin git ya outa here and home?"

"Yes. I just want to get away from here. I need to see my uncle."

"Stay put. I found a horse tied yonder an I'll bring em back here." Sam scurried through the thick grove and retrieved the animal and quickly brought it to Kathryn. With Sam's help she was able to get mounted. Sam got on Snowflake and kept the horse's reins in his hands, leading it and Kathryn toward home.

Rick Barnett drove the buckboard late afternoon into Villa. Grove, leaving Pedro Lopez at the ranch to keep the fire going in the fireplace and to tend to the roast Rick had started before he left, should Kathryn be hungry when they returned. At Pedro's insistence, Rick found himself at the general store inquiring about tablecloths.

"How do you do, Mr. Barnett," said Alice Truitt, who was also doing some shopping.

"I am just fine, Mrs. Truitt. In fact, I'm more than fine, because at eight o'clock my niece, Kathryn, will be arriving on the stage."

"Oh, that is wonderful news," she smiled brightly.

"Yes, it is. I wonder, as long as I've run into you, if you might assist me at pickin out a couple of nice tablecloths. That is, if I wouldn't be imposing on you?"

"Why, I would be delighted."

Together they selected a fine linen with matching napkins and two flowered-print ones. While the clerk wrapped them up, Rick asked Alice if she would like to join him at the hotel for a bite to eat, and she gladly accepted.

Alice was very chatty over their light dinner and inquired if Sam had returned yet from the cattle drive. Rick informed her that he was expecting him at any time, pointing out that he and Jim would be in a hurry this time returning, because they were most anxious to meet Kathryn.

Rick drove the widow home and promised her that he would indeed bring his niece over for tea, for Alice was truly looking forward to meeting her. In fact, she suggested that after Kathryn had settled in, she would like to host a small party for her so that she could meet some of the ladies around town. Rick thought that a fine idea. They said goodbyes and Rick headed back for the stage station.

It was eight o'clock and there was no sign of the stage. The sun was nearly set and dark shadows filled the street. Rick looked around and he seemed to be the only one waiting for a passenger. He paced and fidgeted, then finally stepped inside the small wooden building to check with Peter, the stationmaster, to see if he had any word as to why the stage was late. He had heard nothing. Rick went back out and walked to the end of the main street until he was in a position to see down the long trail that swung up from near the mountains. A small cloud of dust became visible in the distance, and his heart beat a little faster. That must be the stage, he thought excitedly. Finally, Kathryn will be here.

Rick stood and watched the cloud grow larger as the stage got closer. Slowly, he walked back toward the station and turned his head often to make sure the streamer of dust was still heading his way. He poked his head in at Peter and announced, "The stage is coming," with a big grin spread all over his face. He went anxiously back out to position himself for viewing the arrival.

Across the street at the Jack Rabbit Saloon, sat Zeb Taylor, smugly playing a game of poker, as he awaited the news that the stage arrival would tell him. Rick knew the slovenly Taylor was in town when he spotted the fat man's horse tied across the street. This made him uneasy, but he stayed his distance, not wanting to engage in verbal combat with the distasteful man, especially upon Kathryn's impending arrival. That was no way for her to end her journey and be welcomed into her new surroundings; no way at all. Besides this evening Rick only wanted peace and the delightful joy of driving Kathryn to her new home, introducing her to Pedro, and to Sam and Jim when they returned, surprising her with the beautiful room and showing off the ranch.

He nervously glanced at his reflection in the station window. Surveying his image, he thought he looked pretty dandy in his blue-and-white striped, band-collar shirt and black leather vest, and hoped Kathryn would think so, too. He polished the dust off the tops of his boots, rubbing each against the backs of his pantlegs, then tipped his best black Stetson off his face and gave a sideways grin to himself.

The air had gotten chilly, and Rick strolled to the buckboard hitched next to the station and retrieved his fringed buckskin coat from the seat. Hooking the collar with his finger, he slung it over his shoulder and marched back to the front of the station and looked down the trail to judge how much closer the stage had come. About a mile or so to go, he thought, leaning first on one leg, then the other, while butterflies flapped in his stomach. Alone, he watched and waited.

The station door opened and Peter stepped out. "About here, Rick?" he asked, flipping the lid up on his pocket watch.

"Here she comes," pointed Rick, grinning. His grin slowly faded and his eyes narrowed to scope in what he thought he saw."

"Naw," he said aloud the stage got closer, Rick stiffened and knew. It was Jim. His Jim, Jim Miller. Why was he driving? Rick quickly slipped on his coat and ran to meet up with the stage as it slowed its speed a block down the road.

"Rick. Rick.' Git the doc, quick," Jim yelled down. "And the undertaker and sheriff," he added.

"Peter. Go for the doc, and get the sheriff and undertaker," relayed Rick. Peter spun around and ran to Doc Lawton's office down the street.

Jim slowed the stage with Rick trotting alongside to see into the window. The stage stopped and Rick grimaced when he saw the bloody, wounded men and a frightened, wild-haired woman in a dirty, blood-spattered dress. "Kathryn?" he questioned eagerly. "Is that you?" The woman sadly shook her head. Jim jumped down and turned the reins over to the stable hands and ran to Rick's side. Rick, stunned, but in control, had opened the door to offer his assistance.

"Jim, what happened?" asked Rick, ashen-faced. "Where's Kathryn?"

"Soon's we git these people to the Doc's, we gotta go back an help Sam find her."

"What'd ya mean, find her? What's happened to her?" Rick demanded,

Peter and Doc Lawton, toting canvas stretchers, came running up the street, followed by several men and women, some to help, some to gawk. Peter handed his stretcher to one of the men running beside him and left to go back and get the sheriff.

Sheriff Buck McCain was sitting with his feet propped up on his desk reading some papers when Peter burst through the door. "You're needed at the stage station," he blurted out. "There's been trouble." Buck swung his feet to the floor and grabbed his hat from the top of the desk and took his coat off the hook by the door as he hastily followed Peter back to the station.

Someone had gone to Fred Heath's Saloon for Luigi Amato, the undertaker. The sheriff, Peter and Luigi converged at the coach at the same time. Buck pushed his way through the crowd of onlookers and asked who drove the stage in.

"I did, Buck," answered Jim. To Rick and Buck, Jim rattled out just what he did know; about finding the dead man on the side of the road, stopping the driverless stage, the wounded, the hysterical woman, but no Kathryn. Rick felt as though he were going to be sick to his stomach, and he swallowed hard and took a deep breath to get ahold of himself. This was no time for anything but a clear head.

Hidden by the crowd stood Zeb Taylor with a sinister smile on his face. His ears took in the exciting information, that Rick Barnett's niece who was to arrive on this stage was surprisingly missing. Hearing this, Zeb quietly slipped back to the saloon.

The wounded were carried away on stretchers, with Claudette clutching Harold's hand as they trudged over to the doctor's office. Will's body was lifted from the back and taken to the undertaker's parlor. Rick called Peter over. "Peter, could you find someone to ride out to my ranch and tell Pedro what's happened and what we're goin to do?"

"Sure will, Rick," he answered. "And if I can't find anyone, I'll go myself."

"Thanks, ol buddy. I appreciate it."

Jim untied his horse from the back of the stage and went to borrow a fresh mount from the livery stable. When he returned, Buck had just finished examining the coach and was conferring with Rick, he heard, "It's evident the stage has been robbed, which I suspected. I'm going to need all the information and clues I can get my hands on." He acknowledged Jim standing by. "Jim, we got six men who've volunteered to ride along with us. I know it's going to be rough in the dark, but we can't leave that poor girl out there."

"I'll lead the way," said Jim. "Let's ride." Jim sprung on his horse and Rick climbed into the buckboard and made a turnaround in the middle of the street. They sped out of town followed by Sheriff McCain and the six men back down the stage route road.

The night was closing in and the moon had yet to rise, making it difficult to stay on the trail. "Just where are we headin?" yelled Rick, loud enough to be heard above the clomping hooves, rattling wagon and the wind in their ears.

"Back where we stopped the stage," Jim called back.

After several miles behind them, Jim slowed up and the rest followed suit. "It was right around here," pointed out Jim.

"Sam," called Rick loudly. "Kathryn?" There was no response, not a sound. "Jeez, what are we gonna do, Jim? It's all my fault if somethin happened to Kathryn. I shoulda never said she could come out here," he said remorsefully, Overwhelming guilt and worry consumed Rick's being.

"Rick, don't do this to yerself. It's not yer fault...get that through yer head." Jim climbed off his horse to lead him.

"The rest of you dismount and spread out," ordered Jim. "We'll go slow and go up to where me and Sam found all the tracks."

Rick got down from the buckboard and guided the two horses and the wagon, walking some distance back from Jim. In short intervals Rick and Jim took turns calling out Kathryn and Sam's names, then they'd stop, listen and go on. Like an echo the sheriff and the volunteers would also call the names intermittently, then all trudged forward some more.

"Kathryn. Sam," called Rick for the dozenth time.

"Rick? That you?" came a far-off cry. Rick and Jim froze in their tracks. Excitedly, Rick hollered back. "Sam?"

"Yeah, it's me, me and Kathryn." Jim leaped on his horse as Rick scrambled back into the wagon and the two raced down the road toward Sam's voice. The message was spread they'd been found and the sheriff and the other men converged and galloped behind. The moon, in its last quarter, finally crested a peak and dark silhouettes appeared ahead on the road, two horses, two riders.

"It's my Uncle Richard," cried Kathryn to Sam.

"Yeah, Missy...they come to find ya."

Kathryn, so taken aback at bearing the familiar sound of her uncle's voice, began giddily laughing with joy. When near to them, Rick jumped off the wagon, threw the reins to Jim, and ran.

"Kathryn. Kathryn," he shouted until he reached her. He put out his arms, and with her arms clinging to his neck, Rick gently lifted Kathryn from the horse.

"Oh, Uncle Richard, Uncle Richard," she cried, clinging tightly and sobbing happy, tired tears all over his shoulder'. And Rick, unable to hold manly pride back, cried tears of relief.

A snort sounded as Sam blew his nose; and Jim, holding two sets of reins, tried wiping his tears with his sleeves. Buck and the rest of the men caught up and, even in the dim moonlight, the happy grins that spread across the four faces could be seen as well as felt.

"Kathryn, are you all right?" asked Rick.

"I will be now," smiled Kathryn. Jim stepped up and Rick slapped him on the back.

"Jim, meet Kathryn. Kathryn, this is my foreman, Jim Miller."

"I am sure proud to meet ya, Kathryn. I'm jist so glad that Sam here found ya," grinned Jim.

Kathryn reached out her hand and shook Jim's. "I'm glad to meet you, too, Jim." Kathryn knew how terrible she looked and how she must appear to all the gawking men and wrapped herself tighter in Sam's large coat, wishing she could just hide completely in it.

Buck informed the volunteers that they could head on home and thanked them for their help. Rick went over and shook each man's hand and thanked him, too. While Rick was doing this, Buck went over to Kathryn.

"Kathryn, I'm Buck McCain, the sheriff. "I regret all that you've been through."

Kathryn smiled weakly and he went on. "Would you recognize any of the men that held up the stage if you saw them again?"

Kathryn looked horrified at the prospect of ever seeing any of them again, especially the Indian. "I don't know," she answered.

When the sheriff and the others were out of earshot, Kathryn said to Sam, "Thank you for not mentioning what else happened to me back there. I couldn't bear the humiliation."

Sam gave her a squeeze around her shoulders and said in a low whisper, "Kathryn, I'll leave that up to you, about tellin the worst part."

"Thank you, Sam."

Rick came up to Kathryn and Sam. "Kathryn, we're gonna make a bed for you in the back of my wagon. That way you can rest better on the way back to town."

"Good idea, Rick," agreed Sam. Jim helped Sam spread out Sam's bedroll from off the back of his saddle on the floor of the buckboard, and Rick fetched the big, warm blanket he'd carried from home. He walked over and helped her climb in. Although Kathryn had so much she wanted to share and to ride next to her uncle, she gave no protest to this arrangement. She was now completely exhausted. Rick tucked her in, then told her, "We'll be taking rooms at the hotel, and when we get there I'll bring the doc over to take a look at you. Now, try and get some rest, all right?"

Kathryn was about to protest about the doctor but was too tired to put up a fuss. All she could say was, "I can find out about the others then, can't I?"

"Ya sure can." Rick smiled down at her and patted her shoulder, then climbed up in the seat and slapped the reins,

Buck rode alongside Jim and Sam ahead of the buckboard and listened intently as the two explained in more detail how they came to find the dead man and the stage. Then Sam related about the Indian firing at him, being careful not to tie him in with the violence to Kathryn. Buck speculated whether he was involved in the robbery or was just a renegade who happened on the scene. Jim reminded the sheriff of the shooting incident involving Pedro and Rick, and they all came to the conclusion there must be a tie in there somewhere...but how?

Kathryn lay in the bumpy wagon and fixed her eyes on the stars overhead. Her body ached and felt drained, her mind numb. The image of Clint's face kept coming to her. She could picture his dazzling dark eyes, his trim moustache that spread ever so slightly when he smiled at her. Then the image changed to when the bullet struck his back and the horrible look of surprise and pain that showed on his face as he gritted his teeth and his eyes went wide in agony.

She was very grateful that Sam had found her and thankful to now be safe with her uncle, but this way...this way she was being brought to town instead of the way she had planned, the way it was supposed to be, was just so humiliating. Her body felt wretched and her overwhelming feeling of shame and how incredibly dirty she felt seemed more than she could endure. What if her uncle should find out what hideous thing the Indian had done to her? Would she be able to even look him in the eye? It was enough embarrassment that Sam should know. Tears rolled out the corners of her eyes. Maybe her mother had been right, about the West not being a good place for her to be. It certainly had proved already to being dangerous and savage. But how could she face her mother again after this? She guessed she could not, she, alone, had chosen this and now she must see it through. Her eyelids became heavy, and she began to pray for Clint, Claudette and Harold and Manuel, that they be alive and all right, but she did not finish her prayer, as sleep won out.

18

*B*lackhorse breathed an exhausted sigh as he heard the last sounds of the riders and the buckboard pass heading for Villa Grove. Positioned high on a cliff above, nursing his wounded leg and side, he had observed all the activity below. Although it was dark, with only a portion of moon for light, to his knowledge, the party of searchers had not found where he had stashed the small strongbox of payroll money.

With a piece of rawhide for a tourniquet and a hastily concocted poultice, he had stopped the bleeding from his calf. It was a deep flesh wound, as the bullet had chunked out a piece of flesh, but luckily the slug had not embedded. It was not as serious as he first thought, although the pain was intense. He had picked leaves and washed them off not far upstream from where the woman hid, then had covered his wound with them and secured it with a piece of rawhide. While nearby, he had observed the scene when Sam had found her, and Blackhorse reasoned, due to his present condition, he best pick another time to abduct Barnett's niece, when he was in better shape.

Now, feeling safe, he descended from his lofty spot and retrieved his pony tied far back in the woods. Skirting the side of the road nearest the woods he made his way riding toward the spot where he had concealed the box. It was still there. It was the only thing that would appease Zeb after the bungled job. Something small glinted in the moonlight by a bush near the huge rock. He stooped and snatched it up. It looked like a gold pin of some kind, and he put it inside the leather pouch he wore around his waist. He went back to the box. It was heavier now that he was weakened, but he managed to set it upon his pony's back, then he stood on a rock and eased his sore right leg over the animal, and sat himself down. It was late, he knew, by the moon's position, but he must travel as long and far as he could to get back to Zeb's.

Zeb would be mad when he told him he did not have Barnett's niece and disgusted that Cal and Marty were dead, for to Zeb it would mean he would have to find two more men to replace them. The only thing that would ease his wrath would be the payroll strongbox.

It was near midmorning before Blackhorse sauntered down Zeb's long road. Exhausted, he could barely keep his eyes open and was relieved, in a way, when Zeb stepped anxiously out on the porch.

"Good to finally see you, my friend. I have been waiting." His pig like eyes darted behind Blackhorse and swept the area behind. "Where is Barnett's niece?" he demanded suspiciously.

"With Barnett, and the sheriff in town."

Zeb scowled and narrowed his eyes, which left only slits, then spat tobacco on the porch step.

"And Marty and Cal?"

"Dead." Blackhorse pushed the heavy box and let it thud to the ground. Zeb motioned for Jake and Bart, who stood on either side of him, to get the box.

Blackhorse nearly collapsed as he dismounted and clung to his pony till he was able to walk. "Give my pony food and water," he said to Bart.

"I don't take no orders from you, Injun," spat Bart. Had Blackhorse felt better, he would have beaten Bart until he could not stand, for his insult, but for the moment he shrugged it off

"Do as he asks, Bart," ordered Zeb. "Jake, bring the box into the house. Blackhorse, come inside. You and I, we have much to discuss." He spat out his wad of tobacco and went into the house, and Jake followed closely lugging the box. Bart grudgingly took the pony toward the barn, and Blackhorse, favoring his bad leg, limped up the steps and made his way into the house.

It would have been a nice white man's house, thought Blackhorse, if Zeb didn't have so many decorations and ornaments around everywhere. The rooms were large and the furniture big and heavy. Surprisingly, it was always clean, not from any effort on Zeb's part, except for his good sense to have two Mexican senoritas, Lupe and Rosetta, living there, who did all the housework and cooking.

"Get this man some food," bellowed Zeb to Rosetta, a young girl about fifteen years old. He motioned for Jake to put the box next to his feet and said, "I will open that later. Now, we have business to discuss," and dismissed him. He plopped his big behind down on his chair and tackled the food left on his plate when he was interrupted by Blackhorse.

Blackhorse eased uncomfortably into a chair at the opposite end of the long, oblong table and nodded a thank you to Rosetta for the cup of hot coffee she set before him. With both hands he picked up the cup and gulped down nearly all of it. Again he nodded a thank you when she placed a plate of eggs and a piece of salt pork down for him. He grabbed pork in one hand and his fork with the other and took turns biting until he had consumed, in a short time, all the food on his plate.

"Now that yer belly's full, my incompetent friend, you tell me how you could be so careless and stupid as to let a little woman get away from a big buck like you."

Blackhorse explained how they had set up the trap, surprised the stage, how Cal and Marty got shot, that he had had his hands on the niece and the strongbox, but that riders had come. He told that he had sent the stage down the road and that he had little time to get away himself. He said how he had planned on going back for the niece and box, but only one of the men took the stage into town...Barnett's men, he added...and that big Sam had shot him and found Barnett's niece who had run away to hide.

"You are telling me you could not stand up to old Sam?" chided Zeb.

"I was shot in my leg and in my side." His pride refused to admit it was Barnett's niece who got him in the side. "What good would I be to you dead, like Cal and Marty."

Zeb smiled cynically. "You could not speak tales of me," he toyed.

"You would not have the box," countered Blackhorse, not moving a muscle on his face.

Zeb agreed. "Tell me this. Where are Marty and Cal's bodies and their horses?"

"Cal?" Blackhorse repeated, and then thought. "Somewhere on the road between Cotton Creek and Villa Grove. Marty? Who can say? He hung by his boot, the horse spooked and he kept on running."

"How bad ya hurt?" asked Zeb finally but with no concern to his voice.

"Bad enough to rest."

"You want Lupe to take care of your wounds? You rest here?"

"No." With that Blackhorse stood up slowly, prepared to leave.

"I will bring your cut of the money in a day or two." Blackhorse nodded and went for the door. "Lay low," cautioned Zeb. Blackhorse nodded and left to get his pony.

When he had gone, Zeb summoned Bart and Jake. "Ride the backway, see if ya can find Cal and Marty's bodies. Take shovels; bury em deep if you do. Don't want of McCain or Barnett tyin me into this. Now go. I must work on another plan."

Blackhorse zigzagged until he crossed Little Kerber Creek and headed toward the short, narrow canyon that led to his cave. He put his pony in the makeshift corral at the back and painfully scaled the rocks up to his home. Exhausted and weak Blackhorse fumbled around in the dark cave to start a fire. With the dim light the flames provided he set out his medicine to attend properly to his wounds, with trembling hands he cleansed and dressed the torn, bloody flesh. He then took his knife and hacked a large hunk of meat from the side-of-beef that hung from a hook, driven into the wall. Near the fire he picked up a long, pointed stick and worked it through the meat, then propped it across two V-shaped sticks braced on either side of the fire-pit and positioned it across the flame. After he had rested for the remainder of the day, he would have his meat all cooked. With this chore out of the way, Blackhorse sat back on his haunches, watched his supper begin to cook, and stared, into the dancing flames.

As he studied the fire, an unknown fear began to gnaw at his insides and prey on his mind for reasons he could not perceive. His soul could not attain peace when his mind was so disturbed. He stared deeper into the flames and they merged to form the shape of the woman's face. Blackhorse blinked and shuddered. He looked away and saw the flames dancing shadows on the cave wall. They waved and flickered across, up and down and around. Again he felt the haunting when the shadows amassed and conformed to the silhouetted figure and face of the woman. He jerked his head away and the cold sweat over his body made him shiver. His eyes went back to the fire, but the woman's cries of fear and her screams of shame-filled indignation and pain began to ring and echo in his ears.

Why was this happening, he anguished? Why was the image of Barnett's niece haunting him? Why should this even matter to him, just because he had satisfied his flesh's desire with a white woman? She had intrigued him. He wanted her. He took her. In his mind he committed no wrong. Why was he being tormented by her memory? The feeling would not go away and kept gnawing at his innards. He turned his body away from the flames and the shadowed wall to the opening of the cave and was surprised to see how gray and dark it had become outside.

A flash of lightning shone through the open space followed by a, loud clap of thunder that rumbled its way over the hills and canyons. Blackhorse, now in much pain with not only his leg but his mind, crawled toward the opening and leaned his body out halfway and observed the menacing sky. Large drops of rain hit his face and the steady plopping of the water as it bounced on the leaves and creek made a rhythmical yet melancholy sound. He inched himself outside and gradually stood up, letting the rain beat down upon him.

He stood deathly still and watched as more lightning streaked the sky and illuminated the earth below. Gusts of wind began to sway the pines and eerie sounds filled the valley hollows. Suddenly, Blackhorse felt isolated and more alone than he had ever felt in his life. His body shook with each clap of thunder and great fear and shame welled up inside. He did not understand why he felt this shame for he had never felt it before. Nothing much had mattered to him, not since that one fateful day, long ago, as a young boy. He had felt scorn and contempt for others, choosing to distance himself when people got too close. He belonged to no one but himself, and the Great Spirit.

But now he trembled and was afraid, for the Great Spirit seemed angry with him. Standing alone on the ledge, the sky lighted, then darkened his mind began to retrace his life after that terrifying day. He realized now, that he had never, from then on, known complete peace or happiness that nothing had ever really mattered to him. An emptiness throbbed at his insides, and now, for the first time since the tribe was viscously attacked did he finally release his pain.

He raised wet, bare arms to the Great Spirit as the rain soaked his head and dripped off the ends or his braids. At the top of his lungs Blackhorse let out a shrieking cry of anguish that echoed through the dark, rain-drenched hills. He beat on his chest with his fists and continued his mournful wail while his pony, enclosed below, whinnied and pawed the ground in fear. The lightning flashed on and off and the thunder rumbled and clapped in the clouds as Blackhorse unleashed the torment in his soul for the shame of yesterday's deed.

19

*T*he sudden afternoon storm did nothing to cheer Kathryn's spirits. She studied the warm colors and tasteful furnishings in her room on the second story of the hotel as she lay on her back in the middle of the large and comfortable bed. She had wanted Uncle Richard to take her on to the ranch, but Dr. Lawton had been insistent that she remain another day.

Late last night the buckboard with Rick, Kathryn, Jim, and Sam and Buck were on horseback, straggled into town. They pulled to a stop in front of the elegant two-story San Luis Hotel.

"I'll see you tomorrow," waved Buck, and he rode on to his small house not too far from the jail.

Rick woke the innkeeper and secured the rest of them lodging; Jim took charge of the horses and buckboard; and Sam carried tired, travel-weary Kathryn upstairs to her room. He gently placed her—buckskin coat, blanket and all—onto the bed.

"You've been very kind to me, Sam," acknowledged Kathryn, smiling gratefully.

"Shucks. I've only done what anyone else woulda done," he answered. Rick tapped lightly on the door and let himself in.

"Uncle Richard, I know it's late, but is there anyway we can find out about Clint... and the others?" Kathryn pleaded.

"Jim's gonna check when he's done takin the horses over to the livery. He should be back here shortly."

"That's good," she said softly. "Uncle Richard," she asked drowsily, "what has happened to all my things, my baggage and handbag? Do you have any idea?"

"I'll go down to the stagecoach and have a look," offered Sam. He left quietly so as not to disturb the other sleeping guests.

Rick studied his niece lying so helpless and bedraggled in Sam's huge coat, her once-pretty, rose-colored dress now dirty, spotted and torn and her shoes caked with mud. "I'll take yer shoes off and bring some fresh water to you," said Rick matter of factly. "Ya know," he said, as he began unfastening the buttons on her high-topped shoes, "you gave us quite a scare." His fingers trembled as he worked on the many buttons. "When that stage came in the way it did, well, I didn't know what to think or imagine what happened to you. And when I found out you were left out there...all alone." His voice trailed off and he swallowed the lump in his throat. "I just thank God that you are alive."

Kathryn smiled through grateful tears to finally be with her uncle and reached over and squeezed his arm. Rick took her hand in both of his and looked at her fondly, then a puzzled expression came to his face and he asked, curiously, "Kathryn, how did you manage to get away from the stage?"

"I ran," she answered half truthfully."

"You're a very brave woman, Kathryn."

She smiled at her adoring uncle, then her face became pensive as she spoke. "I was so worried whether you would even want me out here...that I would be a nuisance and a burden." Her eyes got misty as she added, "And I guess I am already what I most feared." She looked away and shook her head slightly. She started to cry, saying, "Just look at all the trouble I've caused you and everybody else."

"Kathryn," Rick said sternly, "you are not a burden, and you did not cause the trouble. What happened was not your fault. But ya kin be sure we'll find out whose it was. I jist regret your arrival was spoiled by such awful things...and that you had to suffer and go through the ordeal."

In her mind flashed, if he only knew the worst of the ordeal, and she felt dirty and ashamed all over again. Rick got a basin of water and a washcloth and sat next to her on the bed. He handed her the wet cloth and she lay it over her face for a. moment, enjoying the refreshing coolness, then stroked some of the grime off. Rick watched her with interest and said, "I haven't told you how really happy I am that you are here. It's an honor, knowing you cared enough to travel all this way to come live with me... and share my home. I'll correct that...our home. Yours, mine, Sam, Jim, and Pedro's. Whatever your reasons for leaving Lexington we will talk about later."

"Thank you. I love you, Uncle Richard." He took her in his arms and cradled her.

A knock sounded lightly on the door. "Come in," said Kathryn, in a loud whisper. Jim stepped in and carefully shut the door.

"Any news?" inquired Rick. Kathryn sat breathless, afraid of what she dreaded she might hear.

"Yup. The driver...Clint, is alive, but in pretty bad shape." Kathryn's face froze at this news. "At least right now," Jim quickly added, not wanting to alarm or upset Kathryn more than she was. "The big fellow..."

"Manuel," offered Kathryn.

"Yeah, Manuel. Well, he's hurt bad, too, but not as bad as the doc first thought."

"And Claudette and Harold?" questioned Kathryn anxiously.

"Doc put 'em up here in the hotel. I think they're just down the hall...anyway, guess that Harold just got a nasty shoulder wound, and his wife's not hurt bad, 'cept for some nasty bruises...but she is mighty upset and exhausted. Doc wants to have a look at you, too, Kathryn. He says if yer not too bad off he'd come by late morning. He's got his hands full with Clint and Manuel. Fact he's even got the Widow Truitt over there now, helpin him."

"Yes, I can wait until morning. I don't want to take him away from where he is most needed." Another rap sounded. "Come in," she said. Sam stepped in, his arms full of baggage, and Jim went and quickly shut the door for him.

"I got these out of the stage. There's plenty more there. I don't know if any of em belong to you or not. Take yer pick," he grinned, as he set down three cases. "Oh, is this yers?" he asked, dangling a badly smudged tapestry handbag.

"Oh, yes, it is. I'm so glad you found it." Sam tiptoed over to give it to her, saying, "Kinda heavy, ain't it?"

"It's one of my guns and some of my winnings from a poker game," smirked Kathryn. Three men's eyebrows raised in unison, then they grinned and suppressed their laughter.

"We'd better git and let this tired girl catch some sleep," announced Rick. "And it wouldn't hurt the rest of us either." Jim and Sam headed for the door and said goodnight quietly.

As Sam departed, he turned and gave Kathryn a knowing, sympathetic smile. Rick bent down and kissed her cheek. "I love you. You rest well if you can. Our room is right next door." Rick pointed to her left. "You holler if ya need us." The door closed.

Rick's last words echoed in her ears. She had heard Clint say almost the same thing back in Dodge City. The memory ached in her heart. The room went quiet and the oil lamp pulled long shadows down the wall. Her whole body hurt and ached as she crawled off the bed to use the chamber pot, and she winced in pain in doing so. She looked over at the three pieces of baggage on the floor. Only one was hers; the other two belonged to Claudette. Sam had brought in her larger valise and on stiff aching legs, she shuffled to it and nervously undid the clasp. She spread it open and inspected its contents and let out a grateful sigh when she saw that her father John's Colt 44 was still there and had not been stolen.

She looked and saw her large wad of money she had tucked inside her bloomers. There should be about two thousand, she figured. Five hundred that she had taken out of the bank and one thousand five hundred she had put in from the game on the train. She was happy to see it was there, for she fully intended to pay her own way at her uncle's and use some of the money to invest in her future here. She closed the valise and limped back to the bed and opened her handbag, and it was still full of bills. The derringer she took out and tucked under her pillow, then lay wearily down, still wearing her soiled clothes. She spread the blanket over her legs and snuggled deeper into Sam's buckskin coat and promptly fell asleep.

Kathryn awoke in a puzzled state, then, she became fully alert. "Clint. I've got to go to Clint." With effort she got out of bed and took off Sam's coat and set it on the chair. Sadly, she looked at her torn and dirty dress, but this was no time for remorse. She peeled it off and tossed it on the bed. There was still some water left in the pitcher on the commode and she dumped some in the bowl and hastily washed, then opened her valise. How fortunate for her it was the large valise for also inside were her brush, comb and toiletries and clean undergarments. But, unfortunately, the only dress she had put in there had been the rose taffeta that lay on the bed. Her riding clothes were there, her pink cotton skirt and her tan trousers.

She changed from head to toe, donned the skirt and heavy cotton blouse and pulled on her boots. The torn and telltale chemise, undergarments and dress were stuffed in the bottom of the valise. A look in the mirror was distressing. There were baggy, dark circles under her swollen, red-rimmed eyes. She splashed more cold water on them, then left the room.

Silently she stepped into the strange hallway and descended the wide staircase. The desk clerk popped his head up from the register when Kathryn approached.

"Please tell me how I can get to the doctor's office."

"Hey, yer the lady that was lost from the stage, aren't you?"

Kathryn scowled at him, "Yes. Now, where is the doctor's?" He directed her and she abruptly left and marched determined down the street.

Her hand was shaking when she reached for the handle on the office door. When she opened it, the smell of ether penetrated the air and made her nauseated. She gripped the edge of the desk until the sickening feeling subsided.

The room she stood in was small, with just a desk and a few chairs placed against the wall. There was a closed door that appeared to lead to another room.

"Hello," Kathryn called. The door opened and a tall, lanky and very tired man wearing a bloodstained white coat stepped out.

"Hello. What can I do for you?" Dr. Lawton asked calmly.

"My name is Kathryn, Kathryn Barnett and..."

"You are Rick's niece. I'm Dr. Lawton, Bob Lawton." He stepped forward and Kathryn extended her hand.

"I'm so pleased to meet you. Here, come sit down. You must be exhausted after your unfortunate ordeal." He ushered her to one of the chairs and sat down beside her. "I am very surprised to see you up and around after what all Sam has told me." Her face flushed and she prayed Sam had not told everything. He said he wouldn't. Dr. Lawton continued, "In fact, I was going to come over to the hotel shortly and check you over."

"Dr. Lawton, I'm not here about myself." A look of interest crossed his face as she went on. "I came to see about Clint Davis."

"Clint is in very serious condition, Kathryn," Doc answered soberly. "He has not regained consciousness since he was brought in."

Color drained from Kathryn's face. "I want to see him," she said solemnly.

"I understand. But before I take you to him, I must warn you...he doesn't look very good right now."

Doc stood and helped Kathryn to her feet and led her into the other room. Her eyes searched the dim, curtained interior. There was an examining table and two hospital beds, both occupied. Kathryn recognized the heavy shape and shock of black hair and whispered, "That's Manuel." He was sleeping on his back, snoring, with his face turned to the wall. Thick white bandages were wrapped around the splint on his left leg and his right arm rested on his barrel chest in a sling. "Will he be all right?" she asked in a worried tone.

"He's a tough old bird...I think he'll pull out of this. It is just going to take time to heal and keep infection away."

Kathryn's eyes darted to the far right side of the room, then, she put her hand to her mouth to stop from crying out Clint's name. She never felt her feet move, but she was suddenly at his side. Her eyes filled with stinging tears as she looked upon his helplessness. A blanket covered his lower half and he was propped with pillows to keep him from rolling onto his bandaged back. His arm and shoulder were cut and bruised from the banging he received when the coach went wildly down the road. The tears escaped when she bent over and saw his battered, swollen face with his bottom lip split and his eye blackened.

"Oh, Clint," she cried in a whisper. She placed her hand tenderly on his shoulder, then, gently stroked his arm.

His breathing was so shallow that his chest barely moved, and she bit down on her lip to stop her trembling chin. Ever so carefully Kathryn bent over, so as not to bump his sores, and brushed her lips against his cheek. Clint's eyelids moved only slightly but didn't open. By his ear, in a choked-up voice, she whispered, "Clint, it's me, Kathryn. I'm here...I'm safe. Please, wake up. Oh, please get well...I love you...I need..." She turned quickly away and, on unsteady legs, darted from the room and collapsed upon the floor.

Claudette was summoned to help the doctor get Kathryn out of her clothes and into a warm nightgown, after Rick and the Doc returned her to her room.

Now, confined to the hotel room, Kathryn watched the raindrops splatter against the windowpanes, and it reminded her of the night when Clint had first kissed her that night at the way station during another storm. She could feel his lips on hers, and absently her fingers traced her lips. "Oh God," she cried in prayer. "Please don't let Clint die. Please don't take him from me." A knock interrupted her pleas to God. "Yes," she said, startled.

"It's just me." The door opened and Rick entered, "Whew, quite a rain out there." He took off his damp coat and shook the moisture off his hat and set them across a chair. I came to see how you are feeling and ask if there is anything I can get for you," he smiled.

"Well, there is one thing. Take me down the hall to see Claudette and Harold."

"Huh-uh, Doc said to keep you in this bed for the rest of the day." He came over close to the bed and said, "You know, I never realized how anxious you were to see this Clint fellow, but don't you think you coulda asked me or one of us to take you over instead of going all by yourself? You've got to get your strength back before you go a gallivanting around town," said Rick kindly. "This Clint must be pretty special to you, huh?"

"Yes, he is," Kathryn answered sweetly.

"Well, Kathryn, I'm happy you have found someone special you care about. Let's hope and pray he gits well real soon...so's I can get to know him. And if you think he's special, I'm sure I'll think so too." She smiled gratefully at him for the nice things he had just said. "As for Claudette," Rick went on, "well, she's been asking about you and mighty anxious to see you. How's about I bring her down here?"

Her eyes brightened. "Oh, yes. Please do."

"Be right back." Kathryn sat erect and fluffed up the pillows behind her and straightened her bed jacket.

A rap sounded again. "Come in, Claudette," she called. The door opened, but it was Sam.

"Hello, there. Feelin' any better?"

"Yes, I guess so."

"I thought Rick was coming in here?" Sam questioned.

"He went to bring Claudette down."

"I came to tell him, me and Jim's gonna head back ta the ranch soon's the rain lets up."

"I wish I were going. I'm wondering what my new home really looks like. I've imagined it for so long just how I think it looks."

"From what the Doc said, you'll be able to see it tomorrow," he answered, grinning. Then his face got serious and he glanced nervously toward the door and stepped over near Kathryn. "Since this may be the only time fer a while when we can talk, I'm gonna come right out an ask ya if you confided to the Doc what that Indian did to you? 'Cause if'n ya didn't, I think ya oughta," he said sternly.

Kathryn's face became red just even having the subject brought up. "I'm not tryin to embarrass ya, Missy, so please forgive me fer askin, but I wanta know, so if yer hurt, Doc can help ya."

"I haven't yet," she answered dully. "Actually, he hasn't been able to examine me, other than check me over quickly after I fainted in his office. He was planning on coming over here later this afternoon and hopefully bring me good news about Clint."

"You'll tell him then?"

"Yes. Now, I don't want to hear any more about it. All right?"

"All right," he smiled kindly and nodded his head in agreement.

The door flew open and Claudette rushed in and ran with outstretched arms to Kathryn. They embraced, cried, laughed and cried. "I've been so worried about you," sobbed Claudette.

"And I have been worried about you and Harold, too. How is he? Is he going to be all right?"

"I think so, but he is in a lot of pain, and he was lucky in a way."

"How do you feel getting shot is lucky?" blinked Kathryn.

"That bullet that came through the window could have struck his head or gone to his heart...he could have been killed...like Will," she answered, going pale in the face.

"Poor Will...poor, poor Will," Kathryn said, shaking her head in disbelief.

"Excuse me, ladies," interrupted Rick. "We'll leave you to yerselves. I'll be back in a while, Kathryn."

Sam moseyed over to the bed. "I'm goin back to the ranch, but I wanted to say it was a pleasure meetin you, Mrs. Bartholemew, even if it wasn't the best of circumstances."

"Oh, please, call me Claudette. I and Harold both want to thank you and Jim for saving our lives. Please convey our thanks to Jim, if you would. I don't know how we can ever repay you."

"No need, ma'am...Claudette," he smiled. "I'm jist glad we were there to be able to help ya. But I will tell Jim whatcha said. See you at the ranch, Kathryn."

Both men left.

"Now, Kathryn," began Claudette. "What on earth happened to you? I was in such a position inside the coach, actually, my Harold made me lay on the floor and I was simply terrified with all the shooting and all. Then when Harold was shot," she shuddered at recalling the incident, "he fell on top of me...and stayed that way through a wild ride, until Sam and Jim rescued us. But I heard you scream and holler and, oh, Kathryn...I'm so sorry," she said with tear-filled eyes, "that I could do nothing to help you." She reached over and took Kathryn's hand, and the two women felt each other's concern.

A tear at a time trickled down Kathryn's cheeks, and she needed to share her plight with a woman, a woman who would understand and care for her feelings and understand how ashamed and dirty inside she felt, too. She needed to share the horror, for it was too much to carry alone.

When Kathryn finished her story of her brutal attack, told of her pain, her running, of being abandoned, her fears and Sam finding her, the two sat quietly just holding each other. Finally, Claudette said, as she stroked Kathryn's hair, "My heart is in deep pain knowing what has happened to you, please know this. And, I know it will be difficult, but you must try and put this behind you. You have a new home to go to and a brand new life before you. That is what is important now. And, of course, there is Clint. I believe he will pull through this, with time and prayers. You wait and see."

Kathryn smiled weakly. "You are truly a good friend, Claudette. Thank you for listening to me and understanding and caring. We must never lose touch with one another. I need you in my life and I care about you, too. I just hope I can be as good of a friend to you."

"You have already been that. I do not know how I would have endured this long, tiring trip if it were not for your company, compassion, and your good nature." She embraced Kathryn and said, "I best be getting back to Harold. Although he is doing quite well, all things considered, he is still rather helpless and in a lot of pain. I will see you later. You have a nice nap and get your strength back."

"Thank you, I will."

When Claudette reached the door, she turned around wearing a silly smile. "I must tell you this before I go, about the small fright I had last night when Dr. Lawton and I were trying to get Harold out of his shirt."

"What was that?" asked Kathryn curiously.

Claudette started to laugh as she said, "Snake rattles rolled out of Harold's pocket onto the floor; 'bout scared me half to death." They both giggled and laughed, then, Claudette closed the door behind her.

The sudden rainstorm had subsided and now it was just barely misting.

Rick waved so long to Sam and Jim, then, went into the sheriff's office. He tossed his hat on a small table and helped himself, as he usually did, to a cup of coffee from the large enamel pot perched on top of the woodstove heater. Buck, his scuffed tan boots jutting over the top of the desk, tilted his chair back and thoughtfully observed his old friend. Rick slid a homemade wooden chair next to the desk and plunked his tired body down.

"Figured you'd be over soon as ya could," said Buck, stroking his clean-shaven chin. "Ya know, I've been mullin' over this whole nasty stage business..." He paused and took a slug of his own coffee, then set the tin cup on the desk near his outstretched leg. "Seems no one recognized any of the hold-up men, but then I didn't really expect 'em to. I sent a couple of fellas out early this morning to go find the body Sam and Jim came upon and to bring it back. Sam said the face was pretty blown away, but maybe he's got some identification on him; that'll shed some light on this if he does." Buck set his firm, square jaw and waited for Rick's comments.

Rick sipped the hot, strong coffee, then set the cup down and took out his pipe. After the tobacco lit and the fragrant smoke streamed out of the bowl, he leaned across the desk with a look of rage he'd kept inside until now. "Sam told me about the Indian, too. And I say he was no renegade who happened along."

"What are ya saying, Rick?"

"I'm saying I think he could have been the same one that was on my land who shot Pedro and shot at me, and..." his voice raised, "somehow, Zeb Taylor's mixed up in all this. That's what I'm saying."

"How?"

"I don't know. That's the hard part. I just got this gut feelin...like that same day of the shooting when Zeb conveniently showed up. He wants my land, ya know, and wants it bad."

"Why does he want yer land, Rick?"

"Besides his greed? I don't know...yet."

"Well, Sam couldn't give a real good description, but it did sound close to the one you gave me," reflected Buck. "The thing is, findin him and gettin outa him what he does or might know."

"I can go to Taylor's and snoop around. I don't expect any help outa Zeb, but I gotta start somewhere. Care to ride out with me this afternoon?"

"Ya couldn't stop me," answered Rick.

"Good. Meet me back here around one o'clock. I'm going over to Doc's and see if the big Mexican can tell, me any more. Maybe the driver's come to, and he might be of help." "What about Harold Bartholomew?"

"He said he really didn't get good looks at their faces from inside the coach."

"Well, I'll see you at one," Rick said. "If ya need me, I'll be at the hotel. I must get some dinner up to Kathryn and see how she is doing." He picked up his hat and slapped it on his head and nodded goodbye.

Ernie Smith tapped the spit out of his harmonica, then began playing another tune, as he ambled his chuck wagon along toward Villa Grove. He was in no particular rush to get home and had taken the roundabout route, enjoying his own private vacation from work or worry. Not that he ever worried much; it wasn't his nature. Very little could rattle Ernie. He was happy with his wad of pay he'd received from feeding Barnett's drovers on their way to Fort Garland and knew his brother Herbert had things under control at their farm and wouldn't expect to see Ernie until he saw him drive up.

The strains of "Red River Valley" floated through the air. Ernie leaned back and propped his curled boots up on the dashboard and let his two mules take their own sweet time.

Not far from the outskirts of town Ernie stopped playing and took the harmonica from his mouth. He was distracted by the cluster and squawking of a bunch of crows scrapping over some strange object on the ground. A few scattered as the noisy wagon approached and Ernie jerked the mules to a stop. He grabbed his trusty old 12-gauge shotgun and blasted at the birds, pegged off a few and sent the rest flying off in all directions. He sauntered closer to the object for a better look. "I'll be damned," he exclaimed, as he blinked his gray eyes. "Could turn a man's stomach," he added flatly. He studied on the object and nervously looked around, clutching tightly to his gun, "How the hell'd this git here?" he uttered.

Before him on the sand lay the disgusting and stomach clutching sight he gazed down upon. Flies buzzed and swarmed on the severed human head with its eyes pecked clean from their sockets. The mouth locked wide open showed bashed-out teeth and half a tongue. Shredded strips of blood-dried flesh hung beneath exposed cheekbones and part of the skull was caved in. Muscle, bone and cords stuck out from where the neck used to be. "S'pose the sheriff'll want to see this," he said disgusted. Still somewhat leary, Ernie went to the back of his wagon and pulled out a shovel and a gunnysack and returned to the head. Crows scolded him from tree branches and from a safe distance on the ground, as he scooped up their meal and stuck it in the sack.

He clutched the top opening and toted the head to the back of the wagon and cringed when he set it down on the floor. He set the shovel beside it, looked about, then climbed back into the wagon and proceeded on.

Pulling the reins to the right, Ernie guided the mules to the San Luis Creek for water. Another sight caused him to stop the mules again. "Oh, Lord," exclaimed Ernie. He watched a spooked, crazed horse as it tried in vain to shed its unwanted cargo. It reared, circled and kicked at the twisted, mangled body that must belong to the head in his gunny sack, for the body was missing its. Aggressive, hungry crows dove and attacked at the flesh and added to the torment of the poor beast.

Ernie reached behind him and fished out a handful of carrots from a tin and once again climbed down from his wagon. He spoke in low, easy tones as he advanced toward the frightened animal. "Easy boy, easy now," he kept repeating.

The horse froze and fixed wild eyes upon the approaching figure. Slowly Ernie extended his arm and let the horse see a carrot, then continued to move in closer, all the while repeating soothing words. The horse stayed his ground, with the corpse's leg twisted backwards in the stirrup and the handless, crooked arms curved toward the ground and framed the hollow between the shoulders where the neck used to be.

Finally the horse's head bobbed and he stretched his neck out with quivering nostrils to catch the scent of the strange man and the carrot. The carrot won his interest and the top lip curled back as he opened his large-toothed mouth for a bite. While the horse ate, Ernie stroked the long neck. Another carrot was offered and the horse willingly indulged. Ernie eased his hand toward the saddle and attempted to unfasten the cinch, all the while keeping up his low conversation with the animal.

It took patience and time before the saddle slid off its back, freeing the poor creature of his unwanted burden. The horse was led to the side of the wagon and tied. Ernie trudged back and shooed the birds away while he took his large knife and cut the stirrup with the attached boot off of the saddle. "S'pose Buck'll want this, too," he said, matter-of-factly. He stroked his long straggly beard in thought, then went and got a tarp and rope from the wagon.

Ernie suspended the tied canvas, tarp-bound, pungent remains to the rear of the wagon, gave the tied horse a reassuring pat and climbed back into the driver's seat. His keen eyes looked up at the darkened sky and he could see a storm brewing. "Gee-haw," he shouted to his mules and trekked on toward town just as it began to rain.

The chuck wagon drew a small, curious following as it headed up the muddy street and came to a halt in front of Buck McCain's office shortly after noon.

Buck ushered Ernie into the office and set him down with some hot coffee while he scooted over to Luigi Amato's Undertaking Parlor. Buck returned with Luigi pushing his two-wheeled cart and retrieved the remains of Marty, including the sack with the head. The horse was led around to the back of the jailhouse for the time being. Then Buck explained to Ernie that there had been a stage hold-up, the one Rick's niece was on, and that what he'd found was most likely one of the men. According to Kathryn, he said, one of the thieves had been shot, and when his horse galloped away, the fellow was being dragged along.

"Too bad nobody found him sooner," replied Ernie. "That way I wouldn't a had such a mess to pick up."

"He was that," Buck agreed.

"Well, if'n ya don't need me fer anything more, I think I'll head over to the Jack Rabbit and wash the bad taste outer my mouth." Buck thanked him for going to the trouble of dealing with such a disagreeable task and bringing the remains in, and Ernie replied, "Was nothin," and drove on down the street.

Around one o'clock, Rick and Luigi met with Buck at his office. Luigi Amato was a tall, boney man in his late forties, with a sharp-pointed chin and a long nose, with deep-set gray eyes. His thick, unruly dark hair resembled a bush badly in need of a trim. He helped himself to coffee and took a seat alongside Rick.

"Did you find any identification on the man?" asked Buck.

"Only a busted gold watch with the initials M.B. engraved on the back. Here." He reached into his pocket and produced the smashed watch and turned it over to Buck. Buck studied on it, turned the back over and said, "M.B. Of course that doesn't necessarily mean it was his," he said thoughtfully. "Nothing else, Luigi?"

"Not really. Just the usual scars from gunshot wounds that I most always find on this sort of chap."

"Rick, does M.B. mean anything to you?" asked Buck.

"As a matter of fact, it does. Zeb hired on a hand named Marty Brown."

"Well, that might give us something to go on, besides what I've got out back. C'mon." They followed Buck around the side of the jailhouse to the horse. "Check it out." They looked at the left side and the brand T stood out plain as day.

"Bar T. That's Zeb Taylor's brand," exclaimed Rick.

"Let's go back inside," suggested Buck. They rounded the corner of the building as Art and Paul, the two men Buck sent out in the morning, came riding up with a dead man slung over the saddle on the extra horse they'd taken along. All were drenched from the sudden storm. "Where'd you find him?" asked Buck.

"'Bout a mile or so back from where Jim 'n Sam found all them tracks," replied Paul as he swung off his horse.

"I best go and get my cart again," announced Luigi, and down the street he trotted.

They helped Luigi load up the faceless corpse of Cal and he pushed the cart down to his parlor to join the other two bodies he already had. Will and Marty.

"Let's go inside," suggested Buck. They all got coffee and Paul and Art hung close to the stove to warm up and dry out.

"As I see it," began Buck, "there's still one horse missing. But, most of all, there's still the Indian."

"True," agreed Rick. "But Zeb claims he doesn't have any Indian workin for him. If we could only find that Redskin, maybe we could get him to talk." He took a gulp of coffee and continued. "Kathryn told me she thought she wounded him when she took a shot at him from the driver's seat. And Sam swears he got him in the leg. Maybe he's not dead. Maybe he made it back and is holin' up at Zeb's?"

"Well," said Buck, "let's ride out there and nose around and see what we can come up with." He looked over at Art and Paul. "You fellas up to takin another ride?" They nodded yes.

Zeb Taylor eventually got around to dividing the money in the strongbox. "A couple hundred for Blackhorse, the rest for me," he grinned slyly. "Stupid, ignorant Indian don't know or care nothing about money anyways. This will at least keep him thinking he is doing his job for me." In a way he was glad that Cal and Marty were dead and not in on the take; that way he got their share. Not that he ever divided the spoils fairly anyhow. He shoved the empty box into the closet in his private office and put his share of money into a safe hidden behind a secret panel in the wall. No sooner had he finished when Lupe knocked at the door and informed him that there were riders coming. Zeb grumbled and spit into the spitoon at the side of his big oak desk, strapped on his pair of guns and went outside to meet them.

He wasn't surprised to see it was Sheriff McCain and Rick with him, for he had half expected them. He was just annoyed at the intrusion and knowing he was subject to their suspicions and attacks on his character; but he was prepared for them, in his mind.

"Well, if it isn't Sheriff McCain," he said, as friendly as he could muster. "What brings a busy man like yourself out my way?" He spit a stream of tobacco juice over the side of the porch railing and grinned up at the four mounted horsemen toting an extra horse.

"Got some questions for ya. Mind if I come in?" asked Buck.

"No need for that. We will talk here."

"Suit yerself." Buck cocked his head behind him and said, "This horse belong to you?" Paul tugged the reins and turned the animal around so the brand was showing.

"Yeah, that's my horse. Where did you find him?" he asked slyly.

"Not far from the stage robbery," answered Buck, fixing a stare at Zeb.

Zeb's expression did not change. "You don't say," he exclaimed.

"Ya got a fellow working here named Marty...Marty Brown?"

"I did have. But the ingrate, he quit on me only a few days ago. He got ornery actin and just rode off...on my horse. Why you askin me all this, Buck?"

"'Cause we think it's Marty's body we've found that was shot during the hold-up. Did he have a gold watch?"

"Yeah." Zeb spit again and smiled slightly for his truthful answer.

"Where is the Indian ya got workin for ya, Zeb?" inserted Rick.

"Rick. How many times I got to tell you? I have no Indian working for me. I would not want one of those sneaky Redskins around my place. Steal a man blind and slit yer throat in the bargain." He spit in indignation and looked up. To his horror, Bart and Jake were rounding the bend with Cal's horse in tow. Buck and Rick turned in their saddles to see what had caught Zeb's eye, as did Paul and Art.

Tiny beads of sweat collected on the fat man's forehead and he stretched his mind for a plausible story, which wouldn't be too hard. He was more worried that Jake or Bart would louse things up. They weren't too bright, in Zeb's opinion.

Jake and Bart saw the sheriff and his small posse too late. They exchanged worried glances and had no choice but to continue toward the group gathered by the porch.

"What we got comin here, Zeb," asked Buck, watching the slovenly man's face for signs of guilt.

"Hey," shouted Zeb to Jake and Bart. "Where was it you find my horse that that no-good Cal steal out from under me?"

The two slid wary eyes at each other and knew something was wrong. They knew, too, they had to somehow go along with Zeb's concocted story, for they feared his wrath. They ambled alongside Buck and said their "Howdys" before answering Zeb.

Bart spoke up. "We found this horse a yers wanderin around the hills...west of town, headin this way. Musta been on his way home, Zeb."

"But no sign of that good-fer-nothin Cal," Jake included.

"Are you sayin, Zeb, that both Cal and Marty deserted you...is that right?" questioned Buck.

"Yeah. And it puzzles me so. For I treat my men good, like family. Is that not so?" he answered, looking straight at Jake and Bart.

"Like family," they nodded.

Buck could see they were getting nowhere here. He chose not to let on that Luigi now had both bodies of Zeb's alleged run-.off men. He'd wait on that; for what, he wasn't quite sure, but more would come to surface, he hoped. "Paul, give the man his horse. We best be gittin back to town."

"Many thanks, Buck," smiled Zeb in a somewhat taunting manner. "I am most grateful you take time from your busy job to travel this distance to bring my property. I hope you catch those robbers. We cannot have thieves running around preying on honest folks."

Rick almost gagged on those last remarks. Buck held his tongue. For the time being, he'd play along. Buck tipped his hat and answered, "No problem, just doin my job. And don't you worry, I'll find the culprits," he added stonily.

The four men trotted away back toward town. Buck looked at Rick. "He's a lying bastard, I know. We'll just have to find a way to tie him in on this and trap him."

"I wonder what the shovels were for," Rick said.

"I was wonderin' that myself," answered Buck.

Zeb watched as the men rode out. "Did you find Cal's body?" he asked nervously.

"Naw, an the rain washed any tracks away," answered Jake.

"We didn't find Marty's neither," added Bart.

"Never mind Marty, Luigi's got him. The sheriff's already found him." Zeb pondered on Cal's body and wondered where the hell it could be. Well, no matter. There was no way they were going to connect him with any of this. He would make sure.

"Take the saddles off the horses and take them to the corral. Then go check the west fence line," he ordered Bart and Jake. Zeb turned and went back into the house and slammed the door.

Kathryn just finished with the letter she wrote to her mother, Jolene, with the pen and ink she borrowed from Claudette when Dr. Bob Lawton rapped on her door.

"Hello, Kathryn. May I come in?"

"Why, yes," she answered, as she slid the letter into the already addressed envelope. Black bag in hand, Bob entered and drew up a chair beside the bed.

"Well," he smiled. "There's color back in your cheeks. That's good. You must be feeling better after this morning's fainting spell?"

"Yes, much better, thank you. How is Clint?" she asked fearfully.

"I'm afraid he is about the same as when you saw him this morning. But he is holding his own, and that is a good sign," he smiled. "Now, let's have a good look at you, just to make sure there's been no adverse effects from your plight and exposure." He opened his bag and took out his stethoscope. "I'd like to listen to your heart and lungs first."

"All right," she answered, somewhat reluctantly, for she never had liked any doctor's poking or probing.

"Hmmm, sounds all right," he confirmed. He took out a thermometer and shook the mercury down. "Here." She opened her mouth and he placed the thin glass tube under her tongue. In a few minutes he removed it and walked over to the window to read it. "You have a very slight temperature, but I don't think it is enough for us to worry about it now."

Dr. Lawton put away the thermometer and sat down observing her. "I noticed your jaw and cheek were slightly discolored. How did that happen?"

Kathryn stiffened, recalling the Indian's blow to her face. She also remembered what Sam had told her she ought to do, yet having Sam know and telling Claudette had been painful enough. She didn't know if she had the strength, nor the courage to divulge this shameful thing all over again.

Aware she was avoiding answering his last question, Doc studied the expression on her face, then asked, "Are there any more bruises on your body, Kathryn?"

"Just a few," she answered lightly. "Some on my arms, from being thrown around on the stage, and on my legs."

"May I have a look at them?" Doc asked. She pushed up her sleeves and showed him the bruises on her upper arm. Doc couldn't help but notice the imprints, much like pressure from fingers, but he said nothing. "Now, your legs, please?" She stuck her legs out from under the covers and pulled her nightgown up to her knees. Bob noted that these bruises were mostly on the inside and appeared to go higher. Again, he said nothing. Kathryn pulled her nightgown back down and looked at him nervously.

"Isn't there something you would like to tell me, Kathryn?" he asked, now very concerned. Her face tightened and she turned toward the wall, and her body began to tremble, yet she did not respond. "Kathryn, what's wrong?" Bob heard her snivel and he felt genuine pity. Something here was very wrong and he wanted to help. He reached over and patted her shoulder. "Please, Kathryn, what is it? Tell me. Please let me help you." The sniveling continued. "Whatever it is, you can tell me and it will be held in strict confidence, I promise you."

Doc waited.

At last Kathryn spoke, without facing him, for telling to his face was too much for her. In almost a whisper, she said, "I was attacked. I was raped," Her, body stilled and waited for his response. His hand patted her, shoulder and gently squeezed it.

"I am so sorry, Kathryn. I am so sorry that that happened to you." Bob waited a moment before he continued. "I know it is unpleasant for you to even speak of it, and worse for you to have to remember and recall, but Kathryn...who raped you?"

She remained silent for a moment, then answered shamefully, "An...Indian... one of the ones that held up the stage."

Doc was appalled. His heart went out to his friend's niece. "Does your uncle know?"

"No. And I don't want him to, either. Sam only knows, because he found me, and Claudette Bartholomew does because I needed to tell her. I knew she would understand and help me. But no one else. And I want to keep it that way."

"I assure you, I will not talk of this to anyone. Now, Kathryn, I know this won't be pleasant, but I think it best I examine you down there and see if there is any damage to your tissues or signs of infection. Will you please lie down and pull up your nightgown again?"

"Must I?"

"It is for your own good and health, Kathryn."

"Only if you absolutely think it is necessary," she said reluctantly.

"I do."

Kathryn bit her lip and frowned at Dr. Lawton and lay down, please lock the door, I don't want anyone barging in at a time like this."

Bob went and locked the door. He tried to be as impersonal as possible so as not to upset Kathryn any more than she already was. He was appalled at how bruised and swollen her female region was. There were small tears around the opening and he was concerned they could be infected.

"All right," Doc said, trying to sound cheerful. "You can sit up now."

She quickly pulled her nightgown down and pulled the covers back up to her chest and returned to her sitting position.

"I'm going to go back to my office and get you some salve for you to put on your sores down there. I am going to still let you go home tomorrow, as agreed, but I want to see you in a week to make sure you have gotten rid of any infection. All right?"

"All right."

Doc-snapped his black bag shut, stood up and replaced the chair. "I will be back in a jiffy."

Kathryn sat in the bed and felt ashamed all over again. She could never let Uncle Richard or Clint know, she just couldn't face them. But then her thoughts turned to Clint and she became more worried for him than for herself. What if he should die, she thought? She loved him so very much and in such a short time they had become so close, like part of each other. She knew she could never find another man who would mean as much to her as Clint did, no man who could make her feel as she had when he kissed her, no man who could send those mysterious twinges and goose bumps to her body. She began to cry because she was now a used woman and couldn't go to Clint pure and untouched. He would never want her if he knew that another man had taken her. He, for sure, wouldn't if he ever found out it had been an Indian. He must never find out.

A knocking kept sounding and Kathryn finally realized it and quickly wiped her tears. "Come in," she stammered.

Dr. Lawton breezed in with a smile. "Good news, Kathryn," he announced, ignoring her teary eyes. "Clint has regained consciousness. Mrs. Truitt said he came around while I was over here."

Kathryn's face brightened, then, beamed. "Oh, that's wonderful." Happy tears replaced the sad ones.

"And I thought you would be pleased to know that he has asked about you and for you. He seems most anxious to see you. He was very worried for your safety, and I assured him you were fine and that you were here resting, at my request."

"When can I go to see him?"

"I will come back here this evening after dinner and personally escort you over. How is that?"

"I would like that very much," she smiled.

"Now, here is the salve. Wash very good with soap and rinse clean. Then apply it all around down there. And continue to do so at least three times a day until the salve is gone. I have instructed the chambermaid to bring you fresh water and towels so you may bathe and freshen up. I am sure that will make a difference in how you feel."

"Thank you...for everything," she smiled.

"I must go check on Mr. Bartholomew and his wife, but I'll be back after dinner for you." He waved goodbye and left.

It wasn't long before Kathryn was immersed in a large, oblong metal tub enjoying the delicious warmth of the bath water. She gently washed her breasts and cringed at their extreme tenderness and bruises. She stared at the rest of her body, but instead of crying this time, she became angry at the disfiguring marks left by the Indian. She knew the outside bruises would heal and go away, but the bruises to her very being would always remain.

As she sat in the tub with the dim afternoon shadows drifting through half-closed drapes, thoughts, events and people marched rapidly through her mind. All the new sights, new situations, new people...all of it. And what she had learned and gone through, all the changes in her usual ways of acting, thinking and looking at life... all these changes had changed her. She was different, she knew...she could feel it. The vision of the beautiful, Sangre de Cristo Mountains the first time she had seen them came to her and how intrigued and fascinated she had been as they traveled up, through and over them; and the magnificent view of the sprawling San Luis Park, surrounded by still more majestic chains of mountains. Now, she was nearly home. So close to all she had sacrificed for...her new home and a brand new way of life. And Clint. He was now conscious, and that was a good sign. She would have him, too, in her life...her new life. She did not want that Indian to have the control of her emotions and the power to ruin her life. She would not, could not, let this incident pull her down, let it destroy her. She decided the only answer, the only thing-she could do, was do as Claudette advised, put it behind her.

With this new realization, this awakening, this new attitude, Kathryn was finally able to smile, a somewhat sad yet determined smile.

The water had become chilly. Kathryn stepped out of the tub and dried herself off and salved herself as the doctor ordered. She had no intention of moping another minute in bed and went over to her stack of baggage Sam and Jim had brought up from the stage station where it had been stored. After putting on clean undergarments and petticoats, Kathryn unbuckled the leather straps on her trunk, flipped open the latches and selected a deep blue silk dress with matching cashmere wool shawl and a pair of black, high-button shoes with pearl buttons. She removed her jewelry box and picked out a pair of large pearl ear bobs. After she was dressed she brushed her hair and piled it up attractively. The sun was breaking through the clouds now and filled her room with a bright warmth. She walked to the window that looked out over the main street and saw her Uncle Richard, Sheriff McCain and two men riding into town from the west and wondered where they had gone off to.

Rick glanced up and saw her in the window, grinned and waved and she grinned and waved back.

Shortly, Uncle Richard was in her room. "Why, Kathryn, you look very nice. I'm surprised to see you up and all decked out. You must be feeling a whole lot better."

"Oh, I'm feeling much, much better; and I'm getting very anxious to go see the ranch...my new home.

"We'll head out bright and early tomorrow. How's that?"

"That sounds wonderful," she beamed. She told him about Clint and that Dr. Lawton would be coming over after dinner to take her to see him. "Uncle Richard, would you like to come with us?" Kathryn asked, her eyes once again sparkling.

"I'd like that. Besides," Rick grinned, "I might as well meet this man you are so sweet on, because I'm sure I'll be seeing a lot of him, right?"

"Oh, Uncle Richard," she giggled.

"Are you up to taking dinner in the dining room?" he asked.

"Yes, I would love to do that. Do you suppose we could see if Claudette can get away and join us?"

"Well, let's go rap on their door and see."

Rick felt quite the gay blade and center of attention as he escorted the two young, beautiful ladies into the dining room of the San Luis Hotel. Claudette had welcomed the invitation, and after tending to Harold she happily dressed to leave the confines of the hotel room.

The dining room was nearly filled, but the host found them a nice table near the back. Rick smiled and nodded at the people he knew as they went to their table. Most of the ladies who were dining were quite curious as to who the new ladies in town were. They craned their necks and looked in obvious curiosity and made sure to take in the style and fashion Kathryn and Claudette were wearing. It did not take long for the word to be passed among them that the dark-haired one was Rick Barnett's niece, the very one who had been separated and lost from the stagecoach hold-up. There seemed to be a steady, low buzz as information was told, then shared.

After a tasty dinner, Rick strolled Kathryn and Claudette around the block, then back to the hotel lobby to wait for Dr. Lawton. Claudette thanked Rick for a very nice time and told Kathryn to give Clint and Manuel hers and Harold's best wishes and excused herself back to her room.

Dr. Lawton was amazed at the improvement to Kathryn's looks since seeing her last as he escorted her and Rick to his office. And, he informed them, although Clint had improved, he still had a long way to full recovery; and, he added, the same was true for Manuel. The good news, he said, was that Mrs. Truitt was going to take them into her home as soon as they were able to be moved and continue to do their nursing. This would free up the beds and afford him access so that he could still keep a close eye on them. Harold Bartholomew, he informed them, was doing quite well; in fact, better than he at first had anticipated, but he figured it would be at least a couple of weeks before he could be up and about. He was fortunate, he said, that he had such a dutiful and capable wife to administer to his needs.

They reached the office and Kathryn excitedly followed the doctor toward the back room. Rick chose to linger behind until the two had had their reunion and their private moments before he would meet Kathryn's beau.

Clint, still propped on his side, heard Kathryn enter the outer room, and he was eager and waiting. Finding out she was alive and had survived had removed the heavy weight of fear from his heart. When he had come to at the doctor's office, he was alarmed because he didn't know what had happened to Kathryn or any of the others, for that matter. All he remembered was racing the stage against highway robbers, lots of shooting, a bare-chested Indian up beside him in the coach, and Kathryn's screams. He could still hear her screams in his mind and it brought back the shameful feeling of being powerless to help and the anguish that had wrenched his heart for the woman he loved.

His eyes widened and brightened when he saw Kathryn in the doorway. She paused, then, ran to his side smiling through joyous tears. "Oh, Clint...you're going to be all right. I was so afraid...so afraid you might die...I didn't want you to be hurt... to be hurting, as you are now. I was afraid I had lost you." Her chin shook and her face wreathed the agony she felt, but her eyes revealed her love.

Clint's eyes drank in her face, the face of the woman he had searched for most of his life and found. The woman, who had his heart. The woman he feared he had lost. But she was here now, standing beside him. So much he wanted to say, to tell her, but the right words wouldn't come. All he could do was convey through his eyes that which was in his heart. Breathing was difficult due to the burning pain in his back and lungs, but he took a labored gasp of air, and in a rasping voice said, "I...love you."

Tears crept down her cheeks as she reached for his hand and in a hushed silence they knew and felt the love and passion they shared.

"Clint," she said softly, "Uncle Richard is here. He would like to meet you. Do you feel up to it?"

He grinned and nodded yes. Kathryn motioned for Rick, who was standing patiently next to Mrs. Truitt and the Doc. to come in. "Clint," she smiled, this is my Uncle Richard."

"Sir," gasped Clint, hoarsely, "it's a real...pleasure to...meet you...finally."

Rick reached down and lay his hand upon Clint's, knowing the man was in no condition to shake. "I'm real glad to meet you, too, Clint. And happy to hear you're gonna pull out of this in fine shape."

Clint smiled and started to answer. "I know it's hard for you to talk, Clint," said Rick. "Save your energy. I just want you to know you are welcome at the ranch anytime. So you hurry and get well so we can get better acquainted."

"Thanks. "

Doc stepped in and said, "I think we'd better let Clint rest. He's had about all the excitement he outa have for right now."

"See ya later, Clint, "Rick patted his hand and departed for the other room.

Kathryn bent over and her lips tenderly touched Clint's. "I will come by in the morning to see you before we leave for the ranch."

"Good," he smiled.

She kissed him again, then, turned to leave, She saw Manuel grinning happily from his bed and she gave him a wave and a smile, then left the room.

"Si, you are one lucky man, Clint. That one, she is a good woman."

"I know," he acknowledged, then drifted off into a peaceful slumber.

20

Rays of bright sunshine burst through the window and Kathryn awoke in a dreamy state of happiness. With quickness of thought she became alert for this morning she would be going with Uncle Richard to the ranch, her new life. The very idea charged her with energy and she jerked back the covers and hastened to wash and get herself dressed, and decided to wear the blue one, again. She happily bustled about the room gathering and re-packing the items strewn about. She slipped her hand under the pillow and pulled out the derringer and returned it to her Purse and made a quick count of her money. Her eyes swept the room for a quick check and satisfied that everything was in order, left her room and stole silently down the hall to the Bartholomew's.

The goodbyes were brief, as Kathryn would be coming back to town to visit Clint and them within a day or so. She was just leaving their room, when glancing down the hall, saw her uncle about to rap on her door.

"Uncle Richard," she called, in a loud whisper. "I'm down here."

"Well, yer up and dressed bight and early," he marveled. "Come, let's go grab us some breakfast downstairs."

While waiting in the dining room for their food to be served, Rick said, "After we eat I'll walk you over to the Doc's so you kin say goodbye to Clint, and then I'll come back here and get your things loaded up in the buckboard, and drive down to get you. That sound like a good plan?"

"That sounds like a good plan," she agreed, smiling. She was so excited she could scarcely eat, but Rick, insisted she eat as much as she could, because she needed to build up her strength again. Kathryn frowned and forced down what she could.

They left the hotel and strolled down the wooden sidewalk to the doctor's. The sky was clear blue and the sun warmed up the air from the chilly night before. They nodded and smiled at people who passed and Kathryn received many curious stares from those who had no idea who she was. Rick opened the door for her at Doc Lawton's.

"I'll be back in about a half-hour, that all right with you?"

"That's fine," she said and entered the small whitewashed building.

"Good morning," Miss Barnett greeted Alice Truitt.

"Good morning," Kathryn answered. "How is Clint this morning?"

"He seems to be much better. The doctor is in with him now. Won't you please be seated while you wait?"

Kathryn eased herself into one of the chairs by the wall, and Alice came over by her.

"We haven't been officially introduced with all the confusion, but my name is Alice Truitt. I am a friend of Sam McPeak's and your uncle's. I'm a widow now, but before I was married I did nursing. I was so pleased that the doctor asked me to help out. I do get lonely, now and then," she confessed. "I knew that your arrival was expected, and I was so looking forward to meeting you and having you over for tea. I am so very sorry that you went through such a traumatic experience with the robbery and folks getting shot and killed. It must have been dreadful for you."

If she only knew how dreadful, thought Kathryn. "Yes," she answered. "It is an experience I hope I never have to go through...ever again." Alice patted her arm in a motherly fashion and Kathryn could tell she was a good-hearted woman and probably had gone through much heartache herself.

"Mrs. Truitt," said Kathryn.

"Oh, dear...please call me Alice."

"Well, Alice," she began again. "I want to tell you how happy I was and how much I appreciate that you so graciously consented to taking Clint and Manuel into your home for their convalescence. I know it will be a lot of extra work for you and I want to help you out with some of the expenses, if I may?"

"Oh, Kathryn, that won't be necessary...the doctor is paying me a wage for my duties."

"Nevertheless," Kathryn said, "feeding two grown men, not to mention all the extra work does take its toll. Alice, please promise me that you will let me know if there is anything I can do or get for you, like extra food or whatever."

"You are very kind to be concerned and I thank you. And, yes, I will let you know if the need arises for extra assistance."

Doc Lawton stepped out from the sick room. "Ah, Kathryn, I thought I heard your voice. You'll be pleased to know that Clint ate a small breakfast, and kept it down, and that his temperature is beginning to stabilize. Would you like to go in to see him now?"

"Yes, very much."

Clint's hair was combed, thanks to Alice and he looked handsome to her lying on his pillow, bruises and all. Kathryn tiptoed to his bed and gave him a soft peck on the cheek. His eyes opened and brightened when he saw her.

"How are you feeling today, she asked, searching his expression for clues.

"Better...now that...yer here." It still hurt him to talk and it was maddening for him. There was so much he wanted to ask her, to tell her. But it would have to wait.

"I can't stay long today," said Kathryn. "Uncle Richard will be by for me in a short while, but I had to see you and see how you were doing before leaving for the ranch."

"Finally...going to see...yer new home, huh, gal?" Clint grinned.

"Yes, and it seems like it took an eternity to get here, but I am almost there now."

"Are you excited?"

"Yes, in a way. I just think how different it would have been...my arrival, and you not being hurt...or anyone else or Will dead...." Her voice trailed off and they looked at each other with sadness knowing that Will had given his life for them and would no longer be around. "I just hope the sheriff finds out who was responsible for this tragedy," she said firmly.

"Me, too, Kathryn...me, too." There was sadness and pain in his eyes for the loss of his friend.

"Clint, is there anything I can do or bring for you, before I leave?"

"Yes...there is something..." Talking now was becoming painful and Clint started feeling weak.

"What is it, Clint?"

"Would you...check?" He sucked in air and let it out in short gasps.

"Would I check what?" she asked, becoming concerned he was overdoing. "Check about...Will's burial...with Peter...stage...manager."

"Yes, of course I will. Don't worry, I'll go see him as soon as I leave here."

"I know I can't go...jist wanna know," he answered, his voice becoming strained and hoarse.

"Clint, you are tiring. I'm going to leave now and let you get some sleep. If I have any news from Peter I will leave it with the doctor or Mrs. Truitt. I will see you just as soon as I can get back into town. Now, you rest so you can get well." Kathryn bent over and whispered, "I love you, Clint Davis." They kissed gently goodbye and she left the office.

She looked up and down the street for any sign of her uncle and spotted the buckboard with her baggage loaded on the back, parked in front of the sheriff's office and she walked the short distance and poked her head inside.

"Excuse me," said Kathryn," but I need to speak to my uncle a moment."

"Won't you come in and visit a spell," offered Buck.

"Some other time, thank you," she said to the sheriff.

"What is it, Kathryn?" Rick asked. "Is something wrong?"

"No. I just need to speak to Peter somebody or other, at the stage station. I should not be too long."

"Wait. I'm finished here, for now. I'll drive you over."

They pulled up in front of the station and Rick helped Kathryn down and accompanied her in.

"Peter," called Rick, to an empty room.

"Ya. Be right out." Peter soon came out from the back office. "Howdy, Rick and Miss Barnett, although we've not been introduced yet."

"Peter, this is my niece, Kathryn. Kathryn, Peter Voris," said Rick, gallantly doing the honors.

Peter met her extended hand. He was a quiet yet steady sort of man. An Easterner who fell in love with the excitement and promise of the West. Although only in his late thirties, his light brown hair was thinning and he had a distinct receding hairline, which made his forehead protrude. His features were quite ordinary except for his muscular body, and he prided himself for keeping physically fit, a trait left over from his college boxing days. His sharp blue eyes crinkled at the corners as he smiled now at Kathryn.

"What can I do for you?" he asked sincerely.

"Peter, Clint has asked me to check with you about Will to see what arrangements have been made for his burial."

"Well, Ma'am. We don't know of any kinfolk around here and being he was killed in the line of duty, the company will most likely pay for his burial, here."

"When would that be?" Kathryn inquired.

"As soon as Luigi has his box made and gives the go-ahead," Peter answered.

Kathryn looked at her uncle with questioning eyes. "Lets go see Luigi," sighed Rick. Kathryn thanked Peter, then, asked if he'd post her letter, the one she wrote to her mother.

"I'll see to it that it goes off on the next stage," he said. Kathryn turned the letter over to him and handed him some coins for the stamp, and they left.

Luigi Amaoto's establishment was at the northwest side of town. The windows had dark closed heavy draperies and the place seemed forbidding and eerie. Rich knocked on the front door and Kathryn stood nervously by. She had never been to an undertaker's parlor and she was feeling jittery. It was some time before the door was opened and when it did it startled then both.

"Yes"? Oh, Rick, it's you, and your lovely niece. Do come in."

The room they had stepped into was dim-lit and possessed a peculiar odor, with an arrangement of furniture, which consisted of a sofa, and several seating chairs.

"What can I do for you?" asked Luigi.

Kathryn quickly spoke up. "I'm here to see about the arrangements for the young stagehand that was killed. Will Carson."

"Oh, yes. Poor lad, struck down in his prime. Tragic thing. What would you like to know?"

"When is he going to be buried?" questioned Kathryn.

"He is about ready now, but no particular arrangements have been made, so I was just going to deliver him to the cemetery myself and see that he was put in the ground."

Kathryn thought to herself. It isn't right for poor Will to be buried alone, with no family, friends or loved ones there to cry or pray over him, to send him on his way to his new life in the beyond. "Excuse us a moment," she said to Luigi, and took her uncle aside. "Uncle Richard, is it possible we could come back in a day or two?"

Rick was reading her mind and answered, "Yes, if ya feel up to it, we can."

"Good." Kathryn stepped back over to Luigi and inquired, "Can his remains be kept for two more days?"

"Yes. Why?"

She ignored answering and instead fielded another question. "Has he a proper suit to be laid out in?"

"No, he..."

"Well, if you would be so kind, this is what I propose."

Luigi looked astounded at this determined young lady as she went on. "I would like you to purchase a proper suit for him and see that his grave has a nice marker. I also would like you to see that he has a graveside service, with a preacher. And, I would appreciate it if Mr. and Mrs. Bartholomew and Peter Voris are informed that there will be a service. Can you have this all done and arrange for the funeral to be held day after tomorrow, at say, ten o'clock?"

"Why...why, yes. If that is what you wish."

"It's what I wish, And, I want the wagon bearing his coffin to stop for a few minutes in front of the doctor's so Manuel and Clint can know and say their goodbyes." Luigi's eyes were blinking rapidly, keeping up with the plans and orders this small young woman was making. "And, finally, I know this will cost probably more than what the stage company spends so I want you to take this for your fee and trouble and for expenses connected with the funeral," she said matter of factly. She opened her handbag and turned her back until she had counted out what money she wanted. "Here, this should cover it."

Luigi looked down at the two hundred and fifty dollars in his large pale hand and smiled broadly. "Oh, yes. This should take care of it nicely. Don't worry Miss Barnett. William Carson will have a nice funeral."

"Oh, one more thing, would you please stop at Doctor Lawton's and inform him or Mrs. Truitt what time the procession will be stopping there?"

"Oh, yes. I shall attend to that and all the other things. So do not worry."

"Thank you. Uncle Richard, I am more than ready to go home."

"With pleasure, my dear." He extended his elbow and she slipped her arm through his and Rick escorted her out and boosted her up into the seat. He climbed in and handed her a lap robe. "Here, so you don't get the chills." Kathryn spread the robe across her lap and tucked it firmly around her legs and grinned at her uncle when she was finished.

"Now, Kathryn," asked Rick. "Are you sure, positively sure, there are no more stops, errands or missions you have to attend to before I can drive you hone?"

Don't be silly...of course not," she laughed.

"Well, then, my dear sweet Kathryn, with your permission, I will turn this here tired wagon around and drive you home."

"Permission granted," she giggled. Rick gripped the reins and clucked to the team and the wagon made a u-turn. He drove it smartly down the street, made a right turn at the corner and headed west on the road that led to the ranch.

21

Kathryn surveyed the newness of the lush green land that stretched ahead. Gradually it mushroomed into huge clusters of rolling hills that swept higher as they arched, dipped and became taller and mightier, with valleys and canyons tucked and hidden between them.

The flat land they now traveled had splashes of hearty wildflowers along the side of the road that spilled colorfully over the hills was a picturesque gateway to the beautiful, yet mysterious mountains beyond. This was the place she had thought and dreamed about, dreamed about since her uncle, now beside her, had spoken of and described with a glow in his eyes. And, now, she was here...and she felt overwhelmed.

Turning around in the seat, Kathryn intensely cast her eyes back to Villa Grove and saw how it was dwarfed by the impressive mountains that spread high and wide behind it. She searched out the location of the doctor's office and her heart began to ache knowing Clint was there, and with each mile she was leaving him further behind.

Now, it was just her, alone, sitting beside her Uncle Richard. Nervously, she fingered and stroked the heavy, woolen lap-robe. She felt her uncle watching. She looked up and smiled. Rick returned the smile and his eyes conveyed that he understood. He switched the reins into his left hand, then circled her shoulders with his right arm and drew her beside him. She received comfort from the warmth and strength of this gesture and she began to breathe easier and to relax. The slow yet steady clip-clopping of the two horses' hooves had a re-assuring effect and she snuggled closer to her uncle and felt safe, safe from fear, violence and uncertainty, at least for now.

Rick broke the silence. "Been rough, hasn't it?" he asked softly. She nodded against his shoulder. "Kathryn, it took a lot of courage to do what you've done...leaving a comfortable home, to travel all this way...especially by yourself. I knew you could do it, but that don't make it easy...I know better. And, I know it'll take a while to get used to new things and get aquatinted around here...well, any new place. Just give yourself time. You've been through a bad time of it, just go slow and easy." She looked up at him, smiled and nodded and was grateful for his comforting words.

The wagon crunched along on the gravely road and Kathryn enjoyed the steady motion and peaceful solitude, and the ease she felt with her uncle.

"Ever seen a bull elk?" he asked, out of the blue. Kathryn sat up and replied, "No. Why?"

"Well, if you look to your right you'll see one, with about a dozen cows."

"I see it. Gee, they're a lot bigger than antelope or deer," she remarked.

"Good eatin, too," added Rick.

"How much farther is it to the ranch?" asked Kathryn, when Rick made a left turn off the main road.

"Not much farther," he grinned. "We go about two miles toward those hills, then not quite two into them. We're set in a high valley, and I hope you think it's as pretty as I do."

"Kathryn looked around drinking in the scenery and said, "I think I will."

Around the bend of a small hill Kathryn spotted the ranch. "Oh," she said, I see it. There it is. Oh, Uncle Richard...it looks beautiful."

Rick watched his niece's face glow and come to life with enthusiasm. They approached the entrance gate and Kathryn looked up to read the long, carved sign suspended above. BARNETT CATTLE RANCH, it said. She grinned at Rick for it looked so impressive and important.

"You sure have a lot of cattle," she remarked, as they passed by a hundred or so grazing yearlings.

"There's lots more," he told her, "strung out all over the place."

"Oh, look. Look at all those beautiful horses," she exclaimed. "I can hardly wait to go riding."

They were nearing the house and it wasn't long before Sam, Jim, Pedro and the two dogs came bounding out the front door. Rick slowed the wagon. As he pulled it to a stop in the front, the three let loose with a hearty cheer of welcome.

"Ya-hooo. She's finally made it. Welcome, Kathryn," they shouted in unison.

Kathryn grinned, laughed and thanked them. Jasper and Zeke ran up to greet Rick then ran around the wagon to investigate the new person.

"Well, hello there." she said to the two black and white dogs. They rose up on their hind legs and placed their paws on the side of the wagon and Kathryn reached down and petted each on the head. Sam came around to assist her and his mouth stretched wide between his moustache and beard with a warm grin as he helped her carefully out of the wagon, and they exchanged a private knowing with their eyes.

"Hey, Kathryn," hailed Jim, coming up swiftly behind Sam. "Ya look, I just want to say how glad I am yer here."

"Why, thank you, Jim." And she gave him a hug.

Rick led Pedro by the arm over to Kathryn. "I want you to meet Pedro," he said. He's been mighty anxious to meet you. Kathryn, this is Pedro Lopez."

"Senorita Kathryn. It is an honor to at last be meeting you." Pedro's dark eyes flashed and he bowed courteously.

"I'm very pleased to meet you, Pedro," she answered. She extended her hand to shake. Pedro reached out, turned her hand slightly over and kissed the back of it gently. Kathryn smiled self-consciously.

"Now that," declared Jim," is true gallantry. Wonder why I never thought to do that?"

"'Cause yer not polished, like Pedro," offered Sam. They all laughed, but Jim.

"Well, thanks," huffed Jim, pretending to be hurt.

"C'mon," said Rick, "who's going to lend a hand with these bags?" Jim and Sam grabbed an end on the big trunk, Rick and Pedro each took a valise, and Kathryn had her handbag and retrieved her parasol from the floor of the wagon.

Kathryn turned and faced the big sprawling log house and immediately she loved how inviting and warm it looked and adored the big porch with benches for sitting on warm days. "C'mon Kathryn," urged Rick. "We want to show you your new house." Kathryn took his arm and they followed the men and her baggage up the steps, onto the porch and through the front door.

Kathryn stood and admired the large eating space, kitchen, lounging area, all combined in the one room.

"This is where we spend most of our time when we're not outside or working," Rick informed her. They all paused to see what her reaction would be.

Kathryn looked at the long table before her. There were five chairs, one each on three of the sides, and two chairs at the other. One of the two chairs was different from the others and she knew it was placed there for her, and she felt pleased and accepted. She was surprised to see a beautiful tablecloth with tiny clusters of flowers around the border, and she smiled and her eyes got moist when she saw the large fruit jar in the middle of the table stuffed full of wild flowers. Colorful sprigs of white chokecherry blossoms, brilliant scarlet gila, purple wild anums, clusters of blue asters and stems of white willow. "Oooooh, what pretty flowers. Who picked them?" she asked.

"I did," mumbled Jim. "Thought ya might like em."

"Oh, I do. They're beautiful. Thank you, Jim." He blushed and for once nobody teased him. They pretended not to notice.

She looked at the cozy sofa and stuffed chairs arranged near the huge field-stone fireplace and the big oak desk on the wall to the right. "This is a wonderful room," she said with a big smile.

She looked between the main room and hallway and said, "Why, you even have a parlor." It was a small room accessible from either way as it had no doors. It contained a settee and two armless chairs positioned around a marble topped table with ornate carved legs.

"Rick thought he should have one when we built the house," Jim informed her.

"But, we never have used it," admitted Rich.

"Wait until you see what else," Senorita Kathryn," beamed Pedro excitedly. Sam and Jim were already headed down the hall with the trunk and the rest of them followed. Rick stepped over to the closed door and urged Kathryn to come and open it. She came forward and paused, her hand hesitating on the handle. The four men exchanged anxious glances and waited patiently in anticipation. Kathryn cocked her head and gave than all a curious look then slowly turned the knob.

"Why...why, this is...elegant, absolutely elegant. How...how could you do...how did you know...I mean, how did you men decorate this so, so elegantly," she stammered. The four men grinned.

"You really like it?" asked Rick.

"It's perfect. I love it. Thank you for fixing me such a special room." She took a step onto the dark green rug and her eyes took in the pattern of the rosebuds scattered throughout the weave and intertwined with colors of pink and fuchsia. She took a few more steps to the grand walnut bed in front of her with its headboard against the wall to her right and drew her hand across the white crocheted coverlet. Turning, she smiled approvingly at her uncle and saw Sam and Jim waiting with the trunk suspended between them.

"Oh, that's heavy. Please bring it in so you can set it down," she said.

"Where would you like it, Kathryn?" Jim asked.

She quickly glanced around. "Over here looks like a good place," she said, pointing to the vacant space left of the doorway. They set it down there and Rick and Pedro placed the valises down beside it.

Kathryn was standing in front of the cream colored dressing table with the red velvet chair that stood against the wall across from the bed. "You even thought of this?" she asked in amazement. She glided over to the window and fingered the long floor length pink organdy curtains, parted then and gazed out the window. It looked out over the front of the house with the yard and corral as part of her view. Six or more horses were prancing about, and taking up the horizon rose the Sangre de Cristo Mountains, their snowy peaks like dripping frosting on a cake. She could feel the four men watching her silently from the doorway and she felt all choked up.

She felt so wanted in such a short time. Slowly, she turned around to face them. Big Sam, with his long red hair and bushy beard; Jim, his hair combed down and sporting a recently grown thin moustache; Pedro with coal black hair and clean shaven face; and her Uncle Richard, handsome and muscular, dark sensitive eyes and trim, full moustache, stood grouped in the doorway, all wearing boyish grins on their faces.

She was overcome with their efforts, their quite extraordinary efforts to welcome her to this home. Suddenly, her smile was replaced with weeping as she tried to say, "Thank you...this was far more than I expected."

"You're more than welcome, Kathryn," said Rick, and the rest grinned and nodded.

"I don't know about the rest of you," announced Sam, "but this has worked up my appetite. And, besides, I've been stallin' dinner til ya got here. It'll be ready in about five minutes." He turned and went for the kitchen.

"I will give you some help, Sam," said Pedro, trailing after him.

Jim turned to leave and said, "There's fresh water in the pitcher for you, so's you can wash up, if you like." Beside her stood a varnished pine commode with a large rust and yellow flowered pitcher and matching bowl on top and pale yellow towels, folded and stacked, next to the bowl.

"Why, thank you, Jim. I appreciate that," she smiled.

Jim headed for the kitchen and Rick came into the room and stood beside Kathryn.

"I can't tell you what a great feeling it is having you here, here in this house."

"Thank you. Oh, Uncle Richard. I think this room is wonderful and I really love this house. It's so warm and cozy that I feel at home, already."

"This is your home, " Rick smiled, then said, "Let's go join the others."

"Let me freshen up first. You go and I'll be there shortly." Rick nodded and shut the door, and Kathryn sunk dawn in the green velvet chair by the window. Her legs felt unsteady, her heart racing and she felt so overwhelmed by everything. She studied the chair and ran her palm over the soft velvet. It had a comforting effect and she relaxed for a moment and said a prayer of thanks that she was at last here and she was safe. She smelled the aroma of food drifting from the kitchen and she was all at once very hungry. She washed up, checked her appearance in the gilded mirror above the dressing table and went to join the men. She could hear their deep voices engaged in lively conversation and it sounded good to her ears.

Her place was next to Pedro. He stood to pull the chair out for her and she felt a little hesitant with four pairs of eyes watching as she eased herself down between Rick and Pedro. Little did she know that she was the first woman ever to be in this house. Not only was she important by being Rick's niece, but she was a novelty as well.

Sam had Pedro place the silverware in front of their places and after he'd put food on each plate had Jim serve them. Rick took all this in without comment and was amused as well as pleased that they were going to such great lengths for his niece.

Kathryn hungrily ate the rice, beans and meat topped with a flavorful bar-b-que sauce. "This is delicious," she said to Sam.

"Glad ya like it," he beamed.

"What kind of meat is this, if I may ask? I don't believe I've ever eaten anything like this before."

"It's roast bear, been marinating it for a couple of days. That, and cookin it slow makes it tender and tasty."

"There are bears around here," Kathryn asked, somewhat alarmed.

"Si, Senorita Kathryn," answered Pedro. "Big ones, too."

Wide-eyed, Kathryn looked from Pedro to Rick. "Bears, Uncle Richard?"

Rick chuckled. "Yup. Bears."

"Oh, dear. Am I to worry?" she asked her uncle.

"Naw. They don't usually come too close...but, coyotes and the mountain lion," interrupted Pedro, "that is a different story. Si, Senor Rick?"

"Well...hey, we don't want to be scarin Kathryn off...she just got here." The men all laughed and then Kathryn did too.

"No need to be afraid anyhow," Jim told her. "After all, just look at all the protection ya got sittin round the table."

"Yes," she nodded and agreed. "I do have lots of protection."

"Maybe she not need our protection," said Pedro. "Senor Rick tells me the day we go after those strays that she can shoot good for a woman. Did you not say that, Senor Rick?"

"Yes, I guess I did mention that," answered Rick, winking at Kathryn. "One of these days maybe we can have a shooting contest. What do you say, Kathryn?"

"I think that could be fun," she answered. "Just wait until. I'm rested up, I don't want to look too bad."

They finished eating and Kathryn offered to help with the dishes. "No need," said Sam, scraping leftover scraps into bowls for Jasper and Zeke, who were eagerly standing by.

"I'm going to help," stated Pedro. "You rest," he added, looking at Kathryn.

"In that case I think I'll get started unpacking, then lie down for a while. I'm rather tired."

"Good idea," agreed Rick. "Jim, c'mon out and help me in the barn."

"All right," he answered.

"Uncle Richard, could I speak to you before you go out?" Kathryn asked, heading down the hall. Rick followed her and she stopped near her bedroom door. In his ear she whispered, "Where is the privy?"

Rick grinned and whispered back. "Go out the door near my desk. Ya can't miss it. Anything else?"

"Not at the moment," she replied.

Rick and Jim left by the front door and Kathryn scooted out the back. She then returned to her room and opened the large doors on the armoire, then opened the trunk and began hanging up her dresses and putting away her things, but before she was finished she realized how tired she was. She took off her blue dress and hung it up with the others, and put on her red robe, then lay down on her bed to nap. She slept the rest of the afternoon.

It was dusk when she awoke and was disoriented at first, but then she remembered where she was. She inched out of bed and felt for the matches and lit the small lantern beside her bed, and the room took on a soft glow. She wondered what time it was and reminded herself, to purchase a clock for her room and a new brooch watch as hers was lost sometime during the hold-up. Opening the door a crack she heard hushed voices coming from the kitchen area. Not caring to dress up she put on her riding skirt, white blouse and black flat-heeled slippers, then headed toward the kitchen.

The men were conversing over coffee and Sam jumped up to get her some when he saw her enter the room.

"Did you have a good nap?" asked her uncle.

"Yes, but I didn't mean to sleep this long. What time is it?"

"Don't feel bad about that, Kathryn, you needed the rest." Rick glanced over at the mantel clock. "It's seven-thirty."

"We'll be eatin soon," said Sam, as he set down her coffee in a cup and saucer.

"Thank you, Sam," she smiled. "My, what beautiful china." The cup and saucer were ivory colored fine bone china with a thin gold band around the rims and patterned with tiny green ivy.

"I don't remember us having any dishes like that?" questioned Rick.

"We don't," agreed Sam. "I bought it off of the lieutenant's wife when we were at the fort, trying to sound casual about it. Thought Kathryn ought to have something pretty of her own for coffee since we all do."

Kathryn lifted the cup and admired it and was very touched. "You bought this just for me?"

"Sure did. And I tell ya I was worried sick about that delicate thing bein' packed and carried in my saddlebags. I figured it'd end up in about a dozen pieces for I got it home. Sure was relieved it wasn't."

"What a nice thing to do." Kathryn glanced down at the cup then looked into the big man's eyes and saw tenderness and caring. "Thank you. I will treasure this, always."

They had a light supper of chicken soup and corn bread. After they were finished Jim volunteered his services for clean up and Pedro followed Rick out to check on the horses and lock up the big barn. Kathryn asked Sam if there was any tea in the house and he retrieved a canister of chamomile tea from the pantry and filled the metal kettle with water and set it upon the stove.

"Would you call me please when it starts to boil...I'm going to unpack a few more things?"

"Sure will," said Sam.

Kathryn closed her bedroom door. She got out her muff, sleeping cap and bloomers and removed the money, spreading it out on the bed. She counted what was left, then took $500 and tucked it away in her jewelry box; the remainder, about $6,000, for deposit in the bank. She heard Sam call and went to have her tea.

Jim and Sam watched her as she measured out the leaves into a small strainer

Sam handed her and set it in her new cup, then filled it with the water from the hot kettle.

"That smells kinda good," Jim commented. "Think I'll have me some too. By the time Jim found him a clean cup Kathryn had removed her leaves from the strainer.

"Would you like me to make it for you?" she offered.

"Sure. If ya wanna?" Sam was frowning as she made the second cup and stroked his beard.

"By golly, I haven't had any of that tea for a long time. Think I'll have me a cup, too.

As they were having their tea, Kathryn asked each how they came to meet and work for her uncle. She listened with interest as Sam told her how he'd met Rick at Fort Garland, when for a short time he had been serving as scout for an expedition party, and her uncle had been delivering steers. And, Jim shared with excitement the glorious days of the Pikes Peak gold mining.

Rick and Pedro stomped their feet on the porch and came in from tending to chores. Rick was pleased to see that Kathryn, Sam and Jim were hitting it off, for it seemed so by their happy chatter and smiling faces. Jim got up and excused himself saying he wanted to read in bed for a while and Sam said good-night and left for the bunkhouse. Pedro left without a word by the back door. Kathryn wondered why he said nothing but dismissed it from her mind.

She got up and brewed herself one more cup of tea and took it to drink in the chair by the small fire. Rick was at his desk going through some papers and as she gazed about the room she felt a glow of contentment.

Presently, Pedro reentered through the front door concealing something behind his back. Shyly, he approached her. "Senorita Kathryn, I make something for you for your room...while I was laid up from the gunshot." He handed her a flat package wrapped in newspaper.

"Why, Pedro, what a nice surprise." she said as she accepted the package. Carefully she unwrapped it. Curious, Rick craned his head to see what she was getting because he knew of nothing Pedro had been working on for Kathryn.

"Oh, this is beautiful. It really is." Bashfully, Pedro turned his head away and scuffed his boot along the floor. "You have real talent, Pedro." She studied and admired it and asked, "Is this from this front porch?"

"Si."

Rick could stand the suspense no longer. "What did you get?" he asked, walking over to have a look. Kathryn tilted the picture so he could see the beautiful watercolor painting of the front of the ranch. "Pedro," he exclaimed, "that is very, very good. I knew you had some paints and painted some things, although you've never shown them off...but I had no idea you had so much talent."

Pedro looked embarrassed over all the compliments and fuss, but finally popped out with, "Do you really like it? Do you really think it is good?"

"Yes," said Kathryn, "it is truly a wonderful painting...and I love it. I can hardly wait to have it hanging up in my room. Thank you for painting this for me. And, I will treasure this always, too." Pedro smiled broadly and announced he was going to bed now. He strolled out of the door with a swing to his body.

Rick lit his pipe and sat down opposite Kathryn. He puffed and studied her a moment before he spoke. "Kathryn, what happened in Lexington?"

She had been expecting this and she was prepared, but telling him was going to be difficult. It were as though her mother was defiling Rick's brother John's memory. "What happened," she began, "was Phillip Wheeler, Attorney Phillip Wheeler."

"Is that the attorney your mother retained after old Forrest passed away?"

"Yes. Well, at first things remained as usual, but it wasn't long before his business meetings with mother became more frequent...at the mill, at home, then even at restaurants in the evenings." She stopped and sipped her tea and went on. "As you know I was managing the mill, and I felt good about being successful and doing well the things Daddy had taught me. I felt he would be proud of me helping to promote and see that his business was carried on as I knew he would wish. But, dear Phillip convinced mother that the mill would prosper so much better with a man at the controls and suggested one of his business associates, Achibald Denten, would be the perfect man for the job." She paused again for a sip and Rick lit his pipe. "At first," she continued, "Mother, was hesitant and balked, but the day came when she advised me that it would no longer be necessary for me to work at my office at the mill, and if there was anything personal of mine there that I should go bring it home. I was upset and angry and she attempted to shame me by pointing out that proper ladies should not compete in the business world, most especially, if there was no necessity for them to be working outside of the home. She also inferred that perhaps the reason I wasn't yet married was due to my working in a man's field...and that decent men of good breeding would not want a woman like me for a wife. She suggested further that I keep away from the mill and became more involved in charity and civic affairs, and start hob-nobbing, again, with the girls in the proper social circles, as I once had."

Kathryn looked at the expression of astonishment on her uncle's face while he scratched the stem of his pipe on the back of his neck. She took another sip of tea and Rick said, "Go on" as if mesmerized by her story.

"Basically, I was forced to stay home and I hated it. But, I hated it more when Mother and Phillip began seeing each other socially. He was constantly at the house and kept persuading Mother to make drastic changes in the operations of all Daddy's businesses and holdings. It seemed as though suddenly he was in command and in charge of everything. Then, he stopped conferring with Mother about changes. Instead he informed her what decisions and changes he had already implemented."

"How did you find out all of this," asked Rick, captivated by these revelations.

"I listened outside the drawing room, or any other room when I had the opportunity and kept in close contact, discreetly, with Gorden Hamilton, president of the board of Barnett Enterprises," she said.

"Then, I finally confronted Mother. I told her she was giving all her power and authority and decision making over to Philip and that soon she would lose all control, even her personal business, such as the management and running of the house."

"What happened then?"

"She got very angry and things were quite tense for a long time. Nothing concerning Phillip changed, it just got worse. But, it became unbearable when Mother announced she and Phillip were going to marry." She looked at her uncle and his mind was absorbing all she was telling him with a pained expression on his face.

"Go on," he urged, stroking his jaw and weighing her words.

"Phillip did not like me, needless to say, nor I him. Uncle Richard, I truly believe that he does not love Mother. I believe he wanted to marry her for the wealth and prestige it would afford him. He suspected I knew the real truth, for he was cold and evasive toward me. The more I tried to make Mother see how things actually were, the closer she seemed to be with Phillip. I was feeling like an intruder, an unwelcome guest in my own home." She blinked back tears in remembering how it had been.

"Finally, I could stand it no longer. That's when I wired you," she smiled, sadly.

"Are they married now?" Rick asked, trying to disguise his resentment for his dead brother's widow.

"I imagine. They had a wedding date set for two weeks after I left. I couldn't bear to stay for that."

"I understand now why you had to leave. I'm glad you chose to come here, with me. We are family, dear niece," he smiled. His face grew serious, again. "You still have shares in the stock, don't you?" She nodded, yes.

"I have a suggestion."

"Whats that?"

"First, are you acquainted with a reputable lawyer back there?"

"Yes, Attorney Francis Chamberlain."

"Can you trust him?"

"Yes, I believe I can, and he has a fine reputation."

"When you feel up to it, I suggest you write and retain him to watch over your interests, and to keep you informed of what is happening. That way you can keep your hand in things without having to be there." Rick got up and poured himself a cup of coffee, kept hot on the stove. "Want some?" he offered.

"No, thank you. I'll make myself another cup of tea."

Standing together by the stove, Rick summed up his feelings. "I am sorry your own mother put you through all this heartache, but I'm also glad it brought you out here, because I've missed you, and I love you." He gave her a little hug, then said, "As far as Jolene, I am sorry she's been duped. Let's pray she will discover the truth and come to her senses."

They went back to their chairs and Rick bent over and removed his boots and wiggled his toes in front of the fire. "Ah, that feels good."

Kathryn looked at her rugged handsome uncle and she knew she was going to be happy living here with him, because he was so much like her father had been. She knew she would be included in the goings on here and that she would enjoy learning about ranch life.

They talked a while longer until Rick remarked that Kathryn looked tired and she ought to go to bed. "You are right, I am very tired." She stood up and headed for the back door."

"Wait," Rick jumped up and took the lantern off the hook beside the door and lit it for her. "Don't want you getting lost in the dark," he chuckled.

Kathryn made her way to the outhouse, holding the lantern in her outstretched arm. The sound of an owl from a tree branch nearby startled her and she remembered the conversation over dinner, about bears, coyotes and a mountain lion and she hastily completed her mission. She glanced nervously over her shoulders as she scurried back into the safety of the house.

She rinsed out her cup and saucer and set it to the back of the plank board counter, then kissed her uncle good-night on the cheek. She took Pedro's painting and walked quietly down the hall so as not to disturb Jim. Quickly, she undressed and slipped into her nightgown. As she lay in the dark, her room and the ranch, all seemed strange, yet, familiar at the same tine, and she wondered how this could be? She began her prayers, thanking God for her blessings and asking that He help Clint recover, and fell asleep.

Lying on his back wrapped snuggly under his quilt, Jim stared out at the night through his window above his bed. His eyes skipped from one star to another in his limited view of the sky. Faint glimmers of moonlight cast a soft glow over the objects in his room diverting him momentarily. The silhouetted shapes of his large bureau, hump-back trunk, chair and small desk took on a different appearance. He studied the rough outline of the door, keenly aware that Kathryn's room stood across the hall on the other side and his stomach knotted. Quickly, his gaze shot back to the stars and with great difficulty Jim tried to make his logical mind sort out his quarreling emotions. He was happy for his long-time friend, Rick, that his niece was here to live with him and was now safe. She was beautiful and had a manner about her that drew attention to long forgotten feelings. She was the kind of girl he had wished he had found first. But, Kathryn was already spoken for, that was bluntly and painfully clear. He felt a stab of jealous pain and decided he did not like Clint Davis for meeting her first and winning her love. A private part in his heart felt lonely and hopeless and a bit foolish. He glanced once more at the door that separated him from Kathryn. How close, he thought, yet, so far from his reach.

Jim rolled heavily onto his stomach and doubled up his fist and smashed at his pillow. Frustrated and exhausted his sandy-haired head flopped down and sunk into the fluffed up feather pillow and he went to sleep.

Rick sat and watched the fire in the stillness of the night. He mulled over what Kathryn had revealed, and wondered if there was any way he could help Jolene. Evidently, this Wheeler dude was a real slick, smooth talking hombre. And, poor Jolene, she had always been naive. John had protected her, perhaps too much. Something made Rick fear for her, in what way he wasn't sure, just an uneasy feeling. He felt loyalty to his dead brother's family and decided he would write Jolene a letter, a friendly letter to remain in touch. For somehow, sometime down the road, he believed she would be needing his help. He tapped out the ashes from his pipe over the fire and made his trip outside. Upon returning, he laid another log on the embers and turned in for the night.

22

*T*he men were unusually quiet the next morning so they wouldn't wake Kathryn. The sun was not up yet, and outside it was black as pitch. Huddled around the table they whispered as they talked out the plans of the day while they chowed down their breakfast.

"So, it's settled," said Rick in a hushed tone. "Sam'll stay, fix Kathryn her breakfast and keep her company." The rest nodded in agreement. "I just hope it got delivered," he added, wistfully. "Herman told me last week it should be delivered...today. We'll just have to assume it is."

"Sure hope so, Senor Rick," whispered Pedro, excitedly.

The sun was beginning to rise when they went out to do chores and saddle up the horses. They slipped back in the house for a warmer-up of coffee then strapped on their guns, put on coats and hats and tiptoed out the door. They walked the horses until it was safe to make more noise, then cantered to Villa Grove.

Sam cleaned up and fed the two dogs, then set things out to prepare for Kathryn's breakfast. This done he settled comfortably by the fire with his feet propped up reading the paper and waited for Kathryn to rise.

Kathryn woke and lay in a drowsy state under the warm covers in her new comfortable bed. She looked around and loved her room. It was like her old room, in a way, and that helped. Clint came to her mind and she worried how he was this morning. She wondered if she were on his mind. She hoped so because she could not get him out of hers. Even when she was doing other things he seemed to remain in the forefront of her thoughts and actions, a constant. She was missing his company, his twinkling eyes, mustached smile and the private wink he used to give her...remembering the wink brought a smile to her face.

She was wide-awake now and alert and got up and made her bed. She slipped out of her nightgown and prepared to wash. In doing so she passed by the mirror and paused. She wandered, if by some chance, she looked any different, if she showed any telltale signs that revealed she was no longer a virgin. She wondered if her mother could tell if she saw her. She stared at her face and couldn't tell one way or the other.

When she applied the salve, the feeling of shame came back as vivid as before, and she tried to shake the horror of that nightmare that threatened again to consume her. Why had this happened to her, she asked? What had she done to be punished that way? She felt the guilt and shame as acutely as she had that day, and a cold sweat crept over her body. She sat down on the green chair to gather her wits and strength. The mental image of the Indian's dark face hovering over hers had drained her momentarily, both physically and emotionally. She sucked in deep breaths to relax. Absently her hand parted the curtains and she looked out, soaking up the sights and reminded herself that she had to put that all behind her, and go on. This was today, not that horrible day. Today was new, and different. Today was a new beginning. She sat a while and let that sink in and slowly the corners of her mouth began to turn up a little and she rose from her chair and finished dressing into her pink skirt and white blouse.

She opened her door and entered the silent hall and wondered why it was so quiet. Upon reaching the kitchen she was surprised to see only Sam. "Good morning, Sam," she greeted him. "Where is everyone else?"

"That depends...probably be back round dinner tine, I 'spect. Missy, c'mon over where it's warm and I'll bring ya yer coffee."

Taking a chair by the fire she watched Sam pour her coffee in her new cup and the appearance of this earthy mountain man holding on to the dainty little cup and saucer so carefully nudged her heart. The coffee was delivered across the room without a drop being spilled.

"Thank you, Sam," she said, taking hold of the saucer.

"How bout some buckwheat flapjacks?" proposed Sam.

"That sounds yummy."

Sam reheated the big cast iron skillet and poured the batter in, softly whistling to himself as he waited for the tiny bubbles to appear on the top, signaling him to flip them over. He pulled the small pan of bacon from the oven he'd kept warming and began fixing up her plate.

"Breakfast is ready, Missy." Kathryn moved to the table and he joined her with his coffee. She looked at him with a puzzled look on her face.

"Sam, how come you call me Missy?"

"Just a nickname. When I found ya, you were like a frightened little girl...a little missy. Ya don't, mind, do ya?"

"No...I rather like it. Makes me feel special...closer to you...in a way. Mmmm, these are delicious flapjacks," she praised. "So's the bacon. Crunchy, just like I like it. You're a wonderful cook."

"Thanks," he blushed, modestly.

"Maybe you could teach me to cook sometime...do you think'?"

"You don't know how to cook?" he brightened, remembering the ribbing he'd gotten from Jim.

"No, I'm ashamed to say. We always had a wonderful cook...Franny." Closing her eyes a moment she pictured dear plump Franny, and missed her. "Franny would let me help," she told him, "like roll out cookie dough and press the cut-outs on them, or snap beans with her, shell peas, shuck corn...things like that. I used to spend part of my day visiting in the kitchen with her...we'd talk and I'd watch her prepare deliciously wonderful things." Her mind drifted off, bringing back those times and a sweet sorrow shown on her face.

"Want seconds?" Sam offered, awkwardly, knowing she felt homesick.

"Oh, no thank you. I'm full...everything tasted so good."

"Anything special you want to do this morning?" he asked, with interest.

"Yes," she brightened, "stroll around outside. I haven't had a chance to really get a good look at things."

"Let me clean this up and set the stew in the oven for dinner and we'll take a tour," he said, with pep in his step.

Kathryn went out the back and looked around at the surroundings in the daylight and laughed at herself for being so skittish the night before. The ground off the back porch was flat and sunny and grass struggled to grow, in spots. A little farther over were aspen trees and pinon and some stately ponderosa. She admired the coziness and beauty as she made her way down the gravel stone path to the privy situated back and to the far right from the house.

The privy was large, as far as privies went, and not as dark. This one had a small window at either side, and the traditional half-moon cut out high on the door for light and ventilation. But, Kathryn acknowledged, the smells were just as potent and she made haste in the time spent within its confines.

She listened to the birds chirping as she went back toward the house. Perched in the branches of a pinon, sassy long-tailed, black and white magpies scolded and near a bush she spotted a pair of small mountain bluebirds carrying straw for a nest. The blue on the male was such a bright pretty blue and she stopped and watched them for a few moments. A branch snapped off to her right and she turned nearly motionless in that direction in time to see a large doe and her spotted fawn scamper off. She watched them until they were out of sight then looked back toward the large log house to see Sam smiling at her from the doorway.

"This is a wonderful place back here," she beamed.

"I kinda like it, too. See up over there?" he pointed to the far left. She followed with her eyes where the ground sloped upward, thick with trees, then flattened out again. "Up there's a rock, almost like a bench with a back, and it's a good place to go to do serious thinking...or jist git away fer a while."

"Is that where you go?"

"Ya. I do...'specially when things git ta crowdin in on me. Wanna go see it?"

"Oh, yes. Just let me get my shawl, it's a little chilly yet."

"Better put on sturdier shoes than those dainties, if ya got some," he cautioned.

"I do." Kathryn went back inside and changed into her riding boots and grabbed her black shawl.

Sam was sitting on the back porch along with Zeke and Jasper when she returned. Kathryn and Sam began climbing up the gradual incline with the two dogs charging on ahead of them, and soon they arrived at the top of the knoll. There was a different view from all directions and each one splendid in its own way, with rolling hills or flatland against the background of bold mountain vistas. The sky was robin's egg blue this morning and was dabbled with a few wispy clouds that were nudged along by a gentle breeze.

Back a few feet from where they stood was a weird shaped rock, like a bench, beneath a tall aspen, with a mighty ponderosa close by.

"G 'won and give it a try," urged Sam. Kathryn went over and eased herself down and leaned back. It was a secluded setting, yet it was like a throne with a view.

"I can see why you like coming up here," she observed. "It's so peaceful and private...and thoughtfully beautiful." Kathryn studied the unique formations of rocks with shades of colors embedded in the layers against the backdrop of spreading pines.

Sam was watching her take in the terrain. "Amazing what nature can do, huh?"

"Yes. It's hard to find words to describe how it makes me feel, other than small and somewhat insignificant...for everything is so impressive, or large and commanding or colored so magnificently."

They remained silent for a while just enjoying the calm and the view. Sam had been wrestling with his mind and wasn't sure if he should even bring the subject up, but, him being the only one on the ranch that knew, made him feel somehow responsible now for her well being, and a little protective. "Kathryn?" he said. "Are ya feelin all right...now, after what happened to ya?"

She blushed a little due to the subject matter and cast her eyes down. "Yes, I think so. But, when it comes to mind, it's like it's happening all over again."

He knelt down beside her and patted her shoulder and waited a bit to speak. "Ya haven't told Rick yet, have you?"

"No. Maybe I should have said something that night...now...I don't know how to tell him or how to even bring it up. The whole thing is so embarrassing."

"I think you should tell him...I think he should know," Sam said sincerely.

She looked at him in surprise. "You do? Why?"

"'Cause that way the sheriff and us could put an all out effort into findin that scum and make him pay for what he done to you. And...Rick loves you. And, I think he has the right to be concerned and involved not with jist the good stuff in yer life, but... all the stuff."

"I just can't help but feel that people will look at me funny and treat me differently...if they knew. Either by pitying me or loathing."

"Is that how ya think I treat ya?" Sam replied, with a hurt in his voice.

"Oh, no. I didn't mean you, Sam. You've been wonderful to me."

"Well...then tell me this. Are ya uncomfortable bein around me...knowin I know?" he questioned.

"Actually, no. Maybe cause you found and rescued me, and the kind feeling way you acted toward me. I guess it's having other people know exactly what hideous thing was done...I don't know...it's hard to explain."

"I think I know what ya mean. But, Missy, everyone doesn't have to know...and shouldn't know, 'cause it's none of their business, or their concern...but, you are Rick's concern...do ya understand what I mean?"

She thought a moment before answering. "Yes, I think I know what you mean." Neither spoke for a while. They just sat quietly in thought and enjoyed the beauty and solitude together.

Kathryn touched his arm. "Sam, I will try to find the right time to tell Uncle Richard."

Sam nodded, "Good. Wanna climb down and walk around to the front?" he suggested.

"Yes. I haven't seen the buildings or gotten close to the horses yet."

Rounding the left side of the house they crossed over to one of the large corrals where some of Rick's horses were penned. Inside roaming about were some fine fleshed Morgans, as well as quarter horses. Curious, a few sauntered up to the fence and Kathryn and Sam talked to each one they patted and stroked.

"Mighty fine animals these are," commented Kathryn.

"Sure are," agreed Sam. "Yer uncle sets great store by these critters." Snowflake, Sam's mule, was in a corral further back and upon hearing his voice let loose with a loud, harsh bray. "Howdy, Snowflake," hollered Sam.

"How come you ride a mule instead of a horse?" she asked.

"Well, Missy, I think they're a whole lot more surefooted and dependable up in the mountains and less skittish. I need that when I'm trappin and huntin."

"There's two other ones. Are they yours, too?"

"Yup. I use Ginger and Thunder fer packing in. Well, ya wanna see where Pedro and me hang our hats?" She nodded and followed Sam to the bunkhouse situated left of the barn. He opened the door to a large room divided into three sections. At the far end stood a set of simple-made bunk beds, one atop the other, and both mattresses were covered with a grey, wool blanket. Next to the beds was a long plank board with numerous wooden pegs, used for hanging clothes, holsters and hats.

The other two sections, closer to the door, contained two large regular beds topped with handmade patchwork quilts and two wooden closet-like structures separating the two areas. On Pedro's side, next to his bed, was a wicker chair with a colorful woven poncho draped over the back and next to that was propped a guitar. On top of a small table stood a terra cotta statue of the Virgin Mary with a votive candle on its base, some paints, brushes and a Bible. On the wall hung a Winchester rifle near an ornately carved wooden crucifix. On the floor beside his bed, was placed a bright patterned woven rug in shades of yellow, orange, brown, white and red.

To the right, a distinct cultural contrast. Above Sam's bed hung a large stuffed buffalo head and on the wall next to the side was a tanned deer hide painted with Indian symbols, and a rawhide Indian drum suspended from a nail. At the end of the wall, a gun rack was mounted, holding two Hawken plains rifles and a 12-gauge shotgun, a bow and a quiver of arrows. On his table lay a long knife with a fancy carved handle made from an elk horn. Completing the setting, a bearskin rug sprawled on the floor by the side of his bed.

"What an interesting room," exclaimed Kathryn.

"Well, this bunkhouse is a bit nicer than some I've seen," admitted Sam. "Most are just plain, like it is on the other end there. It was Rick's idea to build a nicer place for his help, or fer folks that stayed here."

They strolled back toward the house and Sam said, "I could go for another cup a coffee...how bout you?"

"Yes, I'd like one. Why don't we sit out on the porch to drink it," she suggested.

"Sounds like a fine idea. You sit and I'll bring em out."

She settled down on the long bench placed not far from her bedroom window and presently Sam came out carrying their cups. "After we're finished would you please hang a picture for me?" asked Kathryn.

"The one Pedro gave you?"

"Yes. I was surprised and really touched that he painted that especially for me. And you know, he has some real talent with art."

"Yah, I think so, too. But he paints, then tucks em away. I'm probably one of the only ones here who's ever seen most of em."

Kathryn selected a place on the wall for her picture so that she could view it from her chair by the window. After Sam had driven the nail and the pretty watercolor hung, she took out the photographs she brought from home. She showed Sam the one of her mother and father taken on their wedding day.

Holding the picture Sam observed, "Rick sure looks a lot like his brother." His eyes remained riveted on her mother, studying her striking features and warm smile.

"Beautiful, isn't she," remarked Kathryn, looking over his shoulder.

She sure enough is. Fact, she's about the prettiest woman I've ever seen. I always hoped to find a lady who looked like that...in my dreams of course," he quickly added. "But, knowin what I look like...and the kind of life I lead...well, I know fer certain no lady like this'd look twice or want ta share my kinda life." He spoke matter of factly, but there was a tone of longing and loneliness that crept out. He carefully handed Kathryn the picture and left the room saying he had to check on dinner.

Kathryn held the picture and her heart went out to Sam. He was such a gentle, caring soul, but he probably was right. Most women, like her mother, would not pay serious attention to Sam, especially without knowing what a decent person he was. She placed the picture on the top of the trunk beside her baby picture and another one of herself taken on her twentieth birthday astride Jackson. She finished arranging and tidying her room and sat by the window to begin a letter to Franny. The sound of riders coming caught her ear and she set down her pen and paper.

"Kathryn," called Sam, "I think ya oughta come here... quick.," Puzzled, Kathryn ran from her room to the kitchen where Sam waited holding open the door. They stepped out onto the porch and Sam pointed down the road.

Coming toward them pranced a handsome, white horse, his head erect showing off a silky flowing mane and plumed tail and pulling a four wheeled, two-seater black carriage. Seated smartly in the driver's seat was her Uncle Richard with a big grin. Bringing up the rear rode Jim and Pedro leading Rick's horse, Charlie.

'Whoa," commanded Rick, and the sleek white horse stopped as neat as you please in front of the porch steps. Rick jumped out and removed his hat with a sweeping gesture toward the horse and announced, "Sir Frosty, I would like you to meet your new owner, Kathryn. Kathryn, dear niece, your carriage awaits."

"Mine? This is mine?" she questioned, her eyes wide with disbelief.

"Yup." answered Rick.

She scurried off the porch and ran to get a closer look at the horse and stroked its neck affectionately as she talked in soothing tones.

"C'mon, git in and I'll give you a demonstration ride round the yard, then you can have a go at it," offered Rick. Giddily, she was helped into the swanky carriage by Sam while Jim and Pedro looked on. Rick drove her up, then back down the yard and stopped again by the porch. "Now, its yer turn," he said, and he handed her the reins. Smiling, she waved to Sam, Pedro and Jim who stood grinning at her from the porch. She clucked her tongue and away they went.

The white horse picked up his hoofs and set them down nobly as he pulled his new mistress up and down the drive and a turn around the yard. Kathryn tightened the reins and the handsome steed halted in front of the steps and she was nearly breathless with excitement.

"Oh, Uncle Richard. What a wonderful present." She turned around to check out the buggy. It was made of fine grade, black leather, and the top was collapsible so one could ride in the open air.

"I absolutely adore it. And, my horse. What a fine, handsome animal he is. But, why did you go and do all this for me?" she questioned.

"Kathryn, I just couldn't see you having to ride to the funeral tomorrow in my old, beat up buckboard. Its' fine for haulin, but not for a lady, especially if yer dressed up fancy and all. Besides, I figured you needed something of yer own to get around in, and a horse of yer own to ride."

She threw her arms around her uncle's neck and gave him a big hug. "Thank you. Oh, thank you. I know I will have a wonderful time driving him into town...to see Clint...and to visit with Claudette...oh, and I will be able to bring her out here to visit me now, too." Rick grinned and nodded as she went on. "And, I can do shopping...and oh, so many things."

That evening Kathryn asked her uncle to come to her room before he retired for the night. She waited nervously behind her closed door until she finally heard his soft knock. She invited him to sit in the bigger chair by the window and she took the small red velvet chair by her dressing table.

Rick eased his body into the comfortable chair and asked, "What is it, Kathryn? Are you sorry you came here to the ranch? Is something wrong?" He felt anxious for her manner was quiet and unfamiliar.

"No, nothing like that," she answered, swallowing hard. "I'm very happy I came here. I love the ranch. It is just that there is something I've not told you...that I must. And, now I feel it's time you knew." Rick sat stiff and alert hanging on her words. "It's something I didn't want anyone to know, but Sam convinced me, today, that I should tell you."

"What does Sam know, that I don't?" he asked, curiously.

"He wouldn't know anything, if he hadn't been the one who found me," she admitted. Rick narrowed his eyes searching his mind and her face for clues of what she could possibly tell him.

Kathryn gulped as she straightened herself up and found her courage to tell her uncle the unspeakable. "Uncle Richard," she began, her voice quivering, "that... Indian...didn't just rob and shoot people...he...he raped me." There, she'd said it. She told. Her body began to tremble as she waited for her uncle's response.

Rick reacted as if he'd been shot. His expression turned from intense interest to one of absolute anguish and his head dropped as he expelled a guttural moan, then, sputtered inaudible phrases. His head raised, inch by inch, and tears of grief trickled down his twisted face.

"No. Oh, my God, no. Oooooh, Kathryn." His outstretched arms shook as he reached out for her. Kathryn hastened to the refuge of sympathy and understanding in the comfort of her Uncle Richard's embrace.

23

Jim had Sir Frosty harnessed up to Kathryn's new carriage and waiting in front of the door when Kathryn and Rick stepped out. Rick helped her in, then took the reins as he drove her to Villa Grove for the funeral. The ride would have been a delight due to the warm temperature and calm breeze except far the fact that today was the day to bury Will and say goodbye.

Rick stopped the carriage in front of the San Luis Hotel and helped Kathryn alight amidst curious stares from on-lookers. Having packed no mourning clothes, Kathryn wore a dark burgundy dress and long veiled bonnet. Rick escorted her to the

Bartholomews' room and Claudette greeted them sedately and invited them in.

"I want you to ride with us to the funeral, Claudette, so we came a little early to make sure you hadn't already gone," said Kathryn.

"Thank you. I had planned on riding with Peter Voris, but attending with a friend is so much better. I will send the bell boy over to inform Peter of my change in plans."

Harold greeted them and said, "Please do have a seat." He was partially dressed in trousers and a loose fitting shirt seated at the window, positioned for a view of the procession when it passed by. Claudette, also lacking mourning attire, wore a chocolate brown dress and matching hat with veil.

"You are looking much better, Harold," Kathryn noted.

"I'm feeling much better, too, except for this wretched pain in my shoulder. But Doctor Lawton says I am progressing well. In fact, he insists that in another day I should begin to take short strolls."

"That's good news, Harold," said Rick, smiling. "Doc's a good man, and he'll have you out and about in no time, you'll see."

Rick and Harold engaged in a business conversation while Kathryn explained to Claudette some of the plans for the funeral.

The three arrived at Luigi's parlor shortly before ten, the designated time. Kathryn sent Rick in to confer with the undertaker while she and Claudette waited outside in the carriage.

"What a fine carriage you have, Kathryn," admired Claudette.

"Thank you. It is grand, isn't it?" she beamed. "Uncle Richard surprised me with it yesterday."

"Perhaps he could tell Harold where he purchased it because we will be needing one too. And, also, a hauling wagon for the big things we purchase for our home."

"I'll have Uncle Richard speak to Harold."

"Thank you, I appreciate that."

Another carriage pulled to a stop behind them and they turned around to see Peter Voris, the stage manager, and an elderly distinguished man who turned out to be the Reverend Small. Soon, several men on horseback and a small buggy drove up and assembled on the street in front of the parlor. Among familiar faces were Sheriff McCain and his two deputies, Art and Paul. The attractive lady driving the buggy drove up alongside of Kathryn, followed by Buck. "Kathryn, I'd like you to meet my wife, Ruth," spoke the sheriff. The women exchanged greetings, then, Peter walked over to Kathryn's carriage.

"I want to express mine and everyone else's appreciation and gratitude for your hand in arranging Will's funeral. You are truly a caring and remarkable woman," said Peter, solemnly.

"Thank you," answered Kathryn, modestly.

Attention was all turned to the side of the building when a steady "rap, tap, rapa-tap-tap," was heard as a soldier beating rhythmically on a snare drum marched out ahead of the small, narrow wagon, driven by Luigi, bearing Will's coffin. Rick scurried out and took his place in the carriage and turned it around and got behind the wagon. Peter Voris with Reverend Small followed them, then Mrs. McCain, and the horsemen who formed a column of twos and slowly the procession made its way down the street in the direction of Doc Lawton's.

On cue, Luigi reined to a stop in front of the office. Peter led the minister over to Luigi's wagon and helped him up. Reverend Small stood silent a moment. He nodded an acknowledgement to Clint and Manuel, propped-up in their hospital beds that had been rolled outside on the walk, then nodded to the rest of the crowd. He cleared his throat and spoke in a deep, resonant voice.

"The Lord giveth...The Lord taketh away. Will Carson has been taken away... from us, back to our Lord. And, we are gathered here today to say farewell to our good friend, Will...who died in service to his fellow man. Will Carson was a good man, a loyal friend, and a worthy employee. He shall be missed by all who were privileged to know him. Let us bow our heads and pray."

Kathryn exchanged sorrowful looks with Clint and Manuel before they lowered their heads. At the utterings of "Amens," Alice Truitt began to sing:

> Rock of Ages, cleft for me,
> Let me hide myself in Thee,
> Let the water and the blood
> From Thy riven side which flowed,
> Be of sin, the double cure
> Cleanse me from its guilt and power.

Alice motioned for the others to join in and the air was filled with their voices singing the last verse:

> While I draw this fleeting breath,
> When my eyes shall close in death,

When I soar to worlds unknown,
See Thee on Thy judgment throne,
Rock of Ages, cleft for me,
Let me hide myself in Thee. Amen.

Sniffing and nose blowing were heard throughout the song, and when it ended the drum began its beat and they moved on slowly down the street, pausing briefly at the corner so that Harold could view the coffin from his window and word his own farewell.

At the cemetery the coffin was lowered into the ground and they grouped together and recited The Lord's Prayer.

Kathryn could not help but notice the two fresh mounds of soil down to the far right, and knew they were the graves of two of the men who had attacked the stage. They were responsible for Will's death and the others' injuries, and she turned back and looked down at Will's coffin, in tears.

The three women tossed purple mums, provided by Luigi, on top of the coffin and the rest tossed in a handful of dirt as Reverend Small recited "Ashes to ashes, Dust to dust." The service was ended with singing:

Shall we gather at the river,
Where bright angel's feet have trod;
With its crystal tide forever
Flowing by the throne of God?
Yes, we'll gather at the river,
The beautiful, the beautiful river
Gather with the Saints at the river,
That flows by the throne of God. Amen.

The group departed and went their separate ways. Rick drove the carriage over to the Doc's so they might visit and console Clint and Manuel. The two were tucked back in their beds and Clint reached his hand out to Kathryn with a look of gratitude in his eyes. "Kathryn, thank you. It was a beautiful service."

"Si, thank you, Senorita Kathryn...very mucho, for what you did for our Will." His sad eyes were red and swollen in tears and Claudette went to him. She took his hands in hers and spoke to him with comforting words.

Then she said, "Harold sends his condolences and says to tell you he misses his new friend." Manuel smiled broadly. "And as soon as he is able, he will be over to visit with you."

"That is good of him," choked Manuel.

"Say, that's quite a rig ya got there, gal," said Clint to Kathryn. "And a real looker for a horse."

"Yes, aren't they wonderful, Uncle Richard got them for me yesterday. Now, I will be able to visit you as often as I can," she smiled.

"Tell him I said thanks for that, too," he grinned back.

Doc and Rick came into the room. After Rick had spoken to Clint and Manuel, extending his sympathy and wishing them speedy recoveries, Doc remarked that his two patients had probably had enough stress for one day and they needed to get some rest, and apologized for having to ask them all to leave.

"When will ya be back, Kathryn?" Clint asked eagerly.

"In a few days," she promised. "I need to do some shopping and I will make a day of it." She turned to Claudette. "Would you like to go shopping with me on Friday and have lunch?"

"Why, yes. I would love to."

Doc interrupted the ladies' conversation. "Excuse me, Kathryn, but I must tell you that by Friday Clint and Manuel will both be over at Mrs. Truitt's, so you will be able to visit then there in much nicer surroundings than a cold impersonal office," he smiled.

"Well, then, we will come and visit you there," Kathryn said to Clint. "And, perhaps Harold will be able to come along, too."

"Yes, that would be nice," agreed Claudette. "He has been most anxious to visit with you both."

"And, I think the outing would do Harold a lot of good," inserted Doc.

"Then it's settled, said Kathryn. "We will be over at Mrs. Truitt's after our lunch, say about two-thirty, if one of you would be so kind as to inform her of our impending visit."

Kathryn kissed Clint goodbye and Claudette patted Manuel's arm and they departed.

The two women made their plans on the drive back to the hotel where they dropped off Claudette. As they rounded the corner to head out of town, Kathryn had a saddened expression on her face.

"What's wrong, Kathryn?" asked Rick.

"I'm going to miss Claudette when Harold is well, and they move up to Gunnison."

"I know ya will, Honey. She's been a real friend and I think she is good for you... and you for her." Rick put his arm around Kathryn and gave her an understanding hug, then handed her the reins. He was impressed with the effortless way she handled the horse. They talked of many things on the way back to the ranch, but in Rick's mind he couldn't shake the anger he harbored for the Indian who had caused so much pain to those he loved and cared for...Kathryn, Pedro...and Kathryn's new friends and beau. So now he had to find this elusive man and bring him to justice.

24

Kathryn adjusted to the rigors and routine of ranch life. She rose early now to eat breakfast with the men, and not once did Jim Miller forget and appear in his woolies in those early morning hours. That first morning, after Kathryn had arrived, Jim presented himself quite tidily, and the other men had to suppress knowing grins so as not to embarrass Jim or Kathryn.

Kathryn began pitching in with the house cleaning, meal serving and clean-up. She stayed in the kitchen when Sam began preparations for meals to watch and listen to him explain the hows and wherefores of his cooking secrets.

This morning they all sat grouped around the kitchen table talking and drinking coffee after one of Sam's hearty breakfasts. Sam gulped down the last in his cup, stood and announced, "Today's wash day. If any of ya wants yers done, ya better git it out to the basket on the porch."

Chairs were abandoned as the men hustled for their bedrooms, and soon the large basket was overflowing with sheets, trousers, shirts, socks and underwear. Kathryn modestly stuffed her soiled intimate belongings into a pillowcase and set them apart from the basket. Sam was alone in the kitchen when Kathryn offered her help with the washing, but added, "If it is all right, I would prefer to do my own things by myself."

Having a notion that women were bashful about their garments and things, Sam replied, "Sure don't see why not, Missy. I'll git stuff set up an show you how it's done here...then I'll leave ya to yer self."

Doing laundry was going to be a new experience for Kathryn, however; for back in Lexington the servants always did the family wash. Being warm outside now, Sam hauled the large copper boiler out from the storage room and took it out to the side of the house and placed it on a grate set over a blazing fire. He grabbed a bucket and toted water from the well to fill the boiler and one of the nearby washtubs set on a crude wooden stand. When the water had heated, he transferred some of it into the other tub and replaced what he'd taken out. This done, he went and fetched the mound of dirty clothes off the porch and Kathryn followed, carrying her bulging pillowcase.

Sam put the lye soap in the boiler and instructed Kathryn. "Ya put yer clothes in here first," he said, pointing to the boiler, "an then, stir em around with this here wooden stick." He produced the four-foot stick leaning against the stand, and continued. "Then, ya lift em out and drop em inta the warm water tub, so ya can use the scrub board." He pointed to a ridged metal sheet set in a wood frame, with two short legs, resting against the stand. "Ya use that to rub the dirt out," he explained. "Then ya pull each piece out and wring it out and put it in the rinse water tub. Stir em around a little...wring em out again, and put em in this here basket." Take yer basket over to the line and hang em there to dry." He pointed to a long rope stretched between the house and tied to a sturdy branch of an aspen tree. He frowned at Kathryn, then smiled as he asked, "Think yer ready ta try it?"

"Yes...I think so," Kathryn answered, a bit apprehensively.

"I'm goin in now to git some bread and biscuits made. Let me know when yer done so's I kin git my pile of stuff washed," Sam said as he headed for the house.

Kathryn watched Sam lumber up the steps and into the house and heard the door clap shut. Her eyes roamed over the kettles of water and her bulging case of soiled clothes. She sucked in her breath and rolled up the sleeves on her cotton print dress and dove her hands into the case, pulling garments out and dropping them into the copper kettle.

Pantalets, camisoles, petticoats, stockings and a corset bobbed and swam around in the large heated receptacle as she slowly stirred the water. After a bit she started fishing them out, piece by piece with the long stick and dropped them into the warm water tub. She set the scrub board against the side and worked each garment up and down the ridges, then plopped them into the cold rinse water tub. By now her dress was wet across her chest, sticking to her skin, and her sleeves were sopped and dripped on the ground. She stopped and rolled her sleeves up farther, well past her elbows and proceeded until all her things were piled in the basket. Kathryn picked up the basket and trudged over to the clothesline and realized how wet her shoes had gotten when they made shucking sounds with each step. She had finished hanging up her things and stepped back to observe her work and was embarrassed to see her pantalets flapping in the breeze like silly white flags. Quickly, she spun around and nervously glanced about to see if any of the men were riding in from the far range. Luckily, there was no one in sight and she felt relieved, until she remembered that Sam would be out to do the washing for the rest of them. Well, she reasoned, there was not much she could do about that, and she guessed that this was something she must accept and get used to. She just hoped that the wind dried her things quickly so they weren't hanging there so long, and could snatch them from the line. She held out her hands. They were red and cold. Her dress was completely wet down to the bottom. She ran into the house to change and tell Sam that she was finished.

The aroma of fresh baking dough smelled divine as she stepped into the kitchen and Kathryn realized that she had worked up an appetite doing her laundry. Sam grinned at the state of her appearance as he turned from the counter.

"Looks like ya really got inta yer work," he chuckled. Kathryn smirked as she looked down at herself and reached up to tuck in a straggling hunk of damp hair and laughed along with him.

"I must really look a fright. I best get out of these wet things."

"There'll be a hot cinnamon roll for you when yer done...if ya want one," offered Sam.

"Oh, yes. I sure do want one. I'll try and hurry," she called over her shoulder as she made a beeline for her room.

After stripping off her wet things she decided to put on her riding trousers and a white cotton blouse. No sense in ruining another dress, she thought. Besides, when her clothes were dry and put away she would have time to spend with Sir Frosty. She carried her wet clothes back outside and hung them up with the others and returned to the kitchen.

Sam was grinning at her when she reentered the house. "I must say," he commented, "that ya sure do look different in that git-up."

Kathryn glanced down at her trousers and boots, then back up at Sam with a frown on her face. "Are you saying I look unbecoming?" she asked quizzically.

"Oh no, Missy. I didn't mean that at all. Different...like cute," he grinned.

"You don't think they make me look like a boy or something, do you?"

Sam shook his head and his beard jiggled. He laughed as he said, "You sure don't look like a boy...believe me."

Kathryn gave a shy smile then sat dawn at her place where one of Sam's large, warm cinnamon-nut rolls sat waiting for her on a plate. A small mound of butter perched on top was melting and dripping down the sides.

Sam poured them each a cup of coffee and sat down to join her with a hot roll of his own.

"Mmm. These are wonderful," she mumbled, with her mouth full and butter running off her chin.

"Glad ya like em. They're one of my favorite things to eat, for sweets. Unless ya count fresh blueberry pie with churned ice cream," he added, smacking his lips.

They finished their treats and Kathryn went back outside with Sam. He to do his wash, and she to take hers off the line, as they were now dry, and to make room for the men's clothes. Feeling a bit self-conscious, Kathryn unpinned her garments as quickly as possible. When the last piece was folded and placed in the basket, she looked up at Sam who was smiling at her as he wrung out a pair of trousers. She knew he was amused at her modesty and hastily retreated into the house with her basket. She set her clothes down on her bed and went out to give the basket back to Sam.

"Do you want any help?" she offered.

"Sure, if ya'd like to. Why don't ya take this basket of trousers and git them hung up while I git these shirts rinsed and squeezed out?"

For the rest of the time Kathryn hung the clothes and Sam washed them and finally the job was finished. "What say," suggested Sam, "while the clothes are drying we saddle up Sir Frosty, an I'll throw one on ol' Snowflake and we take us a little ride?"

"I'd like that a lot," answered Kathryn happily. She ran to the corral and coaxed Sir Frosty over to the gate to put on a bridle, then led him out. Sam found a blanket and saddle and helped her put them on the patient animal. While Sam went to fetch Snowflake, Kathryn stroked the beautiful white horse's neck and talked to him, and as if he understood her words of affection, he nuzzled her arm.

When Sam came riding from around the barn Kathryn placed her foot into the stirrup and swung her leg gracefully over the saddle. Comfortably settled upon Sir Frosty's back, a big smile shown on her face. What a wonderful feeling it was, she thought, to be up on a horse again. And, on my very own, too, thanks to Uncle Richard.

"Ya sit there like ya were born in a saddle," said Sam. "Ya look right comfortable. C'mon, let's go ride out to the east range and find the others."

Sam turned his mule and led the way and Kathryn gently nudged Sir Frosty and followed Sam around the large corral and out into the open field. The sun was overhead, the sky was cloudless while a cool, steady breeze kept them from being too warm. They cantered side-by-side past cows and young spring calves and onto a trail that skirted one of the hills. The scent of wild flowers and moist pine needles permeated the air, adding to the beauty and joy of Kathryn's first ride on Sir Frosty. She looked over at big Sam riding on his mule, and although she adored this gentle, kind man, she couldn't help but wish that it were Clint riding alongside of her, gazing together at the lush countryside, sharing their feelings and thoughts, and planning their future.

At the far west end of the ranch, hidden from view by rolling hills and clusters of trees, another scene less friendly took place. Blackhorse had heard Zeb coming, and two other riders, and reluctantly he started slowly down the steep incline to meet them.

Zeb Taylor bellowed loudly out to Blackhorse, who was now in sight and half way down the side. "Hurry up and git yer sorry, red hide down here."

Blackhorse stiffened at the command and vowed that one day he would get even with this insulting, disgusting, fat man, then continued the climb down.

Zeb heaved his bulbous flesh out of the saddle and waddled over to a large rock and plopped himself down. He gestured for Jake and Bart to dismount and ordered them all to come over.

"Blackhorse...I hate to have ya leave yer guarding post," said Zeb, "but things have taken a bad turn." He spit a brown stream of tobacco juice which landed near Blackhorse's moccasin. Blackhorse bristled inside and pretended he hadn't noticed. "From my sources in town," Zeb continued, "yer the only one they're looking for, now...fer robbin the stage and killin that guard. Yer gonna havta git out of here for the summer...too much activity this time a year. And I can't take the chance of you gittin caught and anyone connecting me with you." He reached in his pocket and thrust some money at Blackhorse. "Here's a couple a hundred dollars...yer share of the take from the heist...that oughta tide ya over til fall. Now, git yer stuff outa the cave and cover up the entrance. Jake, you an Bart start tearin down the corral. I don't want any tracks or traces left around here to draw any suspicion. Now, allaya hurry yer asses so's we can git the hell outer here."

Jake and Bart took Blackhorse's Paint out of the corral and tied him to a tree and began to dismantle the long poles that were staked and tied together. They dragged them out of the canyon and disposed of them by scattering them amongst the brush in a heavily wooded area.

Blackhorse grudgingly made the climb back to his cave. With painful deliberation he began to gather up what few possessions he owned and stuffed most of them inside a large deerhide bag. He took his shovel and threw dirt on top of his small burning fire then doused it with some water. He stood silent and gazed about at the darkened interior of the cave feeling lost and confused. He didn't want to abandon what he had come to believe...that this cave was his home. His mind began to race. He didn't know where he was going to go. He grabbed the bag and took it out, then broke branches and bush stems and placed then across the opening. In a saddened state he descended the steep grade, bending branches as he went to disguise his path. He reached the bottom and got his bridle and put it on his pony, tossed the blanket across its back and then the sack.

All, except Zeb, took pine boughs and dragged them over the corral area and paths. They backed out of the entrance to the canyon to remove any traces of foot and hoof tracks. Zeb inspected the area, then ordered everyone to mount up.

Bart, Jake and Zeb banded together and watched Blackhorse as he gracefully swung his taut bronze body onto his paint pony and slowly and gently guided him toward the clearing.

"Ya stay outer sight, hear?...Least till September," barked Zeb. "Then report to me when ya come back." He spit and wiped his brown chin with his sleeve and added, "Best ya head north and stay there...til the heat is off." The three turned their mounts away and headed back over the boundary line and back onto Zeb's property without a wave or a look back.

Blackhorse sat stiffly on his pony and watched the departing threesome, and pondered this sudden change and turn of events. Something was wrong. Zeb was up to something. He knew it, he could feel it. But what? He knew Zeb still craved to have Rick's land, more so, the gold that was on it. Blackhorse could not believe that Zeb would leave the cave unguarded and just sit idly by all summer without doing something to turn things in his favor. Blackhorse had felt that he was an important part in Zeb's scheme. Why this change of heart? No answer came. Not yet. He slowly turned his pony and headed northwest through the pines.

In the doctor's office at Villa Grove Clint Davis wore a happy, grateful smile when the doc informed him how well his wounds were healing. He had been envious of Manuel, who was getting around now with just the aid of a cane. Manuel's arm wound gave him little trouble, and only the thigh of his left leg caused him some discomfort. The problem with Clint's wound, the doc said, was that part of his lung had been damaged and to remove the bullet had been a very delicate operation. But, he assured him; however, that with proper rest and taking things slow he would be as good as new.

The front door opened and shut and Peter Voris, from the stage depot came in. Peter walked over and shook Clint and Manuel's hands, gently. "I must say," he smiled, "that you two are looking a whole lot healthier than the night they brought you in. I have to admit I was really concerned that we were going to lose you both. Now," he grinned, "it appears that my worries were unfounded. Of course, we owe most of the credit to this fine gentleman here." He patted Doc Lawton gingerly on the back, then went on. "Fellows, one of the reasons I stopped in, other than a friendly call, is this. You know the company hired on men temporarily to fill your places, but now they want to know just when they can expect you to return to work."

Clint and Manuel exchanged looks with the doc for help with an answer. "Well, Peter," said Doc, "I can only take a good guess. Manuel could go back in say...two weeks, give or take, if he keeps on the way he's been going. Clint, here, well...I'd like to make sure he is fully recovered before putting himself in danger of infection. He had a nasty wound, you know, so I'd have to say at lest three weeks."

Clint and Manuel did not look too happy over the news, nor did Peter. They both were too active to sit around for too long, and confinement did not agree with either of them.

"Well, I'll write and tell them what you've said, Doc." Peter turned to the two men and said, "I would like to stay and visit a while with you fellows but there's a stage due in shortly. See you, later." He hurried out the door just as Alice Truitt came in.

"Hello, Alice," greeted Bob Lawton. "Are you all ready for your star boarders?"

"Oh my, yes. And, I must say, I am looking forward to having people in the house again. I don't know why I didn't think of doing this sooner. I guess I have Rick Barnett to thank, in a way. The day he visited I realized how much extra room and space I had in my home, and how empty it really was," she said in a thoughtful tone. New things and a different way of life were finally opening up for the lonely widow and she smiled, knowingly, to herself.

Art and Paul came in after bringing Doc's buggy around to the front. With their assistance, Clint and Manuel were taken out to Doc's and Alice's buggies for the drive, with Alice leading the way.

A large room on the first floor had been turned into a sick room, with two beds and comfortable chairs. Alice had also redone the bedrooms upstairs with plans to take in borders.

Doc made sure his patients were comfortably situated in their respective new beds and settled in. He gave Alice specific instructions for each man and told her to get in touch immediately if there were any problems. He said his goodbyes and joined Art and Paul who were waiting for him by his buggy.

Doc turned the buggy around and headed back to the center of town. He dropped Art and Paul off at Buck's office, then, drove to his own. It was going to seem strange without Clint and Manuel there. He had grown close to them and enjoyed their company. They were indeed two very interesting individuals, he reflected. He had derived great satisfaction from their late night conversations, about life, living, and other topics of various scope and interest.

Doc stripped the two empty beds and cleaned up the room and his mind wandered to Rick's niece, Kathryn, and he wondered how she was. He would know the answer on Friday when she came in for her check-up. Leaning on the broom he became acutely aware of how alone he really was. He wished that he had found a nice wife, like Buck's Ruth. He pulled his watch from his vest pocket and flipped open the lid. It was almost five-thirty. Doc slid the watch back and set the broom aside and grabbed his hat and coat. On foot he headed for the Jackrabbit Saloon for a leisurely, relaxing drink and catch up on the latest news before going over to the McCains' for supper.

25

*R*ick Barnett walked softly down the hall in his stocking feet so as not to awaken Kathryn, or Jim, for that matter. Although, to wake Jim, even if he clomped in his boots outside his door, would be a long shot.

He tossed a couple of chunks of wood onto the remaining burnt ambers and fired up the stove. What little coffee remained was lukewarm and he quickly made a fresh pot and set it on to brew.

Rick slumped down in his chair, lit his pipe and found himself staring out at the still, black morning through the window above the sink. He had always thought himself a strong man emotionally, as well as physically. He had been able to accept and endure hardships, especially in his lean years, and could deal with disappointments and setbacks. Long, grueling days and nights in the saddle while riding the range had given him the opportunity to know himself honestly, as he was, and to be at peace within and with his Maker. But now his emotions and mind were not at peace and he couldn't quell those disturbing feelings or let go of his inner rage.

Hearing about the hideous attack upon his Kathryn had had a deep effect on him, which left him feeling powerless, yet hostile. What puzzled him was, who was that Indian? Where had he come from? Who knew him? Where had he gone? He and Buck knew Zeb had lied, for some time ago, others had said they had seen an Indian in Zeb's company, and hanging around the ranch. But, at the time, no one thought much about it, because Zeb attracted all sorts of unusual characters. Yet, Zeb swears no Indian works for him and that he "wouldn't want one of those sneaky redskins around."

Pipe in hand, Rick leaned back in his chair and absently scratched his chest through his black flannel shirt as he slowly and deliberately began to sort out questions and examined what knowledge he had. About a month ago, the Indian was on his property...and shot Pedro, and at him. But for what reason? What had brought him there, to that spot? Where had he disappeared to between then and the stage hold-up...and attacking Kathryn. The hold-up. How did the Indian tie in with Zeb's old hands, that Zeb claims up and quit on him? How had they met, if not for Zeb? Rick's mind flashed back to the hold-up. Why had Kathryn been singled out? She said that the Indian had asked if she were a Barnett. A niece of Rick Barnett. Now, why would that be important to an Indian? But, it would be important to Zeb. Zeb, who wanted Rick's property. Rick thought back to the day that Pedro was shot and Zeb's gravel voice echoed in his mind. "One day, one day...my friend...you will live to regret your words. You will also regret not selling to me when I give you a fair price. You can count on that."

Rick jumped up and slammed his fist on the table. "That's gotta be it. There's gotta be a connection between that day and Kathryn's attack. And the answers lie with Zeb and on this land. But, what, and why?" He paced back and forth then abruptly sat down and thrust his feet into his boots. He slapped his old grey Stetson over his uncombed dark hair, grabbed his coat and charged in frustration out the door.

Later, Rick waited at the table for Kathryn to finish getting herself ready for their trip into town. It was already eight o'clock and Jim waited out front with Charlie, and Sir Frosty hitched to the carriage. Earlier, Rick had curried and groomed both horses before breakfast and now he was anxious to get to town to confer with Sheriff Buck.

"Are you about ready, Kathryn?" he called for the second time.

"Just about," came the answer from her room. Kathryn gathered up the money she intended to deposit in the bank and stuffed it into her handbag making the sides bulge out. She checked her appearance a final time in the mirror and straightened her blue bonnet, then quickly scurried down the hall to her impatiently waiting uncle.

Jim happily assisted Kathryn into her carriage as Rick swung his well-built frame onto Charlie.

Jim waved goodbye, wishing that he were going along, but he knew Kathryn would be seeing Clint, besides doing lady things with her friend, Claudette.

As they traveled side-by-side down the long road, Rick asked, "Well, how do you like living in Colorado, so far...all things considered?"

Kathryn turned and smiled broadly. "I love the ranch. And, I enjoy living there, I really do. And, the countryside and beautiful scenery makes each day something special to get up to. But, I will admit that there are times I feel homesick for Lexington...and Mother, of course. But, I know, had I stayed, I would have become even more bitter and unhappy than I was. I am glad I am here. I truly am. I just wish that so much tragedy hadn't happened. It affected so many people, and it certainly made my arrival a dismal affair."

"I'll say," agreed Rick. "But, I'm sure glad yer here, now...and safe. I like having you around, Kathryn. The fellows do, too." Kathryn gave Rick a big, happy smile.

"Let's get our plans straight so we can meet when we're through," suggested Rick, as they reached the outskirts of Villa Grove.

"Well first," answered Kathryn, "I need to go to the bank, then I will be picking up Claudette to do some shopping. After that, we are having lunch at the hotel. Then, we're driving over to Mrs. Truitt's to see Clint," she beamed. "Oh, would you like to join us for lunch...around one o'clock'? I think Harold will be there."

"Sure, I'd like that. Besides, I had planned on meeting with Harold later this morning while you gals were doing your shopping. I'll bring Harold down and we can meet you in the dining room."

"I didn't know you were meeting with Harold," said Kathryn.

"Yes. He asked me to get some business information to him the last time we talked," answered Rick, not daring to reveal any more.

"Oh, Uncle Richard, I meant to ask you earlier. The saddle I've been using is fine and all, but I really would like to buy one of my own. Do you suppose there would be time before we come home for you to help me pick one out?"

"Don't see why we can't fit it in," smiled Rick.

Kathryn pulled her carriage to a stop in front of the bank and Rick waved goodbye and said, "See ya around one." Rick went to post the letter he had written to his sister-in-law, Jolene, then on to Buck's office for a visit.

Kathryn entered the bank and asked to see the president. After she introduced herself, she informed him that she wished to open a savings account. Mr. Eldredge about fell over himself, when she handed him the $6,000 for her first deposit. He tried to conceal his eager delight after she divulged that money from her trust account would be transferred to his bank from Lexington. Before departing, she told Mr. Eldredge that she would be most interested in investing some of her money locally, and asked that he keep her posted on any sound prospects.

Mr. Eldredge not only escorted her to the front door, but all the way to her carriage and helped her step in. His day had begun on a dismal note, but he reentered the bank smiling and light-hearted.

Kathryn clucked her tongue as she touched the reins gently and turned Sir Frosty onto the street and headed directly over to Dr. Lawton's office. She had not mentioned to anyone that she was going to have a check-up. It was too personal, which was why she chose to keep this visit private.

She was relieved that the office was empty except for the doctor who greeted her as she stepped in. "It's good to see you again, Kathryn, he smiled. "And, I must say you are looking very lovely today."

"Why, thank you."

"Have you been having any problems?" he inquired.

"No, none at all."

"Well, good, but, I would like to examine you just the same to be sure there is no threat of infection. If you will go into that room," he pointed to a closed door, "to remove your undergarments, then, please get on the examining table...I will be in shortly."

Kathryn was not happy about any part of this, but complied with the doctor's request.

"Well, Kathryn. You have healed quite nicely. I don't think it would hurt to keep applying the salve for another couple of days. And, unless you have any other problems, you won't have to came back in."

Kathryn was relieved to hear that. She quickly redressed after the doctor stepped out so she could hurry to meet Claudette. She said goodbye to Dr. Lawton and drove her carriage over to the San Luis Hotel.

Claudette was sitting on one of the velvet sofas in the lobby when Kathryn entered the building. They hugged and hurried out to do their shopping.

Brows raised and inquisitive eyes watched as the two attractive and stylishly dressed newcomers drove down the street and pulled up in front of the mercantile in Kathryn's smart carriage.

Inside the large store Kathryn and Claudette began looking at the wide variety and array of goods stacked on floor-to-ceiling shelves and displayed along the aisles on the bare hardwood floor. One section devoted to the lady customers carried dozens of bolts of various fabrics for dressmaking and the like, and bins of sewing supplies. There was also ready-made clothing for men, women and children. Another part of the store carried housewares with everything imaginable for running a home. And, there were shelves of shoes and boots to fit everyone, and many styles of cowboy hats as well as colorful ladies bonnets. There were plain sunbonnets in calicos or tiny gingham checks, and a small sampling of showy, fashionable silks trimmed with decorative feathers, plumes or ribbons.

Kathryn and Claudette fingered and examined the merchandise they admired, and talked and giggled as they selected for purchase items they needed, or what pleased their fancy. They tried on different bonnets and each selected a new one, adding to their already full arms. They took their things up to the long counter and informed the clerk they were not finished yet, and would he please begin itemizing what they already had when he was free. Then Kathryn dragged Claudette over to the shelves containing trousers, insisting that for riding, which Claudette admitted she did and loved, that trousers were the best thing to wear, especially in chilly weather.

"But, I've always worn a riding skirt," protested Claudette. "It just seems a little manish and improper."

"Oh, nonsense," argued Kathryn. "And besides, you don't have to wear them around town. You can bring them along when you come out to the ranch and change into them there. Just find a pair that fits...here, here's a nice grey wool and they look like they'd fit, too."

A tape measure hung from a nail nearby and Claudette reluctantly took it down and ran the tape around the inside of the waist then down the inseam.

"Well?" asked Kathryn.

"I suppose they would fit," she answered. "Oh, why not. I'll buy them. But, Harold will be truly shocked...I assure you." The two giggled, imagining Harold's reaction.

Kathryn eyed the boots. "I think I'm going to get me another pair. These are made so much different than the ones I have." She sat on the chair provided, removed her shoes and began trying on cowboy styled boots. Claudette watched, holding onto her trousers and handbag, but soon she was beside Kathryn in the next chair trying on boots too. They each found a pair they liked and that fit comfortably and put their shoes back on.

Kathryn moved over to the stacks of shirts and began rummaging. She turned around to show two flannel ones, for herself and for her friend. Instead, she burst out laughing at the sight of Claudette standing before her in her lovely mauve dress, wearing a silly grin and a wide-brimmed, high crowned, brown felt cowboy hat pulled down to her eyes.

"Howdy," Claudette said, in a deep voice.

"Howdy...to you, too," greeted Kathryn in a lower voice. They both laughed and Kathryn took off her bonnet and put on a black cowboy hat. The two laughed loudly as they tried on different styles and colors, and checked how they looked in the round mirror on the shelf.

Unbeknownst to them, a woman standing by the pickle barrel observed their unlady-like behavior with narrowed eyes of disdain. She was joined by an acquaintance who had finished at the counter.

"Who are those ridiculous women?" whispered the acquaintance, Mrs. Appleby.

"Dear, I have no idea," retorted Mrs. Eldredge, tight-lipped.

"Well...I have heard that there are some new people in town," confided Mrs. Appleby, "that came in on the stage that was robbed. You don't suppose they could be the ones?"

"I really wouldn't know. But, I did hear," Mrs. Eldredge whispered, "that one of the women that came on the stage was supposed to be a relative of Richard Barnett, that wealthy rancher. A niece from back east, I believe. And, I understand, from the gossip, she comes from money."

"Well, I'm sure neither of those women could be from money with such undignified behavior". Mrs. Appleby sized-up the two in question as they continued their playful diversion.

"You are probably right. Oh, did you happen to take a gander at the carriage parked out on the street?"

"Deary, one could not help but see it."

"Who do you suppose owns it?" wondered Mrs. Eldredge. "Surely not one of them," she added, tightening her nostrils and casting her eyes upward.

"I have no idea. But, earlier when I came into town I noticed it parked in front of your husband's bank," confided Mrs. Appleby.

"You don't say."

They quickly hushed as the two women moved toward the counter, their arms heavy laden with trousers, hats and boots, adding them to their existing pile of merchandise. Their bonnets now properly in place on their well coiffed hair and their decorum more subdued, they waited patiently and quietly while the clerk figured out their bill.

"I will pay for my purchases today," Kathryn addressed the clerk, "but in the future I would like them on a charge account, if that is satisfactory with you. It would help me immensely when I have to have my uncle or anyone else pick articles up for me."

"I, also would like to open an account," spoke Claudette with authority.

"Here," said Tommy, the elderly clerk and owner. "Just fill out your names on this paper for my records."

Tommy wrapped their purchases in plain brown paper and whacked on a bell that brought a young box-boy from the back to assist the ladies with their bundles.

Tommy picked up the papers. His eyes stared in surprise as he read the names, then cleared his throat to say, "Today your total comes to $52.50, Mrs. Bartholomew, and yours, Miss Barnett...comes to $69.30."

The other two women had craned their necks so as to catch the names. Their chins dropped as they exchanged horrified looks.

Quietly, but hastily, they left the Mercantile and scurried over to the San Luis Hotel to discuss their newfound information over tea.

Harold and Rick stood up from the table when Claudette and Kathryn entered the dining room in the San Luis Hotel and pulled out chairs to seat them.

In a corner near the front window Mrs. Appleby nudged Mrs. Eldredge, and with burning curiosity watched and tried to catch the conversation from the intriguing and fashionable newcomers. Not wanting to miss a thing, they summoned a waiter to bring then the luncheon special, giving them an excuse for lingering.

The foursome placed their food orders and Kathryn and Claudette related how much fun they had had shopping. When their meal was served Harold gave Rick a sly look. Rick pursed his lips suppressing a grin and nodded a "go ahead" to Harold.

"Claudette," began Harold. "I believe you will be interested in what I'm about to say."

She turned and gave her husband her full attention and asked with alarm in her voice, "What is it, Harold?"

"Well," he answered, looking into her eyes. "After careful deliberation and doing some checking around...I have come to an important conclusion. And, if it's agreeable to you, and meets with your approval...instead of moving on up to Gunnison, I think we should stay here, here in this area, to make our home."

Claudette blinked and her mouth froze partially open. She turned to Kathryn, then Rick and back to Harold. "Really, we could stay here?"

"Yes," he smiled. "I have put some money down on a rather large section of land for mining speculation over by Kerber Creek. The only thing you need to decide is...do you want to live here in Villa Grove or Bonanza, nearer to Kathryn?"

Claudette reached across the table and clasped Harold's hand, with tears brimming in her happy eyes. "Oh, Harold," she cried. "You have made me so happy... so very happy. Thank you." She took a handkerchief from her handbag and dabbed at escaping tears and smiled at Kathryn with a questioning look. Kathryn did not move or say a word and waited with anticipation.

"Harold," announced Claudette, "I'd like it so much better if we could move to Bonanza...nearer Kathryn."

"Oh, Claudette," exclaimed Kathryn. "I was hoping you would say that." She gently embraced her dear friend and the hug was returned.

"When will we be moving?" asked Claudette, eagerly.

"As soon as the house is built, which means my dear, that after we return from visiting Clint and Manuel, we must sit down and decide on a house plan. And, next week we will drive out and select a home site."

"Oh, you will be out our way," said Kathryn, excitedly. "Please say you will have time to come and see the ranch and visit. And perhaps stay for supper," she added, looking at Rick, who nodded in agreement.

Claudette's eyes begged a yes answer from Harold. He smiled and replied, "We will make time."

After their lunch was finished the four rose to leave and Rick made sure that Harold and Claudette went ahead of he and Kathryn out of the door.

The two nosey women parted the sheer curtains, slightly, and peered out to witness Mrs. Bartholomew throw her arms around her husband as she gazed upon her new carriage parked at the front entrance. It had been delivered by Herman Schlump from the livery during lunch as a surprise from Harold, thanks to Rick's connections and assistance. Envy was written all over the two gawkers faces as they sized up Mrs. Bartholomew's carriage parked behind Miss Barnett's. An exact match, except instead of a white horse, there was a beautiful chestnut mare.

Rick helped the Bartholomews into Claudette's carriage then Kathryn into hers and climbed in beside her. The two carriages pulled out and drove to the home of Mrs. Truitt.

Kathryn's excitement was fever-pitched. Not only was she going to see Clint, away from the doctor's office, but her new friend was going to be living nearby. How wonderful her life was now unfolding. Rick slid a look at his niece's glowing face and he grinned with pleasure.

Rick liked Harold a lot. They got on quite well in just the short time they had been acquainted during Kathryn's confinement in the hotel, and had been more than happy to help Harold obtain a carriage for his wife.

A buggy, smaller in size, was on its way from Denver for Harold's use. After uprooting his wife and their grueling journey, and staring into the face of death, Harold believed his loving and devoted wife deserved not just her own horse and carriage, but anything else he could do for her to make her life easier and happier in this beautiful; but rugged land.

By the time they reached Mrs. Truitt's Claudette had control of the reins and was smiling proudly, and Harold wore a grateful, pleased look. The four paraded up to the door. Before they could knock the door flew open. Clint stood fully dressed wearing his own familiar clothes and, thought Kathryn, more handsome than ever.

"I thought you'd never git here," exclaimed Clint, eagerly. He stepped aside to let the visitors enter and ushered them into the parlor where Manuel sat puffing away on a cigar, which he extinguished when the ladies entered the room. Alice Truitt came from her kitchen through the dining room and paused under the arch between the parlor.

"Hello...all of you," she said graciously. "Won't you please make yourselves at home. " She turned and went back to the kitchen.

"Ah, my old friend, Harold...and his most beautiful wife," greeted Manuel, "and of course Kathryn and Rick." He kept his eyes fixed on Kathryn. "I am happy you finally got here today. You are all this hombre talked about since morning."

Kathryn blushed and Clint scowled and jabbed Manuel with his elbow.

"Kathryn," asked Clint. "Would you like to go for a short walk and see some of Mrs. Truitt's flowers?"

"Yes, I would love to," beamed Kathryn.

Harold spoke up. "If you don't mind, Kathryn, might I have a word in private with Clint first?"

"Why yes, of course."

Harold led Clint outside. Kathryn took a chair beside Claudette and the two of them admired the lovely furnishings in the room. Rick engaged Manuel in a conversation over his health and recovery. In a little while Clint and Harold reentered the room and Clint escorted Kathryn out to view the flowers.

Arm in arm they strolled around the house admiring the roses, asters and mums. Clint stopped and took Kathryn in his arms and looked her in the eye. "Kathryn, I have some good news ta tell you and I can't keep it to myself a minute longer. My plans have been changed and I think it'll be for the better." Kathryn's eyes widened not knowing what to expect and a little afraid of what she was about to be told.

"Harold made me an interesting business offer. He wants me to go into partnership with him," said Clint, excitement showing in his eyes.

"What kind of business?" asked Kathryn, her curiosity peaking.

"Mining," grinned Clint.

"Mining, around here?"

"Yes, Harold seems to think so, and so do quite a few others who've got preemptions up and down the canyon area in the Kerber Creek district. I have saved some money over the years...it's not a fortune, but I'm going to invest it into partnership with the mining company Harold is going to set up."

"Clint, that's wonderful. Does that mean you won't be driving a stage anymore?"

"Right, and it means I will be settling around here."

"I hope that I will get to see more of you than if you were driving for the stage?"

"More than you'll probably like."

"I doubt that...very much."

"Before we go full swing into the mining, and as soon as he gives the go-ahead, I'll be in charge of building Harold and Claudette's new house and out buildings." he told her. "Harold will be busy working with a geologist on the land he bought for speculation."

"You know about building, too?" asked Kathryn.

"Sure do. Studied architecture back east for a while...but, the west seemed more exciting, so I quit and apprenticed as a driver. And, I can't say I've ever been sorry. I found you, didn't I?"

Kathryn grinned up at him and gave him a playful squeeze. Clint's eyes focused deep into hers as he drew her close. Their lips met and they kissed.

"We'd better go in now," gasped Clint. "I have a hunch Mrs. Truitt's waitin on us, so she can serve tea."

The happy couple entered the house to the buzz of lively conversation, and Rick went to inform Alice that Clint and Kathryn were back.

Alice strolled from the kitchen gently pushing a handsome walnut tea cart displaying a shining silver pot, cups and saucers with yellow rose buds on them and a two-tiered server laden with scrumptious cookies and pastries.

Kathryn and Claudette exchanged knowing looks of pleasure and a fond remembrance of the charming afternoon teas they both had known so well. Alice poured and Claudette passed the cups of hot spicy tea and Kathryn handed each a napkin and offered around the server so that Alice's guests might choose their own treat.

Alice took her chair and beamed with joy as she surveyed her room full of company. She looked at them and spoke. "I can not tell you what a delight it is for me to be entertaining such interesting people. I am so glad you are here in my home."

The group smiled and thanked her. Kathryn sitting between Clint and Manuel sneaked a quick glance at Manuel and was surprised at how comfortably at ease this stout, rugged Mexican appeared balancing the delicate cup and saucer-and nibbling on a sweet. Manuel caught her glance and sensed her thoughts. In a matter-of-fact tone he whispered, "We take tea every afternoon with Mrs. Truitt."

Harold cleared his throat and said, "For me, this wonderful get-together so graciously provided by Mrs. Truitt is truly a cause for celebration. I have, in my opinion, obtained two very trustworthy and intelligent men to help me begin my business here in this area. My good wife desires to make our home here, which is a fine choice. Instead of Gunnison, I believe this area will boom as the new mining mecca in the very near future. And, to have Clint Davis and Manuel Garcia working with me as partner and business associate...How can I fail?" He held up his teacup and toasted the two men.

"I didn't know you were going to be working for Harold too," Kathryn said to Manuel.

"Si. That Harold is a good man. I cannot go through life riding the backs of stages with a gun in my hand...I need to became more...and Harold has given this Mexican a chance to be somebody," he smiled.

The tea party ended and Harold went to shake Clint's hand. "I'll be back in a couple of days with some papers for you both to sign." Harold extended his hand to Manuel and said, "I am proud to have you for a friend and glad that you have decided to join my company. You both concentrate on getting healed up so we can begin our business venture." With "thank you's" to Alice Truitt and "goodbyes" to Rick and Kathryn, the Bartholomews took their leave.

After their departure more goodbyes were said and a special thank you to Mrs. Truitt was expressed by Rick and Kathryn, and Clint walked out with them to the carriage.

Kathryn gathered up her skirt and Clint helped her into the carriage next to Rick. Clint had a twinkle in his eye and he said to Kathryn, "One day soon I will come to visit you."

"I would like that...very much. We could go riding and I could show you Uncle Richard's beautiful ranch."

"You come out just as soon as you're able," offered Rick. "We'd all like your company. In fact, we could come and get you, if you like."

Clint smiled and said, "Thanks, but I've gotta start doin for myself. I'm beginning to feel like a helpless kid...instead of a man...havin to have people lookin after me. I'm not used to being dependent on anyone."

"Sometimes it's necessary," countered Rick, "but I understand how ya feel. I was laid up once, and it gits to ya after a while. We'll be looking forward to your visit whenever ya can make it." Kathryn smiled and nodded. Rick flicked the reins and they began to move.

"Goodbye, Clint," said Kathryn.

"Goodbye," he waved. Clint watched until they were out of sight then went back into the house, a happy man full of hope.

Rick pulled the carriage to a stop at Joe's Harness Shop next to the livery stable. He and Kathryn entered the establishment and Rick introduced Old Joe to his niece and told him that she needed a saddle.

Old Joe, a thick muscled man in his late fifties was one of the early merchants in the community. He was totally bald and his skin looked too tight for his head, and he walked with a distinct limp from an accident in his youth when his leg got pinned underneath an ore wagon. But Old Joe was not a bitter man. Instead, he was a very jovial sort and got on well with most everyone.

"You'll be wantin a nice looking one," said Old Joe to Kathryn. "Ta look right on yer fine new horse...and I think I got just the one that'll tickle yer fancy." He shuffled around his shop stopping near the back. "Over here," he beckoned.

They followed him over to where he stood pointing and his calloused hand smacked the seat on the one he had in mind. "It's a fine saddle...a Frasier...superb workmanship."

Kathryn checked it over carefully and ran her hand across the seat feeling its soft smoothness. "How much?" she asked.

One-hundred, and I'll throw in a hackamore and a Navaho saddle blanket, your choice of colors."

"That sounds more than fair, Joe," reasoned Kathryn. "May we see the blankets?"

Old Joe led her over to a neatly stacked bunch of colorful woven blankets. Kathryn thumbed through and stopped. "This one, I'll take this one." Old Joe pulled out the one she'd chosen, a grey with black, white and red design. Kathryn fished in her handbag and drew out the money and Rick hauled out Kathryn's purchases and added then to the pile already in the carriage.

They bid Old Joe goodbye and he thanked Kathryn for her business. Rick ran next door to the livery to retrieve Charlie where he'd left him before lunch, and Kathryn took the seat in her carriage. Soon, they were headed back to the ranch after a busy, delightful day.

Jim spotted Rick and Kathryn coming down the road and shouted to Pedro in the barn that they were coming. The sun was beginning to set when at last the two pulled up to the house.

Jim quickly lent a hand helping cart Kathryn's packages into the house. Rick and Pedro tended to Charlie and unhitched Sir Frosty and led them to the barn and into their stalls. The carriage was pushed into its special place in the barn near the double-door opening. Rick lifted the saddle out and Pedro got the bridle and blanket and they placed them in the tack room.

"How handsome Kathryn's fine horse will look with these," admired Pedro.

"He sure will," agreed Rick.

They closed up the barn for the night and hustled into the house and were greeted by the aroma of vegetable beef stew simmering on the stove.

The table was covered with various sized packages and the men curiously gathered around to watch Kathryn open them. She tore open the brown paper on a long bundle revealing several yards of print fabric. Next, she pulled off the lid on the box and held up the pair of brown leather boots.

"What a nice pair of boots," whistled Jim.

"Sure are," agreed the rest in unison.

She pulled the paper off the next package. "Hey, those look like men's trousers," blurted out Pedro, without thinking.

Kathryn blushed, a little. "They are, Pedro. But, they're for me...to make it easier to do outside chores...and for riding."

"Si, I understand," said Pedro, lowering his eyes. "Those long dresses you ladies wear must get in your way. Is that not so?"

"Si, that's so," laughed Kathryn and the rest joined in.

From the shape of a box in front of her the men knew it contained a hat and watched as she removed the top. They were not too surprised when she pulled out a cowboy hat and put it on.

"Well, how do I look?" she asked, with a smile on her face. It was a light tan and contrasted nicely with her dark hair, and the shape proved very becoming.

"I would say you look right smart," offered Rick.

Sam and Pedro nodded and agreed.

"You look very nice in that kind of hat," complimented Jim as he studied the new look it gave her.

Still wearing the hat she opened the package that contained a blue flannel bib front shirt.

"That's a pretty color blue," Sam said. "Hold it up and let's see how it's gonna look." Kathryn obliged.

"It's a good color for you, there's no doubt," complimented Jim.

"Why, thank you, Jim," smiled Kathryn.

She removed the cowboy hat and picked up the last large package. As she opened the second box she said, "In case you think I will only be dressing in men's styled clothing...this may change your minds." She carefully spread apart the tissue and lifted out a fancy pink bonnet with dyed-to-match decorative feathers and deep pink ribbon ties. She placed it on her head and there was no doubt in anyone's mind that she still intended to present herself in womanly fashion when it suited her.

"That is one of the prettiest little hats I've ever seen," said Sam.

Rick looked at her and said, "You look right beautiful in that, Kathryn."

"She sure does, boss," agreed Pedro.

Jim couldn't say what he thought without bringing attention to himself, so he just smiled and said nothing.

"What's all these little packages?" asked Pedro.

"Here," said Kathryn. "You can open this one." She tossed him a small, bulging sack.

"Hoarhound candy," beamed Pedro.

"Help yourself and pass it around," offered Kathryn. "Here, Sam, you can open this one." She handed him another sack.

"Tea," he grinned. He pulled out a decorated tin of imported Earl Grey tea. "I git the hint, we'll be drinking more tea around here," Sam chuckled, and he set it on the counter near Kathryn's fancy cup and saucer.

"The rest of this stuff is just sewing things, like needles and thread and an embroidery hoop, and scissors, so I can get back to my sewing and needle-point, and a couple of bandanas."

She surveyed the table. "I guess I had better put these things away so we can use the table for supper."

"Here, I'll help," offered Jim first. He held out his arms and Kathryn loaded them up. Rick watched as the two trudged down the hall to Kathryn's room, then got himself a cup of coffee, lit his pipe and sat in his chair by the fire to wait for supper.

26

Kathryn was awake and up earlier than usual. After lighting the lamp she walked across her room, parted the pink organdy curtains and peeked out. In the direction of the Sangre de Cristos the grey light of dawn was intruding upon the blackness of night. She watched for a moment to see the grey expand and brighten on the horizon, then let go of the curtain and turned away from the window. She carefully made her bed and set out a pretty cotton dress, washed and brushed out her hair. She put on her robe over her nightgown and tiptoed down the hall to get herself a cup of coffee and plan her work schedule before the men were up.

A dim light shown from the kitchen as Kathryn made her way down the hall and she hesitated. She bent around the corner and saw her Uncle Richard puffing on his pipe and staring deep in thought at the dark kitchen window. She wondered what he might be thinking and if she should interrupt him.

Rick turned his head and smiled. "Good morning, Kathryn. I thought I heard you rummaging around. Come have coffee with me." He got up and filled her cup with hot coffee and set it before her and sat down.

"I thought you'd be too excited to sleep late what with Claudette and Harold visiting today," said Rick. "Your first guests an all."

"Our first guests," she corrected. "But, yes...I am excited. It is so beautiful and the house is so nice that I want to show it off and share it." She sipped on her coffee and looked at her uncle. "Do you always get up this early?"

"Yup. I like the dark and the quiet. It's my thinkin time," he smiled.

"Am I disturbing you?" she asked.

"Nope...I was about all thought out anyway. Besides, we don't get much of a chance to be alone, and it's kind of nice sharing the quiet early morning with somebody special."

Kathryn smiled warmly at him for the compliment, then got up and took the lantern from the hook and lit it. "Be right back," she called over her shoulder, as she headed for the outhouse.

Kathryn quickly returned and Rick had refilled her cup. Rick cleared his throat to say, "Kathryn, there's something I've been wantin to talk to you about and I think this might be a good time."

She looked up at him. His expression was serious. "What it is, Uncle Richard?"

"I want you to know that I have a will, and that a copy of it is in my room in a small metal box. In case anything would happen to me, I think you should know where it is and what it says."

"I don't like hearing you speak of something happening to you...it frightens me," she said.

"I'm not tryin to scare you, Kathryn, it just makes good sense ta me to let you know how things stand." Rick sucked in heavily on his pipe and blew out slowly. Kathryn's eyes followed the smoke until it vanished then looked nervously back to her uncle.

"As you might guess," he continued, "being you are my only kin...most of everything I have will belong to you." Kathryn blinked as he went on. "I have a great deal of money in the bank and this land is worth quite a bit...including all the livestock. But, the fellas are like family to me, too, and I have made provisions for them. They are each to receive $5,000...I didn't play favorites," he added. "As this place will be yours, it is your decision whether or not you want to stay here. There's also some mementos to be given to the ones I've written down and named. I'd appreciate it if you'd take care of that, too."

"Of course I will," answered Kathryn, biting on her lower lip.

"Kathryn," spoke Rick, softly. "I don't mean ta upset you. I'm sorry if I did. And, now that you've been told, we can leave the subject alone. We don't have to bring it up again, all right?"

"All right," she sniffled.

"Now, dry those tears and let's see a smile on your pretty face." Her mouth turned up slightly at the corners trying to put out a smile. "That's a start," Rick said. And she broke out in a grin. A scratching at the door startled her until she realized it was Jasper and Zeke.

"I'll let them in," offered Kathryn. The two dogs bounded in happily wagging their tails and she bent down and gave them each some petting. The sound of Sam's heavy steps sounded on the porch. She and the dogs moved aside as Sam opened the door and made his way toward the pot.

"What gits you up so early this morning?" Sam asked as he slugged down some coffee. "Oh, yah...I almost fergot," he winked playfully, "Claudette and Harold are coming out this way today." Sam began getting breakfast on the stove and Kathryn went to get dressed.

As soon as breakfast was finished and dishes done, Kathryn tied up her hair with a bandana and began her cleaning. She swept, dusted and arranged the parlor, then on to her room. After she had swept and straightened the main room and kitchen area, she stepped out the back to shake the small area rugs.

Jim was in charge of scrubbing the seats and the floor of the outhouse and dumping lime down the holes. He heard Kathryn on the back porch and poked his head out and watched her. She noticed him looking and he nodded toward the inside of the outhouse then held his nose with his fingers and grinned. Kathryn laughed at him and hung the rugs over the railing.

"I can't say I envy your job," she called down to him.

"I can sure think of better things I'd rather be doing," he called back.

Kathryn strolled down toward the outhouse and Jim walked over to meet her. "Jim, I would like to take Claudette riding, if there's time. Do you suppose you could pick out a nice gentle horse for her? It's been quite a while since she has ridden, so it should be one that's manageable."

"That's no problem...leave it to me. Soon's I git done here...which can't be too soon," he laughed. "I'll go bring in Rosey...she's a sweety."

"Thank you, Jim...I really appreciate that. Well, I best get back to my cleaning so I can start cooking supper." Kathryn hurried back into the house and Jim followed her in with his eyes.

Kathryn was done with the housework and Sam came in from doing his outdoor tasks and they began preparing the food for their guests.

Through the opened window Pedro yelled in, "Senorita Kathryn...your friends are coming up the drive." Kathryn quickly untied her apron and hung it on a hook and snatched the bandana off her head as she scooted down the hall to her room to fix her hair.

Kathryn then ran out on the porch and down the steps with Sam close behind. She shaded her eyes with her hand and saw the carriage with Claudette handling the reins and Harold sitting beside her.

Everyone had gathered by the time the carriage rolled to a stop by the porch.

"We made it," declared Harold, with a teasing smile for Claudette. "Hellos" and "glad yer heres" were exchanged as Sam helped Claudette from her seat. Jim helped

Pedro unhitch Claudette's chestnut mare and let it into the corral for water and to cool down.

Kathryn asked, "I meant to ask you your horse's name...but with all the excitement...I forgot."

Claudette watched as Pedro led her horse with a watchful eye and a winsome smile. She turned to answer beaming, "Her name is Molly. She is so special and very smart, and oh, so gentle. I just love her." She turned to Rick and said, "I don't know how to thank you for helping Harold pick out that horse for me, and the lovely carriage. You were so kind to do that for us."

"Heck, I was glad to. I'm happy yer so pleased...makes me feel good."

Rick took Harold on a walk around the place to show him the barns, and explain his general set-up. Claudette removed a small valise from the carriage seat and arm in arm she and Kathryn climbed the porch steps.

Jim trotted to catch up to the women. "Kathryn, did you want me to saddle up the horses for you, now?"

The two women exchanged looks and Kathryn answered, "Yes, please, Jim. We'll be ready to go as soon as I've shown Claudette the house and we've changed into our riding clothes."

"They'll be ready when you are," smiled Jim. He turned and headed for the tack room.

"What a nice man he is," remarked Claudette. "He was so kind to me when he and Sam caught up to the stage and got it stopped...and driving us all into town for help. I don't know what we could have done if it hadn't been for those two men comin along when they did."

"I don't know what would have happened to me either," shuddered Kathryn. She opened the door and Claudette stepped inside the ranch house.

"This is such a cozy room," remarked Claudette, gazing about the kitchen and the main room. "And, what an impressive fireplace." She was taken back by the nicely furnished parlor as they proceeded down the hall to Kathryn's room.

"I do declare, Kathryn. Your room is absolutely elegant." Claudette glided into the room turning her head this way and that, marveling at the colors and quality of each piece. "Where on earth did you ever manage to get such elaborate and fine furnishings around here?"

"Uncle Richard had this all set up in here for me before I arrived," answered Kathryn.

"I must say, he has excellent taste."

Kathryn began to lay out her riding clothes and Claudette removed hers from the valise. They helped each other out of their dresses and proceeded to change into their other clothes. Claudette finished buttoning her trousers over her green shirt, then sat in the chair by the window to slip on her brown boots. From the bed she picked up the grey cowboy hat. In front of the mirror she took pains placing it upon her head, just so, then stepped back and studied the results.

"Claudette, you look very nice dressed in those kind of clothes," remarked Kathryn.

"You really think so...you're not just saying that?"

"No, I really mean it." Kathryn put on her light tan hat and glimpsed at herself in the mirror.

"You look very becoming in your clothes, too. That shade of blue for a shirt is a good color for you."

"That's funny...that's the same thing Jim said." Kathryn smiled at Claudette and said, "Are you ready to make your debut?"

"I guess so," she answered, expelling a nervous giggle.

Rick, Harold and Pedro were leaving the barn just as the two women were stepping out of the house. Harold stopped dead on the spot and Rick and Pedro exchanged curious looks wondering what Harold was thinking and what he was going to say, if anything.

Sir Frosty and Rosey were tied and waiting with Jim at the hitching post, not far from the porch steps, and the women walked directly to their mounts unaware of the gawking men.

Jim assisted them into their saddles and handed them their reins. Turning their mounts they walked them across the bare ground heading toward the barn. It was then that Claudette's eyes met Harold's. She walked her horse toward him warily, with a half-smile on her face. Harold stepped firmly forward when she reined to a stop.

"Are those the clothes you bought at the Mercantile...that you wouldn't show me?" he asked, looking her straight in the eye.

"Yes...they are."

"Might I say...you made some practical choices...and my dear, that you look quite fetching," said Harold, with a gleam in his eye.

Claudette gave Harold an endearing look and bent low from the saddle to kiss his cheek.

"Kathryn," said Rick, "please don't ride too far from the house. And, I think it would be wise for you to take your gun along, just to be on the safe side."

"All right," she swung off of her horse and ran back inside to get her father's Colt 44.

Claudette frowned. "Richard, is it dangerous to ride around here?"

"No more than any other place. It's just smart to be prepared and have some protection."

In a couple of minutes Kathryn came out with the holster strapped around her hips and remounted Sir Frosty. Claudette studied the gun then said, "Kathryn, you'll have to teach me how to shoot one of those things."

"Sure, I can do that. We can try it after we've come back from our ride."

"Oh, Lord," cried Harold. "Now my wife's going to become a gun slinger." The men burst out laughing and Claudette scowled over Harold's remark.

"Never mind them," consoled Kathryn. "Come on, let's ride." They pressed their boot heels gently to their horse's sides and cantered across the flat, heading toward the sloping hills to the west.

Kathryn and Claudette followed the winding waters of Little Kerber Creek for a few miles then dismounted. They led their horses over to the cool running stream for a drink and scooped up some in their hands to refresh themselves.

Watching their every move from a secluded, safe distance was Jake and Bart. They were heading back from checking the cave to make sure Blackhorse had not returned when they heard riders coming. Crouching low, they nodded approvingly over the shapes and looks of the two ladies. When at last the women remounted and rode back toward the ranch house, Zeb's men fetched their own horses tied aways away and rode back to report to Zeb.

Later, the conversation was lively over supper of roast venison, ranging from how well Claudette had handled a firearm for the first time, to the perfect location the Bartholomews picked for their building site, to the mining of gold and silver.

Harold began to fatigue and Claudette suggested it was time they drove back to the hotel. Pedro fetched Molly and Jim helped him hitch her up and they led the horse and carriage up near the porch. Rick assisted Claudette, and Harold climbed in beside her. Claudette slipped on her gloves and gingerly picked up the reins.

"You know," quipped Harold, "she has been so delighted over this horse and buggy that she insists on doing all the driving."

"Now, Harold," smiled Claudette, "I am just trying to get the hang of it so I'll feel comfortable to drive by myself."

She gently flicked the reins and they moved on up the driveway, turning to wave at the close-knit group waving goodbye.

Kathryn turned in early that night tired, but happily content. The others had stayed up at Rick's private request. They were grouped around the table, heads bent curiously toward Rick.

"Boys," Rick began, talking in a low voice. "I didn't want to spoil Kathryn's first day of entertaining, which is why I postponed riding outa here until tomorrow."

"What's up, Rick?" questioned Jim.

"I've got same hunches I want to follow up on...at the far west end of my land."

"Where I got shot?" asked Pedro.

"Yah, around in there," Rick nodded.

"You want I should go with you, boss?" Pedro inquired.

"Naw, that won't be necessary. I want to go alone. But, I don't want Kathryn to be alarmed when she sees I'm not here in the morning. Sam, if you'll throw a few biscuits in a bag for me, I'll take em along."

"What do you want us to tell Kathryn?" asked Jim.

"Tell her I'm out ridin fences. Now, I think I'll turn in so I can get an early start." Rick tapped the ashes out of his pipe and set it down, pulled off his boots and padded out of the room. The remaining three exchanged anxious looks, but said nothing. They stood up and rinsed out their cups and went their separate ways to bed.

Blackhorse stopped to set up camp for the night. He secured his pony and selected a spot for his fire. He scooped out a small pit and circled it with rocks gathered from close by. Twigs, dry leaves and pine needles sparked then flared as broken branches were crisscrossed carefully on top. After heaping on more wood, he took his knife and gutted out the freshly caught trout from the cold mountain stream near his camp. He positioned it on sticks over the fire in such a way that he could turn it to cook evenly and leaned back against a rock to wait and think.

From his pouch Blackhorse pulled out the shiny brooch watch and lay it in his palm. Images of the beautiful woman came to his mind. Was she all right, he wondered? Was she recovered from what he had done to her? Was she living with Rick Barnett on his ranch, or did she go somewhere else? He lay his forehead in his other hand and squeezed tightly with his fingers to stop the agonizing questions. But it was no use. She was special to him in ways he didn't understand. The one thing that bothered him the most was, did Zeb still plan on kidnapping her?

His fish was cooked and he slipped the brooch back safely into his pouch. He held the fish with the stick he had inserted through it and pulled off pieces and popped then into his mouth.

With his pony's blanket he made a bed close by the fire and lay down on his back and watched the stars come to life, one by one to decorate the black sky. He thought of his tribe, or what was left of them. He wondered if they still came down this way to hunt and bathe in the sacred springs.

He drifted off to sleep and while he dreamt he had a vision. In his vision the Great Spirit sent his mother. She appeared in white buckskin, her long black hair flowed out around her head and she spoke to him saying, "My son. Find your people...make your peace. Your heart will have no rest until you cleanse yourself and clear your name. Go my son, before it is too late for you." Her shape became faint and she was gone.

Blackhorse woke and sat upright with sweat covering his body although the night was cold. He stared into the small flames of his fire and knew what he must do.

27

Making as little noise as possible, Rick pulled on his boots and slugged down the last of his coffee. Treading softly to the side of the door he slid his holster off the peg. As he strapped it on, his eyes fixed upon Kathryn's gun and holster she'd hung next to his. Absently he reached down and touched the smooth well-worn leather. His teeth bit down on his lip as memories of his dead brother came rushing to his mind. He could picture John smiling at him with this, his favorite gun, strapped around his middle when they engaged in shooting matches against each other.

Rick shook his head and wandered what John would think of his family now. His beloved wife, Jolene, married to a scoundrel, and Kathryn, his pride and joy, living out west with him. Rick knew the anger and rage John would have displayed over anyone hurting or laying a hand on his daughter he'd held so dear. A wave of guilt rippled deep in his gut. He felt somehow responsible for Kathryn leaving her home in Lexington and for being attacked and raped because it had happened on her way out here to be with him.

He jerked his coat off the peg and jammed his arms into the sleeves, slapped his hat on his head and left the house. In the barn he lit a lantern and saddled up Charlie, then snuffed the flame. In the quiet predawn Rick led Charlie out of the barn and past the bunkhouse before he stuck his foot into the stirrup and swung himself into the saddle. It was barely light enough to see and Rick walked the horse until the sky brightened, then he spurred Charlie to a canter.

Wending his way up and over the hills, Rick recalled how fearful he had been when Pedro got shot, wondering if he would live or die. Long before this, he knew he should have made this quest the day after the shooting; but worrying about Pedro and concern for Kathryn had interfered with his reason and his suspicious mind. Of course, he could have sent Jim and Sam to scout around, but why put them in danger? He had felt bad enough about Pedro. Besides, this was his land and he must find out for himself. Although, he wasn't exactly sure what he was looking for or hoped to find.

The thick grove of ponderosa pines was in his sights and Rick's muscles flexed and tensed. "Whoa, boy," he commanded, softly. He straightened in the saddle and from his vantage point cast his eyes about in every direction before proceeding down to the creek. The sun had risen and a few birds twitted from branches above him and Rick became aware of feeling alone.

Charlie splashed across the creek that drifted lazily. Rick tilted his hat back and turned his head slowly as he searched the area before he dismounted and led his horse over to the same tree as before and tied him. Small beads of sweat collected on his forehead as the memory of that day returned. Drawing his gun he stood motionless, narrowing his eyes as he checked for any strange movement. Alert and on guard he made his way step by step toward the canyon.

Cautiously he retraced his steps, checking the ground. Strange, he thought, fresh brush draggings all over this area. He continued on, looking down, looking up, until he was deep into the canyon. They weren't very thorough, he reflected, as he gazed down upon partial imprints from an unshod pony. The hairs on the back of his neck began to bristle and nervously he spun around. Nothing there. He was still alone. He looked over the ground again, and almost laughed. They'd forgotten to get rid of the pony crap.

Rick stood in the canyon studying the walls and their structure. His eyes traveled gradually up the steep side of the ravine, then back down again. He walked over to the right and noticed more brush sweeps, bent and snapped branches. It looked to have been a path. He decided to climb it, to see where it went. Stretching his leg he placed his boot up on a rock and began to scale the steep ravine. Up and up he climbed until he reached a narrow ledge. He crawled onto the ledge and leaned his back against the side, layered with rock, and surveyed the area below. He was impressed with this viewpoint from where he stood. One could see anything that was coming for miles around or anyone attempting to scale the side without being seen. Still puzzled, Rick scratched the back of his neck and tried to figure out how any of this tied in with the Indian or Zeb, and him.

Rick studied the ledge and saw that it widened by a clump of branches, and he inched his way over to investigate. With his boot he kicked at the brush and it tumbled aside, exposing an opening in the side of the cliff. Rick was fired up now believing he may finally be on to something.

Retrieving a match from his shirt pocket he struck it against a rock. Bending slightly, he checked for evidence of rattlesnakes and any obstructions. Finding none, he crouched down, gun in hand and peered inside. Holding the match in his outstretched hand he saw that the cavity rose high and spread out as it went deeper into the mountainside. He had found a cave.

He blew out the burned down match before it reached his fingers and quickly lit another. Selecting one of the dried branches he lit the end to use for a torch. Slowly, he inched his way inside on his elbows and knees, branch in one hand and his gun in the other, and crawled a few feet before he was able to stand.

Off to his left near the wall, he spotted some sort of formation and took a couple of steps and saw the circle of rocks with a mound of cold ashes in the middle. Extending his arm he moved the torch as he turned slowly, looked down, up and around. The prints in the dirt floor were clearly made by moccasins. On the opposite wall from the fire pit hung a half a side of beef, suspended on a hook driven into the rock. "Probably my meat," Rick muttered. Not far from the meat lay some objects that appeared to be tools and he lowered the torch for a better look. There in the dirt lay a hammer and a chisel. Trailing back were several small piles of rock and Rick studied the wall of the cave with interest.

Toward the back his gaze caught a faint glimmer and he watched his steps as he treaded deeper into the cavity, his excitement mounting. "Wheweee. If this don't beat all," he exclaimed, and his voice echoed back from the depths within.

Rick knew immediately what his eyes beheld. There was no mistaking it. He was looking at gold.

Could it be the Indian had been working this small pocket he was looking at? And Zeb knew? That would tie them in on this together. A cold sweat came over Rick when it finally hit him that this had to be the Indian that held up the stage and raped Kathryn. He bit his lip in anger and narrowed his eyes in hate. Then, he thought, how am I going to prove any of this? The Indian had vanished. Questions and probable explanations raced through Rick's mind as his eyes traced a thin web of veins embedded in quartz leading deeper into the cave.

He slid his gun back into the holster and wedged his stick torch into a crack in the wall then picked up the hammer and chisel. Carefully, he placed the chisel near the thin veins and quartz and whacked off some samples. He unbuttoned his shirt and put the rock samples inside.

Drawing his gun, he then snuffed out the torch in the dirt leaving him in darkness except for the dim light coming from the opening. He walked as far as he could then crawled out into the bright sunlight. It blinded him temporarily and he crouched on the ledge to think while his eyes had time to adjust. To his recollection there were no markings of any mining claim on his maps, or mention of any in the papers to his property, but he would study these in detail when he returned home. If there was no markings or evidence, then he surmised this gold was discovered after he had purchased the property.

"It's got to be Zeb Taylor," he said aloud. "There's no other explanation." Somehow this thought made sense and Rick scrambled off the ledge and made his way back down the steep path.

Still wary, Rick scoped the area on the way to get his horse. Quickly he unbuttoned his shirt and put the rock samples into the saddlebag and secured the flap, then untied Charlie and led him over to the water.

For the first time he studied the creek bottom. By the side of a small rounded rock something flashed in the sun. He squatted down and dove his hand into the water and plucked it out. A nugget—a good-sized nugget of gold. He pocketed the wet, precious metal, and his eyes traveled the course of the flowing creek upstream. Never before had he noticed that the water came from two directions. The main body flowed from a source around and beyond the huge canyon, but a small tributary appeared to be coming from the underside of the mountain cliff. Very interesting, he thought. Could be that the nugget traveled out from somewhere inside the cave. That old feeling in his gut told him more trouble was in the wind. There was always trouble when greed overpowered rights and decency. In the past Rick had seen what greed for gold and claim jumping had led to.

He grabbed hold of the saddlehorn, slammed his boot into the stirrup and swung his taut body astride. He clicked his tongue and pressed his knees to Charlie's side and they quickly crossed the creek. After traveling a relatively safe distance, Rick put away his gun and reached behind him and fished out a biscuit. When Rick finished he set his battered Stetson tight to his head as he gave Charlie full rein and they high-tailed it for home.

Kathryn was on the porch doing some mending when she looked up and saw her uncle coming down off the hill. "Uncle Richard's back," she called to Sam in the kitchen.

"Good...in time to eat."

Rick was evasive and overly cheerful during lunch break. The men wanted to ask him what he had found, if anything, but could tell by his manner he was not ready to talk. The rest of the afternoon Rick spent studying maps, reading papers and going over the abstract to his property.

After Kathryn had gone to bed, Rick met with the men in the barn so that what he had to tell them would not be overheard. They clustered around him eager to hear the news.

"Well?" prodded Jim. "Ya kept us waitin all day...what'd ya find out?"

"I found a cave. And it's been lived in...up until recently."

"Why would anyone be living in a cave of yours, Boss?" questioned Pedro.

"To guard against me finding this, I suspect." Rick reached in his pocket and pulled out the nugget, holding it out for all to see.

"Well, I'll be damned. Gold. There's gold? Here on your land?" exclaimed Jim.

"This explains why Zeb wants yer land so bad," Sam pointed out. "Got any clues as to who was livin in the cave?"

"Sure do. An Indian. And, it's got to be the same one that held up the stage," replied Rick.

"But how the hell did Zeb and that Indian git together...that's what I want to know," said Sam. "And, who do ya spose discovered there was gold there...Zeb, or the Indian?"

"That's somethin we're goin to have to find out," answered Rick. "I'm goin into town first thing tomorrow, and I don't want you fellas lettin Kathryn out of yer sight. There's trouble brewin...I feel it. Who knows what Zeb'll pull next? Just keep her busy and don't let her go ridin off alone, especially in that direction." He tilted his head to the west.

The little group left the barn to turn in for the night. "Sam," called Rick, softly.

"Yah, what is it, Rick?"

"You are the only one here, as far as I know, who knows about the repulsive act done to Kathryn by that Indian. It makes my innards knot knowin there's a chance he's been around here...since it happened...and wonderin if he's got the notion bout tryin it again."

"The second you mentioned Indian, the same thought jumped into my mind."

"Sam, there's a reason, other than the attack, that Kathryn was singled out, and I'm afraid her life might still be in danger. We're gonna have to watch her like a hawk to protect her."

"Don'tcha think we ought to tell her?" asked Sam.

"I don't know. I just don't know what's best to do. I'm afraid she might become upset again...and frightened. I just don't want to cause her any more grief than she's already been through. Let's sit on it til I get back from town."

The assay office was just opening when Rick got to town.

"Dan, I gotta job for you," began Rick. He plunked the rocks onto the counter and fished the nugget from his shirt pocket.

Dan, a seasoned expert in testing metals, looked down at the samples then back up at Rick. "You going back into mining?" he asked with interest.

"I sure hadn't planned on it," said Rick. "But I would like these tested. How soon can you give me the results?"

"I can start on them now. There's none waiting ahead of you. I'll just get the furnace up to temperature then I can get started. If I work through lunch I can have your results done, say about two."

"Hate to have you work over lunch, Dan...but I do need to get back. I'll be more than happy to pay you extra if you do that."

"No problem, Rick. I haven't been real busy lately, but business has been picking up," he added.

Rick stood and watched Dan build up the fire in the small enclosed brick furnace that resembled a baking oven. While Dan waited for the fire to get hot enough, he picked up the samples and took them to the back where he would pound and pulverize them in preparation for the test. He set the nugget on a worktable where his first step would be to file off shavings to be put in lead foil.

"I won't hang around and disturb you or take a chance on someone seeing me here. Dan., It's very important that my coming here is kept strictly confidential. I wish I could tell you why, but right now I can't."

"Don't worry, Rick. This will remain private business."

"Thanks. I'll see you around two."

Rick marched into the sheriff's office and helped himself to Buck's strong coffee and pulled up a chair near the desk.

"Ya act like ya got a burr under yer saddle...what's up?" asked Buck.

"If things were different I'd be sayin I had good news...no, great news. But, it's more complicated than that. Buck, I found out something very important yesterday that sheds light on many things."

"Shoot." Buck tilted back in his chair and clasped his hands behind his head, his favorite listening position.

"I think I know now why Zeb's been so all-fired anxious to buy my place. And, from what I've discovered, it ties Zeb in with the hold-up."

Buck knit his brows together and eyeballed his old friend. "You sound pretty sure...what have you found out?"

"Gold."

Buck bounced forward in his chair. "Where?"

"By Little Kerber, right around the place where Pedro got shot. I've been bothered by that whole thing ever since it happened. It never figured right. Like, where did that Indian come from in the first place, and what provoked him to shoot at us? So yesterday I rode back there to scout around." Rick took a slug of his coffee and lit up his pipe.

"Buck, I found a cave...hidden up in the canyon. Someone had gone to great pains to keep it hidden and cover up tracks. But, I spotted a few, and they were made by an unshod pony."

Buck was leaning on his elbow taking in every word. He took a sip of coffee and urged Rick on. "Did ya find anything else?"

"Yeah. I noticed a path. That's what led me to the cave. There's evidence that the Indian has been livin in it...and knows about the gold. And, then we have Zeb who threatened me when I refused to sell." Rick puffed nervously on his pipe.

"And, added Buck, "two of Zeb's men just happened to quit on him...in time to rob the stage."

"Yeah," agreed Rick. And, the Indian, who Zeb claims not to know, just happened to join up with Zeb's men. And, another strange coincidence, Kathryn said the Indian asked her if she were a Barnett. Asked if she were my niece." Rick pounded on the desk, his anger mounting. "Now, Buck, how the hell would an Indian who was holed up in a cave...my cave...even know about Kathryn coming...or on what stage? There was a reason she was singled out...you know it, Buck."

Buck narrowed his eyes and stroked his chin. "I know Zeb's behind this mess... the problem is...how we goin to prove it? He's a slick one, there's no doubt about it. He gets someone else to steal for him...he benefits without dirtying his hands. You know

I've been tryin to get the goods on that weasel for a long time. But, he always has his ass covered."

The room went quiet while both men sat and thought. Buck stood up and refilled his big tin cup and Rick held his out for more. Buck set the pot back on the top of the wood stove and walked around his office. He paused and looked out the front window, then turned to Rick.

"As I see it...that Indian's our only way of gettin to the bottom of this."

"If he's still alive," Rick added. From the back of Rick's mind renewed anger surfaced. He wasn't sure what he would do to the Indian, himself, if he was ever found and caught. He didn't want to bring shame to Kathryn, but he knew that the time had come where he could no longer keep the hideous act against her a secret.

Buck was studying his expression and knew something terrible was eating Rick. "What's wrong?"

"Buck, I've been holdin out on you. I want that Indian caught for more than just trespassing, shooting and robbing." Rick's face bore the look of hate, and he bit his lip and narrowed his eyes. "What I am about to tell you must go no further than here." Buck eyed his friend, quizzically, and nodded in agreement.

"Buck, the reason Kathryn was not with the others when the coach was stopped is because the Indian took her off of it." He sucked in hard and let the air back out. "He raped her...Buck, he raped her."

Buck was speechless. He didn't know what words to say to express his feelings at the shock, or how to comfort his heartsick friend. All that came out was, "Oh, my God." Buck walked back to his desk and sat down heavily. Neither spoke. Buck mulled the events of what he had just heard around in his mind. At last he ventured to speak.

"Rick, it looks like this to me. Zeb wants your place, or I should say, the gold that's on it. One way or another, that Indian, whatever his name is, was workin for Zeb. How the gold was found is anybody's guess...but somehow Zeb got wind your niece was coming...probably heard it in town, or something. It was perfect, don't ya see? His men, and that includes that Indian, would rob the stage and I think Kathryn was meant to be kidnapped. Only it didn't work out that way."

Rick looked stunned. "Go on," he said. "I think yer on to something here. But, how do ya come up with kidnapping?"

"I've asked myself...why the extra horse? That's how."

"That's right. I forgot all about it, never gave it a second thought. Kathryn was on a horse when we met up. I was just so happy to see her."

"That's right. And, everyone else's horse who was involved, is accounted for."

"Where is that horse? That isn't the one we hauled back to Zeb, is it?"

"No, that was the one Ernie brought in. The one Kathryn rode is at the livery. No marks on him, either. Besides, Sam said he found it tied up near the place where the stage was ambushed, and the others were on horses. It had to be meant for Kathryn. I think Sam and Jim interrupted the plan...that's what I think."

"It makes sense. The pieces are starting to fit."

"What bothers me, Rick...knowin the kind of snake Zeb is...and the fact, that Kathryn is here, will he try it again?"

Rick was silent for a moment, then said, "How we gonna prove what we know, and how we gonna stop that vermint from trying again, Buck?"

"It still comes back to that damned Indian. Somehow, we gotta find him and git him to spill his guts on what he knows."

"Sure thing...but how we gonna find him? Or, how we gonna trap Zeb?"

"My guess is that Zeb'll lay low for a while knowin he's under suspicion. He knows he can't pull anything without drawin me to him," Buck surmised. He got up from behind his desk and walked over to the rack of shotguns and rifles held in place by a chain and lock. He took his ring of keys and fit one in the lock then slid back the chain far enough to remove a Winchester '73 carbine and locked the chain back in place.

Rick studied on this and asked, "What ya up to, Buck?"

"Think you and Sam can leave the ranch for a while?"

"Yah, as long as I know Kathryn will be safe."

"Good. Cause we're goin Injun huntin. Sam's one of the best trackers I ever ran into and we're going to need the best 'cause we'll be followin a cold trail. And, ya best tell Kathryn and warn her so she can be on her guard."

"I plan on that, Buck. I best git goin. I think I'll stop at Alice's and see if there's a chance Clint and Manuel want to stay at the ranch til we get back. I know I'll feel better with more people there."

"Good idea. And, it might not hurt to have Harold and Claudette out there, too. They're workin on their house building out yer way, might be easier for them not to have to travel such a long ways. Ya might ask, anyhow."

"I like that idea. What time you want to git started?"

"Soon as I get things squared away 'round here, I'll be on my way ta yer place."

Rick made a hurried stop and request at Alice Truitt's boarding house. As soon as Rick filled Manuel and Clint in on the story and plans, they both jumped at the chance to come out and be of help. Then, Rick quickly rode over to the hotel and luckily caught Harold and Claudette in.

In the middle of Rick's speech to convince them they were needed to come out to be with Kathryn, Claudette began to gather what clothes and other articles she felt necessary for their stay.

"Now I gotta warn you both. You'll be staying in my room and it's not anywhere near fancy like this is, so ya might want to think it over a little."

"Nonsense," said Harold. "We'll enjoy the company and I'm sure Claudette will have a much better time being with Kathryn and being able to enjoy the outdoors than confined so much to this room."

"Harold's right, Rick. In fact, I am only sorry for the circumstances that are prompting this sudden visit. Don't you worry, we will manage just fine."

"I don't know how to thank you," said Rick, picking up his hat and getting ready to leave.

"We don't want thanks, Rick. What are friends for if not to help out when needed?" responded Harold.

"Thanks," said Rick, gratefully.

Harold and Rick shook hands and Rick said goodbye to Claudette, then left.

Rick walked into the assay office and Dan had a bright look on his face.

"Boy, when you find gold...you really find it," exclaimed Dan. He handed Rick a summation of his findings and Rick leaned against the counter when he'd finished.

"Yer sure? 120 oz. to the ton?" asked Rick.

"Sure am. And 75 oz. on the silver."

Rick pulled out his billfold and handed Dan twice the going rate for the test. "It's still important you keep this under wraps, Dan."

"Don't worry, Rick, I will. I'm sure you'll tell me why when you're able."

"That I will...you can bet on that. Many thanks, Dan. See ya later."

Remembering Sam's request for sorghum and Kathryn's for thread, Rick rode on to the mercantile passing the Jack Rabbit Saloon on the way. He couldn't help but notice Zeb's sway-backed horse tied out front, along with several others, including a flashy Appaloosa he'd never noticed before. The urge to go in was too much. He tied up Charlie to the hitch-rail alongside the Appy. Squaring his shoulders he brushed his fingertips across his gun butt and strolled through the swinging doors and moseyed up to the long mahogany bar. Rick nodded and "howdied" those he knew that were lined up against the bar, then turned to the bartender standing before him.

"Good to see ya, Rick-it's been a while. What'll ya have?"

"Shot a rye, Mike."

"Comin up." Mike set a shot glass down in front of Rick and grabbed a bottle of rye whiskey off the back bar and filled the glass.

Rick lay down two bits and picked up the glass. "Thanks, Mike." He brought the glass to his lips, tilted his head and threw the rye down. He set the glass down for a refill. While he waited for Mike to work his way back in his direction, Rick looked into the mirror that hung the length of the wall behind the bar. Resting his boot on the shiny brass rail he focused in on the game at the poker table behind him, near the wall.

There were six players including Zeb, which came as no surprise. Rick's jaw tightened when his eye caught sight of the slovenly man. He had never hated a man as much as he hated Zeb. Zeb was waiting for his cards to be dealt and his pig-like eyes stared at Rick's back. Then, their eyes met in the mirror. Rick remained riveted, tipped his hat back on his head and fixed a bead on him until Zeb looked nervously away. Rick's eyes shifted to a new man in the game and one he had never seen in town, or in these parts.

A shady looking fellow, thought Rick. He had beady eyes, like Zeb's, only set in a boney face with a bad complexion, and had dirty-looking blond hair that was parted in the middle. He wore a cocky grin and had manners to match. Sitting next to Zeb, he was shining up to him and Zeb treated him like an old friend and this made Rick suspicious.

Rick motioned Mike down and ordered another shot. "And who's the new dude?"

"Frank's all I got. Never did mention his last name. Just rode in this morning, from what I heard."

"That his Appy out front?"

"Guess so. Quite a looker, ain't it?"

"Sure is. What's his business, do ya know?"

"Don't reckon he ever said. But, if he hangs around Zeb too long, ya kin bet it won't be good or legal. He did ask me, though, how far a ride it was to Bonanza. That's about all I kin tell ya." Mike left to wait on a customer at the other end of the bar.

Rick brought his glass up to his lips watching Zeb and the newcomer, then downed the whiskey, set his glass on the bar and walked out of the saloon without a look back.

Rick rode straight to the barn and swung to the ground. He fished in his saddlebags and took out the sorghum and a spool of thread.

"I'll tend to Charlie," offered Jim, coming out of the barn, "if ya want to go right in."

"Thanks, Jim. Could I ask you to give him a quick rub down? Buck, Sam and I will be ridin out of here early tomorrow and I need Charlie fit for some long ridin."

"Where are you going, Rick?"

"We're going to try and track down that Indian," stated Rick.

"I'll get Snowflake in here then, and, I'll give them an extra ration of oats."

"You're a good man, Jim. Sometimes I don't know what I'd do without you. I'll see you up at the house when yer finished. We gotta have a family talk."

Sam was busy with supper as Rick strolled into the house. He didn't hang up his gun, but set it over by his chair by the fireplace to clean after supper.

"Sam, where's Kathryn?"

"Takin a nap, I think."

"Sam. How'd ya like to git away from here for a few days, or maybe longer?"

"Sounds good to me. What's up?"

"You, me and Buck are going to track down that Indian."

"Now yer talkin. But what about leavin Kathryn? I know she can handle the cookin and all, but Pedro and Jim'll be too busy here by themselves to keep a good watch on her."

"That's been taken care of. I'll explain when everyone is here at the table."

Rick's little family sat grouped around the table with anxious eyes fixed upon him. "As you know," he began, "I've been in town...tending to matters of great importance. And most of what I'm going to say is important for Kathryn's safety." He looked tenderly into his niece's worried eyes. Kathryn straightened her back and frowned, unsure of what was going on and wondering what her uncle was going to say.

"Kathryn, the last couple of days, I've done some investigating. First, I found out there is gold on this land."

"Gold? Really, gold?" Kathryn asked, eyes wide in surprise.

"Yes, gold. And it appears it might be a rich deposit, too."

"Where'?" she asked, fascinated.

"It's located at the far western end in a cave. And until recently that cave was being lived in...by an Indian."

Kathryn's expression turned to a look of horror. She glanced nervously about, and her eyes darted then fixed upon the darkened windowpanes above the sink. Her body felt clammy from the cold sweat that crept over it. No, she thought. I can't be hearing this.

Rick put his hand on her arm. "I know hearing this is upsetting, Kathryn, but I have to tell you more. We believe that it had to be the same Indian that held up the stage." Kathryn gasped and her hand flew to her mouth. Rick's arm went swiftly around her and drew her near.

"Buck and I figure that it was Zeb Taylor, a no-good scum and unfortunately a near neighbor, who is behind the hold-up and the gold discovery. We think he meant to kidnap you at that time, in an effort to force me off this place. You see, he's been tryin to git me to sell out to him for a long time, and I never knew why. Now, I do. He must have gotten wind that you were coming and he couldn't pass up the chance to force my hand. I think Jim and Sam comin along when they did prevented the Indian from carryin out his orders. So, all the Indian took was the payroll. But Buck can't prove that without findin the Indian."

"You...think," stammered Kathryn, "that Indian is still around? That there is a chance he is going to come after me again?"

"That's what we're going to put a stop to, Kathryn. Buck is coming out here first thing in the morning and he, Sam and I are going to track him down. Now, because I am worried and concerned for your safety, I have made arrangements that I think will please you."

Kathryn looked at him with questioning eyes. "What arrangements have you made?"

"You are going to have a houseful of company and protection," he smiled.

"Who?"

"Clint, Manuel, Claudette, and Harold."

"They're all coming out here? Really?"

"Yes, and they're all anxious to do so, too. Claudette and Harold can stay in my room, and Clint and Manuel will take the bunkhouse. It will be closer for Harold to get at their building site, and Clint and Manuel for that matter, too. So you see, with Jim and Pedro and the rest, you should be more than safe while we are gone."

"If it weren't such a frightening thing, I should be very excited at having everyone here," said Kathryn.

"No reason we can't have a good time in spite of everything, Kathryn," said Jim. Although he would prefer that Clint be excluded from the company, but that was hopeless, so he decided to make the best of things.

"Yes, you're right, Jim. It will seem like a holiday having all my friends here. It will be almost like when we were altogether on the stage. Except for Will, that is," she added, sadly. "Well, I best get things organized if we are going to have guests." She jumped up, but didn't move. Her face drained of color and her legs felt weak just before she collapsed upon the floor.

Kathryn came to lying on the sofa with four pairs of worried eyes gazing down at her. She felt the heavy blanket upon her body and a cold towel across her forehead.

'What happened?" she asked weakly.

"You fainted," answered Rick. "I'm afraid the news about the kidnapping and talk of the Indian, plus the surprise of hearing your friends all coming here was too much excitement for you."

"Have a sip of water, Missy," urged Sam, holding a glass out to her lips. She raised her head and drank to wet her dry mouth and throat, then put her head back down on the pillow feeling sheepish, yet puzzled. She looked away and tried to put what she had heard straight in her mind. She slid her eyes back to her uncle and asked, "Am I really still in that much danger that I need so much looking after?"

"I can't honestly say for certain, Kathryn. But we are dealing with a ruthless, dirty-dealing man who's known to stop at nothing to git what he wants. It's just best to take precautions...don't you think?"

"Yes. You're right. And, it will be fun, too," she smiled. "And, very nice having Clint around. I miss him."

"I thought you did," grinned Rick.

Do ya think yer up to havin supper, Missy?" asked Sam, gently.

"Yes. I'll be fine in a minute or so. I'll just rest here until it's ready, if you don't mind losing your help for tonight," she smiled.

Jim sat up in his bed and tilted his head toward the door in his room. He wasn't sure what had awakened him and cautiously he stepped out onto the floor. Quietly, barefoot and in his longies, he crept to the door and silently turned the knob. He pulled the door open just enough to poke his head out. He listened, again. The sounds were coming from across the hall in Kathryn's room and Jim realized he was hearing her muffled sobbing. His heart felt heavy and sad. He wondered what was making her cry. He guessed she was afraid. Afraid of the Indian, afraid of being kidnapped. He wanted to cross the hall and go to her, to comfort her. But, should he? Was it his place'? No, he thought, angrily. If he were Clint, then it would be all right to comfort her. Then it would be his business, his concern, his place. Yet, it broke his heart hearing her crying softly, thinking no one could hear. He stood and mutely argued with himself and nervously ran his fingers through his unruly sandy hair. He squeezed on the knob until his knuckles ached, grimaced then reluctantly shut the door.

28

*U*p at the crack of dawn, Clint whistled as he happily packed his things into his leather satchel. He was anxious to be going to stay with Kathryn. He had missed her, missed not being near her, like they had been on the train, on the stage and at all the way stations. He had felt their love grow and he had felt useful and protective toward her, that is, until that fateful day when the stage was ambushed. Sometimes he would wake in the night hearing her screams that day, and he remembered that torturous feeling of helplessness. That incident still puzzled him. Had it been fear that made her cry out or had she been really hurt when the Indian pulled her from the driver's seat? She hadn't wanted to talk of it, her only concern had been for him and the others.

Clint heard Manuel's bedroom door shut, then a knock on his door. Manuel poked his head in with a broad smile. "You are about ready, Si?"

"Yup."

The two walked down the stairs and deposited their belongings outside the door, then went to have breakfast with Alice.

After they finished eating and were having coffee, Alice said sadly, "I'm going to miss having you two around. But I know your place is out at the Barnett ranch now."

"We will miss you too, Senora Alice," said Manuel. "I will miss our tea time the most," he added, dropping his gaze.

"You've been mighty good to us and we wouldn't have recovered so fast without you. And, we have a lot to be grateful for, just knowing you," said Clint.

"Well, you two helped me in many ways. I feel that I am at last living again. That I have a purpose. So, I am grateful to you, too," smiled Alice. "Did I tell you that I am getting new boarders tomorrow?"

"No," answered Clint. "Who are they?"

"A charming young couple with a little baby. They came here from Wisconsin, and are staying with relatives at the moment, but it is much too crowded there. They are going to live here until they get a place of their own built. He is a furniture and cabinetmaker, and she is a seamstress. You might mention that to Claudette and Harold. They may be interested in retaining their services for the new house."

"I'll jest do that. I think they'll be very interested. And, it'd give the fella a nice start here in the area." To himself he thought, and I can use him, too, if things go the way I hope.

A knock on the front door got them all up from the table. "Anybody here going to the Barnett Ranch?" hollered Harold, jovially.

Manuel and Clint hugged Alice goodbye and grabbed their possessions and loaded then into Harold's new buckboard, and piled in. They waved goodbye and headed to the livery stable.

Clint was going to pick up his recently purchased horse. Manuel was going to help the Bartholomews load up their things and drive the buckboard, and Harold and Claudette would follow in the carriage.

"See ya'll there," said Clint. He took along his saddlebag and hurried into the livery, and wasted no time in saddling his new horse, a grey, with black tail and mane, named Smokey.

The crisp morning air was refreshing. Clint whistled and hummed as he rode out of town and felt so happy that he burst into song. He was not happy that Kathryn's life might be in danger, but happy he was going to be with her again, at last. That he would be around to protect her, if the need arose. Now, he felt useful and not a helpless invalid. He felt like a man, a man whole again. And, in love. That was the best part, he thought. About a mile from the ranch gate Clint dismounted and led Smokey over to the creek for water, then tied his reins to a small branch. He wandered about picking some of the flowers that grew abundantly near the bank. When he had gathered a sufficient amount he sat on a rock and pulled some of the lower leaves off of the stems and arranged the assortment to suit him. He then lay them on a paper he'd brought along and rolled them carefully inside. He placed the flowers gently in his saddlebag, leaving the flap open so as not to crush them. This done, he nervously sat back on the rock and pulled the black velvet covered box from his red-checked shirt pocket. Slowly he opened the lid and, the blue sapphire stone sparkled in the sunlight.

Harold had crafted the ring especially for him to give to Kathryn after Clint had explained his intentions and what kind of ring he wanted. It was truly a work of art. Two small diamonds were set on each side of an emerald cut, blue sapphire stone, mounted in a gold band.

Now some doubts came over Clint. What if she turned him down? He felt she loved him, but did she love him enough to want to marry him? Maybe, now that she was here and recovered from the long journey, she might want to look around for better prospects?

Clint stroked his moustache and thought, keeping his eyes fixed on the sparkling ring. He thought along the positive side. He had purchased a tract of land not far from the Bartholomews and had drawn up preliminary plans for their home, subject to her approval, of course. And, he stood a very good chance of making big money, now that he had changed his direction in life by teaming up with Harold. He would be able to support her in a fairly nice style, without her money. But it still boiled down to, did she want him for a husband? He snapped the lid shut on the box and placed it back in his pocket. He would wait and ask her when he felt the time was right. He untied Smokey and climbed back into the saddle.

Kathryn was sitting on the porch taking a break after she'd finished cleaning in preparation for the guests. Sam and Rick were busy packing the panniers, strapped on Sam's mule, Thunder, with the supplies they would need while on their hunt for the Indian. Pedro was in the bunkhouse sweeping the floor and putting sheets on the two bunks where Manuel and Clint would be sleeping, and Jim was in the barn cleaning stalls.

Kathryn looked up. Down the long drive she spotted a lone rider. Blinking and looking again, she recognized who it was and quickly stood up. Using the window behind her for a mirror, she checked her appearance in the reflection then ran down the steps wearing a big smile.

Clint saw her coming toward him and his heart started pounding. She was so beautiful with her hair flowing back and her blue dress swaying and bellowing out as she ran.

"Clint. Clint," she called, her arms spread wide. Clint leaped off his horse and ran to embrace her. They came together holding each other tightly. Kathryn pulled her head from his chest and looked teary eyed into his face and his lips came down on hers. The tender kiss made her knees weak and she clung to him tighter. Clint held her shoulders and moved her slightly away.

"Let me look at you. Oh, Kathryn, I've missed you so much."

"And, I have missed you, Clint, more than I know how to tell you. It's going to be wonderful having you living here for a while; we can do so much together. And, with Uncle Richard and Sam gone, I'm going to feel much safer knowing you are going to be here to protect me," she smiled.

Clint gave her a hug then turned and pulled the paper wrapped flowers from the saddlebag. "Here, these are for you."

Kathryn spread the paper apart, carefully. "Oh, Clint. These are beautiful," she exclaimed, as she gazed happily down at the white, yellow and lavender bouquet.

Leading Smokey by the reins with one hand and holding onto Kathryn's with the other, they strolled leisurely toward the barn.

Unseen at the open door up in the hayloft, Jim stood in the shadows and watched the happy couple. As they approached he stepped back into the hay and sat down, the pitchfork still in his hand. He bent his head down and rested his forehead in the palm of his hand. He tried to shake off the feeling of jealousy he'd felt when he watched Kathryn running to Clint, and their embrace. He knew he had no right to be feeling this way, after all, Kathryn was in love with Clint before she even got here. And, she'd certainly given no indication that she regarded him any more than like a brother. Story of his life. No woman ever took him serious or looked at him in that special way he'd seen exchanged between lovers. What was wrong with him, he asked himself? Was it his looks? His manner...his build? He couldn't answer and jumped up in frustration. He began pitching the hay furiously down to empty stalls below. Clint and Kathryn entered the barn.

Clint looked up at the free-falling hay and shouted up, "Howdy, Jim. How ya doin?"

"Fine, Clint, just fine." Jim leaned on the handle of the fork and smiled down. "Good to see ya up and about. Must feel good for you to be back on yer feet, huh?"

"Sure does, Jim. Sure missed seeing this pretty little gal, too," he replied, winking at Kathryn. "But I knew I didn't have to worry about her too much, 'cause she's been in good hands."

"You bet she has," agreed Jim. "If ya want, you kin put yer horse in that stall, on the end to cool him down, or you kin put him out in the corral, whichever. By the way, that's a fine lookin animal ya got. What's his name?"

"Smokey." Clint removed his new saddle from Smokey and Kathryn told him he could take it to the tack room in the barn. Kathryn walked the horse to the stall admiring him, while Clint carried off the saddle and blanket.

"Come," she said. "I'll show you where you are going to be staying." Arm in arm they walked to the bunkhouse and the hay was pitched down even faster than before.

Kathryn was showing Clint the inside of the house when Buck rode up. Pedro came to take his horse, give him some water, and cool him down for the sheriff. Buck sauntered over to the pump. Rick and Sam had just finished tying the panniers and were about to fill up the canteens.

"It looks like it's going to be a good day to travel," remarked Buck. He'd brought his canteen and filled his up too.

"I kin hardly wait to git going," said Sam. "Since we haven't been blessed with rain there's a good chance we kin pick up the trail, plus I got a couple of hunches of my own."

"That so?" asked Buck, curiously. "What?"

Sam fingered the rawhide string of elk's teeth that hung from his neck. "Chief Stumbling Bear and his small tribe should be heading down for their summer camp, and there's a chance we can meet up with him. I think he kin shed some light on our elusive Indian." Sam nodded to himself, thinking, then said, "Something Stumbling Bear told me once is starting to make sense. I'm sorry I didn't put it together long before this."

"What's that, Sam?" asked Rick.

"Let's wait and see," answered Sam.

The sound of hooves and wagon wheels interrupted the discussion. Down the long drive pranced the chestnut mare, Molly, pulling the fancy carriage with Claudette at the reins, and Manuel not far behind, driving their buckboard.

The kitchen filled up with the entire group. Kathryn poured the fresh coffee she'd made and Sam let her wait on him for a change, giving her a sly grin.

"Now, everyone," spoke Rick. "I don't know how long we're goin to be gone... maybe a few days, maybe a few weeks. Jim'll be in charge of the ranch, you git yer orders from him. Kathryn, if you need to go for supplies, you make sure Clint or someone else goes with you. You two ladies;" he warned, "do not go off by yerselves."

"And," inserted Buck, "Art and Paul'll stop by from time to time, and if you do go to town check in at the office."

All nodded and agreed.

"You all can decide for yerselves how yer going to work things out, when Harold here needs to be at the building site with Clint and Manuel.

"Well," Rick set down his big mug, "we best git goin."

Sam and Buck rose and Rick put his arms around Kathryn. She jumped up and threw her arms around him and he kissed her cheek.

"I'll miss you, Uncle Richard," said Kathryn, her voice quivering. "Please be careful."

"I'm gonna miss you, too. You be careful, and don't ride near the west end," Rick warned.

The three men strolled out ahead of the others and climbed into the saddles on their waiting mounts. Standing on the porch, Clint put his arm around Kathryn's waist, Harold held Claudette's hand, Jim and Pedro went down the steps, and Manuel leaned against the door frame as they watched Rick, Buck and Sam ride west with Thunder in tow. When the three crested the first hill they turned and waved, then rode out of sight.

That evening, after they'd eaten the chicken dinner Kathryn and Claudette had fixed, the group sat around in the kitchen making out a schedule to suit everyone's comings and goings.

It was decided if Clint went with Harold to the building site, Manuel would stay at the ranch. If Manuel went, Clint would stay. If they both needed to be there, Jim and Pedro would do chores near the house. And, they agreed one of the men had to stay within sight and shouting distance of the two ladies.

"And do not forget, Senorita Kathryn," grinned Pedro. "We got Zeke and Jasper to watch and listen for us, too." At the sounds of their names, the two dogs flopped out by the fireplace got up, wagging their tails and joined the group, accepting petting and hellos.

"We should get us a nice dog after we get moved into our house," suggested Claudette.

"I think that would be a fine idea, dear. It would be good company for you when I'm gone and be a watch dog, too."

They sat and talked, making plans and joking. Manuel and Clint shared some interesting and funny stories about some of their stagecoach days, and Pedro decided he liked this Manuel, very much. He also liked the fact that he was no longer the only Mexican on the ranch. And, Manuel made Pedro laugh when he asked him if he had a pretty little senorita hidden away someplace.

"No, Manuel," he laughed. "But I hear there are a couple of fine looking Mexican ladies who cook and clean over at that snake, Taylor's place...but I have never had a look at them myself. They are hardly ever seen in town."

"What are they? Prisoners'?" retorted Manuel, in jest.

"Maybe so," reflected Pedro.

It was late, everyone was tired. It had been a long day and they all turned in for the night. Pedro, Manuel and Clint headed for the bunkhouse, Claudette and Harold went to Rick's room, Jim into his and, Kathryn to hers.

Resting on a log around their small glowing campfire, Rick, Sam and Buck discussed the first day of their search. They spoke in low tones, knowing how well their voices could carry in the open night.

Their first stop had been at Little Kerber Creek with a trek up to the cave that held the gold, which had also been the Indian's hide out. Sam had walked about the area below, with eye squinting deliberation and was overjoyed at the amount of visible tracks a short distance from the canyon. "See these?" he'd pointed out. "Three here that came and went from the same direction. Don't take a fool to know where they came from...Zeb's. And he was one of em...I'd bet ol' Snowflake on it. See how deep this set goes? Fat ol' Zeb. But the pony tracks, here, don't come near this group. Must've been a meeting," he guessed, stroking his long beard thoughtfully. "Then the pony's tracks go off there," he pointed, "alone."

With Sam's cunning and expertise they followed the single trail of prints that began veering north. The tracking was slow and painstaking. They'd lose it, then find it, as the pony tracks zigzagged, first going east, then west, south, never going in one direction for long.

Sam washed out the metal plates and utensils in the nearby creek and left then out in a wooden rack to dry, to be used again for breakfast. Rick and Buck spread out the bedrolls and lay just enough wood on the fire to keep it going, not wanting a large blaze to draw attention. They'd chosen a spot tucked back in a small canyon for their camp, bringing the horses and mules in with them. As night fell upon the mountains the canyon became eerie with their shadows moving on the canyon walls. Sam looked like a giant as he stood over the fire rubbing his cold hands he'd gotten washing dishes in the icy mountain stream.

Rick took out his pipe for an after supper smoke and thrust his legs out to loosen up his muscles. Buck stood and stretched his lean, solid body, drawing his arms high in the air and tilted his head back to get the kink out of his neck. His firm jaw and long straight nose made a striking profile from the glow of the fire.

Buck was a straightforward, straight-shootin man and a fair-minded sheriff. He was a self-educated man, quick with his mind, compassionate with his feelings, who thought things through before taking action. He was well liked and respected in the area, and openly adored by his wife, Ruth. Now, as he sat back on his log seat, he stared at the soft burning fire and wondered how long this hunt would take. He wanted justice served by finally getting evidence on Zeb Taylor who'd been a thorn in his side since he'd become sheriff, five years ago. He hoped the Indian would give him the ammunition he needed, by putting the finger on Zeb. And, now that Rick had disclosed that Kathryn had been raped, he wanted the Indian more than ever. Buck had felt saddened and angry when he had heard, and his heart went out to Kathryn. She was, in his mind, a very brave woman to come out here, alone. And he saw in her an inner strength, courage and an adaptability that few women he knew possessed. She was kind, good-hearted and good natured in spite of her ordeal. Buck admired her tremendously.

Sam announced he would take first watch. Buck opted for the second, and Rick got the last. It was not long before Buck and Rick were asleep. Sam positioned himself on the ground at the entrance with his shotgun resting across his lap, and a pile of small dried branches to feed the fire. The sounds of the night creatures filled the air, far away and close by, and Sam tuned in his hearing for any noise out of place. In a short span of stillness the haunting cry from a near-by Horned owl pierced the silence, then the sound of small branches snapping as the large wings pounded the air as it swooped away in search of prey.

Buck was glad when his turn at watch was over and he prodded Rick to wake up and change places. Rick built up the fire to ward away the chills from the cold pre-dawn hours. After a long spell he stiffly rose and walked silently out to view the sky and the faint hint of sunrise shown far away on the horizon. He built up the fire again, and put some bacon in a pan and set it on a rock near the flames, then filled the coffee pot from his canteen and began to boil the coffee.

Before the sun had fully risen the three were mounted up and back on the trail. The trek across Buffalo Pass, southwest of Bonanza, was difficult, but the trail from the Indian had become easier to follow. They had trudged through forests of pinon, stately ponderosa, leafy aspen, fir and cottonwood, through gulches, across streams narrow and wide and up and down rugged mountain trails. At last they were nearing one of the camps of the Shoshone that Sam had visited many times.

Rick and Buck waited with Thunder in a clearing while Sam rode on ahead to announce their arrival, although their guards were aware of their coming. They watched as he rode just to the outside circle of teepees with his right hand raised in friendly gesture. Soon he was surrounded by several smiling men and women happily greeting him. Sam turned and motioned for Rick and Buck to ride on in. They were escorted into the circle of dozens of teepees amongst many small children scampering and squealing in some happy made-up game.

After meeting the Chief, Stumbling Bear, they were invited to partake of a feast in honor of Sam, their friend. There was a colorful ceremonial dance performed for their benefit and Rick and Buck enjoyed the hospitality as much as Sam.

After the festivities, they were led into the large teepee of Chief Stumbling Bear. A fire surrounded by round rocks burned in the center. The Chief nodded as they entered single file and motioned for them to sit, by the entrance. The Chief sat on a woven blanket across from them and on his left sat Chirping Bird, his wife. Next to her were two Elders. On his right sat the Medicine Man, Moon of Many Faces. Rick found himself in the middle, between Sam and Buck on his right. The peace pipe was lit and passed around before the Chief spoke. He directed his words to Buck and Rick.

"You are in search of my son, Blackhorse," he said, solemnly. "I, too, was in search...for him to bury his grieving past...stop running from his people." He paused and looked for a moment at his wife, then stared deep into the fire they sat around. "Why do you look for my son?" he questioned.

Sam nudged Buck. "I represent the law of the white man in a place called Villa Grove," said Buck to the wise looking chief. "I regret to tell you that your son, Blackhorse, as you call him, shot and killed a man in a stage coach hold up, and wounded others on that stage. I also have reason to believe he works for a very dishonest man, who I have tried to bring to justice for many years. Your son must pay for his crimes, and I am hoping he will help me by confessing his crimes and give the name of the man who he works for."

The chief took in all that Buck had said. "And, how will my son be punished by the white man's law?"

"It is up to the judge when Blackhorse is brought to trial," answered Buck. "He could be sent to prison...or he could be hanged."

Chirping Bird's eyes widened a little as she bit her lip, but did not speak. Sam nudged Rick that it was time for him to say his piece. Rick looked at the mother then the father, swallowed and with steady eyes said, "I want him arrested for raping my niece who was also on the stage coach that was held up and robbed. And, for wounding a man who works for me."

The faces of the chief and his wife did not change expression. The chief nodded that he had heard and had understood. "I cannot pass over what my son has done. These are serious crimes you tell of. Before we speak further, I want you to hear what Moon of Many Faces tells you...so you know about the man you came to arrest."

Moon of Many Faces did not look at them, but kept his gaze upon the dancing flames of the fire. "Blackhorse...whom you seek...was a young boy, nearing his manhood. The tribe was off on a hunt...for the day. Like those his age, stayed behind to watch over the camp...the women, the little ones, the old ones. The camp was attacked...by surprise...by a band of white thieves." Sad in voice, the Medicine Man went on. "Many babies and little ones were shot and killed. Many young men were shot and stabbed as they tried in vain to protect their people and the camp. Many of them, too...died. The women were chased down...beaten and raped...stabbed and shot. Blackhorse...they thought, dead. But, he lay badly wounded...and saw his baby sister's head smashed against a rock. He saw his little brother...not yet of age three...get his head cut off...by a sword, and watched in horror as it rolled in the dirt and the rest of the little boy's body jerked and bled on the ground beside him. He tried to get up to fight, but his leg was broken, his other wounds bleeding bad, and fear...tied him to the ground. He saw his mother being raped...and could do nothing." Chirping Bird's lips pressed together in remembered pain and heartache.

"We return...happy, with food from a good hunt...only to find our village destroyed and many of our women and children dead. The sight of our camp was unspeakable, a bloody mess of wounded and dead bodies. Our horses gone and teepees burned. The boy, Blackhorse, was never the same. He blamed himself for what happened to his sister and brother, and mother. Blamed himself for not being a man. During his manhood ceremony he went on his vision quest, and never returned...until three nights ago."

The three men's heads snapped to attention and they slowly exchanged looks with each other. The Medicine Man was finished with the story and the teepee was silent except for the crackling wood of the fire.

Finally, Chief Stumbling Bear spoke to Buck and Rick. "What you have told me was not news. Blackhorse has confessed his crimes to us."

"Where is your son, now?" asked Buck.

"Repenting for his bad deeds...and purifying his soul," answered Moon of Many Faces.

"I would like to see him and speak with him," stated Buck.

"I will see if he is done in the sweat lodge. If he is not, you will have to wait," replied Moon of Many Faces. He stood from his place and slid through the deerskin flap of the teepee.

The teepee was silent. No one spoke during the medicine man's absence.

It seemed a very long time before the flap opened again. Moon of Many Faces entered and paused while another figure entered and stood behind him. He wanted to turn and see the face of the man he had grown to hate, but instead held his body rigid with his eyes fixed upon the fire. The two men walked behind him and the medicine man returned to his place with Blackhorse beside him. Rick's gaze drifted slowly to his left, and Blackhorse's eyes met his. The two men's eyes locked in a stare, each sizing up the other.

The chief spoke. "My son, these men are here to take you back with them. They say you must pay for your crimes in the white man's world. Have you anything to say to them?"

"Yes, my Father," answered Blackhorse, in remorse. He looked from his father to Sam, Rick and Buck, his accusers. He stiffened his jaw to stop the trembling, and in a low deliberate voice began. "I was a victim, also. I was a captive of the man called Zeb Taylor. I had no choice in my crimes." He went on, telling in detail how he was framed and nearly hung for a murder he did not commit in Gunnison. He told how Zeb and his men had rescued him and brought him to his ranch. From then on, how he was forced to do whatever Zeb demanded, robbing stagecoaches and cattle rustling, always with the threat of turning him into the sheriff. When Blackhorse had finished his story he looked nervously at Buck. Buck motioned slightly with his hand at the chief.

"You wish to speak, Sheriff McCain?" asked the chief.

"Yes, I do. Blackhorse, about the murder in Gunnison...I believe you could be innocent and speak the truth. If, for no other reason then I know what a lying thief Zeb Taylor is. I have been aware of his activities and have suspected him of many crimes in my area...for a long time. Until now I have never had enough proof to arrest him. He is a very slippery man. I want you to come back with us and tell our courts what you have said here, tonight. From what you have said, I have enough to arrest him as soon as I return." Buck studied on the Indian to see how he was taking what he had said, then added, "But you also must pay for what you have done."

Rick motioned with his hand. "Speak," nodded Chief Stumbling Bear.

Rick narrowed his eyes at Blackhorse and in a rasping voice said, "It was you who attacked and raped my niece, Kathryn...do you admit to that?" Rick's fist opened and closed tensely waiting for his admission.

Blackhorse directed his eyes down to the fire, then haltingly raised his head and met Rick's stern face. "The terrible act I did to your niece was wrong...it has haunted me, haunted my soul...day and night," he answered mournfully.

Rick's body trembled and he started to leap for Blackhorse, but Sam and Buck grabbed hold of his arms. Rick tried to calm down, but his temples were throbbing while both his fists opened and closed in angry frustration.

"I was only to take her back as a hostage to Zeb Taylor...I had not planned to do what I did...I could not help myself. His voice was anguished and he beat his fists hard upon his chest. Tormented, he cried out, "Now I am no better than the white man who did that to my Mother...my people. For that, I deserve to die. I am ready to die...for that. His head dropped down from exhausted emotion.

Chirping Bird's face wore a look of fright and she turned to her husband, then her eyes darted to Buck, then Rick. The teepee became silent.

Rick looked at Blackhorse and asked, "Why did you shoot Pedro, my hired hand and shoot at me? Did it have to do with my gold in the cave...that you were living in?"

"Yes, I found the gold after I was living there. Zeb found out. He ordered me to guard the cave, and to shoot anyone who came near...until he could find a way to force you off your land."

"And, was it Zeb who ordered the hold up of the stage my niece was on?"

"Yes, but he mostly wanted us to kidnap your niece. We were to bring her to his ranch, but the others were killed. I could not, as riders came." He looked at Sam.

Buck interrupted. 'Does he still plan on kidnapping Kathryn, his niece?"

"I think if he has the chance. He has his mind set on having the gold in the cave."

"Do you know what happened to the cash box that was taken off the stage?"

"I took the box to Zeb. He took it in his house."

"If you come back, peacefully, and tell what you know, I will put in a good word for you to the judge. You might not get the rope, but I cannot make promises or speak for the judge."

"I will come peacefully. I will help you because my soul is not at peace. I am ready to die...if I must. I will not be a coward, I will take my punishment as a man," answered Blackhorse.

"Good. It is done," spoke the chief. "My son will no longer bring shame to his mother or his people. His honor will be returned, as will ours. Our business here is finished. Moon of Many Faces will take you to your lodging for the night. We will say goodbye to our son, now. You may take him with you in the morning. May the Great Spirit be with you in your journey home and the wind upon your back." Chief Stumbling Bear motioned for them to stand and leave.

Chirping Bird was not happy with the decisions made. Her wish had been for her absent son to remain with the tribe, not face a white man's prison or the final end, by hanging. Her face did not reflect these thoughts or her feelings of sorrow. These she would keep to herself.

Disturbed and restless, Rick's mind fought sleep. He rose from his blanket on the ground and carefully stepped over Sam's sprawled-out form and treaded quietly out of the teepee the three men shared for the night. Standing motionless near the entrance, he observed the circle of cone-shaped silhouettes of deer hides, pointing nobly toward the sky. For a few moments, he was mesmerized by the intermittent grey whispy puffs of smoke that drifted ghost-like from the tops of the teepees and vanished into the night sky. The camp was asleep. The only sounds came from the corral of horses pawing the ground and roving about, and the far off sounds of coyote, owls and the nighthawks.

Sullenly he shuffled to the back of their teepee and found a tree nearby and leaned heavily against it. His guts churned and his head ached from the war going on inside. He had vowed in his heart, when he'd found the filthy savage he would kill him for what he'd done to Kathryn. He hated him. Hated him with a black consuming hatred that was eating away at him, yet, something new was gnawing at his innards. It was his contradiction of feelings. He was angry with himself for feeling, feeling compassion for the young boy the medicine man had told about. He didn't want to feel anything but hate for the rapin', murderin' Indian. But, the picture in his mind of the horrifying acts that Blackhorse had witnessed, so early in his life, kept flashing through his mind. And, he vividly could imagine the young boy's terrors and pain. He shook his head trying to rid it of the picture and thought of his Kathryn. What of her? She was just an innocent victim...Blackhorse's victim. And mostly because of Zeb and that damned gold. Logically, he told himself, Blackhorse was a victim, too. A victim of things beyond his control and a victim of Zeb's. But, that didn't excuse him for what he had done to Kathryn. Angrily, he doubled his fist and struck the tree then scowled up at the moon and hoped the judge would hang Blackhorse. Sadly, he shook his head in frustration and grim-faced he dragged his tired body back to the teepee.

Blackhorse kept his word and traveled the long distance peacefully. They arranged their riding time to arrive close to the ranch at dusk, in case Zeb or his men were riding near the area and be tipped off that Blackhorse was in the sheriff's custody. It was dark when the four travelers approached the last hill leading to the ranch.

Zeke and Jasper were snoozing on the porch and their ears perked up when they caught the sounds of the horse's hooves and began to bark.

Inside the ranch house Kathryn and Claudette were just finishing washing the supper dishes, while Clint, Harold and Manuel were bent over the table pouring over plan sketches to the Bartholomew house. Jim and Pedro rested in chairs by the fireplace, Jim reading Rick's leather-bound copy of *Moby Dick*, and Pedro was sketching a scene with a bit of charcoal, he planned to paint later. Sounds of the barking dogs got everyone's attention and they exchanged alarmed looks. The men scrambled for their guns by the door.

Jim poked Pedro. "You sneak out the back, I'll go the front. Clint, you and Harold stay here with the women." The doors opened and Jim and Pedro went cautiously out, guns ready in their hands. The moon was barely over the tops of the Sangre de Cristos and Jim hesitated to listen as he strained his vision in the direction the two dogs were pointed. He heard the clip-clopping of the hooves then made out the four riders. Zeke and Jasper began to wag their tails.

"It's all right, Pedro...where ever ya are," he called out in the darkness. It's Rick. It's Rick and them comin back."

Pedro came out from behind the bush he was using for cover and walked over to

Jim. "I was a little nervous thinking it might be Zeb or one of his men," he breathed in relief. "Ill go tell the others they can rest easy."

Jim sauntered toward the pump to meet the men and Pedro ran up to the house and poked his head in the door. "It's Senor Rick and Sam, back," he grinned, failing to mention Buck or the Indian were with them.

Kathryn and Claudette lit two lanterns. Grabbing the one she'd' lit, Kathryn went out ahead of the others to greet her uncle and Sam, the rest rushed out behind her.

In her outstretched arm Kathryn's lantern lighted a path for her scurrying feet. She was nearly to the center of the turn-around and stopped dead in her tracks. The light cast upon Blackhorse, wiping his mouth with the sleeve of his buckskin shirt after drinking from the pump. Her scream pierced the air and Blackhorse's ears. The lantern smashed on the ground bursting into flames and Kathryn ran past the others back to the house. She disappeared through the door and ran hysterically down the hallway. In frightened gasps for air, she awkwardly lit the lamp by her bed and kicked her door shut, then pushed her trunk in front of it, scattering the pictures on top onto the floor. Her eyes darted about. She wished she'd grabbed her father's 44 when she passed by the door. She scrambled for her handbag and thrust her hand madly inside for the derringer.

Clint was at her door and Rick came running down the hall.

"Kathryn," knocked Clint. "It's all right...he can't hurt you. Open the door." To Rick he whispered, "She's got something blocking the door."

"Kathryn, honey," said Rick. "We're taking him on into town...to the jail. Now open the door, please."

No sound. Clint put his ear up to the door. "Kathryn," he begged. "Let us in." They heard a rasping sound as she pushed the trunk back far enough to open the door. Her eyes had a wild stare and the derringer quivered in her hand.

"Give me the gun, Kathryn," said Clint gently.

"Give Clint the gun," urged Rick, speaking softly. Kathryn stared down at the gun in her trembling white hand, then jerked her head around to the shadowed window in terror. Her face drained of color and the gun discharged as she crumpled to the floor.

Clint scooped her off the floor and lay her on the bed as the others came bounding down the hall, except Buck, who stayed out by the pump guarding Blackhorse and watching the horses.

"Get a cold towel," Rick said to Claudette. She ran back toward the kitchen and Pedro nervously asked what happened.

"The sight of the Indian scared her, Pedro."

"Must have brought back the memory of the robbery," she replied, half-truthfully.

"Anyone git hurt?" asked Sam, concerned.

"Thank God, no," answered Rick. "The bullet went through the lampshade."

Claudette rushed into the room with the cold towel and handed it to Clint. He placed it on her forehead and patted her cheeks and hands, trying to rouse her. Jim watched until Kathryn slowly fluttered her eyes then went back out to see if Buck needed assistance.

Harold clung to Claudette and they watched their friend lying helpless and frightened on the bed. Kathryn looked puzzled at Clint then her attention went to the crowd huddled in the doorway.

"What happened?" she asked Clint. "Did I faint?"

"Yes, you did," he smiled kindly, happy she seemed to be all right.

Rick stepped up to the bed and took Kathryn's hand in his. "Honey, everything is under control. We only stopped here to let off Thunder. We're headin for town to put Blackhorse in jail. He's agreed to testify to the judge against Zeb. He's not been givin us any trouble, so please don't be upset. You're safe and we aim to keep you that way." Kathryn gave him a weak smile.

"I guess I kinda went to pieces out there. I was so glad you were back I didn't stop and think before I went dashing out. I forgot that you had planned on bringing the... the...Indian...back with you. I'm sorry I caused such a fuss."

"Don't worry about it," said Rick, patting her arm. He bent down and kissed her cheek and said, "We're gonna go now so we can finish our business. You just stay here and rest." He looked fondly upon her face then smiled before he said, "If you didn't like the lampshade I bought you, why didn't you say something?"

"What do you mean?" she asked, puzzled.

"You killed it," he laughed gently. He left the room and Sam waved goodbye from the doorway.

Blackhorse was sitting on the ground, his knees drawn up and his head down. Jim looked with disgust at the man who was the cause of so much trouble, and who had the power to scare Kathryn out of her wits. Rick and Sam came up along side Jim and they, too, regarded Blackhorse. Any compassion they had felt at the camp was diminished from the effect he'd had on Kathryn.

"Ready to go?" asked Buck.

"Yah," answered Rick and Sam. They took their reins and climbed back into their saddles. Blackhorse scrambled off the ground and climbed on the back of his Paint, and the four rode off toward town.

Jim removed the panniers from Thunder, slipped off the bridle and turned him loose in the field. He hesitated going back inside because he felt useless. Clint was watching over Kathryn. He'd just be in the way. He sat dejectedly on the porch steps petting the dogs, prolonging his entrance back into the house.

The streets were aglow as the four men entered town. They avoided the main street, choosing instead to ride down a residential side street to come up on the rear of the jailhouse. They dismounted, leaving their horses tied in the back and walked Blackhorse around to the front. Art and Paul were both in the office and Art quickly grabbed the cell keys kept on a large ring in Buck's desk drawer.

Buck directed Blackhorse and Art opened one of the cell doors. Blackhorse stepped in and immediately sat down on the hard, bare bunk keeping his head down, but flinched when the cell door clanged shut.

"Anything happen around here I should know about?" Buck asked Paul.

"The usual bar fights...that's about all."

"Well, you boys are going to hold the fort down again tomorrow. I'm leavin in the morning for Saguache to get warrants for Zeb's arrest and to search his place. Art, you stand guard now. Paul, git some rest, then switch off. I'm goin home to Ruthy and get me some shut-eye. Rick, ya mind taking the pony over to the livery on yer way outa town?"

"No problem."

"And, tell Herman to keep him outa sight. I'll see you fellas as soon as I git back with the papers. Hey, thanks for comin with me and for yer help."

"No need for thanks, Buck," said Sam.

"What we all are doin is for the good of everyone around here." Rick said. "We jest got a bigger stake in it." Sam nodded and then left.

Dog-tired, Rick and Sam climbed back in their saddles and led the pony back the way they'd come and cut over to Herman Schlump's. After making the delivery they finally headed home, the moon lighting their way.

In the silent jailhouse Blackhorse sat cross-legged on the bunk in his cell. He reached into his deerskin pouch tied at his waist and pulled out the gold brooch watch. Gently, he rubbed his calloused fingers over and over, the smooth top. "Kathryn," he whispered.

Zeb Taylor was fairly well drunked up when he and Frank, his newly hired foreman, stumbled out of the Jack Rabbit, but not drunk enough not to notice the familiar Paint being led to the side of the livery by Sam and Rick. He grabbed Frank and dragged him to the side of the saloon into the shadows. Leaning against the building he spit a stream of tobacco juice in loathing, and slowly tried to grasp the situation. He elbowed Frank.

"I gotta problem. An if I gotta problem...that means you gotta problem. He screwed up his face close to Frank's. "Understand?"

"Sure," he answered nervously. "What's the problem?"

"I wanna know what Barnett and Sam are doin with that Paint? That's what. Now, why would they be comin from the direction of the jail...this time a night? Unless... unless as bad luck would have it, they got my Indian. Naw. I told him to stay gone til fall. But, if he's in jail...for some damn reason...and talks...C'mon. We gotta see what's goin on. If he's there, we gotta stop him from double-crossin me." Zeb began walking in the shadows of the streets, motioning for Frank to hurry up.

"Aren't we going to take the horses?" questioned Frank.

"Jest how much attention do you think I want? Jeez. Think."

Zeb hid in the alleyway and ordered Frank to peer in the front window of the jail, and weaved back and forth til Frank returned.

"There's just one light on in the office." Frank whispered. "I can't see back to the cells. And, it ain't the sheriff who's sittin at the desk."

"It's a deputy, you dumb-ass. Let's go around the other side from the back, there's a window there."

Zeb made a step out of his hand and booted Frank up to the window, which was partially opened. Blackhorse heard the slight scuffling outside and quietly stood up on his bunk and peered out. The two men found themselves staring eyeball to eyeball and every muscle in Frank's face froze in startled fear. Blackhorse quickly gathered spit and let loose with it through the barred window splattering Frank's face with saliva. So startled, he lost his hold on the windowsill, and fell to the ground.

"That heathen son-of-a-bitch," snarled Frank.

"Was it an Indian?" asked Zeb, eagerly.

"Yah," he answered swiping at his face with his sleeve.

Zeb spotted a barrel a short ways away and motioned for Frank to follow him. They carried the barrel and placed it under the window and with Frank's help, Zeb was finally standing on top of it.

Blackhorse stood back from the threatening window waiting and listening.

"Blackhorse?" whispered Zeb through the window. "It's me, Zeb, yer ol' friend.

Kin ya hear me?" No answer followed. "Listen, I got somethin important ta tell ya." Zeb heard a sound inside the cell on his left. He pulled his gun silently from the holster and poked his arm through the bars and the gun cracked, loudly.

Zeb jumped off the barrel. "Let's git the hell outa here." They ran to the back and crossed over to another street then made their way back in the direction of the Jack Rabbit. They stood talking outside as if they had never left. In a minute or two, they walked and talked noisily over to their horses, so they'd be noticed for an alibi. Zeb reached in his saddlebag and took out a bottle of whisky, took a slug and passed it to Frank. Frank took a swig and handed it back.

"You go back inside and have a few drinks. Stay in town tonight and see if you can find out any more on the Indian, and what they had him in for. I'm goin home. Git yer ass out to the ranch as soon as ya know anything. Understand?"

"Yah, I understand."

The shot jolted Art from his chair and he grabbed the lantern and charged back to the cell, and Paul leaped off his cot, where he'd been sleeping in the back room and grabbed his gun. Blackhorse lay crumpled on the bunk, blood dripping onto the floor.

"Oh, God," said Art.

"What the hell happened?" asked Paul, as he stared at the wounded Indian.

"He's been shot. Go look around outside...see if anybody's ridin away."

Art got the keys and opened the cell door, gun in hand. Blackhorse gasped and coughed and a trickle of blood ran out of his mouth and down his cheek. His lips were red with blood and he stared at Art with a confused look.

Paul rushed in. "Streets are deserted...no one's in back. I'm going for the Doc."

Art raised the lantern for a closer look at Blackhorse. His breathing was labored and blood seeped through his fingers where his hand clutched his chest.

"Who did this; do you know?" he asked urgently.

With all the strength he could muster, Blackhorse pointed to the window and choked out, "Z...Zeb...a..."

Art had never been alone or this close to an Indian before and even though Blackhorse lay badly wounded a fear of the unknown came over him. He tried to appear calm and in charge, but it was as if at any given moment this man with long braided hair, dressed in buckskin and beads, was going to suddenly leap up and do something terrible to him. He forced himself to look the Indian in the eye and was taken back by the beseeching gaze he received.

"H...Help...me," gasped Blackhorse.

"Paul's gone for the doctor. Just hang on," he found himself saying with compassion. He knew he should check the wound, knew he should be doing something to ease the man's suffering, but he was immobilized, his boots fixed to the floor.

The door flew open. Doc Lawton and Paul charged through and back to the cell.

"Now that yer here, Doc, I'd better go wake Buck and tell him. Art led a hasty retreat.

"Hold the light higher, Paul," instructed Doc. "There." He cut away at the buckskin and examined the wound. "We gotta get him over to my office. I can't work on him here." Doc looked at the Indian. He knew it was the same one who killed the young guard, wounded the others and raped poor Kathryn. But, the look on the man's face and his pleading, pained expression reminded him that his job, his duty, was to heal people, all people, not be their judge. He couldn't play God, he could only be an instrument. He could only be what he was. A doctor. He reached down and stroked Blackhorse's head. "I'm here to help you, and I'll do the best I can."

Zeb rode his short-cut home. He was sweating even though the night air was chilly. By the time he reached home he was good and drunk and sick to his stomach, and he vomited all over himself and on the porch. Lupe had been asleep but heard him stumble in. She grabbed a blanket to use for a wrapper and went to see what was going on.

Zeb stood in the entrance weaving, and reeked of whiskey and bile. The front of him was wet and vomited food particles clung to his clothes. "Oh," exclaimed Lupe in disgust.

"What the hell ya starin' at?" he bellowed. He reached out and slapped her face in anger, and she stumbled backwards clutching her blanket. Rosetta was peeking out of her door and froze when she saw Zeb strike Lupe. Zeb spotted her.

"Rosetta. Git out here and clean off the porch with a bucket of water. Now." Fearing his wrath she tiptoed slowly from her room.

"You," he leered at Lupe, "Come here." He grabbed her arm and dragged her along toward his bedroom.

"No. No. Let me go," begged Lupe. "Please, Zeb...not tonight. You are drunk and you smell...bad."

"It don't bother me none," he laughed sadistically. "I need comfort...and I need it now." Lupe struggled to free herself and Rosetta stood horrified, afraid and too weak to help her-friend. They got to Zeb's room and he shoved Lupe across the threshold and kicked the door shut.

Rosetta covered her ears to block out the screaming protests and slaps, then ran to fetch a bucket, fearing her own punishment. "I wish we could get out of here," she sobbed, out on the porch. "I hate him. I wish he were dead."

29

Kathryn's chair was empty the next morning at breakfast. Finally, Claudette went to her bedroom, knocked and went in. In a few minutes she returned and reported that Kathryn was not feeling well and didn't care to eat yet.

"Is she still upset over the surprise run-in with Blackhorse?" asked Rick frowning.

"She didn't say, But, I would imagine that has a lot to do with it," replied Claudette. "Maybe I should see if she would like to go with me to see the doctor, perhaps he can help her."

"That's a good idea. Go ask her," urged Rick.

"I'll drive them in," offered Harold, "if she wants to go. I was going into town anyway to order some building materials."

Claudette reappeared. "She was reluctant, but I convinced her it wouldn't hurt to go. I told her if she's feeling better afterwards, we could have lunch and maybe do some shopping. That idea appealed to her," she smiled.

Clint helped Kathryn into the carriage, bent over and gently kissed her and said, "I hope yer feelin better after seein the doc. I'll be waiting for you when you get home."

The Bartholomew's carriage pulled up in front of Doctor Lawton's and Harold helped get Kathryn inside. He told them he would be back in a bit, after he checked on something at the sheriff's office for Rick. He didn't want to upset Kathryn more by saying it had to do with Blackhorse and Zeb.

Both Claudette and Kathryn were puzzled at the nervous and almost annoyed expression on Doc Lawton's face when he walked into the waiting room.

"What are you doing here?" he asked abruptly.

Kathryn was taken back, for she had never heard him speak in that tone of voice. Claudette regained her composure and replied, "I brought Kathryn in because she is not feeling well. Did we come at a bad time?"

His eyes went from Claudette's to Kathryn's. Resigned to the inevitable he said, "I might as well tell you...you will find out sooner or later." He stepped over to Kathryn and took her hand. "Blackhorse, the Indian, was shot last night in his cell. He is back there," Doc nodded his head, "in critical condition. I don't have much hope that he will make it."

Kathryn sat down heavily, unable to speak. Claudette asked, "Who shot him?"

He said the word Zeb to Art, but Buck doesn't know for sure if that is who really did it." He looked at Kathryn. "You are pale. Come with me into the examining room." He gently led her back past the closed door where Blackhorse lay fighting for his life.

Claudette waited in a state of worry in the reception area. Harold came bursting in. "Where's Kathryn," he asked out of breath.

"With the doctor."

"Did the doctor tell you who is here?" he asked tensely.

"Yes, he did."

"How did Kathryn take that?"

"Better than I thought she would."

"Dear, are you going to be all right if I run over to the Mercantile? They are out of coffee at the jail, and I offered to get some for Paul."

"Yes. I'll be fine. You go right ahead." Harold gave her a peck on the cheek and hurried out the door.

Not very long after he had gone Claudette heard a muffled cry. It sounded like Kathryn. She jumped up and headed for the examining room just as the doctor came out.

"Claudette, come help," he motioned. "I need you."

Kathryn was huddled and clutched a white sheet around her drawn up knees on top of the examining table. She was rocking back and forth with a vague look in her eyes sobbing, "No-o, no-oo, no-ooo." Claudette hurried to her and wrapped her arms about her friend and held her close. "What's happened? What's wrong?"

With a sad look Doc answered, "She is carrying a baby."

"Oh, no. Oh, dear Lord...Oh, my poor dear Kathryn." Claudette drew Kathryn tightly to her and stroked her head. Tears spilled down her cheeks knowing the pain and anguish that Kathryn had already been through, and now this shocking blow.

"Clau...Claudette," she gasped. 'What am I going to do. What am I going to do. I could just die...I want to die." She clutched at Claudette's arms til they hurt and rocked her body in agonizing jerks. Her tear stained face lifted and her puffy eyes still shedding teardrops looked helplessly at the doctor. "Why did this...have to happen...to me. Why?"

"Because you were raped, Kathryn," he answered softly and gently.

"But...I, I don't want a ba...beee. I don't want to be...a mother," she wailed.

"I know you don't, Kathryn. And, I am sorry this had to turn out this way. But, there is nothing we can do about it. I wish there was. Even if I could legally do it, you are too far along to abort the fetus. I wish there was more I could do or tell you to make this easier, but there is nothing I or you can do about it. I'm sorry, I truly am," said Doc, wishing he had the power to change this pitiful situation around.

Kathryn looked disheartened at Claudette. "What am I going to do about Clint? How will I ever be able to face him...to tell him? He will want nothing to do with me... now. I have lost him...forever." She began crying again and sniveled, "How will I tell Uncle Richard? Oh, Ooooh. I won't be able to face anyone."

"Kathryn," spoke Claudette sternly. "Listen to me. Just listen, please. What has happened has happened, and it is not your fault. No one who knows you or loves you will think anything less of you or think badly of you, especially for something that was not your fault. You are my friend, my dear sweet friend. I will help you. I will stand by you and help you through the whole ordeal. I promise. We will see this through, together."

"Th...thank you," was all Kathryn could answer.

"Now, young lady," said Doc, kindly. "You get yourself dressed and prettied up. While you are doing that I have to check my patient. When I get back there're things we need to discuss so you can stay healthy through this."

"I will go see if Harold is back, unless you need me to help you right now," Claudette said.

"No. I think I can manage. " Dejectedly Kathryn began to put her clothes back on.

"Harold. Good, you are back."

"You look upset, Love...what is the matter?"

Claudette ran teary-eyed into Harold's arms and sobbed, "Oh, the worst possible thing has happened."

"Here, sit down and tell me."

"Oh, Harold, you must promise not to say anything to anyone."

"I promise. Now, tell me what is the matter."

"Kathryn is going to have...a baby."

"Oh, no. Are you sure?"

"Yes. And, she is very upset I just don't know how she is going to get through this, I truly don't. We have to help her, Harold."

"Of course we will help her, in any way we can."

"She does not want the baby, and she is afraid of losing Clint."

"I can certainly see why she wouldn't want the baby," said Harold, thoughtfully. "She isn't married, but worst of all, the father is an Indian. The poor child will be what they refer to out here as a half-breed. And, Claudette, that will not be a good thing for the child. It will have a hard time fitting into society, or knowing where it belongs. I'm afraid people are not very accepting about anybody that is...different." Harold held Claudette close and said, "I shudder to think how Clint is going to feel about this. It will tear him up inside. Rick, too."

It was one of the hardest things the Doc had to do when he went to check on Blackhorse. He gazed down at the Indian clinging to life, yet anger welled up inside him. This man had ruined a beautiful young woman's life...perhaps spoiled her chances to marry the man she loved...or ever marry. He shook his head in frustration as he dutifully checked and cleaned the deep wound.

The Indian had lapsed in and out of consciousness since he had gotten him to the office. The bullet had gone in deep, close to his heart. He had to send Paul over to Alice Truitt's to bring her over to assist him with the difficult surgery. The operation was touchy and had taken a very long time.

Doc looked at the face of Blackhorse and his eyelids flickered, but he did not come around. He placed the white sheet carefully back over him and went to counsel Kathryn.

He knocked on the door. "Come in," said Kathryn. She was fully dressed and had washed her face and fixed her hair, but there was a defiant expression on her face and a cold calculating look in her eye. "I want to see the man that did this to me," she stated flatly. "The man who raped me and ruined my life."

"I don't think that would be wise. It would only upset you more. Besides, he is unconscious."

"I don't care what you think. I want to look at him. Please take me or I'll go myself."

Reluctantly and against his better judgment, Doc complied and led her through the door to Blackhorse. Kathryn angrily marched into the room then stopped abruptly when she neared the bed. Absently, she fingered the derringer inside her handbag. She stared at the man lying there and he appeared helpless and pitiful, and did not resemble the horrid face of the rape, or the face that startled her so badly last night. This confused, and angered her more. She wanted to remember a face she could hate. This didn't seem right, didn't seem fair.

"Is he going to die?" she asked with no emotion.

"Probably. I would be amazed if he pulled through with a wound like he has."

She studied the features on the face of the man whose child she was carrying and her heart filled with rage. Again, she fingered the cold shape of the derringer. She felt like killing him, he deserved it, she reasoned, but she did not have it in her to carry out her anger in that manner. She was angry because her emotions were trapped between right and wrong, good and bad.

"Let's go," she said. "I have seen enough."

Unnoticed as they were about to leave the room, Blackhorse's eyes flicked open. He blinked to clear his blurred vision, and saw Kathryn. He hadn't been dreaming, he told himself. It was her voice he'd heard. He formed her name with his lips as he slipped back into unconsciousness.

The doctor led Kathryn out to the waiting room and Harold immediately stood up and went to her. Tenderly, he put his arm around her.

"Kathryn," he spoke softly, "Claudette has told me. I am so very sorry this tragedy has happened to you. My dear, you have been through so much already. I do want you to understand and know that you can count on the both of us to stand by you through this, and always."

Claudette's eyes moistened as she watched and listened to her Harold. She was so proud of him, and her heart confirmed she had married a truly remarkable man.

"Now," smiled Harold, "I will buy the two most beautiful women in town lunch at the hotel."

"Oh, Harold, I just couldn't go and face anyone. It would seem like they already know."

"Nonsense. We are going. Besides, I am hungry." Harold ushered the two women out the door and gave the doc a sad smile and a slight shake of his head.

Rick and the men at the ranch were gathered by the corral. He had called them together to make a request. "Tomorrow, Buck is goin to want some help. He's asked me to form a posse to ride with him when he goes after Zeb."

"Ya know I wouldn't miss it," shouted Sam.

"Me, neither," yelled Jim.

"You can count on me, Senor Rick," said Pedro bravely.

"You know I'm in," stated Clint.

"I would not be a man if I stayed behind. His men killed my friend. And the cold air aches my old wounds to remind me of that day," declared Manuel. "Besides, Pedro and me, we might get a peek at those Senoritas he's told me about," he summed up, grinning.

The bunch broke into laughter and Pedro looked a little sheepish, then his face got a serious expression and he remarked, "Who knows, Manuel, they may be in danger, too."

"Good point, Pedro, " Rick commented.

The sound of carriage wheels and horse hooves drew their attention to the long drive. Worried and anxious Clint broke away to be first to greet Kathryn.

It had been agreed upon that nothing would be said about Kathryn's condition. She told them she needed time to sort out her feelings and decide how and when she would break the tragic news, first of all to Clint. In her favor, they knew that tomorrow the sheriff and his posse would be riding over to Zeb's to arrest him and search his place. And, with them bringing the news of Blackhorse being shot, the attention could not be directed to Kathryn.

"Kathryn," smiled Clint, "are you all right?"

"I'll be fine," lied Kathryn.

Claudette, being helped from the carriage by Harold, revealed more on Kathryn's behalf. "Doctor Lawton said she has been through too much since leaving her home, and the strain has taken its toll. She just needs lots of rest for a while."

Clint and Claudette escorted Kathryn into the house, while Harold told the news.

"Rick. And the rest of you," motioned Harold, raising his voice to be heard.

"The Indian was shot last night...in his cell. He's in critical condition."

"Who the hell got to him?" yelled Rick, angrily.

"Art said he tried to point to the window and spoke the name Zeb."

"That dirty, rotten bastard. How did he find out we'd snuck him into town?" came Sam's bitter retort.

"I don't know," answered Harold, shaking his head as puzzled as they were.

"Sure sheds a different light on the situation. I jist hope he hangs in long enough to speak his piece in court," Rick said.

All heads turned when they heard a rider coming. "Good," said Rick. "It's Buck, coming back from Saguache. Hope he's got those warrants."

Kathryn took her supper in her room that night and Claudette joined her, for she felt strangely out of place in the kitchen. All the men were busy discussing Blackhorse's shooting and making plans for the early morning surprise at Zeb's ranch. Buck was put up for the night in the parlor and Rick slept on the sofa as he'd done since arriving back with Blackhorse.

An unexpected late night rain splattered upon the roof of the ranch house and Kathryn tossed and turned in bed, unable to sleep. She threw the covers back and wearily made her way in the dark to the chair by the window. Sadly, she eased herself down and stared blankly out into the dark rainy night. She had an ache in the pit of her stomach and a heaviness in her heart. Over and over her thoughts were, "What am I going to do? What I going to do?"

What could she do? This was not something she could share with her mother. How could she? What had happened that caused the horror she now faced was too shameful. What would her mother think of her now? Their parting had been an ugly, painful scene. Her mother had warned her, hadn't she? She had said, "savage Indians." Savage, savage, echoed in her mind. She put her hands over her ears to silence the sound and squeezed her eyes shut to block out the picture of the Indian's face. A loud clap of thunder jolted her in the chair and the rumble that followed seemed to echo, Clint, Clint, Clint. Soon her tears matched the raindrops that slid down the windowpane. She would have to tell Clint...sometime. But, how, how would she begin? She had kept the rape a carefully guarded secret, but now she would have to reveal that, too. Absently, the palm of her hand found its way to her belly and she pushed it slowly back and forth. A baby. Inside there, somewhere, a baby, a new being, a person, a brand new person was growing.

Her body began to shake and her breath came in short gasps as her fist hammered repeatedly on the arm of the chair with the painful truth that she, Kathryn Barnett, was going to be a mother. A mother, whether she wanted to be or not. She would be shunned...mocked, because in reality the baby, the child would be a...bastard. She bit down on her hand to stifle the scream that wanted to come out and startle the silent house and fill it with her shrieking torment. Her teeth moved, biting down firmly on her nightgown covered arm. The baby would be not just a bastard, but a half-breed.

"Oh, God," she sobbed, "What am I going to do? How am I to survive this?" She held her face in her hands and cried softly.

30

One by one before the sun came up, the men staggered sleepily into the kitchen. Although Harold was picked to stay to guard the two women and watch over the ranch, he had gotten up before the rest and had hot strong coffee ready. Standing in his stocking feet, newly purchased Levis and grey-striped shirttails hanging over his hips, he handed each a cup as they paraded-to the table. It didn't take long for the room to buzz with the undercurrent of excited, nervous energy. Buck revealed his plan of action to the men, but as he spoke he couldn't help but wander if Blackhorse, his ace in the hole, was still alive.

Outside, Jasper and Zeke barked warnings. Rick and Sam charged out with guns onto the porch. Vaguely they could make out two riders...no, three...the third being a buckboard. When they got in shouting distance a voice called out. "Rick'? That you?"

"Yah."

The riders dismounted at the hitching rail and quickly sprang off their horses, and the driver of the buckboard pulled alongside. "Peter, Mike...and...Luigi? What brings you out before sun-up?"

Peter Voris, stage manager, and Mike McDougal, bartender at the Jack Rabbit and Luigi Amato, the undertaker, marched up to the steps. "Art and Paul sent us to join the posse," answered Peter. "And, Mike's got some news to tell the sheriff."

"And, I am at your service in any way, and will gladly haul any bodies back to town...dead or alive," answered Luigi.

They marched inside and Harold got them coffee and made the rounds at the table refilling the cups. Mike took a long drink and leaned against the counter.

"I've got some things to tell ya, Buck, you might find important concerning the shootin of that Indian ya had in jail." The room silenced and the men's attention focused on Mike. Mike was a big man, not unlike Sam, except he had short curly brown hair and was clean shaven.

"Rick, 'member that day you stopped in and were askin about that fella, Frank?"

"Yah, I remember. What about him?"

"Well, he and Zeb were in playin cards night before last. When the game was over they walked out...musta lost. Well, anyway, Old Joe was lockin up his harness shop and happened to see you and Sam bringin that Paint to the livery. It belonged to the Indian, didn't it?"

"Yah, it was his," confirmed Buck. "Go on."

"Old Joe saw Zeb watchin you fellas, then they ducked outa sight. Old Joe thought this suspicious so he crouched by his window and watched em. He sees em sneakin off in the direction of the jail, on foot. Now everybody knows Zeb don't walk nowheres, so he stayed watchin and waitin. Pretty soon he sees em hot-footin it back to the saloon, but they stayed outside making all kinds of noise, like they're tryin ta draw attention to themselves. Then, Frank walks over to Zeb's horse and they take a drink from the bottle in his saddlebag, and Zeb rides off. Frank came back in and the damned fool got pretty drunked up and started shootin his mouth off about gettin rich with Zeb...he didn't say how, and then about him personally gettin even with a 'Barnett' Old Joe came to me the next morning and told me what he'd seen. We both went to yer office, Buck, and that's when we found out that somebody'd shot the Indian."

"Art asked me to come out ta tell ya what I knew and join up with the posse."

Harold spotted Claudette down the hall, scurrying in her robe into Kathryn's room and he quickly poured two cups of coffee and carried them to the room. Rick had been deep in thought, as was Clint. Thinking out loud Rick asked, "What would he have to get even with me for? I don't even know the man...not that I'd want to."

"What did you say his name was, Mike?" questioned Clint.

"Frank."

"Frank, what?"

"He's never given his last name," replied Mike.

"Can you describe him for me?" asked Clint, his eyes narrowing in thought.

"Yah. Kind of a shifty lookin fella, wouldn't you say, Rick?" Rick nodded. "About medium build, dirty lookin light hair...he parts it down the middle...beady eyes, yah, beady eyes, kind of a boney looking face...and rotten teeth. He's not what you'd call a lady pleaser," Mike laughed.

Clint's face was livid. "That could only be one person," he stated tensely. Buck looked at Clint, burning with curiosity. "I'd take on all bets that the man's name is Frank Palmer. That description fits him. Rick, I don't think it it's you he wants to get even with...it's Kathryn." Rick's eyes widened and he set down his pipe and asked Clint for an explanation. Clint related the story of the poker game on the train and about Frank breaking into Kathryn's hotel room in Dodge City to rob her, and who knew what else? "Last we saw him he was behind bars. Either, he was given a short sentence and served his time, or he broke out."

"Who knows if he's at Zeb's or what, but I think after hearing that story...more than one man oughta stay here," said Rick.

"I will," volunteered Luigi. "I haven't had a chance to use this much and I have been itching for the chance." He patted his Colt '38 Peacemaker and smiled. "Besides, my wagon'll draw too much attention. You can send someone back for me when you need it."

"That settles it," said Buck. "Let's saddle up and ride outa here before it gets too light out."

The room was noisy with the shuffling of boots as the men strapped on their holsters, picked up their rifles and grabbed their hats. Rick, Sam, Jim, Manuel, Pedro and Clint rushed out to bring their horses out of the barn and get them saddled. Buck, Mike and Peter were mounted up and waiting as the group began to assemble by the pump. A thundering of hooves was heard as the posse of nine rode out of the yard.

Hearing the men ride off, Claudette and Kathryn stole out of the bedroom but stopped short at the kitchen entrance when they saw Luigi sitting at the table with Harold.

"My dears," Harold addressed the women. "Hand me your cups and I'll pour you some fresh coffee."

"Good morning, Mrs. Bartholomew and Miss Barnett," greeted Luigi. "I am going to stay here with you people until the foray at the Taylor ranch is completed. I hope you do not mind my intrusion?"

"Oh, that is quite all right," Kathryn assured him. "If you came all the way out here to help, you are certainly not intruding. I hope you know that you are welcome anytime, not just in time of trouble."

"Very graciously spoken. I thank you for your kindness," said Luigi.

Harold wrestled with himself wondering if he should tell Kathryn about the fellow, Frank, that he had heard about this morning. He didn't know if her frayed emotions could stand any more shocks. He decided to wait and ask Claudette when they had a chance to be alone. But, he had made up his mind that since he was now in charge he would set down some rules for the women to follow.

"Ladies," he said. "Until the fellows come back and tell us everything is under control, I think we should take some precautions."

"Harold, do you really think we could be in danger, here?" asked Claudette, looking frightened.

"The way things have been going, Love, anything seems possible. I just feel we should be alert and prepared, and use some common sense."

"I agree with you, Bartholomew," nodded Luigi. "With people like Zeb Taylor roaming these parts, it is in one's best interest to be vigilant."

"I believe you are right, there, Luigi. So I guess this is a good time for me to give you something, Claudette," said Harold. He got up and went to Rick's bedroom where they'd been staying and returned shortly carrying something behind his back. "Here," he said, "this I bought for you a while back and I can't think of a more appropriate time to give it to you." He set down in front of her a Colt '31 Baby Dragoon, a small pocket pistol, somewhat larger than Kathryn's Derringer. Alongside he placed a box of metallic cartridges. Her face showed surprise and she blinked her eyes at the shiny new gun.

"You bought that just for me? Why Harold...how sweet of you." She stood up and kissed him lovingly on the cheek.

"Claudette, that's a very nice gun," admired Kathryn.

"Sure is," agreed Luigi. And they watched as she picked up her new gun and pretended to shoot the fireplace.

"I'll show you how to load that thing after we have us some breakfast," said Harold, then added, "if you think you can wait that long."

"Now, Harold, " she scolded, and she set down her new gun to help prepare their meal.

Luigi took out his pocket watch. "They've been gone long enough now to just about be on the Taylor property." They all exchanged anxious looks.

Buck halted his posse when they neared the back side of Zeb's property line. The sun had not yet peaked the tops of the mountains, but the morning light had changed from dark to light grey allowing them to view the lay of the land and pick their positions. They were situated on one of several knolls among a grove of pinon trees facing the back and east end of Zeb's large house.

"What we gotta do," said Buck, "is get the place surrounded at strategic spots before me, Rick and Sam ride down to serve him the warrants. The rest of you dismount and tie yer horses here."

"All right," he instructed, "Manuel, Pedro and Jim...you boys work yer way down around the far west side, and spread out. And, Clint, Mike and Peter...you take the east side here and ease toward the back, and be ready to bring the horses down when the need arises. Watch for anyone sneakin out of the house or tryin to ride out. Better git started, and watch yerselves."

The three remaining waited poised on their horses and observed the scene below. One by one, the men quickly covered ground, bending low as they darted from rocks, clumps of trees and bushes, scanned the area ahead, then scrambled a few yards more.

When everyone was in place, Buck, Rick and Sam circled around and got on to the road to make their approach from the front. They walked their horses to keep the noise down so as not to arouse suspicion and alert them. They rode up to the front porch and Buck dismounted. He strolled up to the door and knocked.

Lupe squinted her swollen eyes to peek between the slit in the kitchen curtains. She let out a long sigh of disgust, "More trouble," she fretted, passing her hand over her bruised jaw. She dreaded waking Zeb and stood fixed to the floor, thinking.

"You awake in there, Zeb?" called Buck, knocking some more.

Lupe's slippered feet dragged in the direction of Zeb's bedroom and then hesitated.

Buck stood determined by the side of the door holding the warrants in one hand and his Colt 44 in the other. Buck jerked his head to his right when he heard the sound of the bunkhouse door pop open. Jake, Bart and three rough and foul-looking men, whom he had never seen before, sauntered out toward Rick and Sam with pistols drawn. Buck slowly lowered his gun and slid it behind his leg and waited for his own men to make their move. Out of the corner of his eye he saw Clint and Mike with rifle barrels aimed and ready, and his eye roamed to Rick and Sam sitting calmly in their saddles. At Bart's signal the motley group stopped.

"And jest what the hell do you want so early in the morning, Sheriff?" demanded Bart.

"That's between me and Zeb," answered Buck, staring him in the eye.

"Well, it's my job to see no one disturbs him...til he says. So state yer business."

"My business...is not your business, Bart. So I suggest you put away your guns and go back in the bunkhouse before somebody gits hurt," replied Buck.

Bart snickered, tilted his head and uttered snidely, "Didja hear that boys? We got the drop on em and they're worried we might git hurt. That's rich."

Manuel had seen the bunkhouse door open and signaled to Pedro and Jim. When the coast was clear Manuel snuck up and around the other side of the bunkhouse. Pedro moved silently and unnoticed to an overgrown shrub directly behind the bunch. Jim watched for Pedro's signal then he inched his way up to the side of the house.

Jake elbowed Bart, and asked, "Now what do you suppose the sheriff's got in his hand?" He cocked back the lever on his gun and started walking toward Buck. "I'll jest take those, Sheriff, and deliver them for ya...so you an yer friends here kin be on yer way.'

"Don't nobody move;" boomed Manuel. Zeb's men froze, figuring their next move when they heard...click....click....click behind them as the hammers were drawn back on the rifles of Manuel, Pedro and Jim. Jake spun around and fired at Pedro and his bullet just barely missed him. A zinging sound split the air, and Jake dropped to the ground. Rick and Sam leaped out of their saddles and hit the dirt with their guns drawn. The rest of Zeb's men dropped their guns as they watched themselves being surrounded by rifles and pistols. Jake clutched his bloody arm and yelled in pain in the dirt.

"Nice shootin, Jim," called Buck from the porch.

"Si," grinned Pedro.

"Rick, Sam...go check the bunkhouse. See if there's any more holdin out," said Buck.

Inside the house Lupe pounded frantically on Zeb's door in fear. "Zeb. Come out. There's trouble and shooting."

"I hear. You think I'm deaf," he bellowed. Lupe heard loud profanity and thumping as the cumbersome man hurried to put on his clothes.

"Don't unlock the door," he hollered at her. "Don't let a damned soul in or you'll live to regret it." She ran from his door aid scurried back to the kitchen window to see what was happening outside.

"Bring yer rope, Sam," called Manuel. "I think these boys want to play, 'Ring-Around-The-Rosey.'" Sam brought his rope and he herded the men in a circle. Manuel came to assist and the two performed some fast and slick rope tying. When they were done, the men were standing shoulder to shoulder with their hands tied behind their backs and to each other in a nice tight circle.

Zeb stomped out and shoved Lupe away from the window. He turned and shouted to her, "Go get Frank down here, now." He grabbed his double set of holsters and strapped them on.

Lupe met Frank charging down the steps, gun in hand. "Where's Zeb," he demanded, and his beady eyes shown panic as he pushed passed Lupe when she pointed to the kitchen.

"What's going on outside, Zeb?" Frank asked waving his arms like broken bird wings.

"That," spat Zeb, pointing out the window. Frank pawed at the curtain and took a nervous look and his stomach knotted at what he saw.

Frank turned white-faced to Zeb. "What are ya goin do?"

"We, Palmer. We. Go back upstairs and git a look out the side windows. See how many there are out there. What ya waitin for? Git."

Frank took the steps two at a time and Zeb picked up his shotgun. Rosetta had been watching through a skinny crack in her bedroom door and was afraid with all the shouting and gunfire. She prayed Zeb would not remember her and call her to come out. Lupe cowered in the kitchen near the side door, wishing she could find the courage to run out.

Frank charged clumsily back down the stairs. "Don't look like but one other man...that I could see...behind the rock pile on the west."

"This is the sheriff," pounded Buck with his fist on the door. "Do I have to have my men break down yer door, Zeb? Or are ya gonna open it peacefully?"

"Keep yer damned shirt on, McCain. I'm comin."

Zeb's mind was confused. Just what was Buck's reason for being here...now? Buck meant business for sure, if he out maneuvered his men and hog-tied them, and wounded one of em, that he knew of. Had Blackhorse spilled his guts before they locked him up? If he did, what all had he told? He never should have trusted an Indian in the first place, he chided himself...shoulda killed him soon as I knew about the gold. Zeb was positive no one had seen him or Frank go to the jail, or seen them at the barred window...so how could anyone connect him with Blackhorse's murder? And, he had explained away the last stage robbery quite well, he thought. So, just what was McCain strong-arming him for? Something...that much was certain. Zeb felt trapped. He needed bargaining power but right now he didn't have any. Then a thought came to his mind.

"Frank. Go hide upstairs and stay quiet...no matter what. When ya see the coast is clear, climb down outa one of the windows and git yer ass over to Barnett's. Looks like everybody from there is here, so ya shouldn't have any trouble gittin at his niece. I don't care how ya do it, but bring her back here and if I'm not here, ya keep her here til I send ya word on what ya should do. It looks like ol McCain might have the notion of lockin me up...it'll be my way of gittin out. Now git upstairs while I open the door, 'fore McCain kicks it open."

"How am I gonna git to my horse with them out there, Zeb?"

"You ain't. Yer gonna walk. Now git."

"This is your last chance Zeb. Open up."

Zeb propped the shotgun in a crevice by the door then turned the key in the latch. He jerked the door open and stepped out. A sneering grin quickly disappeared when he caught the sight of six cold steel barrels pointed directly at his fat chest.

"What the hell is the reason for hounding me so early in the morning?" he demanded, snarling his fat lip down, displaying the gaping holes in his teeth.

"I have a warrant for yer arrest, Zeb," answered Buck as he thrust the papers at him. "And, there's one there to search yer house."

"This makes no sense, McCain. I have done nothing."

"We'll let the judge decide. Now, unbuckle those belts and drop em...easy like." Zeb saw he had no choice in the matter; things were not in his favor this time. He unbuckled his belts and dropped his heavy weapons on the porch with a careless defiance. "Now what, sheriff man?" he said, through glinting eyes, and spat a stream of tobacco juice on the top of Buck's boots.

Buck looked down at the brown stringy blob. With iciness in his voice that matched the look in his eye, he called over his shoulder, "Rick, Pedro, bring another rope." Buck held his 44 on Zeb until the rope was delivered. "Now, Zeb, back up into the house." They marched him into the kitchen and were jolted by the sight of Lupe crouched and shaking on the floor in the corner by a side door. Her swollen black and blue eyes pleaded for help and her bruised puffy cheek made her face look strangely misshaped. Her bottom lip protruded, showing the long scabby split and she turned away in shame.

"Who are you?" Buck asked in a soft sympathetic tone.

Zeb glowered at her with the unspoken warning to watch what she said, then convulsed with rage as Rick shoved him into a kitchen chair and Pedro began tying him to it. "You have no right, you bastard...comin in...disturbin a man's home and tyin him up...like a pig," he bellowed.

Rick and Buck exchanged smirks over Zeb's accurate description of himself. Buck stepped closer to the silent woman and held out his hand to help her stand up. She shrank back, then timidly put her hand in his and rose unsteadily to her feet.

"What is your name?" Buck asked.

"I am Lupe," she answered in a low hoarse voice.

"Did he do this to you?" Buck questioned, pointing to her battered face and nodding toward Zeb. Lupe lowered her head and nodded yes. Buck saw Pedro was done tying the rope.

"Pedro, go call Peter and Manuel...tell em to come in here. Then, you may have the honor of guarding the jail's newest guest."

Manuel hustled into the house. He stopped when he saw Lupe and the condition she was in and his heart softened with pity and his eyes looked sadly into hers. With a questioning frown he cocked his head back at Zeb. Lupe dropped her gaze and nodded once. Manuel screwed up his face and his eyes blazed meanly at Zeb. He took two long steps and backhanded Zeb across the face. "That is no way to be treating a women...

you scum. How do you like it, huh?" He smacked him another good one when Zeb spit tobacco juice down the front of his shirt.

"That's enough, Manuel," cautioned Buck. "But, I do thank you for doing what I'd thought of doing."

Peter rushed in and Buck gave him, Rick and Manuel specific areas to search in the house. They spread out and Rick cautiously approached a bedroom door and kicked it open with his boot. He gripped his gun firmly as he surveyed the plainly furnished and dimly lit room. A sound under the bed alerted his senses and he stepped away a couple of feet. "Come out...I know someone's under there," he ordered. He waited with his gun aimed, then a surprised look crossed his face when the young Mexican girl crawled out shaking like a cornered rabbit.

"Don't be afraid," said Rick. "I'm not here to hurt you." He noticed that she had bruises on her upper arms and on her neck and face and his anger rose thinking of the brutal way these women had been treated. "I'm Rick Barnett...I live on the next ranch over. We're here with the sheriff to take Zeb and his men to jail." Her face gladdened with relief. "You come with me to the kitchen. The other lady...Lupe?" She nodded, yes. "Lupe is there. What is your name?" he asked, kindly.

"Rosetta," she answered proudly.

Pedro's eyes and expression showed surprise when he saw Rosetta enter the room with Rick. Rosetta hesitated in front of him and blushed shyly, then quickly went to the end of the room and sat next to Lupe.

"Hey. Buck. In here," called Peter. Buck hustled to the sound and entered an office. Peter was standing in a closet holding an empty metal cash box with Wells Fargo lettered on the side, and he pointed to two more lying on the floor.

"Well, here's some of the proof you've been looking for, Buck," grinned Peter.

Manuel and Rick came into the room and they all searched for more evidence while Buck toted the boxes out to the porch. Zeb saw the boxes go by and his face grew red with anger. Buck waved to get Clint and Mike's attention. They were still in position keeping watch on the overall scene. "Clint. Mike," he shouted. "Bring down the horses."

Buck went in and called for Manuel. "See if there's a wagon we can use to haul some of these varmints back to town in." Then he stepped closer to Zeb. "Why don't you save us some time and trouble and tell me where you stashed the money that was in those boxes?" Zeb snarled up his face and let fly with a hearty spit.

Buck caught a hand signal from Lupe out of the corner of his eye. She then pointed up with her finger and raised her eyes toward the ceiling. Buck went to look for a staircase and found the door that led to it, and proceeded up the narrow steps mindful of trouble. The upper floor was under a slanted roof and appeared to be used for storage. He slid his eyes around and at the same time felt a draft. At the opposite end from where he stood was an iron bed against an open window with a sheet tied to one of the legs and draped over the sill. Buck rushed to the curtainless frame and looked out and down. The sheet had obviously been used for someone's escape. Who? Buck scanned the area outside, but all he saw was their horses being ridden and led down from the knoll at a fast pace. He rushed back down the stairs directly back to Zeb, staying out of spitting range.

"Who was upstairs, Zeb? Yer new sidekick?" Zeb just curled his lip and sat mute.

"Hey, Buck," yelled Clint as he and Mike rode up with the horses. Buck ran out to see what Clint wanted. "Pedro's horse is missing. Don't know if he wandered back home or what?" Pedro heard through the open door and his heart sank.

"Clint," ordered Buck. "Ride back to Rick's and be careful. I think that Frank fellow was here and has escaped. Tell Luigi to have his wagon ready, we're gonna be needing it for haulin. But tell him to wait there til we come. Ya better git ridin, fast. Be careful, Clint."

Fearful for Kathryn and the others at the ranch, Clint rode fast and hard down the road urging his horse to a speedy gallop.

Buck turned around to see Manuel drive up in a beat-up old wagon hitched to two horses. "Good work, Manuel. Jim...Sam...load these men in the wagon, would ya?" Buck motioned for Mike to come with him into the house.

"Pedro, keep yer gun on Zeb. And Mike, untie him, so I can get the cuffs on and toss him in the wagon with the rest of his garbage." Buck looked over at the two frightened women sitting in the corner.

"Will you two ladies come with me?" asked Buck. They exchanged worried looks and quickly got up and scooted past Zeb. "Hold off on the ropes a minute, Mike," said Buck. He led Lupe and Rosetta toward the office and spoke to them in quiet voice.

"My guess," began Buck, "is neither of you have anything to do with the crimes that Zeb has committed." Wide-eyed they shook their heads quickly no.

"We are not here because we choose to be," explained Lupe. "Zeb dragged me out of a saloon in New Mexico, where I worked...and he win Rosetta in a card game somewhere near the Mexico border. He warn us he kill us if we try to leave."

Buck shook his head sadly. "Do you happen to know where he kept the money that he stole?"

Lupe's eyes brightened and a smirk crossed her face. She headed to the back of the office and waved her arm for Buck to follow. She walked past Peter to a wall, reached up and removed a large picture and set it on the floor. With her fist, she hit a section of the wood paneling and it sprung open, concealing a safe. She turned to Buck and smiled, "Here."

"Well, I'll be damned. Rick. Come on in here," called Buck. Rick arrived in time to see Buck shoot the lock on the safe. The door was pulled open and inside were bank notes from Denver, Kansas City, Santa Fe and others. There were also stacks of bills in different denominations, as well as coins of gold and silver.

"Rick, go bring those boxes back in. You and Peter fill em up, then set them in the front of the wagon. I'm going to put these on Zeb," Buck said, holding up the cuffs, "then we can clear outa here."

The ropes were untied and Zeb had the face of a madman. "Stand up easy," commanded Buck, "and step out here to the entrance, where there's more room." Zeb lumbered out of the kitchen. "Stop, that's far enough. Now, turn around, slow."

Zeb glared at Buck and began to turn. Suddenly, he lunged for the shotgun he'd stashed in the crevice. His fat hands gripped the gun as two loud shots exploded through the air from Pedro and Buck's pistols. The bullets ripped and bore into Zeb's fleshy chest and he and the shotgun slammed to the floor. Zeb's face stiffened grotesquely with a look of pain and surprise as his pig-like eyes stared wildly at his bloody chest. Blood spurted and oozed from the ripped holey flesh, soaking his shirt and. running off onto the floor. His obese body began to shake and jerk. Lupe and Rosetta viewed the scene in horror from the office doorway as he thrashed and gagged out guttural moans. The thick red liquid flowed freely out of the gap in his teeth and traveled down his pudgy chin. His cracked worn boots thumped frantically on the bare wood floor as his bulky frame vibrated and twitched making dull thudding sounds. Zeb gasped for breath and his chubby hands clawed at the air. His arms stiffened, then dropped to his sides. The boots ceased to thump. The glazed rounded eyes stared unknowing as his pants grew wet when he expelled for the last time. Zeb Taylor was dead.

Kathryn excused herself after she had helped Claudette wash up the breakfast dishes, and shut herself in her room. After making her bed she slumped despondently in the chair by the window. She felt badly that she had not spoken to Clint or her uncle before they left on the dangerous raid on Zeb Taylor. She just couldn't face them. It had been hard enough, and so uncomfortable for her yesterday when she came back from town to pretend that she was fine, pretend she was only exhausted from the many ordeals she had gone through. Now, concern and worry over their safety weighed heavily upon her. She shuddered to think something horrible could very well happen to her Uncle Richard, Clint, or any one of the men that rode off with Sheriff McCain. Sam, Pedro, Jim, Manuel...Peter Voris and even that bartender, Mike whom she did not know. This man, Zeb Taylor, had created so much trouble and heartache in the area, and especially to her uncle and her. If he hadn't framed that Indian, Blackhorse, he would not have found out about the gold in the cave, the stage may not have been held up, and Will would still be alive...and she, she wouldn't have been savagely raped and expecting an unwanted baby.

Looking about her room Kathryn saddened even more. She felt undeserving of the beautiful things bought just for her welcome and comfort. Things had not worked out the way she had planned and hoped for when she decided to come west. She felt that she had disrupted and barged in on the tight-knit group here at the ranch. She shook her head and realized that she didn't really belong here. Her uncle and the rest of them did not need the burden of a helpless woman or the shame of having an unwed mother under their roof. And afterwards...a baby. No, a bastard baby...a half-breed. And she firmly believed that Clint would be shocked and disgusted when he found out the truth, if he ever found out. She didn't want him to ever find out.

"No," she spoke aloud, "I won't stay here and face the shame and ridicule. I will leave. I will make up some excuse and leave." But, where would she go, she wondered? Back to her old home in Lexington, by her mother? Heavens, no. There of all places she would never be welcomed. She reached into her letter box, on the table beside her and pulled out the letter she had received from her mother. She had not shared the contents with her uncle or anyone, and cynically reread it to confirm her feelings.

> Dear Kathryn,
>
> I was relieved to find you arrived safely at Richard's. My worrying would have been unnecessary if you had not run off like an immature child. Your absence at my wedding was indeed a socially embarrassing situation.
>
> You put me in a most awkward position, having to explain to your dearest friend, Eileen Mary, your sudden departure. She was quite hurt that you did not have the courtesy to tell her you were leaving and say goodbye. She assured me, however, that, she would inform the other members in your sewing circle and reading group of your extended absence, and spare me the unpleasantness. She is a very considerate person.
>
> Your letter was here when Phillip and I returned from our honeymoon in New Orleans. I am certain you do not care to hear how happy the both of us are, so I will keep my joy to myself. I only wish you had the good sense to

recognize my dear Phillip's wonderful, good qualities, for he possesses many.

I hope you are happy with your decision to live in Colorado, and that you are taking proper care of yourself, although I do not see how this could be possible in such a primitive area. Please give my love to Richard.

Mother

A single tear trickled down her cheek, landed on the letter and blotched the ink on "Mother." Kathryn bit her lip as she folded the letter and put it back into the leather box. She felt so lonely and afraid that she didn't know what to do about anything anymore. Her hand rested on her stomach and the stinging reality jolted her. She had to do something...but, what? Maybe she could go somewhere and find an orphanage. She could have the baby someplace where no one knew her...have the baby and let some orphanage find a married couple who could adopt it. This began to seem like a sensible plan.

Kathryn pulled herself out of the chair and started to remove the pictures from off the trunk top. She opened the armoire and carefully took out the pretty dresses and lay them on the bed, then began to pack the trunk. As she did this her mind ran through names of big cities that she might choose to go to, where no one would know her or her family. New York City? That was, oh, so far away. Maybe Denver, right here in Colorado? It would have to be some place here in the west, some place where Indians lived, then her baby would have a better chance of being adopted. Maybe Wyoming, or South Dakota or Arizona. Then, a brilliant idea came into her head. Sam. Sam could help her...if he would? Her plan slowly unfolded in her mind and she felt a small ray of hope enter her bleak looking situation.

She had barely gotten a good start on the packing when the urgent need to use the outhouse arose. She left her room, making sure her door was firmly closed and walked into the kitchen area and smiled at Claudette. She, Harold and Luigi were engaged in a lively conversation over politics. She headed for the back door.

"Kathryn," said Harold, "if you are going outside, please put on your gun as we agreed upon." Recalling Harold's previous rules she quickly obeyed and grabbed her holster and 44 off the peg and strapped it around her waist. Harold picked up his Navy Pocket '36 lying next to him on the table and escorted her out the back door. They paused on the porch and checked the area before Kathryn proceeded alone down the path to the outhouse. She turned and grinned shyly at Harold standing guard on the porch, then pushed open the door.

As Kathryn stepped inside a hand clasped tightly across her mouth and she felt the hard pressure of a gun barrel pressing into her temple. She tried to scream but nothing came out.

A rasping voice hissed in her ear, "If you move or try anything stupid, I will pull this trigger and scatter your brain parts all over."

It was dim and shadowy inside the small structure and the man held her from behind. Kathryn couldn't see who he was, but she had heard that voice somewhere before. She couldn't remember, fear blocked her memory. Her body stiffened and she felt sick to her stomach. She tried to gulp and swallow, then started to gag on her phlegm. The palm of the hand closed tighter and the fingers dug into her cheekbone.

"I'll take my hand away, if you promise not to scream or utter one sound," Kathryn nodded stiffly, her eyes bulged in desperation and her heart pounded so hand her chest ached. The fingers were lifted one by one, then the palm. She shook and gasped to suck in air then suddenly her breakfast came up and she tossed her head and retched into one of the foul-smelling privy holes.

"Jeez, what the hell ya think yer doin?" snarled her assailant. Kathryn wiped her mouth with the back of her hand and tears of anger and helplessness sprung to her eyes. She wanted to scream out for Harold, but the gun in her back stopped her.

A dull pounding noise got their attention. It was a rider, coming fast. It must be one of them coming back from the Taylor ranch, thought Kathryn. Oh, please, she prayed, let someone come and help me. Her eyes were growing accustomed to the dimness and she slid them to the far right. "You. Oh, no," she wailed pitifully. "Not you."

"Shut up." The gun was thrust hard into her side. "Just shut up or yer dead." He felt the hardness on her hip and reached down and pulled out the 44.

"Kathryn," called out Harold. "Someone's coming. I'm going around to the side to see who it is." Harold didn't wait for an answer. He jumped off the porch and ran to identify who was corning off the hill.

Clint waved his hat at Harold to let him know who he was. When he got within shouting distance he yelled, "Where's Kathryn? Is she all right? Is she safe?"

"Yes," Harold called back. Claudette and Luigi came out the front door to catch what was being said.

Clint reined his horse to a sudden stop and leaped out of the saddle. "Have you seen Pedro's horse?" he asked out of breath.

"Why, no. What's wrong?" questioned Harold.

"We think it's been stolen. We think by Frank...Palmer...and we think he may be coming after Kathryn."

"I escorted her to the outhouse just minutes ago, and was waiting for her on the porch when you rode up," Harold told him. "She's probably still there, unless she's already gone back to the house."

"I'll go round back and check, you see if she's inside," Clint said, hurriedly. He ran toward the back and saw the outhouse door was ajar and trotted back into the house through the back. He expected her to be sitting at the table.

"Has anyone checked her room?" asked Clint.

"No, but I'll go now," offered Claudette. She rapped gently. "Kathryn, dear, are you in there?" There was no answer. After a moment Claudette turned the knob and poked her head around the door. "Kathryn?" She stepped in and was taken back by the sight of the opened trunk, half filled with clothes and others piled on the bed. Claudette put her, hands on her hips and tapped her foot trying to figure out why Kathryn was packing her things.

"Clint. Harold. Come here."

"Was she planning on going away?" Clint asked, worried and hurt.

"She never mentioned a thing about going...anywhere," answered Claudette, misty-eyed, as she suddenly thought of why Kathryn might be thinking of leaving, but she dare not mention it to Clint, not now...not yet. It wasn't her place.

Clint cocked his hat back and scratched the front of his scalp. "I don't understand it. Even so, something has happened to her since I rode up. She's got to be around here somewhere, close by. There wasn't enough time to get very far. C'mon, we gotta find her, Harold. Luigi, you stay here with Claudette, and git yer wagon ready...Buck says he's going to be needin it." Harold was close behind Clint as he charged out the back door. Clint ran to the outhouse just to be sure she wasn't still there and noticed a piece of material hanging from a nail on the inside of the door.

"Harold, was she wearing a blouse this color?" he asked, holding up a blue bit a fabric.

"Yes, she was."

"I think she was taken out of here," Clint said, half-crazed. He stepped out and studied the tracks in the dirt. Her slippers and a pair of boots made imprints in front and went around behind.

"Harold. Bring my horse back here." Clint traced the two sets of tracks, his head jerking as he looked around, ahead and down. They led up the hill and he ran, gun in hand, wanting to call Kathryn's name, but afraid to alert Frank. He crested the small, hill and looked about in every direction. There was no sign of anyone. A lump formed in his throat and the pain in his chest cut away at his heart.

"Kathryn," he whispered. "Where are you?" He shifted his gaze skyward and pleaded, "Why must Kathryn go through so much danger? She doesn't deserve it. God. Please help me find her."

He looked down and saw Harold leading Smokey up the hill toward him. "Thanks, Harold," he called, running down to meet him half way. He climbed into the saddle just as they heard noise and commotion coming off the front hill. They saw the men and horses and a wagonload of men riding down to the yard.

"They're comin' for Luigi," Clint told Harold. "You go tell them Kathryn's been kidnapped...and I'm going after her."

"Don't you want help?"

"Yah, but there isn't time to wait." Clint spurred Smokey on up the hill and Harold ran back down and out to the front waving his arms excitedly.

Rick sprang off his horse. "What's up?" he asked.

"Kathryn's been kidnapped practically under our noses," Harold blurted out. "Clint thinks it's that Frank. I don't know how he could have snuck in here without Zeke or Jasper hearing him...but he did. Rick. I'm sorry. I have failed you." Harold's face was twisted in remorse and anguish. Rick took Harold's arm and looked him straight in the eye.

"It's not your fault. I know you did all that anyone could have done. It's not your fault...I do not blame you for what happened. Now, where is Clint?"

"He's following the trail." He pointed back in the direction Clint headed.

Buck was quickly beside Rick and put his arm around his dusty shoulders. "We'll find her," he tried to reassure him. Buck turned to the men and said, loudly, "Manuel and Sam. Would you help Luigi transfer Zeb's body to his wagon, and put Jake in there with him?" He turned back to Rick. "With Luigi, Mike and Peter, I think we can manage to git these fellows back to town. Your main concern is to find Kathryn and Frank. I'll be back to help just as soon as I git things taken care of."

Buck jumped back on his horse. "Let's go," he nodded. He and Peter were on horseback, Luigi and Mike drove the wagons, with Mike's horse tied behind Luigi's wagon.

All right, now," called Rick in a shaking voice. "Let's get organized. Where was she last, Harold?" Harold instantly filled him in on the details, his voice also shaking, but his was from guilt that he had been a failure at the most important job.

"Boss which way would he go with only one horse we know of?" asked Pedro.

"I'm tryin to figure that out."

"Would he be stupid enough, or smart enough, depending on how ya look at it, to head back to Zeb's?" inserted Sam.

"Or to town," countered Jim.

"We'll split up," decided Rick.

"I'm going, too," declared Harold, firmly.

'What about Claudette? She shouldn't be left here alone," Rick reminded him kindly.

Unnoticed by the clustered group, Claudette had quietly been standing in the background. "Don't worry about me," she stated. "It is Kathryn you must worry about."

The men turned abruptly. Claudette stood holding onto a shotgun and her new small pistol protruded from her apron pocket. "I'll stay here and watch over the place. Both doors will be kept locked. Now quit wasting time. Find Kathryn."

She spun on her heel and marched up the steps and into the house and slammed the door, hard.

Harold's mouth gaped open, then he exchanged surprised looks with Rick. Rick said, "You heard the little lady, let's go."

Harold ran to the corral for his horse. Pedro was behind him for a temporary replacement for Midnight; in a matter of minutes they were saddled and mounted.

"Sam, Pedro and Manuel...head back the way we came," said Rick. Without a word they were off.

"Jim and Harold...check out the short-cut toward town. I'm going to follow Clint."

What had a short time ago been a crowded yard was now empty. Claudette watched them all ride away, then set the loaded shotgun on the table where it would be handy, then proceeded to lock and bolt both doors. This done, she sat nervously in a chair and worried. She was too full of anxiety to remain seated long and began pacing back and forth in the kitchen. This was the second time she didn't know what happened to Kathryn, or where she was. What did that horrid man want with her, and what was he going to do to her, she fretted. Kathryn was in no condition to be anywhere, much less dragged someplace against her will. She must be very frightened, thought Claudette. And her emotions were too fragile and raw besides being with child. This ordeal could very well do her in. A shivering sensation came over her and she rubbed her hands up and down her arms. She felt useless. She wanted to be out there helping to look. But, someone had to stay here...and what if Kathryn escaped, somehow, and came back? Somebody should be here waiting for her. Her, eyes glanced at the stove. Food. They would all be hungry. Kathryn should have some warm soup fixed for her...and she would need to be put to bed. Bed. She hastened to Kathryn's room and snatched the dresses off the bed and hung them back in the armoire. She closed the lid on the trunk and replaced the pictures.

"I will not let her run away," she spoke aloud. "I will not." She stomped her foot in angry frustration, then went to prepare soup for Kathryn and a hearty meal for the men.

Pedro's horse began to froth at the mouth and his coat was damp with sweat, and still Frank angrily slapped the reins against his neck and spurred him on. Frank sat behind Kathryn, his arms stretched and wrapped tightly around her and his body pressed her forward squeezing and hurting her, as they rode recklessly in the direction of Zeb Taylor's ranch. She was powerless to escape from the crazed man and all she could do for the moment was keep her balance. They were coming onto a hill and Midnight slowed his pace in his efforts to ascend the rough sloping ground. Kathryn was bent forward and the saddle horn dug painfully into her stomach. Her face brushed Frank's arm and she opened her mouth and clamped her teeth firmly into his fleshy arm and bit hard. He howled in shock and his reflexes jerked, then loosened his grip on the reins. She slammed her elbow back with all the force she could muster into his gut still grinding into his now bleeding flesh. Then quickly as she released her teeth, she twisted in the saddle and shoved him off the back of the horse. Terror-stricken she grappled for the reins and dug her slipper heels into Midnight's side. She headed him into the grove of trees at her right, and rode as if the devil himself were behind her.

Sam broke away from Pedro and Manuel and veered left down a small ravine then up a gentle sloping hill. He figured he was about halfway between the two ranches and kept his eyes peeled and his gun in hand. Just yonder through same pines he glimpsed a blur and urged the mule to speed up, keeping his sights on the image. A loud splitting-snap and a shrill whinny sounded and the solid image sunk to the ground. Sam rode Snowflake hard up to the ridge. What he viewed just ahead stopped him short and the hairs on the back of his neck bristled. With his hand wrapped around the gun butt his eyes darted about for signs of Frank. He whipped his buckskinned leg over the mule's back and rapidly covered ground over to the crumpled body of Kathryn. Nearby, Midnight lay whinnying and snorting as he tried to stand up. Sam dropped to his knees fearing Kathryn was dead. She lay so still. He pressed his fingers against her neck to find a pulse and put his hand next to her nose and mouth for signs of breath. He got both. "Oh, Missy," he breathed, as he swatted away his tears. He studied the mean gash on her forehead caused by the low hanging branch she'd ridden into which flung her off the horse. Dirt and blood were smeared over her forehead and cheeks and he gently lifted off the long strands of blood-soaked hair that lay across her face.

"Kathryn? Can you hear me?" She lay so still. Sam backed up several steps and fired three shots in the air to signal his location and need for help, then trotted back to Kathryn's side. He felt for broken bones and watched her eyelids closely, hoping they'd flutter and open.

Frank's boots plowed clumsily through the sandy soil as he staggered for cover cradling his broken left arm with his good one. His head was bashed on a rock when he went off the back of the horse making him feel dizzy and unsteady on his feet. Blood from the split in his head spread down his face causing him to blink to see where he was going. The sound of horse hooves coming his way froze him momentarily. He scurried then tumbled behind a thicket. He rocked back on his heels, sucked for air and hoped he had not been seen. Laying his injured arm on his knee, he reached for his gun. The holster was empty. He reached for the front of his belt for the 44 he'd taken from Kathryn, but that too was gone. Cold sweat gathered across his forehead and mixed with the blood. Frank stroked his forehead and eyes and wiped his hand off on his pant leg. Something shiny caught his eye and he saw the sun's rays striking the barrel of a gun not far from the bush. Painstakingly he flattened himself and inched toward the 44. With his fingers he raked it to him. He could see the oncoming rider, and lying prone he pulled back the hammer, then got the rider in his wavering sights. He squeezed the trigger. The exploding shell cracked the air and boomed through the hills. Frank's ears were ringing and he blinked away the dripping blood. The rider was still coming toward him. He had missed. Consumed with panic he jerked the hammer back and fired again. Once more, he missed. He rolled back behind the thicket and peered through the branches. Paralyzing tremors came over him when he glimpsed who the rider was. That fella Clint that had decked him in the hotel room and dragged him to jail in Dodge City. Then he saw another rider crest the hill behind the first. He didn't want to be captured. He was afraid to be sent back to prison. Other men had done hideous things to him there. A wave of raging heat flashed over his skin then a cold sweat chilled him and the muscles of his buttocks and sphincter tightened from traumatic memory. Once again he pulled back the hammer on the pistol. With a shaky hand Frank shoved the gun into his mouth and surrendered, to death.

Rick and Clint did not dismount. Clint dropped his head and shook it in disgust at the gruesome sight before them. "What a pitiful way to die," he said.

"Frank...right?" said Rick.

"Yah...it was Frank."

They sped their horses off through the pines in the direction of the three fired shots.

Pedro and Manuel arrived near the scene together to see Sam carrying Kathryn in his arms with Snowflake tagging behind.

"Ss...S...Sam," stuttered Pedro. "She is not..."

"No. But, she's been knocked unconscious and hasn't come around." Sam nodded back of him and said, "Yer horse is lying back there. Don't know how bad he is...I'm sorry, Pedro." He began walking, again.

'I will ride like the wind and bring her carriage back," said Manuel. "It will take too long to carry her so far. Pedro," he said sadly, "go see to your horse."

Manuel split as quick as lightning and Sam kept walking toward the ranch.

Pedro knelt beside Midnight. "Si, my friend. You will be all right." He gently stroked his neck while he felt the injured leg.

Rick and Clint swooped down over the hill and dismounted quickly. Before they could even ask, Pedro told them, "Sam is carrying Kathryn until Manuel comes with the buggy." He gulped and swallowed hard trying to appear and sound brave.

"Is his leg broken, Pedro," Rick asked him, somberly.

"I'm not sure, Senor Rick."

'Rick, I'll help Pedro. You catch up to Sam and Kathryn," offered Clint. "And we'll be behind you shortly."

Rick nodded and rode off. Clint's guts were in a knot with worry over Kathryn and what condition she might be in. But Rick was her flesh and blood kin, after all... it was more his place to be there than himself. While Pedro comforted his horse Clint examined and felt the crippled leg.

"I'm sorry, Pedro...but his leg's broke...broke real bad."

Pedro's face screwed up and he shut his eyes tightly and dropped his head in sorrow.

Clint stood up and went over to the sad boy. He patted his shoulder to give him some comfort. "Do you want me to do it, Pedro?" he asked softly.

"No...Senor Clint. He is my horse...I must be the one."

Pedro walked to the horse he'd been riding and pulled the Winchester out of the doeskin scabbard. He pushed his black hat to the back of his head and walked slowly and softly behind his beloved horse. He bent down and petted his head.

"Adios, my faithful amigo." With his shaking finger he lightly stroked an X between Midnight's ears and eyes. He rose, taking his time while keeping his eye on the spot where the X crossed. He lowered the barrel of the rifle aiming at the cross and strained his watery eyes. He sucked in his breath and held it, then slowly squeezed back on the trigger. The loud crack filled the air and the large black horse quaked and his big eyes stared visionless.

Pedro turned and walked away a few feet, still holding the rifle. Clint heard him sniffle and saw him wipe his face with his sleeve. Pedro was hurting bad, but Clint knew he needed to be alone for a bit. He knew how he felt. This scene brought back the memory of what he had to do to his horse when he was fifteen. Clint unbuckled the cinch and tugged the saddle off Midnight and set it aside.

Pedro reached in his pocket and pulled out a large red handkerchief and blew his nose, noisily. He turned around and looked at Clint then down at his lifeless horse, then gazed sadly back at Clint. He walked to the other horse and slid the Winchester back in the scabbard. Clint stepped over and patted his shoulder.

"I'm sorry, Pedro," he said. "I know it hurt a lot to do what you had to do. It takes a real man to do that to his own horse...takes courage."

Pedro smiled weakly. "Thank you, Senor Clint. We better ride fast now and find out how our Kathryn is...Si?"

"Si, good friend."

31

*T*he carriage, driven by Manuel, led the way into the yard, with Sam supporting Kathryn on his lap in the back seat. Rick, Clint and Pedro rode alongside and just behind.

Once briefly, Kathryn had opened her eves on the ride down. Dazed, she blinked, then her eyes focused for a moment and she said, "Sam?"

"Yah, it's Sam. You had a nasty fall, Missy. Yer gonna be fine...soon's we git ya home and fixed up," he assured her.

Her eyelids closed shut, then, sprung open with a pained expression. She mumbled, "Baby," then slipped back into unconsciousness again. Sam pondered on this the rest of the way home.

Claudette peered out of the curtain when she heard the low thumping of horses' hooves and breathed a nervous sigh of relief. She unbolted the front door and flew down the porch steps, her hand clutching her chest nervously. The carriage halted and Sam awkwardly got out, carefully balancing Kathryn in his arms. Claudette's hands clasped over her mouth as she uttered a mournful cry. She quickly turned and hastily ran ahead to hold the front door open, then scurried down the hall and flung Kathryn's bedroom door open.

She turned back the covers and Sam lay Kathryn gently down. Claudette went to the basin and soaked a washcloth and returned to Kathryn's side. As she swabbed the dirt and blood from Kathryn's face, she looked up at Sam.

"What happened?" she whispered and bit her teeth down on her lip to stop from crying.

"From what I could see she smacked into a low branch. She was goin pretty fast."

"She needs the doctor," Claudette said, firmly. She turned her head and saw the doorway full of worried looking faces.

Rick stepped into the room and looked with alarm at his niece. "Claudette, do you think we could take her into the doctor's or send someone for him?"

"I don't think she should be moved and jostled about anymore, Rick," Claudette answered.

"I will ride into town for the doctor," offered Manuel. Without waiting for a response, he charged down the hall. Within a minute or so, the sounds of his horse were heard galloping down the road.

"And, I will ride out to find Jim and your Harold, and tell them to come back home," announced Pedro. He ran out of the house and was soon on his way.

Clint knelt on the floor beside the bed. Tenderly he took Kathryn's hand in his. His eyes were moist and questioning as he gazed at her delicate, quiet face, Absently he slid his thumb back and forth across the top of her limp hand. While in his mind burned many questions. Why was she packing her things? Where was she going? For what reason? But, he couldn't ask, because she couldn't answer. He looked with love upon the woman who'd stolen his heart.

"Kathryn," he choked. "I sure hope you kin hear me. Yer gonna be all right...you jest gotta be...Oh, Gal, I love you so," he whispered.

Rick looked at the emotional man and his injured niece and his throat lumped up so that he could barely swallow.

"Gentlemen," said Claudette, in a low voice. "I want to get Kathryn out of these tight and dirty clothes and try keep her as comfortable as I can until the doctor gets here. Rick, could you bring me lots of cold water, and Sam, I've started supper. Would you be so kind as to finish it for me?"

"You betcha, Claudette," answered Sam, and he left for the kitchen.

Clint got to his feet and bent over Kathryn and softly kissed her cheek, then he and Rick left the room together.

In about an hour Buck rode in with Jim, Harold and Pedro, having met them on his way back out. Buck rushed in to inquire about Kathryn and shook his head in sympathy when told she was still unconscious. He went out to the barn with Rick and helped harness up a team of horses to the buckboard and they got an old blanket to wrap around Frank's corpse. Rick threw a couple of shovels into the back so they could bury Pedro's horse.

Sam stayed behind to finish cooking the supper and lend Claudette a hand. He watched through the kitchen window as once more Rick, Buck, Jim, Pedro, Harold and Ciint headed out, up and over the hill. Sam turned away from the window and checked on the roasting beef and finished peeling the carrots and potatoes Claudette had left.

Claudette removed Kathryn's soiled slippers and loosened her shirt, then proceeded to take the dirty wool trousers off. She shut her eyes and pursed her lips when she saw the spots of blood on the inside of the trousers. Having gone through miscarriages herself, the telltale signs brought back painfully sad memories. She looked at Kathryn lying so still, and her breathing was so shallow. Was she going to lose the baby from the hard ride and fall? This being a distinct possibility, Claudette was now only more concerned then ever for Kathryn's health and well-being, but a remembered sadness washed over her. A baby. How badly she herself wanted to have one. How hard she and Harold had tried to begin a family. And, here was a situation where a wee little one may be fighting for its very life...but was virtually unwanted. As she folded the soiled trousers and lay them aside she realized how torn her emotions really were, between her dearest friend's health and possibly her life, and also for the life of the innocent baby inside her. Was it a little boy, or a little girl, she wondered absently. She quickly shook that thought away and fetched a towel to tuck under Kathryn, then drew the covers back over her, and tucked them around her warmly.

Sam went to check on Kathryn and Claudette and stood silently in the doorway as Claudette lay a cold compress across Kathryn's lacerated forehead. Kathryn's fluttering eyelids gave her a start, then, she watched as her eyes opened fully with a frightened expression. When they focused on Claudette they took on a look of confusion.

"Kathryn," spoke Claudette, gently, "can you hear me?" Kathryn started to nod, but winced in pain, instead. Her eyes drifted slowly around her room, then back to Claudette.

"Why am I in bed? Why do I hurt so?"

"You had a nasty fall, Kathryn...off Pedro's horse. Do you remember?"

Kathryn lay thinking and Claudette noticed Sam smiling from the doorway. She exchanged happy smiles with him and motioned for him to come in. Kathryn saw Sam's big imposing figure and beard and forced a smile on her hurting face, then her expression froze in remembering.

"Oh, yes. Pedro's horse...I was riding...riding hard, away from that horrible Frank. I was so afraid. I thought he was going to kill me." Her eyes darted back and forth. "Where is he?"

Sam knelt down beside her. "He's dead, Kathryn. He was shooting at Clint. And for, some reason, turned the gun on himself. Ya won't have to worry about him, anymore."

Claudette offered her a sip of water then Kathryn asked, "Did everyone come back safe...from the raid at the Taylor ranch?"

"Yes, we did, Missy...thank God."

"Where's Uncle Richard...and Clint?"

"With Buck and everybody else to git Frank's body...and bury Midnight."

"Midnight'? Midnight is dead?"

"Yah. His leg was broken pretty bad...Pedro had to shoot him."

"Oh, no. Poor Pedro...poor Midnight." A sad look crossed her face. "Sam, it is my fault his leg got broken...I rode him too hard."

"No, I think Frank probably rode him a lot harder before you did...enough to tire him out, bad...makin it easy for him to stumble. Pedro doesn't blame you.""

"I want to make it up to him...just the same. Somehow...somehow I will."

"Kathryn," asked Claudette, "Could you eat a little soup? It's all made."

"I'm not hungry...I feel kind of squeamish...and a little bit dizzy."

"That's understandable, with what all you've been through," answered Claudette. "We'll see what the doctor can do to help you with that when he gets here. Manuel rode into town to get him."

Sam smiled and said, "I'm sure glad yer awake. Ya sure gave us all a scare. I'm gonna leave ya to rest. I'll be back later to look in on you."

Claudette waited until she heard Sam make noise in the kitchen, then turned to say, "I don't know how to tell you this...but...I was washing you up and trying to make you as comfortable as I could, and...and discovered that you are bleeding some down there." She pointed and watched Kathryn's face carefully to see how she was going to take this news.

Kathryn gave her a funny look as she weighed the words in her head and let them sink in. "Did I lose the...baby?" she asked bewildered.

"No. Not yet."

"Does that mean I am going to?"

"I don't know...I really don't."

Kathryn looked puzzled. "May I have another sip of water, please? My throat is very dry."

"Yes, of course. Let me get you some colder and fresher. I won't be but a few minutes." She picked up the rust and yellow flowered pitcher and hastily retreated.

After Claudette left the room, Kathryn in great discomfort sat partially up and lifted the covers to examine the large towel between her legs. There wasn't as much blood as she expected, yet, it was evident something not good was happening. She covered herself back up, and a strange uneasiness washed over her. Her aching head tried to sort out what was happening to her and to make peace with her spiraling emotions.

The circumstances had changed. There was now the possibility she could lose this baby...and her immediate troubles and worries would be over. She would not have to face the coming months in shame...or without Clint. For she was sure in her heart that he would reject her, solely upon the idea she carried another man's child...an Indian man's child...conceived out of wedlock, with brutal force.

If there were no longer this baby within her, she could get on with her life... rebuild, put this all behind her, and begin anew. But, what was she going to rebuild? So much, too much had changed since leaving Lexington, that she wasn't sure at all, anymore, just where her own life was going. What she did know, was that she was surrounded by loving people and knew above all else that she was in love with Clint, and it was with him that she wanted to be with, to shape a future.

Low in her abdomen she felt a strange twinge, a tugging dull ache. Her mind began to focus to her insides. She tried for a moment to imagine what kind of a little being was in there...how tiny and helpless that small growing thing was. Not unlike, she thought, a little foal dependent upon its mother. Then, Kathryn became curious as to what it might look like...if it were born...if it lived. Was it already a boy or a girl? Which, she wondered? Suddenly her eyes widened. She could hardly believe she was actually caring or feeling concerned over something, that when told existed, had upset her so terribly bad. But, something inside her did exist...and now, maybe not for long. She felt all mixed up, torn apart inside and out, and she started to cry.

Claudette came back with the fresh pitcher of water. "Oh, Kathryn...Honey... what are you crying about?"

"I'm not sure...I'm so confused...please help me. I feel so twisted and knotted up inside."

Claudette poured water into a glass and offered it to Kathryn, then filled the bowl. She squeezed out the washcloth and gently swabbed her, face. "Hush, you don't have to cry...things will be better."

"I just don't know what I'm going to do, Claudette."

"Is that why you were packing your things?"

"Yes; I have to leave...don't you see? I can't face Clint...or Uncle Richard...or anyone. I'm too ashamed."

"Are you ashamed to face me?" questioned Claudette.

"Well, no...not you. You understand."

"What about Harold, and the doctor?"

"Claudette, that is different. You know what I mean."

"If we understand, and can accept what happened...something that was not of your doing...or choice, something that was forced upon you, don't you think Clint, your uncle and anyone else here will understand as well, and love you just the same... the same as Harold and I do'?"

"I don't know..."

"I know it won't be easy, and I'll be with you if you like, but I think you owe it to Clint and to your Uncle Rick to be honest and tell them."

"I know you are right, it's just that I do not want to face the shame."

"The shame is not with you...it is with that Indian...Blackhorse."

Kathryn looked at her and thought about that and also wondered why she was the one who had to suffer and pay for something that he did. It just wasn't fair.

"Kathryn, where were you planning on going?"

"I had a plan. I was going to ask Sam to see if the Indian's people would want to adopt the baby. I was going to have it someplace else, where no one would know me."

"I see. Does Sam know, yet?"

"No. But he does know the Indian's people. But, things have changed...it may not be necessary. Oh, I'm so mixed up...there's been so much tragedy...so many people have been affected...I'm so tired."

"I think you had better try and get some sleep. Doctor Lawton should be here in a little while, I hope. I'll leave the door ajar and come peek in on you." she smiled.

"Claudette?"

"Yes?"

"You are truly the best, most loyal friend I have ever known."

"Thank you for saying that, Kathryn. You are very special to me, and the best friend I have ever had."

Kathryn smiled sleepily then closed her eyes.

Claudette sat down at the table in the kitchen with a worried look upon her face. Sam brought her over a cup of tea and sat down beside her with a cup of his own.

"How's she doin?"

"She's more alert...but it is hard to say how serious her injuries really are until Doctor Lawton arrives. Oh, I do wish he would get here."

"He should be along anytime soon I think," Sam replied. He took a sip of tea and sat his cup down. "Claudette, somethin's been botherin me," he whispered softly. "And maybe you kin help me."

"I'll try. What is it, Sam?" She viewed him curiously because he was acting so secretive.

"On the way back down with Kathryn," he looked up to be positive they were truly alone and continued, "anyway...she came to fer a second and muttered the word, 'baby'...what does that mean to you?" He arched his brows questioningly, and Claudette felt as if he were challenging her to be truthful. She pursed her lips tightly in thought then diverted her attention to a sip of tea.

Sam studied on her and asked, "Why would she say that?" Claudette's face flushed and she looked Sam straight in the eye.

"I think you must ask her that yourself, Sam."

"I will. But, I kin tell ya this much," his face saddened, "from the way she's been actin...faintin and gettin hysterical an all, I think our little gal in there is expecting a baby...am I right?" he asked, tensely.

Claudette lowered her eyes and got up from the table and walked outside. She had promised not to say anything to anyone. Now, how was she supposed to answer this question so bluntly put before her? She sat wearily down on the bench on the porch and wished Harold would come home. She needed him and his common sense strength.

Sam sat very still in his chair. He knew he had gotten his answer. "Damn," he muttered. "Damn, that lousy Blackhorse. Oh, God...poor Missy. Please help that poor girl."

He sat for a long time just staring into space, and outside Claudette sat on the porch staring toward the hill.

Noises came from the direction of the hill, stirring them both off their chairs. Sam grabbed a bunch of cups and set them out knowing the men would all want a hot cup. He looked at all the food and recalling the long, tragic day, wondered if anybody would even be hungry...but, knowin this little family he figured they'd manage to put away a pile of food, despite all that had gone on.

Claudette waited at the bottom of the steps and watched as Buck, driving the buckboard with Frank's remains, pulled far and away from the house. The buzz of flies swarming on the covered corpse made her stomach churn and she stepped back up onto the porch to wait for Harold and the rest.

The men clustered around her and she told them that Kathryn had regained consciousness, and before they went to barge in on her, she told them that she was asleep and still not feeling very well.

An exhausted weary group of men paraded through the door and eagerly took a hot cup of Sam's coffee, and Claudette motioned for Harold to step down the hall with her while she peeked in on Kathryn.

"I am so glad that you are finally here, Sweetheart," she breathed. Harold put his arm about her waist and drew her close He knew by her actions and her tone that something more was troubling her. "Wait here a minute," she said. She tiptoed in and checked on Kathryn, then shut the door, leaving it open a few inches to hear her if she called or cried out. She led Harold by the hand to Clint's bedroom and shut the door.

"What's the matter, Claudette?"

"Harold," she said softly, but in a frightened tone, "I think she may lose the baby, and I can't talk to anyone about this but you."

Harold put both arms around her and held her close. He knew that in part, his wife was reliving the loss of the babies she had carried. He knew, also, now that a portion of their new home was ready to be moved into, and she wanted to be carrying her own baby. And, even though the baby Kathryn carried and was in danger of losing was part Indian, to Claudette it was still a baby.

Finally he asked, "Did you find out why she was packing her things?"

"Yes. She was going to go away and have the baby someplace else and, oh, Harold, she was going to have Sam see if that Indian's people wanted to adopt the baby." There were tears in her eyes and Harold held her, tighter.

"Love, if that is what she wants, there isn't anything we can do about it...you know that, don't you?"

"Yes. It's just that I think a baby needs its mother...the most."

"I know...I know."

The sound of riders coming took Claudette to the window. "Oh, thank the dear Lord. It's Manuel with Doctor Lawton. You go greet him with the others. I will be in Kathryn's room so I can speak to him privately and tell him what is happening."

Bob Lawton entered the house carrying his doctor's bag. Rick filled him in on what happened as he walked him down to Kathryn's room. Rick returned to the kitchen and sat beside Buck.

"Buck, this has been a day to end all days."

"You kin say that again. We took care of a lot of business, though. And now we don't even need the Indian to testify against Zeb. If he makes it, which looks doubtful...I will still have to put in a good word for him; as promised. Especially since he came peacefully and volunteered to tell all he knew. I'm just wonderin if he can get a fair trial here though...and I'm not so sure he'll be treated like the other prisoners if he gits a sentence instead of the rope. But, we'll have to see what the judge says and does."

"How bad off was Jake?' Rick asked.

"I hauled him to Doc's and he patched him up. He's back at the jail now. The judge oughta be in town next week and I kin get the jail cleaned out. It's a might crowded."

"Well," said Buck, as he tiredly stood and stretched, "I best git Frank's body to Luigi while I kin still fight off the flies and the smell. Tell Doc to stop by and fill me in on Kathryn when he gits back. Many thanks fer the coffee."

After Buck left, Rick slumped in his big chair by the fireplace and solemnly lit his pipe. Across from him sat Clint staring sullenly at the ceiling with his coffee cup resting on his knee.

Over and over in Clint's head popped the picture of Kathryn's dresses laid out on the bed and some in the open trunk. Why was she leaving? Did Rick or any of the others know and didn't know how to tell him? He was afraid to ask at this point, with Kathryn lying in there, injured. And, where had she planned on going, he kept asking himself? What felt worse was why she hadn't said anything to him, or even hinted she was thinking of going. Had he done anything to offend her? He didn't think he had. Had someone else? He couldn't imagine who. Maybe all this danger had been more than she could bear. She had been through far more than her share...far more than just about anybody. He took a sip of coffee and looked over at Harold seated at the table. Harold caught his look and Clint instantly felt that Harold knew...knew something he didn't. Not being able to stand that, Clint got up and headed for the back door.

"Harold," he said, "could I speak to you outside?"

"Sure," replied Harold. He got up and immediately felt he was going to be put on the spot, but tried to act natural so as not to draw attention or suspicion.

But Sam, rolling out biscuit dough, sensed that something big was agitating Clint and would try to get satisfactory answers out of Harold. He felt sorry for Clint when he'd been told the truth and the whole story concerning the woman he loved. Sam wondered how he would take it, and what effect it would have on him and on her.

When the two were well out of earshot, Clint asked straight out, "Do you know why Kathryn was packing to leave?"

"Yes, Clint...I'm afraid I do. But, it is not my place to tell you. That has to come from Kathryn herself.

"Does Rick know?"

"I don't believe so. As far as I know, Claudette and I are the only ones."

"Well, tell me this...was it something I did that has caused her to want to leave?" Clint said with a hurt expression.

"Heavens no, man.'" Harold put a consoling hand on his shoulder and added, "From what I know and see, that woman loves you...loves you very much."

"Well, what then?" begged Clint.

"I cannot betray her trust, Clint. But I will confide to you that she is dealing with something very serious...and when she tells you, she is going to need all the understanding you can muster. This my man, will truly be a test of your love."

Clint looked at him feeling even more confused and curious.

"I'm sorry that I can't be of any more help to you than that."

'I understand...and I respect yer position and yer loyalty. Thanks jest the same. Here, would you mind taking this in for me? I need to be alone fer a spell." Clint handed Harold his cup and walked away, his head held down.

Sam looked up when Harold came back without Clint. He nodded to him in a knowing manner, then, went back to his cooking.

"Well, Kathryn," smiled Doc kindly. "I guess you've given everyone quite a scare."

"I sure didn't want to," she answered.

"You've gotten a nasty gash there on your forehead. It's going to give you headaches off and on for the next few days, but I don't think you have any serious injuries that won't heal up. Now, as far as your other problem, I see the immediate bleeding has stopped. But, I want you to stay in bed for a few days, just to be on the safe side." He pulled the vanity chair up close to the bed and sat down.

"Kathryn...does anyone besides Claudette and Harold know that you are pregnant?" he asked her directly.

"No," she answered.

"Don't you think it's about time you told...no matter how difficult? Especially to that nice man who loves you so much?"

"Well, he won't...when he knows."

"You are sure of that?" questioned Doc.

"Pretty sure, yes."

"Well, you will find out one way or the other...best to know, than to wonder."

"You make it sound so...so easy," she began, as tears spurted from her eyes, "as if it's not the worst thing that has ever happened to me."

Doc patted her arm, "Now, come on. I am not saying that at all. What happened to you was terrible...unspeakable...something you, or anybody else does not deserve, ever. And, the results have injured not just your body...but your mind and your feelings. But, Kathryn, I truly believe that facing up to this...sharing this sorrow with those you love and trust will make things easier for you and unburden your mind. I'm sure having Claudette know has eased your pain somewhat." He looked at her for a moment, then asked, "Would you like me to tell, for you?"

Kathryn's face grew thoughtful and her eyes cast down while she gave this suggestion some serious thought. Doc exchanged helpless looks with Claudette, who was sitting in the green velvet chair by the window. All was still and the summer's evening breeze drifted through the window and filled the room with the fresh scent of pine.

"Yes," she said at last, very softly. "If you would at least tell the others for me... but, I will tell Uncle Richard and Clint myself...in here, privately."

"All right...whatever you wish." Doc closed his bag, stood up and replaced the chair. "Do you want me to send in Rick and Clint together, or separately?"

"Together. I don't want to have to say what I must...twice. Once is going to be hard enough."

"I will send them in, and I will tell the others. I'll be back in a day or so to check on you...unless I'm summoned sooner. Good night, Kathryn."

"Good night...and thank you."

"Don't mention it. Claudette, are you coming with me or staying here?"

Claudette looked at Kathryn for an answer. "Stay here with me, please," asked Kathryn. "I need you to be with me through this...if you don't mind?"

"Of course, I'll stay, Kathryn."

"Ah, Doc," said Rick, jumping up from his seat. Clint also rose, being back just a short time from his solitary walk. "How is she?" they both asked in unison.

"I think she is going to be just fine," he answered. His eyes shifted from Rick to Clint as he said, "She wants to see both of you now."

The sound of hurrying boots echoed down the hall and Doc sat warily down. "How bout a cup of your good coffee, Sam...before I talk to all of you?"

"Sure thing...coming up," answered Sam. Sam thought, while he filled Doc's cup, that he could almost guess what the doc was going to say. If he told what he felt he might, Sam would feel relieved to have his suspicions out in the open. It would be easier to deal with and to help Kathryn.

The door to Kathryn's room opened and two eager faces peered in. Clint and Rick had smiles that quickly disappeared when they saw the woeful expression on Kathryn's face and the nervous look on Claudette's. They stepped in and Rick quietly shut the door. He and Clint felt awkward and uneasy due to the somber atmosphere. Claudette encouraged her with a calm nod and a comforting smile to go ahead and speak.

Kathryn pulled and straightened the covers around her and fidgeted with the hem on the blanket. Rick finally spoke "What is wrong?"

"I...I have something I must tell you."

Rick instantly sat down on the bed beside her and Clint stood directly behind him, his eyes full of confusion and anxiety. "Kathryn," said Rick, "Jest tell us what's the matter." He and Clint both looked helplessly at Claudette.

"Kathryn, whatever it is that has you so upset...please tell us so we can help you," pleaded Clint.

With dread in her eyes Kathryn looked up at Clint, then to her uncle, then back to Clint. "Clint, there is something I have kept from you." She glanced at Rick. Rick knew she was finally going to tell Clint what happened during the stage robbery. And, he wondered why, now? He knew he was about to feel sorry for both of them.

"Clint, " she began, again. "When the stage was held up and stopped...and you were wounded...that Indian...Blackhorse pulled me down from the seat."

"That part I vaguely recall," he added. "And I heard you scream, then I remember nothing. That's when I musta passed out," he offered. "What's that got to do with now, gal?"

"I was too ashamed to tell you...what else he did to me Clint." She dropped her eyes and her face pinked.

Clint thought a brief moment with brows raised, then they lowered as his jaw gaped open and color drained from his face. Claudette was behind him with a chair.

"Perhaps you had better sit down," she said. He willingly obliged without taking his eyes off Kathryn.

"Oh, God...oh, Kathryn," he muttered at last. "Why didn't you jest tell me? Why did ya suffer with this, yerself?"

"I told you...I was too ashamed."

Clint's stomach was knotted. His emotions went round in his head in a dizzy circle. He felt sorrow, outrage and also hurt because he hadn't been told. And, it was obvious to him that Claudette and Rick knew, and who knew who else? This woman he loved, whom he tried to protect...he felt he had failed. Now he couldn't find words to say to comfort her and this upset him too.

"And...there is...more, "Kathryn stated, crying . "Uncle Richard...Clint." She threw her arms around Rick. "I'm going to have a...a...baby." She sobbed and cried all over Rick's shoulder hanging tightly to his neck. Rick's arms held her close as he cried silently with her.

Clint's eyes snapped shut and he shook his head not wanting to believe what he'd heard. When he opened his eyes there were tears he couldn't control. He reached out and touched Kathryn's hand and her fingers squeezed his.

She moved away from her uncle's grasp and pleaded, "What am I going to do? I'm an unmarried woman...that is going to have...a half Indian...baby."

"Kathryn," spoke Rick, with a lump in his throat. "You won't go through this alone...ya know that. We'll see this through together. I know this is something you don't want...but we'll accept what is...won't we? We're Barnetts...remember?" He forced a fragile smile to her face and took her handkerchief from her hand and caught the sliding tears. "We will talk on this more, later, Kathryn, when yer stronger. Try not worry and upset yerself...everything'll work out...you'll see. Right now, I think you and Clint here need to be alone." He laid her down on the pillow and kissed her cheek.

"C'mon, Claudette, I'll buy you a cup of coffee." he smiled. He held out his hand to her and escorted her to the door. Before he closed the door he reached over and patted Clint's back in a gesture of sympathy.

The door clicked shut and there was an awkward silence. Tears jerked down Kathryn's face as she waited for Clint to tell her they could never more be. Not after this terrible news. In a daze, Clint rose from the chair and walked over to the window. He parted the curtains and gazed out. The moon was high in the sky, giving light to this otherwise bleak night.

"Why couldn't you really tell me, Kathryn? he asked dully.

"I told you...I was ashamed to," she blurted. She raised her head and studied his strong, straight back, wide shoulders and thick dark hair. He was hurt and angry... she could tell, but she couldn't find words to ease his mind...not when her own was so confused

"Is there another reason you didn't want to tell me?"

"Yes."

"What?" he asked, still staring out the window.

"I...I was afraid you wouldn't love me anymore. That...you wouldn't want me... after what another man did to me." She was too numb and too afraid to cry. Her heart pounded as she waited for the terrible words she imagined she would hear.

Clint didn't answer. "Telling you I was raped...would have been bad enough... enough to lose you...but, now," she said, bitterly, "I won't have to wonder because no man would ever want me now." She started to sob, feeling sorry for herself, then said loudly, "I hate that Indian. I hate what he did to me. I hate what he's done to my life. I hate this baby."

Clint spun around and his actions startled her. "You can't hate the baby, Kathryn. It is an innocent victim of what happened."

"But it will be a half-breed, Clint," she protested.

"That baby is a part of you, too. Think about that." She lowered her head. "Kathryn...I'm hurting, too. I'm hurting cause you didn't believe and trust in my love. Did you honestly think I could just stop loving you'?" He didn't wait for an answer, but marched around and sat next to her on the bed. He placed his large hands firmly on her shoulders and waited for her to look him in the eye.

"I love you...no matter what." He narrowed his eyes and they pierced hers as he asked sternly, "Have you stopped loving me because of what happened?"

Her eyes grew big in disbelief of his question. "No, I couldn't."

"Then how, woman, do you think I could stop loving you?"

"I...I...thought what happened...and a...baby would change that," she stammered.

"Well git that notion out of your head...once and fer all." He pulled her closer looking deep into her eyes and brought his lips to hers. Her arms went hesitantly around his strong back, then she pulled him close pressing her fingers into his skin. She could feel the same passion coming from Clint as before and it made her spine tingle, once again.

Very slowly the long kiss ended and Kathryn looked tenderly at Clint with brighter eyes, "Oh, you do still love me," she cried.

"Of course. And don't ever forget that. Now, I think you and that baby need some badly overdue sleep." He lowered her back on the bed and tucked her in. "I'll come back later and check on you. You jest git some shut-eye." He brushed his lips across her cheek, then put the chair back by the dressing table and quietly left the room.

Heads slowly turned with curious, sympathetic stares when Clint entered the kitchen, wondering how he was handling the news. With a squared jaw and determined gait he went to the stove and poured himself some coffee. He took a big slug, then set his cup on the counter, turned and looked at the group. "She's going to need all the comfort and understanding we can give her now. But, you all, love her too, so that won't be hard." His eyes drifted to-Rick. "I planned on askin her to marry me...before this news...and I still aim to, if she'll have me. That is if you have no objections, Rick... to me bein' yer niece's husband."

Rick stood up from the table and walked over to Clint. He slapped him on the back and said, "Yer quite a fella, Clint. I'd like to shake yer hand." The two men's hands clasped firmly as they exchanged looks of mutual trust and understanding.

32

In the dark hours before dawn, Rick awakened stiffly on the sofa then sat up, yawned heavily and stretched his muscle-kinked back. Although he was very fond of Harold and Claudette he was glad they were moving into their new home by the end of the week. He missed the privacy of his own room, but mostly he missed his bed. He fumbled for his pants and pulled them on and found the clean socks he'd draped across the sofa arm. Striking a match he saw his way to the table and lit the wick in the lantern. After stoking the stove and making the coffee he leaned back in his chair.

He was grateful for this early morning solitude, apart from so many people talking and being busy in his own house. Deep in thought he puffed on his pipe waiting for the coffee to brew. He reflected on how his life had turned upside down since Kathryn's urgent telegram. So many adjustments, changes, and life-threatening situations. He had never regretted she had come. What ate at him the most was how he felt responsible that she had been raped on the way to get here, and the resulting pitiful consequence. Had he turned down her request to come, he kept telling himself, she would not be in this "fix" and her life would not have been in danger. Nothing now could change what had happened. All involved would have to accept and learn to live with what was, regardless. Even her mother, Jolene, when eventually told. Rick shook his head imagining her ire.

Rick expelled a weary sign and felt some relief that life was gradually returning to normal around the ranch. Sam and Jim had begun rounding up the steers that were going on the next drive to Fort Garland. Pedro was busy doing minor repairs on the out buildings around the ranch. Clint and Manuel were gone most of the day putting the finishing touches on the Bartholomews' house. Rick stayed indoors much of the time looking after Kathryn and going over his record books. During these times he had debated with himself about whether to go back into mining or not. He wondered if putting himself through the hassle of taking the minerals out of the ground would be worth it in terms of his peace of mind? He had grown to appreciate the satisfying and more tranquil life of cattle ranching and the rewarding benefits he personally attained deep in his soul. He really liked living this way. He would sit on his decision for a while, at least, no rush as far as he was concerned. The gold and silver would and could wait.

Kathryn was confined to her room, for the most part, and slowly she felt better physically, although her emotions were fragile and she found herself in tears when least expected. The headaches were less frequent or severe and she was grateful for that.

This morning Kathryn sat by the window and watched the sun as it inched its way over the jagged peaks of the Sangre de Cristos. She had a shiver when her mind recalled the reappearance of Frank Palmer and the terrorizing ride on Pedro's horse. The thought still struck fear in her heart even though he was no longer a threat to her. She had never known anyone to carry hate or a grudge so long, or go to such extremes for vengeance, except perhaps, Zeb Taylor, whom she had not met. And, from what she had heard and knew, he was capable of all sorts of dirty-dealings. In fact, she figured, with some logic, she wouldn't be carrying this baby if it hadn't been for Zeb's greed for her uncle's gold and the power he had over Blackhorse.

No one in the area had mourned the deaths of Zeb Taylor or Frank Palmer. Kathryn reflected that it was a pitiful tribute to one's life to live so poorly and dishonestly, that when it came time to depart from the world it merely meant welcome relief to most, instead of the grieving sad ache, one had for those they cared for and loved who would no longer be with them.

The sun had now crested the mountain peaks and the sky turned a beautiful robin's egg blue. Kathryn spied Sir Frosty and watched as he romped and pranced about in the pasture enjoying the sunshine that warmed his back. She strongly felt the desire to go out, put a saddle on him and take a long ride by herself. That notion, she knew, was out of the question. She rested her hand on her stomach and breathed a sigh of dismay and looked away from the window. Her gaze drifted to the photograph of herself as a baby, wearing a white smocked dress with tiny embroidered flowers on the yoke. A happy-faced infant smiled back at her with trusting, innocent eyes. The infant appeared content, perhaps knowing that she was loved, cherished and wanted. What of these things would she be giving her own baby? If its picture were taken, would the expression convey the same messages as her own photograph? Kathryn pondered on that and briefly felt a pang of guilt for all the ill feelings she had been harboring toward this baby.

She wondered how had her own mother felt when she found out that she was expecting? Was she happy...pleased...fulfilled? How different their situations were. Her mother was married...very happily married to her father. They were of the same race. What of this child? Its parents not married, its mother white, its father Indian and they didn't even know each other. She thought then about the fact that Blackhorse had killed at least one man, that she knew of...Will. And; he had tried to kill Pedro and Uncle Richard. She was aware of why he had done these things, and it frightened her to think that Blackhorse had the thirst and capability to carry out these deeds. She worried whether this appetite for murder could be an inherited trait. Or, had Blackhorse been motivated by what fate life's circumstances put in his path, forcing his actions only to that of self-preservation? These questions haunted and perplexed her.

She shook these dreadful thoughts from her mind and slowly eased herself over to the dressing table. Picking up her silver handled brush she began stroking the tangles out of her hair. Eyeing her motions in the mirror she studied the features of her face. She watched as a faint smile appeared when she recalled the other night when Clint so gallantly and firmly declared his love for her. How blessed she felt that she had found someone so special to love, who truly loved and cared for her so completely. Nothing that had occurred had affected his feelings and devotion for her.

Kathryn put down her brush and rested her elbow on the table and thought about her difficulty in facing the other men at the ranch. She had been relieved, in a way, that she had been confined to her room for a few days, so she wouldn't have to walk into the kitchen, look at their faces and see the pitying expressions in their eyes. She didn't want pity...not anymore. As Doc Lawton had said, she was going to have a baby and there wasn't anything he or she could do about it. And, Claudette had said, "What had happened had happened." She had to be strong and brave now, for herself and the baby. As Clint had pointed out, quite bluntly, she couldn't hate the baby...for it was a part of her...and an innocent victim. With all these revelations coming to light over the past few days, Kathryn knew, deep down, that she would love this tiny creature growing inside of her.

Sam had been the first to come to see her. "Missy," he said "I'd give anything if this all hadn't happened to ya. I hurt for all ya've been goin through. Ya jest hold yer head up now and you'll make out jest fine. Ya've got a good heart and a fine spirit. Things'll seem different to ya after a spell...mark my words. Now, jest let me know what I kin do fer ya, and consider it done...ya hear?" He'd given her a big hug and a smile and left the room

Later that day, Pedro shyly came to her room. He'd worn a sad face and acted nervous. He didn't know exactly what he should say to a lady he admired who had been savagely attacked, and he was uncomfortable, because he had never been this close to a woman who was going to have a baby.

"Pedro, please sit down," she'd told him. "First, I want to say how very sorry I am about Midnight."

"It wasn't yer fault, Senorita Kathryn. It was that lousy Frank Palmer's fault for stealing him in the first place, to come and do harm to you. I am sorry for you...about that. And, I am also sad for you...for what that Indian did. That was bad...very bad. A thing he should be ashamed for...forever. When the doctor tells us that you are going to have a baby...because of that...that sin against you, I feel very sad...for you. I feel bad that night when I go to bed. I get on my knees and say a prayer to the Blessed Mother of Jesus to help you and your little one." His dark eyes brightened and sparkled. "Then, I think to myself, this is one very lucky nino. He will have such a wonderful mother. And, you are very pretty...and the nino will be of good looks, too. Also...you are very brave and very smart, and you will teach it many things. So now, I do not feel so sad...only a little."

"Oh, Pedro. That's the nicest things you could have said to me. Thank you. That has made me feel so much better. And, thank you for your prayers. I certainly do need them." She reached under her pillow and said, "Please hold out your hand." He had done so, and she placed five hundred dollars across his palm. "I know this cannot bring back Midnight, but, please take this and put it toward a new horse."

"No, Senorita. I cannot take such an amount of money. Besides, Senor Rick, he has said for me to pick out any horse I like here from the ranch."

She hushed him. "You keep it...I insist. Put it toward a new saddle or do whatever you like with it. It is yours."

He started to protest again, then, thought better of it. He did not want to upset an expecting mother.

Quite late that same night, Kathryn sat up in bed leafing through one of Claudette's *Harper's* magazines when a soft knock startled her. She called out in a low voice, "Come in." The door opened partially and Jim poked his head into the room.

"Am I disturbing you?" he asked, nervously raking his fingers through his hair.

"No, that's all right. I was just reading a bit. Come in."

He had refused the offered chair, preferring instead to stand, then pace. "Are you feeling any better?" he questioned, in a concerned manner. When she nodded yes, he continued speaking, "Is there anything...anything at all I can get for you or do?"

She had shaken her head and replied she was fine, as fine as she could be, all things considered. He inched his way to the window and stared out, absorbed in deliberation. He itched the side of his leg and turned to her with serious blue eyes.

"I want ya to know I feel mighty bad for you and for what yer goin through." He swallowed hard to rid his throat of the burning lump that had formed, then went on. "I know you and Clint git on real well...and it don't take much to see how ya feel about each other...but, there's somethin I still gotta say." His eyes darted to the window and then straight back to hers, and declared, "I care for you, too."

Kathryn's eyes popped wide open as he continued. "I just want ya to know...that if things ever change between you...that it don't matter a hoot to me that yer gonna have a baby...cause I think the world of you. I'd be happy to help ya raise it and be like a father for it...just the same. His face had reddened as he blurted out, "I'd marry you, Kathryn...if ya'd have me...and be mighty proud to do it and have you for a wife."

Kathryn blinked in disbelief and surprise. She tried to find words to say to him, but she just sat there with her mouth half open and nothing came out.

Jim gulped then said, "I know I ain't as good lookin as Clint...I just want you to know in case things change...that you kin count on me. That is if you'd want to...or if you need to."

Her voice came back. "Jim, I had no idea that you had any special feelings for me. You have kept them hidden quite well. You have taken me by surprise and I don't know what to say." Jim began making his way toward the door.

"No need for ya to say anything. I just had to come and say my piece. And, I think ya outa know that I cared for you from the start...and I still do...more than ever. So, now ya know." His hand was on the doorknob and he added, "Can I ask ya one favor?"

"Of course Jim, what is it?"

"That you keep what I said just between us. I don't feel much like havin folks jokin about me...behind my back...or to my face...that I'm in love with a woman that already has been spoken for."

"I don't see why anybody needs to know what you have said, Jim. Love is a very special thing...not something to joke about. Yes, I will keep this to myself."

"Thanks," he smiled. He took a couple of steps closer to the bed and his eyes traveled over her face and his gaze revealed his earnest heart. He bent closer and very gently kissed her cheek.

"Have a real good night's sleep." He turned away abruptly to leave.

"Jim?"

"Yah?"

"Thank you for saying those nice and sincere words, it meant a lot. You are a very special person to me." He grinned sheepishly, closed the door and went across the hall to his own room.

Kathryn picked up the brush and resumed brushing her hair. She deliberated on that late night scene and what Jim had said. It must have been difficult for him to come forward, especially at a time like this. She knew, too, that for a while she would feel a little on edge whenever she was in the presence of both Clint and Jim.

The sound of a boot kicking lightly on the bottom of the door brought Kathryn back to the present.

"Yes, who is it?"

"It is your breakfast, Senorita Kathryn," Manuel's voice responded.

"Oh, please come in," urged Kathryn.

Manuel strolled in carrying a tray laden with scrambled eggs, thin slices of fried ham, biscuits, apple juice and coffee. He set the tray on the table by the window and she sat herself down in the chair.

"Oh, I don't think I can eat that much food," she exclaimed.

Manuel handed her a flowered napkin. "You eat what you can little lady. You must get your strength back." He cocked his head to one side and studied her with a discerning look. She looked quizzically up at him.

"You are one very brave woman, Senorita Kathryn. You have endured mucho and still you so nice to everybody. I, for one, owe you a great apology that is a long time overdue. Had my shot been on target the day on the stage, like it should have been...I would have killed that slime of an Indian. Then, such a fine lady that you are, would not be in such a way...as to becoming a mother. I regret my bullet missed. Again, I apologize to you."

"Please do not blame yourself, Manuel. What happened is not your fault," and she found herself adding, "any more than it is mine."

"Gracias, Senorita. You take a little burden off my shoulders. But, I will always feel I could have done my job better...to my dying day."

"Do not carry such a burden, Manuel. It will not help or change things. You must forgive yourself."

"I will give it some thought and pray on it, if that will make you feel better."

"It will," she smiled. Taking a bite of eggs, she noticed something different about Manuel. "There is something about you today...yes, there is a certain look in your eyes...they are twinkling."

"Si. I think I am in love," he admitted, rolling his eyes.

Kathryn stiffened slightly and held her breath. After Jim's declaration she was not sure how to react, or what she was expected to answer.

In a quiet voice she asked, "In love?"

He leaned his heavy frame gently against the bedpost. "Yesterday...me and Pedro we go over to see how little Rosetta and the lovely Lupe are getting on." His eyes brightened and Kathryn relaxed and grinned.

"And, how are they getting on?"

"Oh, mucho better...now that Zeb can no longer beat them. But, they worry. They not think they can stay in a place that does not belong to them. But, I tell Lupe I would like for them to stay. But, Senorita Kathryn...can they be allowed to do such a thing? What do you know of these laws?"

"I don't know. I will try and find out for you."

"Gracias. If there is a way...that would make a happy man of me...Pedro, too," Manuel grinned. "Now you eat your breakfast before it is cold. I must go to work now."

He left and Kathryn laughed at herself for her foolish and vain thinking that Manuel might have been in love with her.

The clippity-clopping of hooves drifted through the open window. She craned her neck to see who was coming. It was Buck and Doctor Lawton riding up on their horses.

"I want you to take short walks, starting today," instructed Doctor Lawton. "You seem to be doing a lot better...it shows in your face. I am pleased, Kathryn."

"Maybe it is because I have been shown a great deal of love and understanding. And, do you know something? I am feeling somewhat resigned to my condition and the only thing I can do now is try and be brave and make the best of this. I have no other choice," she smiled pensively. "Do you realize that you never told me when this baby was to make its entrance into this world?"

"Around the end of January, the first part of February." he smiled broadly.

She thought over that date and time of year and nodded. Doctor, why is the sheriff here? Is there more trouble?"

"Not really. He came to talk to Sam...oh, I might just as well go ahead and tell you...I guess it concerns you as much as anybody else."

Kathryn became curious. "Tell me what?"

"Blackhorse is not improving. I don't think he will live to stand trial. He is convinced that he is going to die and has pleaded with me to have him taken back to his tribe so he can die amongst his people and be near his parents."

Kathryn let this information sink into her mind. So this man, this Indian who had wronged her, this father of her unborn child was going to pay for his deeds after all. Perhaps there was justice in this, she thought. The child would never know its father, and somehow that had never mattered to her anyhow. She wondered if this was God's way of dealing with this? If he did die, she would never have to worry or fear that he could harm her again, or interfere with the child.

"What do you think is best?" she questioned him.

"My honest opinion is that he should be permitted to die with his own people, and I hope that does not sit too badly with you."

"I think that he should, too," Kathryn answered softly and calmly.

"I'll tell Buck and Sam that you said that. It might help them with their decisions. Unless something unforeseen occurs, I will see you next week." He patted her on the am and took his leave.

Later, in the early afternoon Rick and Sam came to her room.

"Missy," began Sam. "We need to talk."

"Of course, both of you sit down." Kathryn was propped with pillows against the headboard of her bed. Sam took the chair by the window and Rick swung the small vanity chair out toward the middle of the room.

"Since any decision about Blackhorse directly affects you," Rick told her, "we need to know yer feelings about Sam tottin him back up north to die."

"I have given this idea a lot of consideration," answered Kathryn, "ever since the doctor told me why Buck was here." She paused and looked from her uncle to Sam.

"Do you think he is going to die, too?" she asked them both.

"It looks that way, Kathryn," responded Rick.

"I'd say so, the way he hasn't healed up, like Doc thought he would. Seems he jest don't have the will to live...and Doc said he can't seem to rid him of the infection from that gunshot," Sam said.

"Sam?" asked Kathryn. "I want to know how you feel about taking him back?"

"I'm kinda mixed up there, Missy. I'd planned on goin on the cattle drive, then packin up to head for the high country, to do my huntin and trappin. But if I go... someone else'll have to take my place. But I don't suppose that's the part ya needed to hear?"

"No. I want to know how you feel about taking Blackhorse. Is this something you want to do?"

"Missy...I understand his people and respect their ways and customs...and the chief is my friend. Yet, inside...I hold a lot of anger for what's been done to you. No way would I want ya to think I'd be bendin over backwards on his behalf. I hate fer you ta think I was goin over ta the enemy...so ta speak, or takin up sides with Blackhorse... cause that's not what it's all about. Ya see, it's more like grantin a dying man his last wish. And, honoring the customs of different people, particularly a tribe of people I happen ta know. Jest don't want ya harborin a grudge against me about this...and if it don't sit well with you, or if it upsets ya in any way...I'll tell Buck, no."

Kathryn had listened closely to what Sam had said. She frowned for a moment, then spoke slowly, with conviction. "I do not want to stand in the way of Blackhorse's dying request. Regardless of my bitter feelings...I honestly believe that he be permitted, if possible, to die in the midst of his own people...if he lives long enough to do so. It is the honorable thing to do. And, no, Sam...I will certainly not harbor a grudge."

"Then it is decided," said Rick. He got up and put his arms around Kathryn and gave her a reassuring squeeze. "Yer quite a gal, my dear niece."

"She sure is that," Sam chimed in.

"When would you be going, Sam?" asked Kathryn.

"Probably in a couple of days. It'll take me a day at least to git all my stuff together and it'll take Buck a little time to clear it with the judge...which he sees no problem in doin...considering the man's goin to die anyhow."

"How long will you be gone?" she asked Sam.

"A couple of months...or so. Then I go back up...later on in the winter."

"Do you come home for Christmas?" she asked.

"Sure do," he winked. "My favorite time, cause I git to bake up a storm. And this year will be even more special...you'll be here with us to celebrate."

The rest of the day and into the night, Sam busied himself with cleaning his guns, gathering his traps and setting them out to be packed. The next day he sent Pedro into town for supplies while he got clothes washed and baked food to take and some to leave behind for the others. He assembled his camping gear, tent, bedroll and cooking utensils and packed them in the paniers. Later in the evening before the sun robbed him of light, Sam fashioned a travois from long poles and deer hides that would be used for transporting Blackhorse.

Kathryn rose this morning with a lot on her mind. This was the day Sam would be leaving as soon as the doctor delivered Blackhorse to the ranch. She selected a dress to put on and became agitated because she could not fasten the buttons. Her waist and stomach had become too thick. She opened the door and called for Claudette.

"What am I going to do?" she wailed.

Claudette eyed the protruding tummy and the space in the back where the buttons refused to meet. "We are going to have to make you some maternity clothes, that is all there is to it. In the meantime, I have a couple of dresses you can borrow that are a little big for me. They should do you nicely until then." She scurried out of the room.

Kathryn removed her dress and hung it back up knowing it would be a long time before she could fit into that or any of her other clothes. Claudette returned and Kathryn chose a yellow cotton print and she smiled when it closed around her just fine.

"Thank you, Claudette. I would have had to wear my robe until I got new clothes, if it wasn't for you." Kathryn gave her an appreciative hug and they went to join the others for breakfast.

This was also the day that Harold and Claudette were leaving to move into their new house. Kathryn felt sad at breakfast, for she knew how empty the house would seem without Claudette. They would visit one another, but that wasn't the same as having her under the same roof.

She knew, too, just how much she would miss Sam and her eyes got misty whenever she glanced his way. He was such a giving, unselfish man. He had principles and the courage to live by an honorable code he imposed upon himself. He was inconveniencing himself to make a long, out of the way journey with a dying man, one whose deeds he loathed, to grant a last request and to return an old chief's wayward son back to him, if only for a short time.

"I think I'll take my coffee out on the porch," announced Kathryn. She picked up the cup and saucer Sam had given her and left the house.

Clint frowned and rose to go after her. "Wait a few minutes, Clint," suggested Claudette. "I think she needs a few minutes alone."

"Yer right. I guess I'm wanting to be too protective."

Soon Jim stood up and stretched. "Sam, ya want me to bring Thunder and Ginger up to the barn for ya?"

"Yah. Thanks. Doc oughta be here in a little while. I need to get the paniers loaded on and the travois hitched up."

Jim stepped cautiously out onto the porch and Kathryn glanced up and smiled. "You all right?" he asked.

"Yes, I think so. Just needed some fresh air." She looked away and stretched her vision across the expanse of land before her. "I like sitting on this porch...the view is so beautiful."

"Yah. I like it, too. Well, I best git Thunder and Ginger for Sam." His boots clumped down the steps and out toward the right side of the barn.

She watched him go. Jim turned and looked back at her when he got to the corral and flashed a smile and a wave, then vaulted over the fence. He was a nice man, thought Kathryn. She wished he did not care so much for her, for she knew she could never return his feelings.

Small clouds of dust stirred up far down the road and caught Kathryn's eye. She sipped her coffee nervously and watched as the shape of a horse and buckboard became clear. It was apparent who was coming with the Paint hitched to the back. The muscles of her legs felt weak as she walked back into the house. With a look of trepidation and a quivering voice she told Sam, "They're coming up the drive."

Sam left his food packing and went to her with his arms opened wide. She allowed herself to be folded into his big, warm embrace and buried her face into the softness of his buckskin shirt catching the scent of the familiar musky odor.

"Please be careful, Sam," Kathryn pleaded.

"Don'tcha worry none 'bout me. You jest take good care of yerself...ya hear?" She nodded she would, against his chest.

The sound of the horses' hooves and the buckboard slowly traveling past the house toward the barn made Kathryn stiffen. Clint was by her side and Sam told him, "You take her and hang on to her, Clint...I gotta go help Jim and the Doc."

Sam headed out the door followed by Rick, Pedro and Manuel to give their assistance. Kathryn turned to look out the window and saw Blackhorse propped up in the back of the buckboard and the Paint nuzzling his arm. Clint wrapped his arm around her shoulder and tried to draw her away. "Please don't look. Seeing him is only going to upset you again."

"No...I'm all right," she answered, in barely a whisper. Behind them, Harold was helping Claudette clear the table of the breakfast dishes and they exchanged worried looks. Kathryn watched apprehensively as Blackhorse was lifted, with the aid of a blanket under him, off the buckboard by Sam, Rick, Jim and the Doc, and placed on the travois. She saw Doc bend close to Blackhorse's face then turn and look toward the house. He motioned to Rick to come over and gestured to Blackhorse. Rick cocked his head intent on what Doc was telling him, then Doc gestured once again, toward the house. Rick walked a short ways away and Doc followed. Then Rick nodded and headed for the house.

"Kathryn," Rick said gravely. "I said you would not come out, but Blackhorse insisted I at least ask ya..."

"Come out...for what?" she asked.

"He wants to apologize ta you for his wrongs against you...before he dies."

"I don't think I want to face him."

"That's what I thought. That's what I told the Doc." He turned and went back out to deliver the message.

There was more talk between Doc, Blackhorse and Rick and much hand gesturing. Then Sam joined in. Next, Sam headed for the house with long, heavy strides.

"Missy...that Indian's gittin himself plenty worked up. He claims he needs to see ya so he can tell ya how sorry he is. We told him there was no way you were comin out. He's rantin and ravin that his soul is tormented and begs we ask ya again. Is there any way yer up to hearin him out? If not, I'll jest ride him outa here."

"Clint? Will you take me out there?" Kathryn asked in a steady voice. "Are ya sure that's what ya want to do?" Clint asked. "Something tells me I should."

Claudette clasped Harold's hand firmly. "Sam?" she questioned. "Do you think this is wise for Kathryn?"

"I dunno." Sam shook his head looking concerned at Kathryn. Kathryn reached for Sam's arm and tugged at Clint's and bravely headed for the door without a word. Her steps were determined as she walked in the direction of the travois, hanging onto the arms of Sam and Clint with Claudette and Harold close behind. As they neared the barn area there fell an uneasy stillness over the assembled group. Rick froze in place, Jim, Pedro and Manuel stopped what they were doing, as if suspended in space.

Kathryn walked within a few feet of Blackhorse and stopped. She expected to be frightened, but the pitiful condition and appearance of the Indian and the pained expression in his eyes eased the anticipated fear. Blackhorse's heart beat rapidly when he had seen Kathryn step out of the house, and he thought it would stop when he saw she was with child. Was it his, he wondered? Now, she stood before him with vague accusing eyes and still she was beautiful to him, but he dare not convey that thought or betray his heart. He took a deep breath bringing sharp pains to his chest. His dark eyes tried to express his sorrow and his lips spoke the words he so desperately needed to say.

"I have wronged you...Kathryn," he began with labored breathing. "I regret my act of force upon you." Stabbing pains, like knives in his chest, caused him to pause for a moment, then he went on. "I am sorry...very sorry, and ashamed...I had...no right.' I am scum...dirt be...neath your feet. My death is...my punishment."

Kathryn's body remained rigid as her gaze drifted aimlessly over this now pathetic creature. His "act of force" had all but ruined her life. She had carried a hate and fear inside of her since that time, and now...now she wasn't sure...wasn't sure what she felt. She recalled the horrifying things her uncle had told her, after returning from the Indian's village...the sickening things this man had witnessed as a young boy, and also how he had been framed to do another man's unlawful bidding. Kathryn's eyes met Blackhorse's hopeless, pleading eyes, and she knew that the hate she had clung to, for so long, could consume and destroy her. To hate forever would not change her personal dilemma. The hate had become a burden. She wanted that burden no more.

Slowly she reached out her hand and lay it gently over his. In a trembling voice she uttered, "I...forgive you...Blackhorse."

Blackhorse closed his eyes and took a deep, hurting breath, then, released it very slowly. He knew he should feel unmanly for the tears that escaped out of the corners of his eyes and disappeared into his hairline, but the relief, her forgiving, had brought to his tormented mind and soul was too strong to keep trapped inside. "Thank you, Kathryn," he said hoarsely. "May the Great Spirit...forgive me...too." Blackhorse paused while he painfully gasped for more air. He stole a quick glance at her swollen stomach, then looked deep into her dark, sensitive eyes, trying desperately to touch her-soul.

"May the Great Spirit...heap many blessings...upon you...and your life be full and...rich with happiness." The corners of his mouth curved up as he gave her an awkward smile then turned his face away. With tears in her eyes, Kathryn gently squeezed Blackhorse's hand, then slowly stepped back.

Kathryn turned around and looked first into the understanding eyes of her Uncle Richard, shifted her gaze to Sam who smiled proudly at her, then to Clint's anxious face. She looked again at Sam and sadly said, "Goodbye, dear Sam. Please be careful...and return to us, soon." She reached out to Clint and said, "Would you take me in, now?" Clint felt her body shaking. He bent down and scooped her up in his arms and carried her back toward the house.

Sam silently watched Kathryn for a moment, then shook everyone's hand as they bid him farewell. The mules headed out with Sam astride Snowflake leading the way; Ginger next with the paniers, Thunder pulling the travois carrying Blackhorse, and the Paint bringing up the rear. The little group watched as they crested the hill. Kathryn watched from the doorway, cradled in Clint's arms, as her dear friend, Sam, in his floppy leather hat, turned and waved, then slowly disappeared over the ridge.

This was a day for farewells. By mid-morning, Claudette and Harold gave Rick their thanks for putting them up for so long, and carried the last of their personal possessions to Claudette's carriage. The buckboard was drawn up behind it, chock full of new household items and supplies.

Claudette and Kathryn had a private and tearful goodbye in Kathryn's room, and reminded each other of just how close they were going to be living to the other.

Manuel piled his things at the back of the buckboard, anxious to move into his own little cabin Harold had built for him, so that his right-hand man would have his own place and be available when needed. He climbed up into the wooden seat, and grabbed the reins. Flashing a big grin to Pedro he said, "You come by to visit, me, my good amigo." Then he added, laughing, "You and I...we go courting...together. Si?"

That got a chuckle out of Pedro. Nodding and grinning, he shouted, "Si."

Before Claudette could get behind the driver's seat of the carriage Harold grasped her elbow and guided her around to the other side. "My dear, he said, gallantly, "I would like the honor of being the one to drive you to your new home.'"

Claudette smiled affectionately and allowed herself to be seated. Harold masterfully took the reins and clucked his tongue and led the way across the fields.

Kathryn waved to her friends from the drive until they were out of sight. With great tears in her eyes and a feeling of exhaustion she went to her room for a good cry and a nap.

Late that afternoon Kathryn walked by herself up the sloping knoll behind the house. The air was warm with a balmy breeze blowing out of the south. She stood and surveyed the impressive view and remembered the day she had come up here with Sam, and a sadness washed over her because she was missing her friend already. She walked over to the bench-shaped rock and wearily sat down. She watched the birds for a while then watched some wispy clouds go by. She thought to herself that life was indeed a mystery and the more she thought she knew about it, the less she seemed to understand. For a long time she pondered her own purpose here on earth.

Clint took long strides up the incline and stopped when his eyes met Kathryn's. He tilted his black hat back with his thumb, lowered his eyes and frowned at her.

"I've been lookin all over for you. I've been worried." He didn't wait for an explanation, but finished the short climb to the top and came to sit down beside her. He put his arm around her shoulders and pulled her close to him. For a while the two just sat together enjoying the comfort of each other and the view without saying a word.

Finally, Clint broke the silence. "Kathryn," he said. "There's something you and I have to talk about, now."

She turned and studied his serious expression. "Don't look so glum, gal. What I've got to say will make you happy...I hope."

"What would that be?" she asked, curiously.

"Kathryn...I love you...more than anything else in this world. You are my world. The first day I saw ya...back in Lexington at the train depot...I felt in my heart you were the woman for me. And nothin that's happened has changed my mind. I don't come from a rich or fancy background, but I come from good people, and I do aim on makin real good money. But, gal...all, the money I could ever make, or hope to have, wouldn't mean a darn thing without you in my life...and by my side. What I'm tryin to say, my dear, sweet Kathryn is...will you marry me?"'

Kathryn looked up at Clint's sincere expression and saw the honesty in his pleading dark eyes and tears began to glisten in hers. "What about the baby?"

"It'll be ours. Yours and mine. Anyway, who else would know different," he chuckled. "Look at us. We both have dark eyes and dark hair and with any luck at all it'll look jest like you. And, even if it doesn't...so what?"

"But...but..."

"No buts. All I need to know is do ya love me? And will ya marry me?"

A smile crept across Kathryn's lips as she looked into the eyes of the man she loved so dearly...so desperately. "Yes. Oh. yes. I would be proud to marry you."

Clint grabbed her rather clumsily and held her tight to his body, then bent down and kissed her with warm passionate lips. He held her close again, not wanting her to see him blinking back his own tears of rejoicing happiness and relief. With his left hand he reached into his shirt pocket and pulled out the black velvet box and let go of her a moment so that he could open it. With jittery fingers he carefully removed the ring. Kathryn blinked and stared at the ring and her moist dark eyes sparkled almost as much as the twinkling sapphire and diamonds in it.

Clint picked up her left hand and as he slid the ring on her finger, he said, "I've been carryin this around for a long time. Now, it shall be where it rightfully belongs."

"Oh Clint," she breathed. "It is beautiful." She reached up and threw her arms about his neck hugging him with joy.

"Gal, you've made me so happy...I could bust."

"Oh, Clint, I truly do love you."'

"Kathryn, I've another surprise," he announced.

"Another surprise? What kind of a surprise?"

"I've bought us some acreage not far from Harold and Claudette's place...I hope you'll find it to yer liking...for building our home, " he smiled.

"You did?" she asked astonished. "You bought it just for us?"

"Sure did. And, I've already started workin on our house plans...but, I need to see if ya like my ideas and if they meet with yer approval...and to tell me what you'd like so l can draw them up right."

"Oh, Clint. My world has seemed so bleak and full of troubles for so long and now it's as if a rainbow has come into my life. I am so happy. So full of hope and love."

"I'm glad...so glad to see you smiling again. Now, what I want to know is...how soon can you be ready to get married?"

She patted her stomach with resignation and a smile. "Considering we are working against time...I'd say as soon as possible." She thought for a moment, then her eyes brightened. "We can have the wedding here at the house. We could ask the Reverend Small to perform the ceremony...Uncle Richard can give me away...Claudette can be my matron of honor."

"And, Harold can be my best man," grinned Clint.

Kathryn was giddy with excitement and giggled and laughed as she stood up. "Come," she urged. Let's go tell Uncle Richard first. Then, do you suppose first thing in the morning we could hitch up Sir Frosty and drive over to Claudette and Harold's...to tell them and Manuel?"

"I don't see why not," he grinned.

Clint held her close and they stood silent atop the sloping knoll. The sun hovered over the mountains to the west, casting a golden glow upon the earth. Above, the sky was a soft bluish-grey with splashes of orange and yellow and traces of small feathery clouds that barely moved against the gentle breeze that blew.

"I love you, Kathryn," he whispered in her ear.

"And, I love you, Clint," she answered with a smile.

Clint took her hand and gently guided her back down the knoll.

"Clint?" she said, when they'd reached the bottom.

"Yah ?"

"How long before we could move into our house?"

'Well, let me think a minute." He stopped and stroked his moustache, then turned to her with an idea. "We could do what other folks have done. Get one big room built, live in that while we build and add on to the house." And he inserted, "I can make it as big as you want." He checked her expression to see what she thought of his idea.

"Yes, let's just do that," she beamed. "How long would the one room take?"

Clint frowned, then answered, "Around three weeks...give or take, oughta make it livable, but I'll need some help."

'What's this I hear about needin some help?" asked Rick, leaning against the open back door.

"Oh, Uncle Richard. We've got some wonderful news to tell you," beamed Kathryn.

Clint and Kathryn walked with Rick into the house to make their announcement and plan their hasty wedding.

In Lexington, Kentucky

"KATHRYN JOLENE BARNETT AND CLINTON CHARLES DAVIS—RECENTLY MARRIED AT BARNETT RANCH," read the telegram that quivered in Jolene Barnett Wheeler's hand.

www.ingramcontent.com/pod-product-compliance
Lightning Source LLC
Chambersburg PA
CBHW031155050726
47495CB00019B/1744